A
HEADFUL
OF
SKYE

Dear Daisy,
It's lovely to have met you.
I really hope you enjoy ♡

First published in 2023

Copyright © Willow H. Wood

www.willowhwood.com

Willow H. Wood has asserted her right under
the Copyright, Designs and Patents Act, 1988,
to be identified as Author of this work.

A catalogue record for this book is available
from the British Library.

ISBN: 978-1-7392033-0-6 PB

ISBN:: 978-1-7392033-1-3 eBook

A
HEADFUL
OF
SKYE

WILLOW H. WOOD

Dear Mitch,
This one is for you and me,
No matter how heavy the rainfall,
I love you.
Willow

OBITUARIES

If you asked Mayu to describe her identity, she would have asked you to clarify the word's meaning. In Mayu's eyes, it was everything that cannot be captured by neural nets or quantified by basic surveys. She'd tell you that identity is not your achievements or even your name.

> *My identity,* she'd say, *is that I love the smell of singed dust on a hot radiator. My identity is feeling content to have red bean soup in the autumn, my feet cozy under the kotatsu and falling asleep where I sit while Yūta watches TV.* Here, she'd fight not to cry. *My identity,* she'd continue, *is that I must wear fluffy socks in the house and I love to sit at work half an hour early with a book—except I rarely read the book and often start working early.*

Mayu would explain that she reads symbology into everything, from targeted advertising, to the wind rattling the *emas* exactly when she pauses to admire everyone's wishes. *I am terrified of fire and feel nervous around candles.* No one will remember these things. Her obituary will one day state that she had a doctorate in neuroscience and worked in the field of machine learning. Hopefully, they'd call her fair and hardworking, followed by her advances to coma therapy.

As Mayu stared at her husband's obituary, she suddenly wished his goldfish was still alive, too. *His identity,* she thought, *is gone.*

1

"**Y**ŪTA!" SHE SCREAMED, heart hammering against her ribs. "Listen—stay with me!"

Mayu tried to grip Yūta's arms and shake him—he stood right in front of her—but her hands passed through his body. She swept at him again and again, catching nothing, snatching at only the air and memories.

"Fight it," she cried. "Snap out of it, Yūta!"

He continued staring over her head, unaffected, taking shallow, forced breaths as if about to pass out. She knew that if he didn't come back to her, he would be gone forever.

They stood on the edge of a small pier at sunset, the sea glistening. It was one of Mayu's favourite memories. Yūta had proposed to her here, the wind mussing his black hair and tugging at her skirt so sharply she had to hold it down.

Desperate, Mayu focused on increasing the sensory stimuli. Maybe she could shock him into waking up. Straining her mental reach, Mayu intensified the moment until sea salt stung her nose, the wind lashed the skirt around her hips, and even though the sea itself lapped peacefully against the shore, the sound of waves roared around them. The sun gleamed across the water in shards of blinding light, forcing Mayu to shield her eyes.

"Yūta, you have to try!"

For a second, his gaze met hers.

Was it working?

Mayu's throat clogged. "Do you remember? I said yes." Her voice cracked. "Focus, my love. This isn't real, but *I* am. This is our history."

As she spoke, an oppressive black veil returned—a smothering darkness she'd been fighting to keep at bay. It fell from the clouds to the ground, covering the houses on the shore and extinguishing all light. As it spread, it obscured all it touched, and no matter how hard Mayu tried, her memory wasn't strong enough to resist it.

Every cell in her body screamed *grab Yūta—shake him, slap him—or it's all over!* Mayu clawed her hands and shook them at Yūta instead, as if to rattle some sense back into him, "Try, damn it!"

Her limbs trembled. How could he leave her? She tried once more to grab him and make him see sense. "Stop it. *Stop it*!" she screamed, "You're letting it win!"

The wall of black consumed the sun, the sea, the sand, and the pier beneath her feet—until nothing remained except the two of them, in total darkness and utter silence. Only Yūta was visible, his outline glowing like he'd become a dim candle from another world.

Mayu held her tongue, spluttering on words, her gaze fixed on his face. Yūta's pupils disappeared, and he let out a long, hollow sigh.

"NO!" His head dipped, and Mayu watched him slowly fall. The colour in his clothes, his face—all turned grey. She made to catch him as he fell backwards, but he fell through her fingers as a wisping trail of breath.

And then he was gone.

᠅

"Mayu! Oh, thank—"

She opened her bleary eyes and felt tears on her skin, dripping into her ears.

A heart monitor beat a staccato rhythm in time with the thumping in her chest, but all Mayu heard was the other one: the long, unending flat line.

"Yūta …" she whispered. Batting away the medical staff who surrounded her bed, Mayu tried to heave herself off the mattress, forgetting about Morpheus, the dream machine she was still hooked up to.

"No, Doctor," said a nurse, gripping her shoulder and forcing her down.

"Get off me—*ah*!" Needle-sharp barbs twisted in her forehead, triggering spasms of paralysis down her neck and sharp tingles through her body. Reaching up, she touched the probes embedded in her skin. The wires attached to them resisted her movement and bound her to the machine beside her.

Glancing at the bed nearby, Mayu took in Yūta's sleeping—no, *dead*—form. He already looked pale.

She fell back onto her pillow and closed her eyes, squeezed them shut against the real world. Mayu had never failed to guide a coma patient back to consciousness. Why Yūta? Why *her* Yūta? She needed to wail but didn't have the energy; she felt stuffed-up and drained, and the bed seemed to spin—maybe her whole body was spiralling apart—she was barely aware of the specialists disconnecting her.

Mayu clenched the mattress as they dislodged the

hair-thin probes in her brain, feeling only a slight, cold discomfort as they slid out of her skin. When only the drip line tethered her, she made to get up again.

Her bones crunched and creaked. Her legs throbbed and dragged. Had they replaced her knees with lead?

"No, Shirakawa," said Doctor Fukushima. He held her shoulders. "You have been sedated for two weeks. Don't overdo it."

"Two weeks?" she croaked. Mayu glanced at her colleague's round face, his features twisting and mashing with the spinning in her head. His oval glasses had slipped down his nose, and she saw that his eyes were bloodshot and tired. Mayu breathed deep, felt the air rasp in her throat and hoped that, maybe, she was still dreaming. The fight wasn't over yet.

Moving hesitantly, Mayu struggled against her colleague's hands until, giving up on pacifying her, he helped her to sit. In the wall opposite her bed was a window of glass. It danced with charts and numbers written backwards—the results in constant flux. Behind the patterns of information sat a small team of scientists. Her team.

They stared at her silently. Her lead biomedical engineer, Momo Kuramochi, covered her mouth. The room gleamed with sterility and functionality. Mayu scrunched her eyes shut and, with a desperate force of will, tried to summon a lush field overlooked by mountains. She believed in it, wanted it desperately—any second a breeze would kiss her clammy cheeks and Yūta would hold her hand.

"We need to get you checked over." Fukushima sounded crystal clear, his voice clanging around her ears.

"A field…" she whispered, covering her ears, "A field and mountains."

Someone's hand found her shoulder. Opening her eyes, Mayu's spirit crumbled at her unaltered surroundings; the faces staring at her with unwanted confirmation.

Mayu clamped her trembling lips shut and looked across at Yūta's body.

"We'll take care of him," said Fukushima as the staff draped a sheet over her husband and wheeled him out of the room. Fukushima stood by her bedside, his lab coat glowing beneath the room's blue, purple, and yellow lights. "You did all you could," he said.

Mayu hung her head, her shoulders jerking with the effort of containing her despair.

2

NO MATTER HOW dark or twisted a dream could be, it used to be just that, a dream; Mayu's playground; her office. Despite having no artistic talent to brag about at school, her imagination overflowed, more vivid than her skill with words or a canvas. Science made more physical sense, something that could be described, calculated, measured; while her dreams were intangible, from another world, in a language she couldn't paint or describe.

Since Yūta, in every nightmare in which she died, she felt death's coldness close around her throat. She'd lurched awake, half leaping off her pillow and sucking in a huge breath like a free-diver breaking the water's surface. It became a pattern within a week. After two, she stopped reaching for comfort from the empty space beside her.

Waking with less of a gasp and more of a fitful shudder some morning or other, Mayu blinked at the indistinct darkness of her room. Not ready for another tense dream with maybe a moment's reprieve, she eased out of bed, tugged on a sweater, and slid open the bedroom door, letting her fingers trail across the frosted glass panes. Hazy pre-dawn shadows filled the open-plan living room and kitchenette beyond.

Her stylish but compact apartment in the Sky High Living block featured ceiling to floor windows, here and in the adjoining office, which made it feel less like a state-of-the-art shoebox. In the streets far below, cars were mere dots, but the height didn't bother her. Mayu enjoyed pressing against the glass to look down on it all. She marvelled at the man-made towers, their constellation of windows glimmering around her like stars until midnight, when all non-essential lights went out.

Pushing aside the pile of take-out boxes in the kitchen, she found the teapot. It smelled of fermented leaves and, if she was being honest with herself, even mildew, but roasted green tea would be strong enough to mask that.

She'd just brewed a cup and brought it to her lips when a ringtone echoed inside the office. Mayu had turned down almost all visitor requests, barely answered her phone and pretended that even family and non-legal emails were going straight to spam. She looked at the clock in the sitting area. Not yet 6 a.m. She stood there, watching the second hand *tick, tick* away every moment she did nothing.

Shuffling across the apartment, sliding along on blue fluffy socks, she crept into her office and watched the computer flashing with an incoming call. She stared at it blankly, like she'd never seen the name before and let it ring until she'd settled herself into the desk chair. She accepted the call. A video feed sprang to life and an ageing man stared out at her, the text box waiting beneath. Mayu barely recognised her own face in the corner.

"Hello, Fukushima," she said softly, nudging a plate of week-old cake crumbs away from the camera.

"Good morning, Mayu. I'm so sorry to call this early, but you know how it is." Her co-director removed his glasses and rubbed his bleary eyes. "How are you?" His face always looked rounder without glasses—and weary, the shadows under his eyes no longer hidden.

She shrugged and only said, "Yeah," sipping her tea, waiting.

"Yeah." He sounded strained but quickly hid it. "Listen, I need to ask…please come back to work."

A shiver shook her.

"I know it's only been a month, but our sponsors are putting on pressure, saying it's not profitable to recover only a few patients each year. We have to 'think more like a business or find a new partner.'"

"But I can't submit to the procedure too often."

"I know, that's what I told them. The brain can't take too much messing with—beyond what you already do. Seventeen patients in eight years? That's amazing, I said so. They suggested we hire more staff, but they aren't offering more money. Apparently, their assets in neurological tech aren't providing the income to cover our work." A glimmer of light caught the edge of Mayu's monitor. She looked towards it, through the windows that yawned a view of Tokyo's skyline. Sharp beams of sunlight streaked the clouds, a florescent yellow globe peaking over the distant mountains, burning the rest of the sky orange.

She watched the giant, battery-powered sky ships as they sailed among the smog, emerging from the grimy dawn, like whales gliding through water and breaking the surface to breathe. They left a path of clear sky in their wake like a reverse contrail, sucking pollution into their hulls ready for processing. Even from afar, Mayu could make out the animated screens on one ship's side proclaiming the benefits of this recycling process, which would see the constituent compounds turned into hydrocarbon, then carbon nanotubes, and ultimately, hydrogen fuel cells for the production of eco-friendly cars.

"Mayu?"

Blinking, she tugged the sleeves of her sweater further over her fingers, swapping her cup between hands. She savoured the warmth of it through the knitted fibres. Fukushima was leaning closer to the camera when she looked back at him.

"Please come back as senior director," he said. "Come back and complete Matokai's training. He'll be ready to take over your role by the time we start our next case. I've forwarded the patient's outline to you already."

"Okay." Mayu watched as a familiar news banner danced under his face. She absentmindedly registered the outdatedness of their work app. The news banner had been introduced to the app just before its providers had ceased giving updates, so the links were always the same, never refreshed, just like the unfashionable silver-blue colour scheme with its false sheen around the edges.

She stared at the image of a diamond-encrusted necklace, reciting the headline in her head before the familiar words popped up: *6 Billion Yen Stolen in Smash-and-Grab Jewel Heist.* If only they had six billion yen to spend on their research.

"Should I look into finding more staff?" he asked.

"Okay."

She heard a gentle sigh. "The new patient is based in England, so we get to travel for our next project—I remember you saying you wanted to move abroad not so long ago."

"That was a joint wish," she whispered.

Her thoughts were elsewhere, undisturbed by Fukushima's string of condolences.

"A London hospital?" she interrupted.

He frowned. "Yes."

"We'll arrange a conference," she said, gaze drifting off again. "We can find a second sponsor by releasing a statement about our work. We could include the patient and get a journalist or documentary writer to cover their treatment. It may encourage donations."

A smile illuminated the deep creases in Fukushima's face. "That's a brilliant idea."

Indeed. She felt a spark of thoughts flowing after the idea. There were people she hadn't spoken to since last year who could help, who could put her in touch with the right groups to host such an event.

"I'm sorry I haven't visited."

It was a considerable effort to tear her focus away from the tea leaves circling around her cup but she looked up. "It's okay." She even managed a smile.

The doorbell sounded like a shriek in the night and she jumped, staining her yellow sleeves in dark tea. "I've gotta go."

"Alright." Fukushima stayed leaning close to the camera like he wanted to protest otherwise. "I'll talk to you soon."

She hit the 'end call' button and the video feed died with a series of cheerful pops.

The doorbell shrieked again. She sighed, getting to her feet, running her hands through her unbrushed hair. She straightened her sweater, unsure who to expect, as she padded across the soft cream carpet of the living room to the front door, flicking the light switch as she went. Strips in the ceiling blinked into life as she moved past the sensors.

Mayu checked the spy-hole and saw a young woman with bobbed hair and long mascaraed eyelashes glancing to each side in the hallway. She recognised her visitor from the pastel pink tips of her hair.

"Momo," she said, opening the door. The young woman was dressed for work in pencil skirt and black tights. "What are you doing here?"

Clutching a small white box to her chest, Momo Kuramochi launched across the threshold and flung one arm around Mayu's neck. "I know it's super early, I'm so sorry, but I couldn't go another day without telling you. I had to tell you before I went to work."

"What are you talking about?"

She allowed Momo to kick off her shoes before struggling into the living room where she disentangled herself from her colleague's grasp. The apartment always seemed to shrink in size when Momo visited. For a small individual, she took up a lot of room.

Momo set the white box down on the coffee table, next to a bouquet of withered tulips. Then she went to pick it up again but paused and gestured for Mayu to sit down.

"What's wrong?" Mayu sat and Momo fell into place beside her. One inch closer and she'd be sitting in Mayu's lap.

"I've been offered a job with Halcyon," she said. Silence hung between them for only a second before she went on, "Do you want tea? I'd love a cup of tea. I'm gasping, actually." Momo jumped off the couch and headed into the kitchenette. She filled the kettle and flicked it on.

"What? When did that happen?" How could Momo want to leave them? Leave her?

Avoiding eye contact, Momo busied herself by clearing the dirty plates and cutlery in Mayu's kitchenette. "Um, three days ago. They said their PTSD dream therapy has almost reached an impasse, and since I designed half the algorithms that measure, control and interpret coma brainwaves, they asked if I'd help them develop it full-time. They've even offered me an apartment in Munich, but I told them we're also at a critical—"

"Stop, stop." A ringing filled Mayu's ears.

Momo froze, staring at the plates she'd put in the sink. "Do you want it?"

After a moment's pause, Momo finally looked at her. She didn't nod, didn't smile, but Mayu read her answer from the tiny twitches in her face. Abandoning the plates, Momo retrieved a letter from her bag and handed it over. It bore the Halcyon logo—a bird soaring free in the outline of someone's head. Going straight to the salary offer at the bottom, Mayu felt the blood drain from her face. It was what Momo deserved, much more than Mayu could ask their sponsors to pay.

"Please forgive me." Momo blushed and rubbed her arms. "I didn't seek it out. And I haven't accepted it."

"You should," Mayu said softly.

Momo's eyes widened. "I can't. We're struggling for staff!"

"I won't tell anyone until you've made up your mind. But if you want to go, I'll handle Fukushima and—"

"No, I don't want to create more trouble for you."

"Momo, I'd do anything for you. Don't be silly. You should consider their offer. Besides, you're great and all, but you're not the only Bio Engineer in the world." She smiled, trying to keep the joke light, but ended up staring at the small altar in the corner of the room, Yūta's photo smiling back at her.

She curled into a ball at the end of the couch, feeling ashamed of wearing a yellow sweater instead of something more suitably sombre. Momo glanced at the shrine too.

"How have you been holding up?" she asked, almost inaudibly, as the kettle started rumbling.

Mayu shrugged, her eyes grew hot, and a sickening, breathless feeling tightened her chest. She had to start being okay at some point.

Momo knelt beside the coffee table and picked up the white box. "Here, this is for you. I don't really know how to give it to you. I'm sorry."

"What is it?"

"Just…open it."

The box felt lopsided as whatever lay inside slid across the bottom. If this were a gift, Momo would be squirming back and forth as if about to pee her pants, but instead, she bowed her head and clenched her hands demurely in her lap.

Chewing on her bottom lip, Mayu ran her fingers over the enveloped lid and pulled it open.

"The hospital wanted them collected," Momo explained. "Reception said they couldn't reach you, but I knew you wouldn't want these things thrown out."

Mayu stared at the dog-tags engraved with his name. She burst into tears, her throat straining to hold back any wailing noises. "Thank you."

"Hey, come here," Momo murmured, stretching out her hand in offering.

"I'm sorry."

"I said, come here, idiot." Mayu chuckled as her friend deliberately made her natural Osaka accent thicker. She always did that when trying to break uncomfortable tension. Most of the time, she didn't understand half of what Momo said during her performative wise-cracks, but it always made her smile regardless.

Clutching Yūta's work-tags, Mayu crawled into her friend's arms. They entangled their legs and fell over sideways onto the plush carpet, but Momo didn't let go. Her arms cocooned Mayu, allowing her to shrink into her chest like a tiny child.

They lay like that for a while, Momo stroking Mayu's hair—so still that the lights switched off and cast the room in dull morning glow—until Mayu couldn't bear the snot blocking her nose and pushed away. Untwisting their legs, Momo bounced to her feet.

"No, no. I'll get it." She raced to the bathroom, returning with a roll of toilet paper, but paused mid-step, staring at Mayu wide-eyed.

"Did you feel that?"

Neither of them moved, listening, waiting. A second later, Mayu felt it.

She swiped the TV remote off the table and they both scrambled to her bedroom doorway. They shoved back the sliding screen and sat opposite each other, backs pressed against the doorframe. Stretching her arm out to get the signal past the couch, Mayu aimed the remote at the TV, turning it on and changing channel.

Another tremor vibrated through the floor, but the weather warning station had nothing about an impending earthquake.

Aside from unwashed bedding, a musky smell of after-shave filled her bedroom. She'd sprayed the pillows, the curtains—even used his cologne as air-freshener. She saw Momo resist the urge to cover her nose.

"There's no one else like him," Mayu croaked, watching the woman on TV present reports and predictions.

The floor shuddered this time. Mayu shut her eyes and clenched her fists.

"New alert," said the reporter, "an earthquake of 7.5 magnitudes hit Ojiya, Niigata Prefecture, five minutes ago. The quake is being felt across the Kantō region. If you hear sirens, please follow…"

She felt Momo place a comforting hand on her leg.

"I don't think I'll love anyone else," Mayu whispered, her face hot and damp again.

"Do you want me to stay over for a few days?" Momo asked, voice strained.

"No, it's alright."

Something soft bumped against her leg: "Here." She took the roll of toilet paper from Momo's outstretched hand, her friend's expression warm like summer rain.

"If you are in Tokyo, be on alert," said the anchor, "but

any tremors in the city should subside quickly and, at the moment, there is no cause for serious alarm."

As Mayu mopped her face and blew her nose, Momo returned to making the tea, teetering en route as the floor quivered. She took out Mayu's glossy black tea set—the one with a winter poem written in red and white calligraphy across the pot and cups.

"I'm not sure I can come back to work," Mayu said. "I don't think I care anymore. And what if no one else wants to sponsor us?"

"We'll find a way," Momo said, opening a sealed bag of tea. "And of course you care. You've put your life into the project. I don't want to hear otherwise."

The promise of grassy sencha brewed in a clean pot soothed Mayu's nerves a little. She had invested eight years in the Parallel Dream Project—just thinking about that and the progress they'd made blew on the embers deep within her gut.

"Hey…" Momo stopped arranging the tea tray, her whole body stiff as she picked up four empty pill packets from underneath a chocolate wrapper. "Mayu, this is a lot of painkillers." A terrible notion filled her eyes; Mayu could see her train of thought jumping from one conclusion to the next.

"I've had a lot of headaches," Mayu explained, staring at the wall. "Crying does that."

"But still …"

"I'm fine. Leave them alone."

"One of—you're taking tramadol? Are you sure you don't want me to—"

"*Leave it*, Momo. I'm fine."

Mayu hugged her knees and kept her eyes on the TV, the carpet, anything that made her look deep in thought. Given her knowledge of drugs, it hadn't been hard to discover what medications mixed reasonably well, without a serious risk of killing herself. She'd found a combination of painkillers that made her face numb, her body float— something to make the world feel distant, apart from the insatiable thirst for water that came as a side-effect.

She heard Momo snivel and suppress a sigh. After a few minutes, Momo carried over a tray and knelt down on the far side of the table. She had a knack for pouring tea without spilling anything, which is why the black tea set only came out when Momo visited. It had calligraphy across all the pieces, the set so ornate-looking that Mayu feared to break it, but she always trusted Momo to handle it with care.

Mayu moved from the bedroom doorway and sat cross-legged across from her.

"Fukushima can carry on as acting Senior Director," Momo said, passing a cup of tea.

"Okay."

"You found sponsors before, you'll think of a way to generate money again."

Mayu nodded.

"Meanwhile, you and I are going to rediscover your *pizzazz*, you hear?"

The end of Mayu's nose tingled, her eyes growing wet.

Momo's face softened. "I know you don't want to be a Dream Guide again. You went through so much and… We understand." Sighing, she added, "I'm not leaving you for Halcyon. I think I knew it deep down."

"But the pay rise! You've got to think about yourself, too. I know you want…"

Momo's expression grew tender, pinning Mayu's words to her tongue.

"Our team needs me more than I need money," said Momo. "Maybe I can help Halcyon in other ways, but from home, with you."

Gratitude filled Mayu to bursting, a genuine smile she hadn't felt in a long time reshaping her entire face. She closed her eyes, regained composure. They sipped their tea in silence, watching the sky ships make fading patterns in the clouds. The pictures on Mayu's walls rattled as the last shockwave hit the building. With resources spread thinly, due to the cost of climate control and disaster prevention, they still couldn't get funding from the government. Perhaps that would improve in another five years.

"I don't suppose you've looked at the latest patient file Fukushima has marked as a priority candidate, have you?" Momo asked.

"I was hoping it would read itself," she replied. Mayu pressed the hot ceramic to her forehead and winced, rolling the cup over her faded bruises. She had only guided seventeen patients back to consciousness, but the procedure was starting to leave her skin calloused and discoloured by the small, pink prick marks left behind by the probes.

"Well, I think you'll like this one. It's in England. Weren't you saying how much you'd like to work abroad once in a while?"

Mayu forced a smile. "What's so special about this case?"

"The girl has degenerative narcolepsy. She passed out

at the top of a flight of stairs one day, smashing her head on the way down. She's been comatose for almost a year."

As if waiting for the hard sell, Mayu peered over the rim of her cup. "And?"

"*And* doctors can see brainwaves spreading from her hippocampus."

Mayu's lips parted and she lowered the cup a little.

"We've seen that in induced comas, but never in a patient whose coma was caused by trauma. She could be the best study in PDE we've found yet."

Hook, line, and sinker, Momo had her by the tails of her lab coat. Huffing into her cup, Mayu muttered, "Momo Kuramochi, you always did know how to cheer me up."

3

Two months later

WHEN MAYU AND her team finally landed at Heathrow Airport, the first thing she noted was the rain. England glistened with grey puddles. The rooftops sloped at jaunty angles, most of them speckled with terracotta chimney pots. There were red brick houses with white window frames, and as they'd flown over Westminster, Momo pointed out the vermillion road leading to the palace, like a permanent red carpet defying the destruction of east London.

The London Lakes drew the eye in ways the royal road couldn't and they stared at the shimmering grey pools in silence. With rising sea levels and frequent storms across the UK, the Thames had burst its banks. The water had surged twenty miles inland leaving a trail of destruction. Whole districts had not only been flooded but submerged in sinkholes as parts of the underground tube network collapsed. Mayu had heard that areas further away, like East Tilbury and Canvey Island, were still completely submerged. She shuddered, struck by the certain devastation that seemed to loom over humanity everywhere in the world. '*Are we too late*?' she always wondered when faced with the evidence, all too aware that Tokyo could be wiped off the earth in the event of a major tsunami.

There was no time for sightseeing or worrying, however. Mayu threw her bags into her hotel room, changed her shirt, brushed her teeth, tugged out her speech notes and raced back to the lobby. Fukushima paced the worn carpet, waiting, and Momo sat slumped in an armchair. She'd had a tablet glued to her hand for the entire flight, reviewing Halcyon's quantifications for variability in neuronal spike trains. Fukushima berated her for not sleeping and, judging from her glazed eyes, Mayu suspected that Momo regretted it too. Only Mayu knew why she'd insisted on working. Momo had agreed to act as a temporary consultant to Halcyon, but they both knew their team would see it as a breach of business interest—especially Fukushima. They would have to keep it quiet, at least for now. Mayu trusted her.

"Know where we're going?" Mayu asked Fukushima.

"Nope," he looked down at Momo, took her elbow and tugged her onto her feet. "But hopefully our contact does. Come on, Kuramochi, wake up!"

Momo groaned. "I'm awake, I'm awake. Why don't you pester the others?"

As she said it, their two missing colleagues scurried out the elevator. Richard spread his arms wide and announced in (what was probably) an awful English accent, "G'day Guvnor!"

"What did he just say?" whispered Momo.

"No idea," teased Mayu. "Richard, how many times have we told you? Don't yell about drugs in public."

He leaned back and chuckled. "Drugs are legally my profession," he said, reverting to Japanese. "You want morphine? Or something more comatose?" His grasp of the language was impressive, but it was still tinged with a distinct American twang. He grinned at them and his face creased with the echoes of every smile he'd ever given, dimpled cheeks, eyes decked with crow's feet, and a general aura of warmth.

"You alright, Fukushima?" asked the young man beside Richard, their up-and-coming Dream Guide, Tomoya Matokai. He didn't own any tailored suits and yet he always wore one to work, no matter how baggy the jacket looked on his narrow shoulders. Combined with his fluffy black hair, he had a soft, huggable appearance, hiding the true sharpness of his mind.

"Yes, just brilliant," Fukushima snapped.

Richard slapped a hand on Tomoya's back. "He's just salty you're gonna kick back and relax for the next two hours."

"If only I spoke better English," Tomoya pretended to lament.

Fukushima clapped his hands to regain order. "Come on, or we'll be late. Have we got everything?" He rearranged his glasses, jiggling them on the bridge of his nose in agitation.

"I've triple checked," said Richard. "Everything will be fine."

A three-foot-tall hotel service bot led them outside. It had a pixelated expression with huge blinking eyes and an oval body, rolling down the front steps on flexible caterpillar tracks that adapted to the terrain. Speaking in exuberant chimes, the bot showed Mayu and her team to their waiting cab. The electric, driverless vehicles set off as soon as the doors shut. They crawled through London's traffic, Fukushima wringing his hands together like he was trying to make rice cakes, until Mayu pinned them to his lap.

"If we're late, we're late," she said. "We've done what we can."

The sky grumbled in disagreement, as darker and thicker clouds gathered overhead. When they eventually pulled over, outside a grand, cream-coloured stone building, a flutter of nausea unsettled Mayu's stomach. Her palms sweated and she did her best to slide out of the car like an empress. She regretted wearing heels.

Rain pelted them as they regrouped outside the main doors and, before Mayu had finished pinning her name badge onto her jacket, she was standing in the wings of the conference theatre. Oh hell, it was huge. Oh *hell*, she had to speak a lot of English. There had to be at least eight hundred people present.

She saw Momo and Fukushima sliding into the seats in front of the stage, separated from the crowd. They both looked at large, standing tablets that connected wirelessly to the on-stage screens. On-site I.T. staff handed them electronic pens and logged them in. Somewhere in the audience, Tomoya sat in safe obscurity, while Richard waited with Mayu in the wings.

"You nervous?" he asked.

Mayu ruffled her new fringe to make sure it covered the scars on her forehead. "Are you sure you can't do the whole thing?" she replied.

He chuckled, leaning backwards and nodded. "If it's any consolation, half of them are just press and most of it will go over their heads."

"That's not much help. They'll coin a ridiculous term far from the point."

"Come on, you've got the easy part," Richard cried as the lights dimmed and an excited hush rippled across the audience. Momo, wriggling in her seat with nerves, caught Richard's eye and waved to him.

"*Wow*," she mouthed.

He pulled a stupid face in reply.

The audience settled down with a series of coughs and squeaks as the chairman walked onto the stage from the opposite wing. His greying hair and watery eyes looked bright beneath the spotlights.

"Good day, it's a pleasure to welcome you to this innovative exhibition," he said.

Mayu immediately tuned him out. She stared at her notes, the cue cards trembling in her hands. Even Richard was taking deep breaths now. She seriously needed to pee.

"It's my pleasure to introduce," said the chairman, "Doctor Richard Lanagan." He spread one arm wide to the wings and Richard, putting on an easy smile, strode across the stage to a spectacular round of applause. The sheer volume of noise made Mayu's head spin.

"Thank you, thank you," Richard said into the microphone. "It's a pleasure to be here, even if it is raining as usual. I've heard the English would sooner learn to breath underwater than cancel a conference with free hot tea." The audience tittered but Mayu couldn't muster a smile.

In a calm and concise manner, Richard spent the next

ten minutes explaining regular neural activity. Behind him, on two massive interactive screens, were images of the human brain. Certain sections glowed and were highlighted in turn, Momo and Fukushima controlling the displays to match Richard's pace. The two of them stood up now, leaning over the digital tabletops that controlled the live screens. They used charts and equations to complement Richard's talk and, occasionally, Momo drew science-puns in the corners, lifting Richard's presentation with a splash of humour. Mayu almost forgot that she would be taking over soon.

"When a patient has been deemed comatose," Richard was saying, "the predominant brainwaves, or frequency, that we can detect when measuring for cerebral blood flow are called Delta waves." He had finished explaining the properties of the brain stem and cerebral cortex and how their synaptic functions could lead to a coma if weakened or damaged. He was building up to introducing Mayu. He went on about electrical signals and Momo highlighted a map of the brain on one of the screens.

He explained that some brainwaves are emotional, and that Delta waves are survival messages that tell the body to heal. "But we have discovered a brainwave that combines our emotional subconscious with healing." It was time to drop the greatest discovery of Mayu's life…to people who mostly had no idea what Richard was talking about.

"The precuneus is involved with episodic memory, reflections upon the self, aspects of consciousness and, most importantly, visuospatial processing, or spatial-temporal reasoning: your perception of reality. We already know it's possible to trick the brain into feeling as if it's entered another world with the development of Virtual Reality. Now we can do it directly within a coma patient's mind."

Mayu started counting her breathes. She'd crossed her legs so tightly it almost hurt.

"When a patient is comatose, we thought the deepest level of consciousness was a flat line—a stage between life and death. But by using anaesthetic drugs, we can recreate a coma deeper than a flat line and, when the brain goes so deeply unconscious, cortical activity revives. Signals from the hippocampus start to spread across the brain's outer-most layer."

Momo selected parts of the brain to make it glow and little synapses pulsed weakly from a hidden fissure between the cerebral hemispheres towards the front of the brain.

"This activity is so faint, and the deep level of conscious-ness so specific, that it has previously gone undetected; until it was discovered by Mayu Shirakawa."

Richard planted himself on the stage, replacing the microphone in the lectern. He asked the audience if they could guess what part of the brain was used to connect all these intricate neurons and signals. "I'll give you a clue, it deals with episodic memory." Mayu was surprised when someone correctly called out, 'the frontal gyrus.'

"This new waveform drives both sleep and dreams, we call it Parallel Dream Energy—PDE, Parallel brainwaves or, simply, Parallel Energy. The coma patient is now no longer totally unreachable. They will still not respond to any physical pain or stimulus but, if we heighten the inten-sity of their Parallel brainwaves, their dreams will become more intense."

Mayu forced a grin, trying to psyche herself up for

the moment, slapping her cue cards against her hand and bouncing on the balls of her feet.

"The coma patient is in a very vulnerable state when we heighten the Parallel frequency. Their spatial-temporal reasoning stops working correctly and it breaks down all perceptions of reality, time and space. Their dreams are so vivid, so intense, that they might as well be in a parallel universe, which is why we call this frequency Parallel Dream Energy.

"But, the amazing thing about this," Richard continued, "the *truly* amazing discovery, is that Parallel Energy can be shared between humans."

Here, Fukushima and Momo began working in tandem between the big screens, linking and animating two images of the brain. Mayu swelled with pride. They'd spent hours preparing these overhead special effects, and their meticulous attention to detail and timing was paying off.

"Using a machine that facilitates our work—the Morpheus—we can forge a synaptic connection between a coma patient and someone with naturally high levels of Parallel Energy, who we will call the Dream Guide.

"By putting the Dream Guide into a deep sleep, basically a comatose state, we can then manipulate their neurons to absorb, *and process*, the coma patient's dreams. But the Dream Guide doesn't just experience the coma patient's dreams; they can interact, walk, and talk with the patient."

Richard paused to allow that information to sink into the silence. He clasped his hands together, beaming with glee.

"My colleague, Doctor Shirakawa, will now elaborate. Thank you."

The audience clapped. Richard strode towards Mayu and, holding her head high, she stepped out from the wings to meet him. She smiled, cameras flashed and, as he crossed her path, they paused to shake hands.

"You'll be fine," he said.

Mayu just forced a wider grin and nodded.

Unlike Richard, Mayu clung to the lectern to hide her trembling, leaving the microphone in its stand. The audience settled again, black tiers of invisible faces. She silently thanked the lighting crew.

"Good evening," she said, trying to steady the nervous tremor in her voice. "Thank you for being here." Taking a deep breath and letting it out in a rush, Mayu told herself this was just extreme practice for her talk tomorrow with the Mansfields. She would have to explain all this again to the parents paying for the dream therapy.

"As a Dream Guide, it is my job to simulate day and night for the patient, and by the end of each 'day' the patient should feel exhausted; this is a good thing. By simulating an environment of restfulness in between periods of adventure and exercise, the patient's neural pathways are reignited. The team in the real world watch out for these spikes in brain activity to stimulate them further with chemicals, nutrients and electro-pulses that refocus the brain's healing capabilities.

"Think of it as layers of consciousness that the patient must be helped through before they can finally wake up. At each stage, the brain compartmentalises trauma and begins to distinguish between reality and imagination."

Mayu smiled, remembering how one patient had been convinced that books could fly and were a normal means of transportation in the first layer of his dreams. This had been fun until he kept sinking into the pages when it teetered on the edge of a nightmare. Luckily, he had been easily distracted by using his fascination for game shows and portraying him as the luckiest contestant to ever play Spandex Splash.

"But reality is a fragile thing," Mayu explained, "and when the fabric of your world is threatened—especially in such an internal way—the brain can shut down in panic. It's my job to control the dreams, to ensure they are safe, and to effectively cocoon the patient within my own mind to protect them from their demons. If I fail…"

She swallowed hard, seeing Yūta's lifeless eyes staring back at her within the blinding lights. His outline loomed out of the audience, a black silhouette cut into the air, two glaring spotlights for eyes. Mayu sucked in a breath and squeezed her eyes shut. When she opened them again, he was gone.

4

THE CONFERENCE WAS a storming success. Mayu and Richard were ambushed by the press outside their hotel for the next few days. Medical directorates wrote long emails wanting to discuss the ethics of their work, and for more evidence to support their claims. Two new sponsors made serious inquiries and two more showed interest. The BBC wanted Mayu and Richard to do a live radio interview. Everywhere she turned, Mayu felt scrutinised and increasingly tight-chested, unable to escape the inevitable mention of her husband's death. Her first failed patient. Every time someone brought it up, a wedge of guilt drove deeper into her heart.

While Richard handled the brunt of public relations, increasingly redirecting enquiries to their office in Tokyo, Mayu and Fukushima got to work studying Skye Mansfield's medical records—their real reason for being in London.

The hotel had given them a small business room with a high-definition television. Despite its limited capacity for a maximum of six people, the room was clean and quiet. Here, they spent most afternoons discussing Skye's condition. Her personality profile and medical history had been collated into a physical binder for their colleague, Tomoya Matokai, to study in-depth. Each team member had read it, but only Tomoya had to memorise all of it. Currently, it had a plethora of multi-coloured sticky notes curling out from the binder, extra data graphs, and restaurant coasters tucked between the pages—handwritten notes written on the back of these water-marked placeholders. He had to know Skye's interests and fears; the personal details that would give Tomoya inspiration when shaping their dreams. Out of habit, Mayu's brain had latched onto these extra details anyway whenever she studied the documents.

Skye Mansfield was the daughter of two wealthy diamond experts, whose business had international recognition. She was a dancer, who was also good at art, confident and independent, but she was known to have confidential difficulties at home and had displayed behavioural problems at school.

"The more I read about her cataplexy," said Mayu, flicking through some of Skye's early medical records, "the less I like the idea of heightening her PDE."

Fukushima put down his pen and took off his glasses. He was making notes about possible similarities between the girl's brainwaves and those of past patients. "I think severe cataplexy was the cause of her permanent sleep," he said.

"I agree," said Mayu.

Not only did Skye have narcolepsy, a brain disorder that caused sufferers to fall asleep at inappropriate times, but she also suffered from episodes of muscle limpness. Anything that triggered sudden, intense emotional reactions made Skye Mansfield's body collapse—particularly feelings of shock, fear, or stress. Heightening a coma patient's Parallel Energy was always risky, as any failure on the Guide's part could mean a fatal seizure for the patient. This risk would be doubled for Skye.

"If we trigger too much of the wrong emotion," said Fukushima, "it could kill her. Even *you* can't control everything that happens in a Parallel Dream." He rubbed his eyes and clasped his hands on top of his notes.

"True, but maybe…she could theoretically be one of our easier subjects."

He tilted his head in question and Mayu dragged over his laptop from the edge of the table. It was wirelessly connected to the television and currently displaying their out-dated work software. She left the multiple chat channels with their staff, blind to its recycled news updates, and opened their shared online files. Knowing exactly where to look, Mayu soon opened the photo of a black and white brain scan. A glow surrounded Skye's brain, a visible whisper of PDE. Mayu stood and traced her fingers over the aura on the television screen.

"She's already showing signs of naturally high Parallel Waves," she said, "as good as if we'd put her in a coma ourselves at the lab. Don't you see? If she's already showing PDE, we don't have to use as many drugs to enhance them. Tomoya won't have to work so hard to forge a new reality that they can both accept. Well, hypothetically. Maybe her dreams will be *easier* to control because of it."

Fukushima didn't look convinced at first, but she saw his mind working behind those tired eyes, saw him draw together why it seemed possible Skye's cataplexy could be negated. "So, it's like when you and Matokai share a dream, you can control the environment more easily because you're both naturally perceptive." Straightening his shoulders, he nodded, chewing on a smile he didn't quite want to give.

Just as Fukushima opened his mouth to speak again, the meeting room door swung open. Tomoya Matokai burst in with fresh coffee. He grinned at Mayu, his features almost cloyingly cheerful.

"I'm sorry, Shirakawa," he said. "They didn't have vanilla flavour, but I got you caramel. I hope that's—well, I hope it's similar. If not, you can buy a vanilla plant and make the syrup yourself, because I think the barista would skin me with her teeth if I complained."

"It could be worse," Mayu replied, smirking as she took the warm cup from him. She cradled it close to her chest and closed her eyes. The scent of rich, sweet coffee filled her nose. She let the soothing smell tingle to the tips of her fingers.

"Let's go," Tomoya tapped his foot for emphasis, "Richard and Kuramochi are waiting." He made to scoop up Fukushima's notes into one mound of paper, but the man batted away his help, preferring to have everything in order. Tomoya looked at Mayu and rolled his eyes, hefting his multicoloured binder off the table, plastic sheets sticking out of the top and bottom.

Before long, clutching Yūta's dog tags beneath her shirt, the whole team was ascending in a hospital elevator. Sterilised corridors flashed beyond the green glass shaft, the floors so starkly white that they glowed beneath the lights.

"The coffee from the vending machine here tastes like…" Richard paused, and Mayu suspected he was biting back a vulgar word, because he muttered something quick in English. "It tastes like dirt. I'll go out to buy something real later, if you all want one too. My treat."

"Haven't you had enough today?" said Momo, pushing hair out her face. "Your breath stinks."

"Why are you complaining?" he replied. A wicked grin came over him and Richard bent down to her height. "Are you saying I should stop leaning over your shoulder?"

Momo stiffened and shoved him aside. "Yes, it's annoying."

Richard laughed and patted her back. "I'll be sure to buy some gum."

On Momo's other side, Tomoya held his notes in one hand and a bag of snap peas balanced in the middle of the pages. He was getting close to the end of the folder and he had a red pen behind his ear, ready to make more notes. His chomping echoed off the reinforced glass walls.

"Miss Mansfield plays the cello," he said. "Maybe the two of us could play a symphony off Kiyomizu-dera's balcony. I'd pay to do that for real." He chuckled and Mayu smiled back, picturing Tomoya and Skye performing atop the ancient Kyoto temple. Mayu could only imagine him in one of his baggy suits.

"Oh…" He pulled a snap pea away from his mouth. "A couple of weeks before she fell unconscious, her best friend died."

"Shit." Fukushima clenched his phone like he hadn't heard any of them speaking. "Our sponsors are pulling out. They've lost almost everything from one of their investments. They've given us a month to get our affairs in order and find someone else."

The elevator arrived at the top floor and everyone stood

there for half a second, Momo's breathing louder with each intake of air. Maybe she was regretting not taking Halcyon's offer after all. Not ready to think about their sponsors—or lack of—Mayu avoided Fukushima's expectant stare and led the way to Skye Mansfield's private room. Momo launched into a volley of questions behind her, few of which Fukushima could answer.

Skye's room was larger than most private quarters and well lit. Large windows on the far side let in early autumn sunlight and looked down on central London. And there, in the centre of the room, slept the twelve-year-old girl, who should have had rounded cheeks and rosy skin. Her bronze hair lay flat and bedraggled over the pillow, her chest rising and falling as the breathing apparatus pumped oxygen down her throat. A monitor over her bedside measured the electrochemical impulses in her brain, showing only four cycles per second; incredibly low.

Sitting by the windows, in two faded red chairs, were Mr. and Mrs. Mansfield. They rose and shook Mayu's hand.

"Are *all* of you here to help Skye?" asked Mrs. Mansfield.

Mayu didn't miss the woman's displeased grimace. "Yes. It seems like a lot, but each of us is a necessary part of the team. We are here to see Skye together, firsthand, so that we can all see what we are dealing with in person. I hope you understand?"

Mr. Mansfield nodded, "Of course. What do you need from my wife and I?"

"It's alright, leave it to us, my team will check her vitals and the strength of her brainwaves, but now I must speak with you alone."

As Mayu said this, Fukushima bowed and headed over

to Skye's monitors. She wished for a second that Keiji was with them, a serious man and a prominent member of their team. He would have supported her during 'The Talk' with the Mansfields. Over the past two months of coming back to work, Mayu had found his steady, deep voice and quiet, unassuming manner calming, a quality that Momo couldn't quite equal. It made sense that Keiji should stay behind in Tokyo to oversee the lab. Aside from his agreeable nature, he was effectively a senior member of the team in terms of experience.

Fukushima unhooked the medical report hanging from the end of Skye's bed, Momo began testing the girl's pupil dilation and physical condition. Tomoya sat down with Richard to take notes, ask questions, and compare charts.

"Pardon?" said Mr. Mansfield.

"Please," Mayu gestured towards the hall, "come with me."

Without a second glance, Skye's parents did as requested and followed Mayu out of the room. "We'll find somewhere to sit," she said, making sure to smile. Why couldn't Richard do this bit? Her supplementary English from college felt so thick and stilted. Language didn't matter in dreams; communication happened on a much more instinctive level, one that Mayu wished translated into the real world.

They chose a table on one of the balconies overlooking the main lobby. The hospital was structured like whipped ice-cream. It had thirty floors, each one spiralling above the ground floor reception. Five glass elevators connected the floors, positioned like pillars around the circular lobby.

Mayu sat straight-backed and clasped her hands in her lap. "Before we talk about the treatment, I just have one question. Do you know what made Skye fall down the stairs? Her file doesn't say."

"Oh…no," said Mr. Mansfield. His wife lowered her eyes, her expression a mask of neutrality. Mayu searched desperately for comforting words, but the awkward silence made her thoughts slide into useless static.

"I should…I should have kept a better eye on her," his wife blurted. "She'd only just started the new spring term at school and they said she pushed herself too hard in sports—ran herself into the ground with her cataplexy, or something about too much dance. Normally she gets back up and at it, but this time she didn't come around for a whole day, so she got returned to us. She'd only been back to school for a week and had to come home again. Anyway, she'd been home for maybe two days and just… I heard this terrible thump upstairs and I *knew*, call it mother's instinct or whatever you like, but I *just knew* she'd hurt herself. And there she was, lying at the bottom of the attic stairs."

"I see, I'm very sorry," Mayu replied, taking a mental note to tell Tomoya: avoid attics, stairs, and excessive sports in their dreams. "Has anyone talked to you about this procedure?"

Mrs. Mansfield took her husband's hand.

"Not in detail," said Mrs. Mansfield. "What will happen?"

"In simple terms please; we're not doctors," added Mr. Mansfield.

"Normally," Mayu began, "we insert probes into the

patient's forehead. This is not damaging, do not worry. What we do is heighten one of her brain frequencies. This makes her dreams intense but open to suggestion.

"Tomoya, one of the team, will be put into a coma state nearby. We do the same thing to him—put probes in his mind." She tapped her forehead in three different spots. "Their brain frequencies will then be connected and Tomoya will act as her Dream Guide. He will enter her dreams to convince her to wake up."

"How?" blurted Mrs. Mansfield. "Or is that a difficult question?"

Mayu's shoulders relaxed. She'd given this spiel once already at the conference. She explained the process of reigniting neural pathways through exercise and imagination. The experience would seem so life-like that, to start with, Skye would not be able to distinguish between reality and dreams. "For all intents and purposes, Skye and Tomoya will exist in a parallel world of their own making. However," Mayu heaved a sigh and took a moment to choose her words. "You must understand, if we do this, there is no going back. Skye will either survive, or she will not. There is no in between."

Mrs. Mansfield's eyes widened. "No margin at all?"

"Your daughter's narcolepsy and cataplexy are conditions we've never encountered before in previous patients, which makes the risks higher." She thought of Yūta's face, covered in bandages and burn marks when they first brought him into the hospital. "Once Skye's consciousness is connected to Tomoya, she will become dependent upon his ability to control their perceptions of reality.

"When the fabric of your world is threatened—especially

in such an internal way—the brain can shut down in panic. It's violent, it causes a seizure, and the patient can die. This can happen at any point, so the Guide must keep things… controlled."

Staring at the couple's stunned faces made it harder to keep talking. An ache to run away filled her, but she held her head high.

"We had one patient who came close to shutting down but who pulled through, they described it as fatal sleep and we have adopted the term. We encourage patients to go to sleep and wake up fresh within their dream, but somehow…our patients sense whether it will be the last time they go to sleep. So, there's always a good chance we can avoid it. There are clear signs Tomoya will watch for.

"If we start this, even just to test if Skye is receptive to Parallel stimulation, there is no going back. We must ride through the storm until her brainwaves either resettle and there is no change to her condition, or she wakes up."

Mr. Mansfield looked at his wife and kissed her hand. She started weeping, sniffing hard to avoid making a scene. Mayu swallowed the lump in her throat.

"If you need time…" she whispered.

Mrs. Mansfield gripped her husband's hand tight against her chest, just as Mayu used to do with Yūta whenever they murmured promises to each other.

"This is going to cost a fortune and, what, it's fifty-fifty? I want a percentage." A stern, unflinching mask settled on Mr. Mansfield's face. "What's the likelihood of success?"

"When we do this," Mayu said, "it's not just Skye's life that will be at risk, but Tomoya's as well. That's why it's expensive. It's a dangerous job that only we can do." He stared without blinking, waiting for a direct answer. "I can't give you a percentage yet."

"Why would you advertise such a dangerous procedure?" asked Mrs. Mansfield, her blue eyes shining as glossy as her pearl earrings.

"Because it works." Only one death out of seventeen.

"What about the dreams?" Mrs. Mansfield asked. They shared a tight-lipped glance, sniffing through their aristocratic white noses, when a dull buzzing noise interrupted the moment. Mrs. Mansfield eased her hand out of her husband's grip and pulled a cell phone from her pocket.

"Excuse me," she said and clopped off down the corridor, answering the call.

Mayu felt her bottom jaw jutting out in distaste.

"Bloody hell, I'd rather kill her in her sleep peacefully than give her a seizure," Mr. Mansfield muttered, dragging a hand down his face. He looked tired and distracted, his gaze darting over the glass balcony and around the central shaft above the lobby.

"We…" A gnawing doubt crept into Mayu's gut. "We're highly successful." The success rate came from Mayu's work as the Dream Guide. She couldn't speak for Tomoya's chances, and it felt like promising false hope. She squashed the feeling, ashamed of doubting one of her best employees.

"That girl always has been trouble," Mr. Mansfield sighed fondly. The light in his eyes snuffed out again as he looked at Mayu. "A family friend is paying for Skye's dream treatment. We don't want his generosity to be in vain either."

"That's a risk he will have to take. We all will."

The way Mr. Mansfield narrowed his eyes made her mouth go dry. A lean man with hollow cheeks, he looked as clean cut as the diamonds he sold. Mayu clenched her hands in her lap and tried a reassuring smile. It only seemed to aggravate him.

It did surprise her to learn that the Mansfields weren't paying for Skye's treatment. From Skye's background profile, she knew they dealt in sourcing diamonds for numerous international jewellers. Since they were obviously well-off, Mayu had assumed they had the money for Skye's treatment and more left over to burn in the streets—especially since their family home was up in Scotland. The couple had transferred Skye to London when she first fell unconscious, as if under the impression that no other hospital compared to this one.

Taking a deep breath, Mr. Mansfield pursed his lips and folded his hands on top of the table.

"We're aware that Skye's dreams will be like another world. Now you're telling us that if her cataplexy is triggered there, it could have unforeseen consequences." He tilted his head, no longer just a father, but a businessman about to extract what he wanted—a man who probably got his demands often and who did not respond kindly when denied. "If we do this, I want you to promise that your man can suppress any bad memory or nightmare Skye might dally with. She's always had a wild imagination and a lot of nightmares."

Her skin felt like it was humming with the effort to appear calm.

"Can this Tom side-track her, or not?" His eyebrows quirked up as if punctuating an ultimatum. "My girl is challenging, a good liar and prone to melodrama. Given her conditions, can he keep someone like that in check? Doctors have warned us that she might not be the same when she wakes up, that she'll have memory failure. But we came to *you*. I want her back the way she was."

"She already has high Parallel brainwaves, but—"

Mrs. Mansfield returned and without sitting down interrupted, "Let's just do it. That was Fabio. He said go for it. We've got to take our best shot at waking Skye, and he'll pay." The businesswoman flicked a finger at the corner of her eye, fighting the wobble in her lip.

"Really?" whispered Mr. Mansfield, searching his wife's face.

"He said…seeing Skye awake again will be payment enough."

Mr. Mansfield gripped his wife's hand and spoke with his eyes, a silent conversation that was testimony to a long, well-weathered relationship.

"Alright then," agreed Mr. Mansfield, smiling at last. It didn't make him look any more genial. "We'll leave her life to you, Doctor."

Mayu nodded, eager to get away from them. "We'll do our best."

She bowed slightly, slipped out of her seat and covered her mouth as she strode away. She should have been firmer; she should have told them that Skye might not wake up as the same girl who fell down the stairs. Thank the stars Tomoya was going under instead of her. If they failed again…or maybe that's why they'd failed Yūta—she should not have insisted on being his Dream Guide, she should have accepted Tomoya's offer, his logic. *I'll be less emotionally involved*, he'd said, *you know that's always best.*

Instead of returning to the team, she dived into the toilets, picked a cubicle and sat on the toilet lid. Mayu tugged out Yūta's dog tags and doubled over, clutching them tight and squeezing her eyes shut.

"Yūta, I'm sorry," she wheezed.

"Don't over-think things," she imagined him saying, murmuring to herself in the deepest voice she could manage. "Come on, Doctor Shirakawa. Stop worrying. We got this."

"We got this." But they weren't a duo anymore. There was no "'we.'" She felt a scream build inside her throat. Good old Mayu. Special Mayu, with her special brainwaves. "Come on, you baby," she told herself, "Stop being pathetic."

A creaky squeak echoed in the bathroom as someone entered and Mayu held her breath.

"Mayu? Are you alright?"

Momo.

If she stayed quiet, maybe…

"Don't make me check under the stalls. I saw you sneak in here."

"Hello, Momo," she sighed. Putting on a brave face and wiping her eyes, Mayu opened the door. She jumped back as Momo charged into the cubicle and dragged her to the mirrors where the light was brighter.

"Oh, Mayu!" Momo rose up on tiptoes and wrapped her arms around Mayu's neck. "You should tell me when you're upset."

"Get off," she muttered, pushing Momo away. "I'm fine; I just wanted to think, in peace."

"Are you sure?" Momo peered up at her, combing her fingers through the pink-tipped strands of her hair. "You've been doubting your work a lot lately."

Mayu made a show of washing her hands.

"You don't contribute as much to discussions," said Momo, softly. "And you've stopped criticising Matokai when he goes off topic. It's driving me nuts! Your notes are so…quiet too. I don't know, there's no bold suggestions in the margins."

"Stop it." It came out harsher than expected, clearly audible in the empty bathroom. Shame radiated across every inch of Mayu's skin. Even if the ceiling collapsed on top of her and ended this interrogation, it wouldn't crush the frustration and guilt filling her every muscle. "I'm fine."

She yelped in surprise as Momo wrapped her in a firm embrace, pinning Mayu's arms to her side.

"You're not a failure, Mayu," she whispered into her shoulder.

Mayu hung her head as another surge of heat hit the back of her eyes, but she did not let it win. Biting her tongue and inhaling deeply, Mayu stared at her reflection, pushing her chaotic feelings somewhere dark and isolated. Even if she couldn't believe Momo, she had to act otherwise, before the whole team felt like they were standing on shaky legs. They had a job to do.

5

I T HAD BEEN two months since she came back to work but Mayu was finally finding the energy she needed, she was turning up for everything at least fifteen minutes early again. The hospital's quiet lobby should have been a perfect place to read her novel while she waited for the rest of the team, but she didn't get past unlocking her Porta Book's homepage—merely stared at the television in reception.

It was broadcasting a weather warning. Mayu read the subtitles that warned of gales, building stronger over the next few days. In two weeks, they could be looking into the face of a hurricane unless the winds blew themselves out.

Two weeks. What if Tomoya didn't rescue Skye before that? No, he was good, better than good, and he always surpassed Mayu at everything, given time. Her average was four days; this would be no different. Still, what if?

She had taken two weeks trying to save her husband. This time they didn't have two weeks, not if a hurricane was coming. Her heart started thumping—not fast, just hard, painful beats. She wondered whether she should intervene and take over as the Dream Guide. She touched her forehead, the skin no longer bumpy, hiding the recovery going on beneath. A hurricane would affect power. They needed a dedicated back-up generator.

A blur of movement caught the corner of her eye.

Dressed in a fresh suit, Tomoya marched across the floor, panic written in the taut line of his mouth. When he said good morning to her, it sounded like he was greeting an ex-girlfriend he'd hoped never to see again—quiet and abrupt. In fact, his breathing came in harsh puffs. Mayu tucked her Porta Book away and uncrossed her legs.

"What's wrong?"

Tomoya had a habit of mincing his words, but without any hesitation he fell into the space beside her and spoke so fast she almost didn't catch it.

"I ran ahead of him. In the cab—I was in the back—next to Richard. I didn't mean to look, but I did. I saw a weather warning about a hurricane on his phone."

"So did I." She gestured towards the television.

"It could arrive in the next couple of weeks. We don't have the funds to stay here until the storm has passed."

"But if we go home," said Mayu, "the cost of getting here, transporting our equipment, *then* getting everything home again means we will lose more than if we waited it out."

Tomoya rubbed a hand over his mouth, until he was fully massaging his jaw. "Shirakawa, I don't think I can bring her back in less than a week."

Panic threatened to swallow her, because if he believed that, then Mayu would have to take over or they'd all go home to a crushing debt and, potentially, no job. "You can do this," she said. "You're very capable. In practice, the last three times you pulled me back in a day, or just over. I will find us another source of income, perhaps by tomorrow and then we can put it off until the storm passes. But if that's not possible, you *will* be okay. Okay?"

With a calm exhale, Tomoya's shoulders relaxed.

Mayu watched Fukushima arrive, he nodded 'hello' across the room. Fixing an amicable smile, she nodded back, thinking the same thing as everyone else: who would take on their massive expenses when the world was falling apart?

৵

Mr. and Mrs. Mansfield signed the appropriate paperwork and Momo measured their daughter's head for the probes. A glass wall, that was in fact a monitor, partitioned her bed from the control area where the team would work when monitoring Skye and her Dream Guide.

Tomoya and Fukushima set up Morpheus, the main machine, which had been specially flown in from their lab in Tokyo. It was positioned between Skye's bed and the empty bed that awaited Tomoya.

Richard and Momo checked that Morpheus responded correctly on their monitors and that certain charts overlapped on the glass screen without glitching. Momo, seated at the main monitor, tossed her head back, showing off the elegant lines of her jaw and neck, "Richard, would you take a look at this?" she purred, batting her long, fluttery eyelashes.

He looked up from where he knelt in the corner, optimising the main circuit board and switches. It took a moment for the words to register, his vacant eyes suggesting that he was still thinking about circuitry. With wires draped over his shoulder and glasses for close-up work, he looked wiser. He peered over them at her. "Is there a problem, *Mochi*?" he asked, getting up.

Momo scowled at the pet name, but not in the same way she used to; a devious little glint in her eyes. Mayu could remember a time when Momo snapped at any man who dared to shorten her surname to '"Mochi," but Richard got away with calling her "sweet rice cake" as if they were childhood friends. Most of the time.

At the back of the room, Mayu hid a smirk and chewed on her thumbnail. She sat at the writing table sifting through paperwork, her phone always within reach.

"Let's have a look," said Richard, engaging in his usual habit of leaning over peoples' chairs, one hand on the tabletop monitor. Momo leant back in her chair to explain the problem to his left cheek.

Harsh winds outside battered the windows, bringing dark, sooty clouds with them. When she looked back at her phone, the text she had written to their colleague in Tokyo still said 'pending'.

"Oh," she began, addressing the others, "someone's coming to fix the ceiling hooks—"

The wind punched against the glass, shrieking like a runaway train. All the lights flickered, including their monitors.

"When do we get that back-up generator?" Fukushima asked Mayu, kneading his hands together.

"They said tomorrow."

"Good. We don't have the money to delay. We will get everything ready to begin tomorrow."

Everyone looked at Tomoya. For a smart man, he

didn't hide his feelings very well. His throat bobbed and his lips stretched thin. "Are you sure we can't—I mean, what if Mayu finds new sponsors? Can't we wait out the storm?"

Fukushima kept his face neutral as he asked, "Mayu, is there anyone who'll sign us on within the next forty-eight hours?" His tone suggested that he expected a negative answer.

"Not yet, but I'll keep trying," she told Tomoya, trying to sound confident and upbeat.

"Well, I—I should get on with reading Miss Mansfield's profile," he said.

They toiled until late afternoon, going over every item on their checklist and each component of the machine that would merge Skye and Tomoya's brainwaves. Tomoya grew distracted as the day went on, when he joined them at the machine he became a hindrance, his mind preoccupied with his role the next day.

Mayu shrank with guilt, pretending not to notice, withdrawing into her own thoughts. Under the artificial lights, surrounded by soft murmurs and the whistling outside, she felt increasingly drained. She stared at the tablet in front of her, at the hundreds of unopened emails, from other doctors, from their sponsor, from potential new sponsors, it seemed pointless.

"Are you going to just sit there, Mayu? You haven't made any calls."

The quiet words slapped her. She looked up at Fukushima, unable to reply. Tomoya peered at them from the other side of the table.

"You've been spacing out all day. Have you got an update on funding?"

Blinking fast, she looked back at the tablet. She didn't want any of these sponsors. They reeked of meddling and moving them away from coma therapy, of outsiders dictating how she should do her job. The only decision she'd made was to approve a new intern for the lab back at base. Her Head Neuropharmacologist, Keiji Obinata, had messaged to say that his interview with the graduate had been 'highly promising,' which made it easy to respond, 'sounds great, get her started'. Maybe hiring new staff was not a priority but, feeling stubborn, she told herself that their business wasn't over until it was over. She shook her head at Fukushima in response. He grumbled his disapproval but went back to his own work.

"Tomoya," she said around four o'clock, "you should go relax."

"I…are you sure?" He hunched over Skye's file, as if to hide the papers he'd been scribbling on. From the glimpses she'd had of his notes, it wasn't to do with Skye's procedure. "I mean, there are still things to do. I don't mind."

Momo had said she wasn't criticising him enough, so she mustered some sense of responsibility and replied, "You've spent too much time on your own pet projects rather than on Skye's profile," but it sounded weak, because really, he'd probably memorised Skye's medical conditions, personal details, school reports, even blood-type, in one reading. "We'll manage. I…don't think I'll find us new funding within a week. I'm sorry, Tomoya. We'll have to start testing tomorrow." She offered an apologetic smile. "Go on. Take the folder and I'll visit you later. You can do this."

Like a ghost going through the motions of a past life,

Tomoya gathered up the papers in one disorganised pile. "Thanks for trying, Shirakawa." He bowed and Richard opened the door for him as he went.

By eight o'clock that evening, Fukushima deemed everything was ready for preliminary tests the next day.

"Everyone, make sure you get proper rest," he said. "It may be the last we have for a while. Who knows how long it will take to wake this girl up."

"What if Matokai takes longer than four days?" said Richard, skewing his mouth and folding his arms. The wind seemed to moan the same question.

"He won't," replied Fukushima. "The odds are on our side. And we can't afford to let this take longer, not just because of some storm. We'll only bury ourselves in more debt if our stay here is prolonged. Mayu, did you settle anything this afternoon?"

His tone made her clench her handbag like she might swing it at him, "And what if I haven't?"

Everyone froze, but Mayu did her best to stare Fukushima out.

"Are you serious?" Fukushima said carefully. "What's with your attitude?"

"What's with your *tone*? We can't pick a new sponsor in one afternoon. Don't suggest that I'm not doing anything. I'll just pack up and leave if that's what you think."

"Of course I don't. We depend on you." Anger began to slip through his words.

"I'm sick of you breathing down my neck today! What's your problem?"

His eyebrows shot high, revealing anxiety and disbelief. "I'm just asking for progress, not a contract, signed and stamped! We're supposed to be a team. Don't you care about that anymore? If we don't choose a new sponsor for ourselves swiftly, someone will take the project by legal obligation, like the Department of Defence, probably for interrogation research. How can you not see that? All our livelihoods are at risk, not just yours!"

It took a moment for Mayu to compose herself as the truth of his words settled between them.

"I might get some coffee. Anyone want coffee?" murmured Richard.

Fukushima huffed, focusing on Mayu. "I'm not sure you're taking your role seriously anymore."

"Hey, what's gotten into you?" Momo back-handed his arm, "Of course she is."

But if Mayu was honest with herself, Fukushima was only pointing out what the others were willing to excuse. Sure, she turned up on time, early most days, but she wasn't putting in the effort. As they argued, Mayu pulled on her coat and left without a word, relieved that their voices were silenced when the door clicked shut behind her.

6

OUTSIDE, RAIN LASHED the sidewalk. It soaked Mayu's coat the second she stepped outside, a wall of water so thick that squinting didn't make the edge of the sidewalk any easier to see. She told herself it didn't matter if she caught a cold waiting for a taxi; it would suit her mood.

Finally, locked in her hotel room, Mayu curled up on the bed. She reached for her phone, opened the contact details for her colleague, Keiji Obinata, and stared at the digits for a few minutes, just wanting to hear a detached voice from everything that was happening. Some part of her recognised that it was weird to call an acquaintance from across the world just for late night chit-chat.

She flicked through her photos instead. Most related to her work, specialised equipment and charts from the lab, but some were of Yūta, and the yellow tulips he used to bring home. He would buy them on unimportant days so it always surprised her. She smiled at a picture of the first beautiful, buttery bouquet he'd brought home. She swiped the screen; a snap of them together appeared. Yūta stood tall, at six-foot-three, smiling sheepishly at the stranger she had persuaded to take their picture. A winter sky glowed around his mussed black hair, softening the angles of his face. Mount Fuji loomed in the background, majestic and capped in snow. Mayu had both arms wrapped around Yūta's waist. Her head barely came up to his chest.

"Mini and Mighty claim this bridge," he had muttered.

"Make sure you smile!" Mayu laughed, looking up at him just to make sure.

One click and that second was captured, frozen in time.

Although the brain can retain enough information to fill a house, even working at minimum capacity, Yūta's voice, the smell of his clothes, had been lost. The sensation of his body engulfing Mayu from behind—even that was fading. She squeezed her eyes shut and searched for that feeling deep within her heart. A gentle whisper lay against her skin; a blush of heat momentarily warmed her; Yūta was still there.

Except he's not, is he? Death bled insidiously into her thoughts, the unforgettable memory of its slow, cold flow as it claimed Yūta. Terrifying, and yet somehow calming. Just before she had come round, as death tore their dreams apart, a blissful peace had filled her. She had wondered whether it was just the anaesthetic but if, in dreams, death felt like falling into a coma, maybe it wasn't so frightening.

She reached into her suitcase and took out a selection of painkillers.

✄

That evening, Mayu found Tomoya in his hotel room, slumped on the couch, the cushions plump, plum-coloured and comforting. She avoided the empty space beside him, opting for the firm armchair. His eyes stayed unfocused and his attention distracted, so Mayu resorted to reading a complementary magazine as the wind and rain buffeted the windows.

"Skye likes ballet," whispered Tomoya, his mind clearly unable to rest. The cream clock on the side table blinked over to nine-thirty and Mayu lowered the magazine.

"You used to like dancing," he said.

As much as Mayu wanted to forget about her high school culture club, if it made Tomoya feel more at ease… She thought back, feeling the warmth of the dance hall in summer. She would end up drenched in sweat, her feet sore from spinning on the springwood floor.

"That was a long time ago," she mused. "I'm surprised you still remember."

"You should have seen yourself." Tomoya blushed and hunched his shoulders. "My friends went to watch Etsuko, but I always thought your technique was better. I didn't stare, I promise. I just…remember."

Dancing came as naturally to Mayu as ice-skating on concrete: that is, it didn't. She ruffled her fringe, unsure what to say. "I never took it seriously," she said. "Etsuko wanted to dance; I went because I had to join a culture club. It seemed logical to pick one where I could go with a friend."

Tomoya leant forward, his arms on his knees. "Yeah, but you were focused. And you always danced by yourself, in the sunniest corner of the room, like you wanted to challenge yourself. I mean, now I know you can't resist sunlight even if it means cooking to death, but I always admired that about you; your focus, that is."

"Where is this coming from?" Mayu asked, forcing a nervous laugh.

"Nowhere! It's just that…" He hung his head and looked away. "Why did you hire me?"

Super-smart Tomoya doubted himself. Mayu's lips parted in surprise, but nothing came out.

Folding up the magazine, Mayu reached over and patted the back of his hand. He pulled back, his wide eyes reflecting the lamplight, but allowed Mayu to place her hand on top of his. Tomoya looked away again. *Think, Mayu, think!* She was distracted by the wind outside, it had rediscovered its wailing voice, and by the tingling sensation in her cheeks from her earlier combination of painkillers.

"I didn't know you in school," she said at last, licking her not-quite-numb lips, "but I knew your name. Tomoya Matokai… Tomoya Matokai… Three years younger than me and yet some bumbling kid was the smartest in our school?"

He met her gaze, clearly unsure how to take this. Mayu grinned.

"I wanted to know why I always came second. I wanted to be loved like Tomoya Matokai. 'Oh, he's so thoughtful!' the teachers used to say. Even Etsuko, she used to dance hoping you'd ask her out one day you know."

"What?" He tried to laugh, his ears red. "You could have told me that eleven years ago!"

"Yeah, well, I couldn't let the perfect Matokai have my best friend too, could I? The first time I remember meeting you properly was at university. Do you remember? I was so mad. I couldn't believe you'd made it onto the same course as me. So again, Tomoya Matokai… Tomoya Matokai…

Your name followed me around no matter where I went. But when I met you, I couldn't stay mad."

"I remember now," he murmured. "You asked me some weird questions."

Ah yes, not her shining moment. "The point *is*," she hurried on, "your dedication and talent shines above the rest. You're smarter than me; you get things done. That's why I hired you. I can see you're having doubts, Miss Mansfield is your first patient, but I know you're capable of anything you set your mind on, even helping this kid."

Tomoya snuck a glance at her and held her fingers, returning the firm grip. "I see." His touch felt clammy. "It's ironic, right? That's exactly what I thought of you. Thanks, Shirakawa. I think."

Mayu's mind filled with dancing—flashes of spinning, blankets of sunlight, swinging her arms through dust motes, twisting and panting. Had Tomoya been there in the shadows of the hall, watching her instead of Etsuko? Just out of view, despite Mayu's futile efforts to pretend she was dancing alone. They could have been friends, if she hadn't been so proud.

Clearing her throat, Mayu sat back in her chair and Tomoya sought for something to do. For a while he chewed on the end of a pencil Mayu had lent him yesterday. 'Loaning' Tomoya a pencil was pretty much a permanent grant.

"Shirakawa," he said, pushing the pencil above his ear and grabbing his pen instead, twisting it in his fingers, "I've got to be honest. I'm still not sure about being Skye's Dream Guide. I want to be, I really do, and I think I can do it…" He picked up his precious black folder, splurging with multicoloured tabs and scrappy bits of paper. "But I think I'd feel better if we had a back-up plan—something more than succeed or fail."

Mayu closed her eyes heavily for a second, sucking on her dry tongue. "Well, we haven't come up with anything yet."

"I know. But I've been thinking about how I sometimes get stuck between realities," he went on. "When we share practice dreams, sometimes I see something different to you. I can't quite penetrate your perceptions."

"That's not unusual. I can't do it all the time either."

Tomoya scribbled a harsh line on the cover of his folder, the ink invisible on the black, but a deep rivet showed in the lamplight. "I know. But you still gain control much quicker. If I get stuck between realities with Skye, that could be it. We're either both in a coma forever, or one—or both of us—die!"

The plain, polished room shrank in size as Tomoya's panic flared at last.

"Calm down," said Mayu. "Tell me what you've been planning."

He flipped open the folder, unclipped the binding, and handed her a number of sheets. The first page had a pencilled diagram of three people connected by Parallel Energy. Mayu's eyes widened as the algorithms clicked together.

"If I need help, if I get stuck, or it looks like I'm sinking," Tomoya gushed, "I think we can connect three people. We can connect you to Skye and me, and you can pull us through."

"But we've got no way of implementing this without

proper testing." She flicked through the other sheets, absorbing his neat handwriting, the myriad of images, and her own formulas.

"I need *something*," he said.

Skimming the last page, Mayu tore her gaze away to look at Tomoya, and found a vulnerable face watching her, an expression she saw every day in the mirror.

"It scares you, doesn't it?" he said softly. "Being a Dream Guide again."

Taking a deep breath and trying desperately to wet her tongue now, Mayu refocused on his papers. "Let's call Obinata. If we give him your notes, he can test it for us at the lab, but that doesn't mean we can use it yet."

Tomoya sagged into the couch for the first time and his shoulders relaxed. "So long as he keeps you updated." With that, he sprung out of his chair to fetch his computer tablet. Their work chat app was ringing by the time he sat back down, the inevitable 'smash-and-grab' news banner rolling along the bottom. He grabbed a bottle of water from the table beside him.

"You sound thirsty, do you want this?" He offered her the bottle.

Mayu moved to the empty space beside Tomoya, a video feed opened just as she got settled.

A man with broad, stony shoulders stared back at them. "Guys, it's four in the morning!" he grumbled.

"Oh, sorry," Tomoya's whole body cringed. "I forgot."

Keiji Obinata didn't twitch, but Mayu noticed the subtle flare of his nostrils as he sighed. His dyed, platinum blond hair looked flatter than usual and his eyes were soft with sleep. Keiji had such an angular, judging face, but she had warmed to him when they'd first met three years ago—something about him seemed honest, and boy, had she been right about that. He'd seemed overly reserved in the beginning, but she soon learnt he was just private, and considered everything he wanted to say before speaking.

"You've got five seconds to convince me it's important."

"Right. So. I've got this theory I really need you to run tests on."

While Mayu drained the entire bottle of water, Keiji sighed often, but sat there patiently, listening. The windows in the hotel room rattled, the glass seemed to buzz with pressure and Mayu snatched Tomoya's wrist, staring at the windows, afraid they might burst at any second. She tried hard to focus through the drug-induced numbness taking over her whole face.

"What was…guys your…hello?" Keiji's face froze on screen as the signal cut out.

Just as the lights flickered, the doorbell rang—the sound was meant to imitate a burst of songbirds. It was shrill and abrupt, an odd quirk for a hotel room. Mayu jumped up, dragging Tomoya away from the windows, and answered the door. It was a small service bot holding out a pamphlet, its blue, pixelated eyes curved in a joyful expression.

"Good evening," it said. "Wind speeds could amplify in ways that may affect this building's health and safety. If you hear an alarm, please follow the instructions in this pamphlet. If you have any questions, please summon me, ring reception, or speak to a member of staff. Thank you for your cooperation."

It turned left and rolled along the corridor to the next room. Mayu met Tomoya's shrewd eyes, gripping the pamphlet.

"Maybe we need two generators," he said, voice hoarse.

7

I N SKYE'S HOSPITAL room the next day, Mayu sat at the control station twisting her wedding ring around her finger and watching Tomoya through the towering glass monitor. Momo sat beside her, leaning over the computer bank to analyse the details scrolling past.

Yesterday's storm had eventually died down, leaving sporadic showers and mild wind. Sunlight faded in and out between the clouds, casting intermittent rays of light into the room that bounced off the panels of their dedicated generator.

Standing in the corner out the way, Mrs. Mansfield tapped at her smart phone. She didn't glance up at the team, the monitor, or even her daughter, but moved her thumbs across the flickering screen with deft speed. At least Mayu knew when to stop working, Skye's mother was dressed in a business suit again; a pencil skirt, a blue corded jacket, and a tasteful gold necklace twinkling with emerald stones. It was awkward to have her present, Mayu was grateful she didn't understand Japanese.

On the other side of the high-tech glass screen, Tomoya sat in a supportive chair for this testing phase, as Fukushima strapped him into a simulation helmet.

"You calibrated it already?" Mayu asked Momo.

"Measured it out first thing," she replied. "Marked up Matokai's head, set the grid equations, input his standard PDE—we're good to go. Just need Fuku to insert the carbon claw probes."

Clapping his hands, Richard leant over Momo and hit the microphone button. "Looking good, Matokai," he said, his voice filtering into Tomoya's helmet.

Tomoya tried to look up and Fukushima slapped his shoulder.

The helmet covered Tomoya's eyes and nose; fulgent blue lights on the helmet indicated that he was fully conscious. Wires that would soon connect him to Skye trailed out of the helmet's crown, curved up towards hooks in the ceiling, and then back down to Morpheus. Electrodes with carbon claws were already piercing the girl's forehead, ready to begin testing.

Skye's mother finally looked up and caught Mayu staring. Mayu darted her gaze back to the others. She heard Mrs. Mansfield clear her throat and then her high heels clicking across the room towards her. Conjuring a smile felt like forcing together incorrect jigsaw pieces, her mouth skewed into tight alignment, but Mayu did her best as the woman stopped beside her and folded her arms.

"I'm just telling my husband you're beginning testing," she said. "And Fabio."

"Ah." Mayu chewed her inner lip. "Your friend is very generous."

Nodding, Mrs. Mansfield's smile was thin, her gaze fixed on Richard's back. She swallowed hard. "We've been friends a very, very long time. Long before Skye. He introduced us to the world of diamonds, in fact. Without him, we wouldn't be in this business at all."

Perhaps the Mansfields could be potential investors in the Parallel Dream Project, she wondered.

"It's absurd, having a business *and* a child, but we did it. Do you have children?"

There was a momentary blank where Mayu wanted to disappear; dissolve into nothingness. "No."

"Smart. Don't have children and don't get a dog. Terrible commitments." Mrs. Mansfield tittered at her own inappropriateness, until she saw Mayu's unfeeling stillness. "What's the helmet for?"

Rousing herself to follow the woman's head-jerk at Tomoya, she said, "It's to test a patient's reception to electro stimuli. It is not immersive, just a brushing of consciousnesses. Physical observations are often not enough—even chart readings can't tell if a patient has reachable dreams. We suspect Skye will be fine, but it's best to follow procedure."

"I think we're ready," said Fukushima, no longer fiddling with the helmet. "Matokai, don't do too much. Just observe and do as instructed, you hear?"

"Yes, sir."

Taking off his glasses and wiping them on his lab coat, Fukushima nodded at Momo, looking grim. Mayu stopped twisting her ring. Richard hit the microphone button again.

"Okay. We begin in five, four…"

Mayu bit her lip.

"One. Introduce electrical stimuli."

Fukushima, still standing between Skye and Tomoya, powered up the Morpheus. Lights blinked across its surface and, instantly, one of Skye's brainwaves undulated across the glass wall monitor—her PDE. So far so good, no negative spikes.

Beside the brainwave graphs, yellow glowing veins spread out like spider webs. They expanded and pulsed into a twistable, 3D render of Skye Mansfield's brain.

"Live images rendered. Increase strength," said Richard.

Fukushima altered the settings.

"Careful," Momo pointed to a reading at the bottom of the screen, "blood flow around Skye's brain has increased."

"I'll manipulate the left probes accordingly," said Fukushima.

Richard swiped across a tabletop monitor and the charts on the main screen changed. They moved to overlap each other. "Parallel Dream Energy readings have increased by three percent and rising," he reported. "Heart rate unchanged. Blood flow steadying."

"You'll get to talk to him again, won't you?" asked Mrs. Mansfield, glancing from Mayu to Tomoya, looking anxious. "Properly, I mean."

"Yes. After he's made contact with Skye and we bring him back for stage two."

"My husband and I…perhaps we should have mentioned, Skye loves hide and seek… Not just hiding herself but finding hidden objects…and hiding them too. Perhaps that's something that your colleague could use…or ask her about…" Mrs. Mansfield fidgeted in discomfort, "…in the dream world, I mean."

"Oh. Well, I'll let him know after testing then." Mayu turned away. "Sorry, I have to concentrate now."

Skye's mother returned to the corner of the room and resumed tapping on her phone, although it didn't consume her attention this time. Her eyelashes were thick and curled, bringing a sharp severity to every glance she flashed their way.

Taking a deep breath, Richard glanced across at Momo. She nodded at him.

"Increase strength," he said.

"I'm feeling a little nervous," Tomoya whispered.

Tucking a pink strand of hair behind her ear, Momo squeezed Richard aside to get to the microphone. "Believe in yourself, or I'll come in there and rough you up. You still owe me a bowl of *champon*. Get this right, and I'll wipe your debt clean."

"You know not to bet against me."

"That's the spirit."

"Increase strength," said Richard, reclaiming the mic. "Skye's PDE is at 10 percent and rising, condition stable." He turned to Mayu. "Alright, on my mark." Then into the microphone again, "Matokai, we're about to inject the epizodaphine. You shouldn't feel more than a sting. If anything feels wrong, anything at all, just say so."

"Understood," Tomoya replied. He clenched the armrests. "I'm ready."

"Try to relax." Richard nodded at Mayu, who initiated the injection sequence.

In the chair, Tomoya gritted his teeth and squirmed slightly.

That should be me, thought Mayu.

Tomoya's readings came up on the glass wall next to Skye's, and Fukushima joined everyone behind the monitor. For the next few minutes, the team whispered and altered settings from behind the glass. Eventually, Tomoya's jaw went slack and his hands draped over the armrests, relaxed.

"Can you hear me, Matokai?" asked Richard.

Everyone grew still waiting for his reply. Even Mrs. Mansfield's thumbs paused as she looked up under her lashes. She might not have understood their words, but the sudden hush around the room translated that the time for jokes was over.

"Yes," Tomoya whispered.

"Very good. How do things feel?"

"Floating…"

Richard scribbled something down. "That's nice. Your heart rate is a little jumpy. You sure you feel okay?"

No reply.

"Do you know what you have to do?"

No reply. Tomoya's heart rate and breathing continued to speed up.

"Matokai, do you—"

"Shirakawa?" Tomoya said.

Richard glanced across at Mayu. "Huh? You gotta focus, Matokai. Do—"

"Please let…Shirakawa speak."

Nobody moved. They all stared at Mayu. Her cheeks burned so hot they had to be glowing. Richard broke the silence with a surprised chuckle.

"Shirakawa, I think someone's on the phone for you."

"Shut up," she murmured, taking his place at the microphone. "Tomoya, it's me."

A nervous smile twitched at Tomoya's mouth. "You've…been here."

Ah, now she understood. "I have. I know it seems scary, but you're fine. You're not trapped; we'll set you free in a minute. Just take a deep, calm breath."

Mayu shuddered, watching his chest rise and fall. The test phase was the worst. Dreaming, but still aware. Trapped and immobile, barely able to speak, unsure what was real or if you'd ever escape the darkness. What if the team forgot about you?

"We'll give you a good shake in a minute," she reassured. "You are not trapped, and we're not going anywhere. You'll be able to move again, I promise."

"Thank you."

On screen, his heart rate started to calm.

"I'm right here. I'm real. Take a deep breath and let your body relax. Just sink into your thoughts."

Tomoya's current semi-conscious state was not unheard of; many people experienced it, although unintentionally, all over the world. Doctors called it 'sleep paralysis'; patients called it terrifying. Mayu could relate to the latter. She and Tomoya were lucky, most people in sleep paralysis could not speak at all, for Mayu, and probably Tomoya, it was possible with enormous effort, at least, during testing.

"Do you know what you have to do?" Mayu asked. Almost half a minute passed before Tomoya replied. "Find Skye."

"That's correct. We're about to merge your Parallel frequencies. Remember, the girl is sensitive to shock and fear. Be gentle."

There was no confirmation, but Mayu was confident that he had understood as the lights on his simulation helmet turned yellow. His brainwaves were ready to merge.

The others stared at her, waiting.

"Do it," she said.

Numbers began counting down on the glass monitor.

A new chart appeared in the top corner with two fluctuating lines gradually drawing closer together—Tomoya and Skye's Parallel Dream Energies.

The two connected.

Tomoya's hands clenched; Skye's cerebral blood flow spiked. Mayu knew that if it increased too far it might cause an aneurysm, followed by a seizure.

"Tomoya, can you tell me what's happening?" she asked with forced composure. "Stay calm, don't force anything."

"Skye's not responding to stimuli," said Momo. "Electrical pulses fading fast."

"Tomoya," Mayu said again, "can you *talk* to me?"

His lips moved but nothing came out, only bursts of harsh breathing.

"Matokai's blood pressure is rising," Momo warned.

Mrs. Mansfield sensed the urgency in their voices and folded her phone, looking anxious now and poised to get involved. Sensing this, Mayu turned away, shot back to her workstation, focused on her controls, and increased the dose of epizodaphine.

"What are you doing?" Fukushima hissed. "Too much and you'll put him under for good!"

"He needs to calm down and help the girl to help himself, or they'll both suffer," she snapped, aware of their spectator reacting to the tension.

Just then, Tomoya's hoarse voice whispered, "She's all alone. I can see her."

Taking a deep breath, she quickly moved back to the mic, Mayu purred, "Good, that's good. Don't fully merge with her, Tomoya, okay? You're just there to observe and keep her from slipping away. What can you see?"

Tomoya's teeth clenched and the muscles in his neck tightened. Out the corner of Mayu's eye, she was aware of Richard's corresponding tension as he clenched his fists on the desk.

"What can you see?" she repeated quietly.

"She's on a tower. Darkness is…coming."

"Oh no," whispered Momo. "Her Delta waves have dropped below one cycle a second."

The girl's mind was dying.

"What's happening?" demanded Mrs. Mansfield, striding over and hovering near them, her lips pursed as if preparing to give orders. Richard sounded strange and unfamiliar when he spoke in English, but he raised his hands and uttered something in a reassuring tone to placate her.

Closing her eyes, Mayu gripped the microphone tight. "Listen carefully" she said. "You have to shape that girl's world. Don't engage. Don't make her aware of your presence. Just bring her away from that darkness gently. You can do it, Tomoya, take her to a different land, just like we practiced."

"I will."

Everyone fell silent, watching Tomoya and listening to the rhythms of his monitor readings. Momo whimpered and clasped her hands tightly in front of her mouth.

"He can't do it," she whined.

"He can," Mayu growled in the back of her throat. She believed in him. She really did. He could do it. He could—

A shrill, warning ringing sent waves of fear cascading through the team. Seizure. Tomoya shook in his chair, Mayu almost yanked out the mic and threw it into Momo's lap as she sprinted around the glass monitor to Tomoya and gripped his wrists tight. Fukushima was right on her heels. He wrapped one arm around Tomoya's chest to pin him into his chair.

"You'll be okay, Tomoya," said Mayu. "You can do this."

"Skye is stabilising," Momo said.

"See," said Mayu. "I knew you could do it."

Her relief turned to shock as she saw blood dribble down Tomoya's cheek and drip onto his shirt.

"Abort the connection!" she ordered.

"But the shock—" Momo started.

"What is going on?" Mrs. Mansfield shrieked. "Speak English, all of you!"

Mayu ignored her—looked straight at Momo. "Do it now."

The lights on top of the helmet blazed red and a valve at the back opened with a hiss. A deep humming filled the room as the connection between Tomoya and Skye was forced apart.

"I got him," Mayu said to Fukushima.

He nodded and let go of Tomoya's chest. He reached up and gently pulled off the helmet. Mayu gripped Tomoya's cheeks to steady his head. Setting the heavy helmet aside, Fukushima said, "I'll check on Skye."

Mayu stared at the blood oozing from small burn holes on Tomoya's forehead. *It should have been me.*

"Jesus!" said Mrs. Mansfield. "This is a bloody farce. Do you know what you're doing?! This is—" The words blurred into noise as her voice rose and the words tumbled out too fast for Mayu to follow.

After Tomoya's shakes subsided to tremors, Richard brought out the first aid box and together they dressed Tomoya's wounds. Mayu tried checking his pulse.

"I can't find it," she croaked.

"Let's just get him out of here," Richard replied. He scooped his long arms under Tomoya, lifted him from the chair, and carried him out the room.

Mayu went to follow before remembering she had another patient. "How is the girl?" She went to Skye and leant over the bed. Focusing on Fukushima's reply felt like deciphering white noise, especially with Mrs. Mansfield still shouting at him from the opposite side of the bed.

"She's stable," he said in English, holding up a hand to implore Mrs. Mansfield to be quiet, "but she won't be for long."

8

MAYU STARED DOWN at Skye's pasty face. So young and smooth, cow-lick eyelashes, thin pink lips, freckled cheeks. A storm cloud of guilt threatened to break Mayu's careful composure, anxiety crackling through every nerve.

Momo managed to silence Mrs. Mansfield and herded her to the other side of the room. She spoke rapidly but calmly, staring into her eyes with an unnerving intensity. But Mrs. Mansfield quickly pulled away to make a phone call.

Fukushima turned away from Morpheus to stare at Mayu. "It was a mistake to use Tomoya, we can't change that now, but we can still rescue the situation, you must take over or the girl will die."

She stared at him. "I can't."

"You can. Her Parallel waves are stronger than expected—too strong for Matokai, he didn't stand a chance—she's almost as receptive as you."

The only sound was Mrs. Mansfield gabbling into her phone. Mayu couldn't face any of them, couldn't face Fukushima's solution.

"It's too soon to put me under," she said.

"It's not." Fukushima's determined frown softened. He gently squeezed her shoulder. "You've been in the clear for a few days now."

He said something else she didn't hear. The floor was swaying.

"Shirakawa."

"I can't." Maybe Tomoya's burns weren't as bad as they appeared, maybe all he needed was a few hours of cooling gel and rest, and he'd be ready to carry on.

"Then the girl will die."

Mayu felt sick, she clenched her fists, searched for a defence as her head spun. "You can't put all this on me! You shouldn't have grabbed a job like this just to appease our sponsor's quota," she panted. "You didn't think, Fuku-shima. You didn't think about us! We could've waited. Asked for more time. We could've developed better tests. Found a less fragile patient for Tomoya's first task. What was the rush?"

"That's not the issue. You haven't had your head in the game since coming here."

"So this is my fault?"

"You're going to fix this," interjected Mrs. Mansfield, targeting Mayu and Fukushima again. "You promised you could bring Skye back. You *will* bring her back. We…we *need* her!" She began taking deep, dramatic breaths, conducting herself by rising and lowering her hands with each inhale and exhalation.

Mayu looked down at Skye again, nestled against the pillows. The edges of the room darkened and the floor continued to sway. Fukushima dealt with Mrs. Mansfield, explaining Skye's condition and the steps they would take next.

"I need some air," Mayu said as she fled from the room, her lab coat billowing.

Only Momo heard. She made to run after her, "Mayu, wait—" but Mayu hurriedly closed the door in reply.

A commotion further down the corridor guided Mayu to where Tomoya was being treated. Richard had set him down on a bed for the nurses in the emergency team and had stepped back to give them space. Mayu crept into the room, her back pressed up against the wall.

"What happened?" one nurse asked.

"Partially imbedded electrodes caused the wounds," replied Richard.

The nurse's eyes widened.

Mayu watched as another nurse checked for Tomoya's heartbeat. "Shallow pulse," she announced. "Irregular breathing," said a third, as she moved to get a ventilation mask.

Tomoya's eyes cracked open and he let out a confused, strangled moan.

Mayu sagged in relief. She crept out the room again, trapped in a spiral of dread. No one bothered her as she paced to one of the balconies and pulled out her phone. There was only one person she wanted to call, one person who'd know how to reassure her, and he was dead. Of course she wasn't going to abandon Skye Mansfield, but for a good half a minute, Mayu stared at the plunge on the other side of the balcony—down to the hard lobby floor.

Without registering what she was doing, Mayu hit the call button. It rang three times.

"What's up?"

Her lips parted, but nothing came out.

"Hello? Doctor Shirakawa?"

The lobby floor turned hazy as heat built in her eyes. "Obinata," she croaked, "I'm sorry. I just…need to talk."

Keiji hesitated only a second. "Alright."

It didn't take long to explain what had happened.

"So now you've got to take over," he said.

"She's a difficult patient." Mayu felt like a punctured lifebuoy, barely keeping afloat. "If Tomoya couldn't do it—Tomoya can do anything…" She sniffed, clinging to her dignity, holding herself afloat a little while longer.

"What are you afraid of? Skye was his first patient, wasn't she? You've got years of experience. You'll be fine."

"Yeah," Mayu whispered. "Probably."

"You'll rescue Skye without a problem."

"I don't think she's the one who needs rescuing." Another piece of herself sank to the hollow pit of her stomach. Leaning against the glass banister until it dug into her chest, Mayu stared at the lobby floor again. Keiji's answering silence conveyed he understood.

"I'm sorry about Yūta."

The way he said it eased an unspoken ache in her throat.

"I can't imagine what that's like, losing someone you loved the way you did. However, all life is a choice."

Mayu pressed the phone harder to her damp cheek. "Huh?"

"I never knew my parents, so I didn't understand that I was missing out, or that it was odd to be brought up by two old people. I was ten when I first realised: maybe this isn't normal. I call my guardians 'Granny' and 'Grandpa,' although they aren't blood relatives, so they never talked about what my parents were like—they didn't know. They still don't.

"When I asked, 'Why do people treat our family differently?' Granny said that my mother, whoever she was, collapsed on their doorstep after ringing the bell. When they opened the door, she was dead and I was the baby in her lap. I think Granny expected me to cry, because then she said, 'Loved ones are like trees. They cannot feed the leaves they hold forever, and when the leaves are separated from their loving branch, they must fly on the wind or they will drop and ferment into the earth below.'

"She meant that I had a choice. I could cry if I wanted to, but I either had to carry on building the life we shared, or let the sadness hold me back." Keiji let out a deep sigh. "But like I said, I didn't know my mother. It's hard to feel burdened by a memory you never had."

Mayu viewed him in a new light. How could he speak about it so casually?

"I never knew," she said.

A shift in his voice hinted at a smirk. "It's not much of a conversation starter."

She almost laughed. "No. I guess not. Thanks, Obinata."

"You know…you can call me Keiji, I don't mind."

A real smile lit Mayu's face and she rubbed her eyes dry as best she could. "I'll let you get back to feeding the ducks, or whatever it is we pay you for."

Mayu returned to Richard and Tomoya. More nurses had arrived to help; Tomoya was made comfortable until he could be fully assessed. Mayu hovered by Richard, close enough to smell the woodsy and citrus notes of the Italian cologne he'd bought in Duty Free, until one of the nurses allowed them to approach.

Outside in the corridor, Mayu heard footsteps. From the sharp *rat-tat-rat-tat* pace she guessed it was Momo. No time left. She approached Tomoya's bedside and, just as she touched his hand, Momo burst through the door.

"Is he okay?" she asked, going pale at the sight of Tomoya's breathing mask. She was frozen in the doorway, unable to run in and hug him, an invisible force holding her back. She tore her gaze away from Tomoya—hair framing the disarray in her eyes.

"Mayu, you have to come back. Skye won't last more than two hours. We can't—I know it's hard—but please don't…" Her whole body seemed to beg her. "We have to *do* something."

By 'we' Mayu knew very well she meant 'you'.

Mayu squeezed Tomoya's hand.

"S-sorry," Tomoya whispered.

"It's not your fault," soothed Mayu. "You did nothing wrong."

"But the darkness…"

"You suppressed it. The girl is fine."

Tomoya's eyes shone glassy with strain and pride. "But did Momo just say…"

"Don't worry, Tomoya. I'll take over."

A flicker of concern. Then he tried to smile, staring at her with the respect that had built up over many years. He squeezed her hand in return. "You won't be alone. You can do it as a team. With Yūta. Just remember, don't use real memories."

Mayu's eyes widened.

Why had *she* never thought of it like that? It felt hard to breathe. She barely managed 'goodbye' as a nurse ushered them out.

She followed Richard and Momo back to the girl's room in silence. They found Fukushima with Skye, waiting for them alone. Mrs. Mansfield was nowhere to be seen.

"How is Tomoya?" Fukushima folded his arms tight against his chest.

"He'll have burnt a lot of cells," said Richard, "but he's alive."

"Shit." Fukushima rubbed his temple, looking drained. "Mrs. Mansfield has gone to wait for her husband in the lobby. If we mess up any further, it won't matter who wants to sponsor us, we won't be deemed fit to run the project by ourselves."

The empty bed beside Skye, waiting for her Dream Guide, loomed behind the glass screen. Mayu felt resigned, but the fresh memory of Tomoya's pride—in himself and in her—compelled her to prove that she was worthy of his respect. He'd completed the worst phase; the rest would be like any other case she assured herself.

Blinking hard, Mayu approached Fukushima. He hovered in the centre of the room as if he hadn't moved from that spot since she left. Without a word, she removed her lab coat and changed into the scrubs folded up on the end of the bed. The starchy smell reminded her of her grandmother.

"What are you doing?" he asked.

Mayu sat on the edge of the bed, trembling. "What does it look like?"

Pushing his glasses up his nose, Fukushima peered

down at her, the lines in his face deep and forlorn. When he spoke, it was so gentle it made Mayu's eyes sting. "Her mother is furious," he said. "If we don't succeed, we lose more than Skye—they'll make sure of it. You can do this."

She glared at him, every burden burning her up inside, wanting to scream. "You want to prove we should keep the Parallel Dream Project? Then deal with her parents. You can find sponsor candidates. Now put me under."

Mayu glanced at Momo beyond the glass, standing by her console. Hesitantly, Momo nodded to show that she was ready to recalibrate the probe graph. Mayu lay down, glanced at Skye, immobile beside her, and looked up at the projector above her pillow. It projected a grid onto her face to calculate exactly where the probes had to be inserted into her forehead.

Choosing this didn't make it seem any fairer she thought, remembering Keiji's words. She pulled up the covers and settled down, staring into the pale-yellow lights recalibrating the fit for her facial structure. Morpheus already held Mayu's cranial measurements and data regarding her previous sessions, so it took barely two minutes to pinpoint and align the probes. Fukushima pushed needles into her inner-elbows, the drugs made her feel heavy and she felt herself sink down into the mattress, a useless, leaden doll. How long would she be under this time she wondered?

Fermenting leaves…

The drugs gradually calmed her pulse, pulling her down, down into numbness. A particular numbness that she hadn't realised she'd been trying to recreate; a loss of control of her body, her feelings faded and worries muted.

Mayu's body was sinking into the earth, the sunlight blurred into uneven patches. The air became water. What was the point of saving people?

Ferment.

What was the point of waking up?

A child's voice cried out, "Hello?" It echoed and faded. "Is anyone there?" It wavered with hopelessness, meek and lonely. "Anyone…?"

9

THE DIM PATTERN of light and the smell of
rotting apples dispersed at the sound of the voice—a
girl's, high pitched and spiked with fear. Sinking
and resigned, Mayu ignored it. Her forehead throbbed, a
migraine. Couldn't she just sleep?

"Where is everyone?"

That girl again.

"Please…I'm cold."

A grey sky came into focus, like a fire had spread across
it leaving billowing smoke… Where was she?

Floating high above the ground, she saw an endless
ashen land, drained of colour and life. On the distant hills,
just a few ruins, the crumbling remains of past buildings.
Nothing but the wind.

A flicker of light, growing to a dazzling glare, caught
Mayu's attention. She squinted as she noticed the remains
of an old clock tower behind her, a giant diamond hovering in the air above it. Light sparkled off its hard, angled
surfaces, yet its centre was cracked and dark. No, not dark,
it held something—a tiny figure, deep in the diamond's
heart, arms hugging its knees. A girl.

Letting the wind blow her forward, Mayu swooped

down and floated above the shining stone. Below it, the clock tower stretched away, her eyes drawn down to its base, where strange white stalagmites encircled it like lumpy wax drippings, but each exactly the same.

"I'm sorry!"

Mayu looked back at the girl who'd spoken only to herself.

"Hello!" Mayu called, her cheery greeting whispering over the rooftops.

The girl gasped and her head jerked up from her knees. Her gaze shot right through Mayu, looking up at the empty clouds with large, confused eyes, and Mayu reeled back, recognising her.

Skye Mansfield's lower lip trembled and Mayu remembered her mission.

She strained to make herself tangible to the child until she felt as obvious as an airship, a clear mass in the air. Sharp, hot pain lanced her skull and murmurs of softer, easier dreams caressed her weary body. Giving into them would be so nice…

Lurching away from the feeling, Mayu stopped struggling and the murmurs abated. A blur of movement distracted her on the ground, and she squinted at the stalagmites. They seemed to be softening, white minerals trickling like wax over their lumpy surfaces, each one positioned closer to the base of the tower than she remembered a moment ago.

She studied Skye. If Mayu could not penetrate this level of her mind, she'd have to change tack and lure Skye to her. Focusing on the atmosphere, she sensed an agitated vibe. Perhaps she couldn't reach Skye because the girl feared anything new in this barren landscape. Looking for clues, Mayu noticed Skye's clothes: a buttery-beige sweater with a crest on the left breast. A stiff white collar poked out around her neck and the grey, pleated skirt was accompanied by long grey socks and sensible brown shoes; a school uniform.

Reaching out, she brushed invisible fingers over the diamond's surface. Skye's teeth chattered with cold as if feeling the wind and, again, Mayu noticed the waxy stalagmites changing shape, shifting closer, and tightly surrounding the tower. She sensed images: grey classrooms, shared desks, a muddy playing field, cold knees, twisting corridors, hidden stairwells…

As all this flooded Mayu's mind, she extended her mental reach. She felt static and electric tingles crackling over her skin: Skye's mental current. It hissed as Mayu tried to absorb it, and she cringed.

Looked down.

Heart stopped.

One of the tall, waxy drippings had a head—tipped back to show a blank, featureless face, appearing to stare at Mayu nonetheless. It didn't move. Neither did she.

Gasping, she tore her gaze away and knocked on the diamond. "Skye, I'm here to rescue you!"

"How?" Skye crossed her legs, searching the rooftops for Mayu's physical form.

"You need to come to me."

"*How?*" The girl tensed as if coiled to strike. "Can't you see I'm stuck?"

"No, you're not! You just—" Mayu glanced downwards.

The wax head had become a human face with eyes, wide, icy and unblinking. "You must break the diamond."

"*Break the diamond?* The hardest thing ever! Are you stupid? I can't!"

Visualising Skye's school building on a clear patch of ground nearby, Mayu encouraged Skye's currents to merge with her again, and a building took shape across the street. Old and prestigious, black roof shingles and stone walls, a construct that appeared to be a cross between a manor house and a fort. It looked as dreary and lifeless as everything else so Mayu strained to imagine warm, glowing lights in the windows. The wax figure looked at it, and back to her, a furious accusation in its eyes. A ripple of movement; all the wax figures tilted back their heads, eyes springing open.

"Skye…" she whispered, doing her best to sound soothing.

The girl spotted the warm lights and familiar architec-ture. "My school?" she said to herself.

Mayu bit her inner cheeks, pushing against a boiling, burning sensation in her bones. "You…you've got to get to class, you're late!"

"Oh no! But I'm stuck!"

Their connection was still weak. Whatever Skye believed: that was reality. The hazy dream landscape, no matter how surreal, was absolute truth unless Mayu could take charge and change Skye's perception. For now, she'd have to rely on the power of suggestion.

"Look at your skin, it's made of diamond."

Skye raised her hands and narrowed her eyes, examin-ing them front and back.

"You see it, right? You're indestructible. And what's the only thing that can cut diamond?"

As Skye turned her hands palm-down again, light glittered over her fingers. "Another diamond."

Success. Time for motivation. "Skye, you're going to be late!"

Skye smacked the wall of gemstone tentatively, as if punching a younger sibling she didn't really want to hurt. On the ground, the wax figure that had opened its eyes first punched its fingers into the clock tower. The crunch of fingers piercing stone made Mayu's stomach lurch, especially as it continued to stare at her.

Would criticism or encouragement spur Skye on?

"I can't!" The girl bunched her hands into fists.

Another punch and crunch—wax fingers into stone.

"Skye, you must! You'll get an award if you can; the school's relying on you."

Not looking entirely convinced, Skye tried again, her punch reverberating like she'd struck a gong. Below, eight wax figures now punctured the side of the building with their bony white digits.

Next tactic. "Useless! You call that a punch? You hit like a baby!"

"Hey!" Scowling like a feral brat, Skye whacked the iridescent surface in front of her until it cracked.

With a rumble, so did the clock tower, and every wax figure started scrambling up the sides of the building, limbs hauling themselves up with frantic urgency, heads bent back, eyes fixed on Mayu. She strangled a cry in her throat. *It's just a dream. It's just a dream.*

"Pathetic! You couldn't smash an ice cube!" Mayu roared.

The answering growl was half lion, half girl as Skye punched again and again. The crack zigzagged up through the diamond towards its surface. The white figures were halfway up the tower now, getting faster, closer, eyes larger, pupils expanding, like two exploding black moons obscur-ing a white sky.

"You'll—you won't—" Mayu tried, throat strangled, unable to look away from the creatures. So close, so fast, they were burning from the inside out with something she didn't understand.

"I'll what?" Skye growled, panting.

With one final punch, the diamond shattered. Light burst outwards, dizzying. For a second, Mayu was disorientated and blind. Skye's scream brought her back. Mayu flew closer, close enough to see irises twitching in the figures' faces as they grabbed the ledge of the clock tower. The roof crumbled and collapsed, and Skye was gone, falling.

Mayu shot down the dark shaft into the tower itself, reaching Skye just as she hit the ground. She wobbled on her feet, lost and stunned, but not afraid. She still hadn't seen the wax figures, good.

Mayu blew a gust of air at the brick wall and visualised a door appearing in the darkness. It flung open onto the grey world outside. Skye's school was visible across the road.

"Run!" The urgency in Mayu's voice made the girl tense. Above, a waxy face shot its gaze to the bottom of the well. "Go!"

With a leap, Skye obeyed. The wind lashed her auburn hair and her eyes shone. A series of thuds echoed behind them as the wax creatures jumped down into the tower, and Skye hesitated.

"Don't look!" Mayu barked.

Now clearheaded and determined, Skye ran full tilt across the road. Slapping footfalls chased them. Skye whimpered.

"You're made of diamond, don't be afraid." Mayu reached into the space in her mind that would accommodate Skye, linking them with psychic threads, but a burst of static rent the air. "Don't be afraid of *me*," she added.

Glancing back at the waxwork figures, Mayu frowned. All but one had halted to crouch in the diamond debris. Lifting shards of stone they pressed them into their malleable bodies—into their eyes, their stomach and their arms. All but one.

Skye burst into the foyer of the school, which looked nothing like those Mayu had attended. The floors were half carpet, half stone, a plush couch stood on one side beside a grand fireplace, with a smart reception area on the other. Checking over her shoulder, Mayu saw their lone pursuer drawing closer on bubbling, fluid legs.

Mayu tried to plant her feet firmly next to Skye, but a force repelled her, like the north ends of two magnets. She needed a physical symbol, something to snap Skye into a rational layer of consciousness.

"This way." Flying up the nearby stairs, Mayu left a trail of sparkles and chimes for Skye to follow. The girl clattered after it, tripping on the first step and scrabbling up the rest on all fours.

Behind them, the foyer doors slammed open, Skye

screamed, a dull whining shook the walls like chronic tinnitus. Skye hesitated; fear weighed her down and the stress began to trigger her body's shutdown reaction. When Mayu looked back, she had collapsed on the floor.

"Skye, get up!"

A white face leered up the stairs, its sharp aristocratic nose a prominent feature. Mayu imagined the walls cracking inwards and they obeyed, forming a protective barrier of stone and wood between Skye and the impending danger. Moaning, the girl started moving again, crawling forward as the creature threw itself against the rubble.

Challenging her imagination, Mayu took hold of the synaptic charge in the air, like seizing a piece of string that would tie the two of them together. As she dived into a semi-rendered classroom, that connection fizzled into her brainwaves and fought to repel her meddling.

"Don't give up," she called to Skye. "Faster!"

Mayu erased the classroom walls around her and redefined them into one of her own memories. Wooden walls appeared, a new roof rippled overhead, but the back of the room looked broken, the ceiling and wall long collapsed from rot. Knotweed sprouted from the floorboards and a laburnum tree stood just beyond the fallen wall, its lemon-yellow flowers springing open and drooping inside. But the weight of the world seemed to grow heavier and the ringing noise filled the school around her.

Mayu heard Skye running down the corridor towards her. The repelling force became suffocating as she grew closer. Looking out into the corridor she saw the creature explode through the barrier of rubble, stumbling forwards and chasing the girl on its hands and knees, each limb pounding the floor. The resentment in its eyes sent Mayu reeling back into the room, away from the door.

Closer. The pressure in Mayu's head felt crushing.

"*Confirmed exposure reactions.*" Momo's voice. "*There are six Parallel waves. Body temperature at forty-two Celsius! It's killing her brain cells!*"

Through the coma, the muffled voices of concerned colleagues reached her, only heard between merging layers of consciousness. If she woke, Mayu knew she would never be sure whether she had heard these voices or also dreamt them. But she couldn't help listening, distracted, identifying each voice.

"*Begin harmonisation sequence.*"

Fukushima.

"*Beginning. Phase three: stimuli neuron fusion.*"

Momo.

"*Connection to closest Parallel Dream measures at eleven…*"

Richard.

Skye burst into the room. Mayu collapsed into the knotweed as Skye groaned in pain on the other side of the room. A waxy hand reached in, brushed the girl's shoulder. Summoning all her strength, Mayu made the door slam shut, just as two unblinking eyes appeared in the doorway.

Blinding golden sunlight hit them. Above, squeezing through cracks in the rotten ceiling, dropped curtains of lilac wisteria. Mayu inhaled the perfume, clutching the knotweed under her, hands trembling with pain. She sent the wisteria dancing as a distraction, letting loose a purple shower of petals.

Breathing harder, she felt a great weight force itself

into her body. She struggled not to fight it, allowing Skye's mind to fuse with hers. When the suffocating pressure passed, she relaxed into the cushioned floor, gentle wisps of steam spiralling round her from the warm blanket of weeds.

Only the leaves rustled.

A short distance away, Skye's careful breathing reached Mayu's ears. The girl shuffled closer over the broken wooden floor. Exhaustion sat on top of Mayu's chest like a heavy rock; she needed time.

She needed a decoy.

Closing her eyes, Mayu conjured a replica of herself. This was her world now, distanced from the pain and injuries she had suffered. Her double stood by the laburnum tree, a healthy vision of her normal self, and she made it smile.

Skye gasped.

Unable to see Skye from her real position on the floor, Mayu hoped her gasp was positive, the recent terror of their struggle dissipating.

"Hello!" Mayu made the apparition sound gentle and cheery. Then she made it turn and walk away, down the hillside, calling back: "Come with me, Skye."

"Wait!" Skye ran past, not noticing Mayu hidden amongst the weeds and petals. Mayu made the vision sweep off, always just out of reach, heading towards a water mill that she knew lay at the bottom of the hill.

With Skye safe for the moment and out of the way, Mayu took a few deep breaths.

She felt heavier and heavier…

The allure of a deeper sleep beckoned.

Get up.

Struggling into a sitting position and up onto her feet, Mayu pushed through the knotgrass, swept the wisteria branches aside, and headed past the remains of the rotten wall and to the laburnum tree.

There, at the bottom of the hill was the abandoned water mill. Beside it flowed a shallow river and further upstream was a small weir. The old fishing bridge spanned halfway across the river, its sun-bleached wooden structure standing over the water.

Mayu spotted Skye scampering down the hill, she had nearly reached the river. The exhausted ache in Mayu's body became secondary to the magic at her fingertips. Settling into her dream, *her* world, Mayu willed herself across the distance. The laburnum tree disappeared and the scenery shot past in a blur. Grinning, Mayu stopped her teleportation on the mill's stone platform, next to the creaky steps that led up to the fishing bridge. The river flowed gently past behind her.

Mayu's apparition strode into the mill and through the open doorway that led to the fishing bridge. Just as it walked into her body, rejoining with its source, Skye jogged through the empty mill and out onto the platform. The girl skidded to a halt, opposite Mayu, stunned. Such wide blue-green eyes and angelic round cheeks.

"What the hell's going on?" Skye squealed.

Mayu raised her eyebrows.

"Well, you gonna answer me? Who are you?"

Regaining her smile, Mayu bowed her head and held out her hand. "I am Mayu Shirakawa, it's a pleasure to meet you, Skye."

10

BROW CREASING, SKYE hesitated, stepping back. "You know my name?" She played with the sleeves of her sweater, twisting them around her wrists. "You a stalker or something? What do you want?"

An uncomfortable spark stabbed into the back of Mayu's mind, and she fought to keep a serene expression. "Now, now. There's no need to panic. I understand—"

"Where is everyone else?" Skye practically screamed it, her question ricocheting around the empty building behind her. Red in the face, she clenched her fists and pinned her arms to her sides. "What the hell, hell, *hell,* is going on?"

"Let me speak," Mayu ordered, like a schoolteacher trained at keeping her temper in check. "Your parents sent me."

Skye's face darkened and her big eyes grew even rounder.

"They sent me here to help you," said Mayu. "I'm sorry, I have some bad news."

"Like everyone's dead? Are you gonna kill me? Who are you even supposed to be?"

"Will you stop interrupting me?" Mayu wrinkled her nose.

Skye hunched her shoulders, managing to pout and glare at the same time.

"Skye, you're currently very unwell."

"Are you stupid? I'm clearly—"

"Hey!" Mayu pressed a finger to her lips, jumping forward a step, and Skye clamped her mouth shut. "You are in a coma. This is a dream, not the real world." She took a calming breath. "You've been asleep for almost a year. No one can wake you, so—"

"Oh right," Skye interrupted, backing away. "You're crazy. You're a crazy person."

"No, this is the truth. If you—"

"Nutter!" Skye cried before spinning on her heel and running away.

Her rejection sent another spike of discomfort through Mayu's head as Skye's mind tried to tear itself free, but Mayu couldn't let that happen, the shock and instability would cause it to shut down indefinitely.

Mayu growled. Clenching her fists, she teleported around the building, cutting off Skye's escape. The girl collided with Mayu, winding her, but she managed to take hold of Skye's shoulders.

"Let go!" Skye shrieked, now frightened.

"I'm not here to hurt you," Mayu reassured. "Please calm down or you'll seriously injure us both."

A second later, Skye's jaw went slack and she slumped in Mayu's grip. Fumbling at the sudden switch in energy, Mayu shoved her hands beneath Skye's arms and managed to keep her on her feet. In a heartbeat, Skye regained her strength, raised her head again and regained her composure.

"How did you… What do you want?"

"I'm here to help you."

"Get *off*!"

"Just listen!"

Skye stomped on Mayu's foot. The blow didn't hurt, but the action sent sharper pains deep into Mayu's skull, and she let go with a cry. Clutching the back of her neck, Mayu fell to her knees.

"This is a dream, and I'm here to help you wake up."

Skye backed away, her hair blowing in a breeze.

"If this is a dream," the girl shot back, "then how are you real? You're holding your head instead of your foot, you weirdo."

"This is a different sort of dream. This is our reality, but it's not the only reality. It's a parallel world—our world."

"You're crazy!" Mayu heard a wobble in Skye's tone now. "Where am I?"

The ache in Mayu's head subsided. Getting to her feet, she sighed, pitying the girl's fear. "If this isn't a dream," she said gently, "then how can I do this?"

Mayu found it came easily, she focused on a giant panda and, in the blink of an eye, she became one. Skye staggered backwards, staring at Mayu with disbelief, awed and petrified.

"You see," said Mayu.

Skye shrieked. "Talking!"

"Yes, I can still talk." Sitting on her furry behind, Mayu examined her paws and wriggled her feet. Being an animal felt so comforting. "You have been asleep for a very long time and I'm here to guide you back to the real world. It may take a few days, but…"

Skye's legs buckled and the girl collapsed in a heap.

Getting onto all fours, Mayu padded over and rolled Skye onto her back. The girl didn't bat an eyelid, out cold. With a heavy sigh, Mayu waited, hoping this wasn't going to happen all the time—with luck there'd come a point when Skye could accept their bizarre reality and believe. When Skye finally squinted up at her, Mayu shifted to shade her from the sun.

"You okay?" asked Mayu.

Skye tried to nod. "Yeah. My limbs don't feel so good."

"You'll get over it," Mayu teased.

"Gee, thanks, Mum."

At least the shock hadn't been too severe.

Watching her blink clear her blurry eyes, Mayu bent closer. The girl held her breath, stiffening as if expecting to be eaten. Mayu smiled, hoping her thin black panda lips didn't look too sinister.

"Am I dead?" Skye whispered.

"No, you're not dead. But you're not awake, either."

The world around them held its breath as Skye lifted one hand and stroked Mayu's fluffy face. Her tiny hand grew more confident, exploring an ear. The soft caress released Mayu's tense shoulders. Exhaling deeply through her wet nose, Mayu morphed back to herself.

She helped Skye to sit up next to her and brushed the grass off her back. They sat in silence for a heartbeat.

"How do we wake up?" Skye asked, pulling up her socks.

Faced with the creative challenge ahead, Mayu's spirits lifted. "By having fun!"

"What?"

"You'll see."

Skye scrunched her nose. She had a cute thinking face. "That's not an answer," Skye said.

Just as Mayu opened her mouth to reply, a shadowy figure strolled through the reeds further downstream, behind Skye. It sat down out of sight before Mayu got a proper look. Skye twisted round to see what she was staring at.

"What's wrong?"

"Nothing, I thought I saw something, but it was just the reeds." Rising to her feet, Mayu reached down and pulled Skye up with a new vigour. Mayu put her hands on her hips. "Alright, this is our world. We might see some strange things that we're not expecting, but we can mostly go anywhere we want. You can *be* anything you want too, anything at all. Our world is defined by our imagination."

"This is nuts. You're really crazy."

"Didn't I just turn into a panda before your eyes?" Mayu reached over and pinched Skye's cheek—hard.

"Ow! What was that for?" She staggered out of Mayu's reach, cradling her pink skin.

"Does it feel real now?"

A mischievous glint lit Skye's smile and Mayu regretted explaining.

"We're dreaming?" the girl said.

"Yes."

"And I can turn into anything?"

"Well, almost anything. Sometimes the mind tries to limit itself, especially if you're not used to manipulating the variables of deep sleep and—" Skye's head tilted and her eyes conveyed disinterest of the finer points. "Y-yes, almost anything."

The smile came back. "How?"

"You just will it to happen."

"Because this is a dream?"

Mayu nodded. Closing her eyes, Skye screwed her face up in concentration, and Mayu took a step back in case she transformed into a dragon or something equally outrageous. "Don't overdo it," she said. "This is your first time."

"What, dreaming?" cackled Skye.

There was a loud *pop* and a blast of thin smoke. Mayu coughed and waved the initial blast out of her face while the wind carried away the rest.

"Skye?"

"Meow." She looked down and saw a chubby ginger cat in the grass. It giggled. "I've always wanted to be a cat." Kitty Cat Skye waddled closer and Mayu felt laughter fill her chest. "I really am a bloody cat!" Skye's laughter was almost a shriek, and Mayu winced at the piercing decibel. Beaming and purring with pride, the cat lifted her fat little face into the sunlight. Shuffling closer, she wove between Mayu's legs and pretended to mew.

"What should we do first?" Skye asked, eventually plopping down in front of Mayu's feet.

"I thought we could visit the sea. It's over that way." Mayu pointed over Skye's head to the horizon, where the sea was hidden by the hills.

"What?" groaned Skye. "I'm not walking a million miles just for that."

"Have you forgotten that we can be anything? We can *do* practically anything too."

Tilting her ears forward, Skye managed to have a scrunched, thinking face even as a cat. "Oh, *I* know!"

Bouncing onto all fours, Skye ran around Mayu's legs, in and out, until she stopped directly between her feet.

"What *are* you—"

Before Mayu could finish, there was another pop and puff of smoke. The ground fell away from beneath Mayu's shoes as she was jerked up into the air, shrieking. She fell forward onto something solid and soft. "Stripes?" she whispered.

As the smoke cleared, Mayu gasped. She was sitting on the back of a tiger—a *giant* tiger, bigger than a four-wheel drive. Skye laughed again, the noise vibrating deep within.

"This is so cool. I'm a bloody tiger!"

That word again. It was an English swear word, wasn't it? Mayu couldn't bring herself to care. Being the responsible adult didn't figure high on her agenda as Skye's shoulders rolled under her hands and her orange body swaggered as she walked.

"I'll get us there," cried Skye. "Hold on."

Mayu dug her hands into Skye's fur as the tiger lunged into a run. Willing away her fear, Mayu convinced herself that she was a trained tiger jockey—riding on the back of a powerful, lurching cat was easier than riding a bike to work. In moments, Mayu released her grip and slowly lifted her arms above her head. She laughed, her body moving in tandem with Skye's sprinting haunches.

"You're a natural," Mayu cried.

Her stomach dropped as Skye leapt down the crest of a hill, wind whipped at Mayu's cheeks, and she grabbed hold of Skye's fur again.

"Don't panic, you scaredy-cat!" Skye jeered.

The lush countryside rolled past and the glimmer of

the sea grew gradually closer as Skye ate up the distance. Sunlight bounced off the waves and clouds glided inland on coastal breezes. Mayu smirked, not prepared to let Skye have the upper hand in this adventure, not yet.

"Careful," Mayu said, "we're approaching a cliff edge."

"Doesn't it just lead into the sea?"

Clever, sneaky child, Mayu had a suspicion that she planned on running and diving into the water if she said yes.

"I'm not sure yet, let's see."

Salt and seaweed hit Mayu's nose, the pungent smell redolent on the rising wind, which grew stronger as they approached the cliff. Her hair beat about her face, whipped into tangles, and for a second Mayu's mind wandered—she saw Yūta standing on the edge of the pier, unresponsive to her intense sensory stimuli. She shook her head, noticing that Skye was slowing down.

They padded closer to the cliff edge, the ocean rolling and crashing far below. Mayu spread her mental reach—out into the ocean, up into the calm sky, and pulled her idea into shape.

Just as Skye stepped forwards to look over cliff edge, a vibrating, ethereal song washed up to meet them. Skye's fur rippled, she gasped, and before she could form the question, a magnificent pod of blue whales soared upwards over the cliff edge, blocking out the sky.

They surged past in a vertical streak to the heavens as silver stars spiralled down to meet them. Not real stars, but star-shaped, five-pointed, sparkling lights.

"Wow…" whispered Skye.

Without warning, she transformed back into a girl

and Mayu fell to the ground. She grumbled as she picked herself up, tempted to retaliate by turning Skye into a frog but, seeing the wonder in Skye's eyes as she stood, tiny and awestruck, watching the spectacle open-mouthed, Mayu couldn't remain disgruntled.

The last whale ascended with an undulating song and Skye spun on the spot to gaze after them as their fluked tales propelled them through the clouds. Far above, they regrouped and surfed on the air currents.

Squealing with joy and flapping her arms, Skye said, "Did you do that?"

"Nope, not me." Sometimes magic was better without a cause. "We can't predict everything, remember?"

"*Wow*! Let's go!" Skye hunched down, scrunched her face, and then jumped up like a spring, stumbling as she landed on her feet again. "What?" She jumped again, flapping her arms. "Why can't I *fly*?"

"It's one of the hardest things to accomplish," Mayu explained. "Flying dreams, even when you are in control of them, are often weighted with self-doubt. Don't forget, you're asleep, Skye. You're in a…" She faltered on repeating 'coma' again. "You're impressive, I mean, you can turn into a tiger, that's more control than most people who are at your level of consciousness."

For the first time, Skye's lips turned down into a heart-wrenching pout. She folded her arms, hugging herself. "I'm really in a coma? That means I'm almost dead, doesn't it?"

"No, it just means we need to wake up a few times in the dream world before you can wake up in the real world." Mayu brushed Skye's hair behind her ear and put a hand on her shoulder.

"I don't know how that works," Skye said.

"You don't have to. That's why I'm here. Come on, let's not think about that right now." She turned Skye around to face the sea. "We can't go up, but have you ever wanted to breathe underwater?"

The effect was instant. Skye's eyes lit up, her smile blossomed; she seemed to swell like a balloon, pumped with excitement.

"I can be a fish?"

"You can be a human."

Skye gasped. "I can be a mermaid." She tiptoed to the cliff edge and peered over as far as she dared. "That's a long way down, and the sea will sweep us into the rocks…"

Mayu nodded, impressed with the analysis, even if the girl was wrong. Holding out her arm (although it was just for show), Mayu willed the sea to stop thrashing and it settled into a calm, Mediterranean blue.

"Let's run off the edge. We'll fly."

Skye didn't look so sure, she backed up a few paces. "You just said flying was hard."

"Yeah, but I'm a pro."

Even a middle-aged mother couldn't have pulled off the derisive look Skye gave her. Mayu stopped herself from rolling her eyes.

"Ready?" asked Mayu. "And, go!"

She seized Skye's hand and they charged, leaping off the edge. As Skye's hesitant jump dragged them down, even Mayu had momentary doubts about making it, but gathering her courage, Mayu willed them upwards. Skye shrieked in disbelief as they swooped up and levelled out over the radiant blue water, until Mayu cried, "Time to go swimming!"

"But how do I breathe?"

"You'll figure it out."

"What!"

Sea water swept over Mayu's face and engulfed her body. Skye's hand slipped from hers and Mayu somersaulted to check on her. The blue depths shimmered all around, empty. She felt a pang of dread.

The familiar, calming sensation of breathing underwater dampened the initial fear. A shadow flickered in the corner of her eye. She looked up to catch a glimpse of a male silhouette, swimming gracefully above. Mayu peered at his outline, which blurred like a bad television signal, and as he reached the surface he vanished in the sparkling light.

A stream of bubbles rushed up Mayu's back and she turned to see Skye spiralling past. She swooped underneath Mayu, flapping a long, sapphire tail. An utter natural. Skye's Parallel Dream Energy had to be putting out fantastic readings, at least an 8.3. Mayu bet that Momo and Fukushima were having a field day recording the results.

Smiling, inhaling the fresh sea water that tasted nothing like salt, Mayu kicked her legs and watched them gel together. A scaly, peach-coloured tail appeared, from her hips to her ankles, while her feet grew into large translucent fins. Her shirt washed off into nothingness, leaving peachy scales over her breasts. She felt ridiculous.

Dreaming like this hadn't happened in years. Her patients had lacked a colourful sense of imagination. They'd clung to their dignity even in their dreams and their minds hadn't strayed anywhere so magical.

"I'm queen of the sea!" Skye cheered, her voice garbled and distorted. She stretched her arms wide, embracing the silkiness of water on skin, and then suddenly lunged at Mayu, who jerked back in surprise.

"I'll race you!" said Skye.

Mayu laughed, bubbles tickling her tongue. "You're on, don't expect a head start."

"I won't need one, you haven't got a chance!"

Giggling, Skye shoved Mayu backwards and flipped overhead. She shot off, leaving a stream of white bubbles behind. A cheat!

With powerful strokes of her tail, Mayu shot through the water, propelled forward at an exhilarating speed. If she were running on dry land, Mayu would already have keeled over gasping for breath like an old car tyre. Perhaps she'd missed her true occupational calling as a professional mermaid.

The endless blue spread before her, painted with Skye's jet stream. The girl looped and curved a path ahead. Now she was just showing off. Pushing harder, Mayu gained distance and then waved as she flippered past. A determined scowl flashed across Skye's face. Tittering, Mayu shot onwards, corkscrewing like a fighter-kite.

She looked up at the surface of the sea as it refracted ribbons of sunlight and she rocketed towards it, not losing her advantage. Up and up, until she erupted from the sea, arms held out behind her. The cold air rushed over Mayu's skin, from her head to her fins, and her breath felt like the first she'd ever taken. Lashings of purple and orange decorated the horizon, and pink clouds hung in the air.

Mayu completed her arc and splashed back into the sea. Skye had caught up a little, her gaze so serious that one might have thought a shark was snapping at her tail. Just as Mayu dived down to carry on her winning streak, another flicker of movement caught her eye. She looked up, squint-ing against the light, her breath caught in her lungs.

Hanging above her was a merman, his emerald fish tail swaying beneath him. His black hair rippled in the water, light-patterns playing across his arms. With the bright halo of sunshine around him, Mayu couldn't make out his face.

"Are you—"

As soon as she spoke, he plunged, an arrow flying into the black depths.

"Wait!"

Mayu swam after him but slowed on seeing a glittering trail of emerald scales in his wake. Red tinged the water. Swallowing the nervousness rising in her throat, she let herself drift back up, eyes fixed on the scales as they scat-tered like petals on the wind.

"Mayu! Did you give up?"

She jerked around, startled by Skye's voice. The girl's blue tail sent her bobbing in Mayu's direction. She couldn't get distracted. Glancing downwards one last time, she saw no sign of him; the scales had shimmered into nothingness.

"Who was that?" puffed Skye, next to her.

"You saw him?"

"Obviously, I'm not blind."

"Just an apparition." A bleeding one.

"Someone you know?" Skye tilted her head, bronze hair fanning out around her.

Mayu hesitated. "Our dreams are peopled by those we know in real life, even if they wear a face we don't recognise."

For the first time, Mayu saw a hint of concern in Skye's expression, concern for *her*. Sweeping her hair out of her face, enjoying the weird, tingling tug on her scalp, Mayu floated past Skye and beckoned for her to follow. "Let's go somewhere else, the sun is setting."

"Already?"

"I promise you'll love it."

She saw the girl suppress a smirk as she followed Mayu's fins. Mayu turned her mental concentration onto producing a small island. She'd done this a few times before and, depending on what she focused on creating—land structure or population—the difficulty of the feat altered. Creating a population always gave Mayu much more pleasure and so that was easier to construct.

Far ahead, the beginnings of her work began to grow; rock grumbled out of the seabed, piercing the surface above. She pictured parts of her grandmother's village, traditional town houses and people dressed for a summer festival.

All the while, creatures swam up from the dark ocean depths. Majestic, purple fish with glowing yellow stripes floated below them, each as big as a bus. Skye stared at them in awe.

"They aren't dangerous," Mayu said.

"So I can touch one?" Without waiting for an answer, Skye swam down to one of the giants with her arm outstretched. Her fingers grazed its back and she pulled away squealing. "It's weird!" she reported. "It's so weird!" Skye took hold of its dorsal fin and stroked the fish like a pet.

"I'd ask, 'Can we keep it?'" Skye said, "But I think it will be happier here."

Mayu said nothing, grinning, not about to remind her of the whales, now swimming among the stars somewhere. Just in case. They didn't need a giant, glowing fish bobbing behind them at every turn.

The seabed came into view as the depth decreased. With a sonorous hum, the purple fish turned away. Skye let out a loud, bubbly groan of disappointment, "Do they have to go?"

The girl's involvement with their world made Mayu giddy, but she focused on the island almost fully emerged in the near-distance. Skye gasped.

"My school, Mayu! My school's down there." "Wait, what?" She looked down in time to see Skye's fins swimming down towards the seabed. "Skye!" The giant fish waited for her, their glowing stripes illuminating a bubble settled on the sand—a protective barrier for a building sitting on the sand.

Abandoning her island creation, Mayu spun around, lashing her tail furiously to try and catch up but, before she could reach Skye, a sharp pain hit the back of her skull and burnt right down to her fins. Dazed, she glanced down to see her shiny scales peeling off—leaving a sparkling trail behind her.

Ahead, Skye reached the sea floor and pushed one hand through the bubble. It sucked her in and skinned off her tail as she entered, leaving a plume of sapphire scales drifting up through the water. She landed face first on the sand, as dry as a shell on the beach.

"Skye!" Mayu called, diving through the bubble's roof and losing her tail too, "Are you alright?" She tumbled to her hands and feet on the sand, running to the girl who stumbled upright on shaky legs, looking down at her feet in surprise.

"I'm fine. Do I look like I need babysitting?"

Mayu slowed, "Just checking."

Rolling her eyes, Skye didn't wait for her to catch up, but marched haughtily towards the school, "Check something less obvious."

Before she could catch herself, Mayu sneered at the girl's back and strode after her.

Inside, none of the lights were working, the corridors were dark and gloomy, masked in blue shadow. Skye led with the confidence of being in familiar surroundings, but it felt odd to Mayu to imagine her living here. The ceiling towered above, fine art dotted the walls, and they passed stately furniture and trophy cabinets with awards engraved with the names of those long since forgotten. Even the stacks of square lockers in the hallway looked grand—the doors finished in polished oak.

"Do you really want to be *here*?" Mayu asked.

"I just want to see my locker."

"But why?"

"I just *do*."

Mayu's sigh was masked by the shriek of a bell. Doors up and down the corridor banged open and children poured out, all wearing the same uniform as Skye. But none of them had real faces, each one a roughly cut crystal head of polygon shapes.

"Who's that?" Skye asked. "I've not seen *that* teacher before."

Dressed in a suit, even in Mayu's dream, Tomoya Matokai had emerged from one of the classrooms, his hands casually stuffed into his pockets, an exaggerated grin on his lips. He wore no tie, his collar unbuttoned and falling open; the laid-back look suited him. A few doors down, Momo stepped out into the hallway as well. She carried folders under both arms and pretended to buckle at the knees, wobbling as if not strong enough to carry them.

"Today was the worst," Momo said to her.

Just as Mayu explained to Skye that they were her colleagues, a girl pushed through the throng of other children. Defined, unlike the rest, she had thick black hair, eyes dark as night, skin ochre amidst her predominantly pale classmates.

Skye went rigid.

Flashing a grin, the girl edged closer, a question written on her face, as if to ask Skye why she looked ill. With a chuckle, she paused at arm's length then shot her hand forwards to hit Skye on the arm.

"Tag! You're It!" The girl's Scottish accent was as striking as the glint in her eyes.

She ran off.

"Stop—Henri!" Skye shouted, sprinting after her.

"Hang on—this isn't—" Mayu snatched at the back of Skye's sweater and missed. "We should go. This isn't what I meant for us!" But Skye ignored her. The crowd of faceless students blocked Mayu's path and, in seconds, Skye had vanished around the corner.

"Oh, for the love of—"

"You're It!" Skye's voice again, but behind her.

Mayu turned. Silence. The children had vanished, only a steady *drip…drip…*echoed down the corridor. Looking back to where she'd seen Skye disappearing, the corridor was nearly deserted too, only Tomoya and Momo remained. They stood by their classrooms, no longer smiling, the corners of their mouth tinged green with algae.

Tomoya's lip curled, "So much for you being the best Dream Guide."

11

RIGHT. AMAZING. THE job had barely begun, and the fabric of reality was already out to get her. Mayu grasped for the knowledge that it was all a dream, that Tomoya and Momo were not rotting teachers in this school at the bottom of the ocean. But the knowledge grew uncertain when confronted with Tomoya's scorn.

"Skye, we need to go," she called.

A child's laughter skittered across the walls, everywhere and nowhere all at once. Mayu groaned. Beyond Tomoya and Momo, dappled blue and yellow light shone from the end of the hallway, like sunlight on the water's surface. Taking a deep breath, she shuffled forward, looking straight ahead.

Her shoulders tensed as she approached Tomoya. He didn't look at her, but said, "If you hadn't been so arrogant, if you'd let *me* be his Dream Guide, I would have saved him, and I would have had the experience to help Skye."

Mayu hesitated for a fraction of a second, guilt knifing her stomach, before pushing on past him, eyes fixed down the hallway.

"She doesn't care," said Momo, "so long as we all pretend it was the right decision."

The air felt thick and stagnant as Mayu tried to make them disappear, or even to talk like normal, smile like normal. But she couldn't get control; Skye's Parallel Energy was bat-tling against her, strong and overpowering, like a headache she couldn't subdue. She needed to be more careful, she couldn't indulge the girl with links to her real life again.

Momo lunged as Mayu passed her, dropped her folders, teeth bared, "*Perfect* Mayu!"

Shock and fear slammed together, trembling through her in waves and escaping from her mouth as unintelligible noises. She shut her eyes and when she looked again, Momo and Tomoya were standing still behind her, their backs to her. She hurried round the corridor towards the light. The ghost of a girl stared into the depths of her locker.

Mayu took a steady breath. "Skye?"

The girl slammed her locker shut and the light was extinguished, leaving her in darkness. It made Mayu breathless. *Keep walking.*

One step forward, a brief grinding noise followed her. Another few steps, again, a dull screech of metal, like a keening animal dragging itself across the floor. Turning to look behind her would reveal nothing, it was too dark. *Keep walking.*

She had to focus on Skye, she had to pull her back, like two souls entwined in one body. The next metallic screech stretched longer, coming closer.

A soft green light glowed from behind her. She suppressed a shiver, not wanting to look.

"Where are you?" cried Skye.

Mayu whipped around and stifled a scream, staggering away from the stack of lockers moving up behind her.

Then laughed, *lockers*! She'd been stalked by *lockers*, the green light glowed behind them.

The end of the hallway loomed ahead of her, with an emergency exit door, the sign on it read: *home.* She hedged around the lockers, keeping her back to the wall, and set her sights on the promise of freedom. Before she could reach it, the green light vanished. She was plunged into pitch blackness again, the breath catching in her chest.

"Where are you?" Skye's voice sounded melodic, like they were playing hide and seek. A breeze flickered past Mayu's right shoulder, snatching with it some part of her memory. Hide and seek, it seemed important. The voice seemed important, something was pressing down on her mind and making it hard to think.

"Where are you?" The voice was closer.

No. Getting out, that was important, getting home.

The light reappeared ahead of her, Mayu jogged to it. She could hear footsteps running after her. Tomoya materialised out of the shadows, blocking the door marked *home.* The green light made his skin look sickly, his eyes hidden in deep, shadowy sockets.

He strode towards her, Mayu skidded to a stop, turned and fled into the darkness. Her skin felt like ice, it prickled. She had to keep going. The emerald light ebbed and flowed, reappearing just before she walked into another locker blocking the middle of the corridor. It towered over her like a man's shadow. Mayu slapped a hand over her mouth, suppressing a cry of terror. Her blood pulsed so hard she barely heard the child-like whisper over her shoulder, the voice full of hunger.

"Found you."

If she could have, Mayu would have wrenched the locker off the floor and sent it tumbling behind her, flattening whatever was there. Instead, struggling to breathe, she sprinted around it and made for the green light.

The door grew closer. *Home, home, home.*

Mayu threw herself against the bar-handle, swung out, and yelled at the hole revealed behind it, tiptoeing on the edge of falling through the doorway. Two graves waited beyond the exit. One was filled in, its headstone bearing the name 'Yūta'; the other was empty, a dark wet pit in front of a slab of stone, already in place, and engraved with 'Mayu'.

The same bloodcurdling, metallic screech echoed behind her. Glancing backwards, she saw the stack of lockers again, rushing at her. She begged herself to vanish. Evaporate. Fly. But she was stuck like a lump of clay on the edge of the doorway. It was going to ram her, smash her and break her bones. Instead, the stack of lockers halted an arm's length away, the central locker snapped open, someone burst out, someone she almost recognised, leaping at her face. She screamed, swiping them away, and fell.

Muddy walls came up around her and air finally filled her lungs as she hit the bottom of the grave. Mayu stared upwards. Waiting for the thing that had escaped the locker as it hissed, "Where is it?" The voice was ragged, but familiar. She shivered. A fine powder started falling. At first, Mayu thought it was snow, until she licked a flake off her lips: salt. The whirling patterns calmed her. Maybe she was dead. That could be nice.

Pressure started building down her arms and, raising her hand to her eyes, she saw worms bulging and wriggling under the skin. Despite immediate revulsion, the sight made her curious, until the falling salt changed colour and she tasted soil. The dirt fell heavier, threatening to bury her alive, and bile rose in her throat. No, she didn't want to die like *this*, cold and suffocated.

A girl's head appeared over the edge of the grave and Mayu shrieked. The girl shrieked back. With a curse, Mayu took a shuddering breath. Sitting up, she saw the gravestones were gone, replaced by yellow tulips, the grave was just a ditch of sand, and nothing wriggled beneath her skin.

A sharp zap hit the back of Mayu's head, and maybe the girl's too. They both cupped the back of their neck, looked at each other—recognition sparking in their eyes.

"Skye, we have to go."

"But I—"

"We're leaving!"

Skye helped Mayu to her feet. She held the girl's hand in a crushing grip as she ran for the bubble's membrane. As they pushed through the gelatinous surface and breathed in sea water, their legs turned back into fishtails. Skye tugged her hand free, but Mayu heard her following.

"Why are you so miserable?" Skye called. "I want to go back!"

"We're only going where I say we're going from now on, understand?"

"No, that's not fair."

Mayu spun around, still shaking off the last tremors of fear. "It is fair, because I'm in charge. So you will do as you're told."

"I got to see my friend. I want to see her again!"

"You can't control what's happening around us Skye, you made a nightmare!"

"No, I didn't! You're lying."

"I'm not. You're a strong dreamer, but that doesn't mean you know what you're doing, it could put us in danger." Mayu took a deep breath, clenched her hands and then released them. "Don't run off without me ever again. Ever."

"I'll go wherever I—"

"Enough!" Mayu rarely shouted. It made her tremble and hurt her throat. Lowering the volume, but losing none of the steel in her voice, she said, "We could die in one of these dreams, *especially* in a nightmare."

By the blanched look on Skye's face, Mayu felt sure she'd got the message.

"Come on."

Turning, Mayu led the way to the island she'd started building what felt like hours ago. As she entered the shallows, her tail flicking the sand with every stroke, her legs morphed back to normal and her speed dropped like an anchor as they kicked weakly behind her. "Skye, you might want to change back now," she called, but the girl darted ahead. When Mayu caught up, wading through the waves with her head out of the water at last, she tried not to feel exasperated. Skye had beached herself. Mayu emerged from the surf in shorts and a T-shirt, staring down at the girl, hands on hips.

"Very smooth," she said.

Skye flipped her tail back and forth as if to fan herself.

"Are you going to ignore me now?"

Skye sniffed.

"So you're just going to stay beached until, what, a firefighter comes along?"

"A firefighter?" Skye repeated with disgust.

"Yeah, someone strong enough to pick you up and rescue you from me."

With a '*hmph!*' Skye hid her face against her shoulder and carried on fanning her tail. The setting sun turned her scales into jewels in the orange light.

"Is that a yes? And then what? You get to do whatever you want?"

"Just shut up!" Skye snapped. "*Knights* rescue people, anyway, not stupid firefighters."

"I mean…"

"There's no fire here, is there? No. So I don't need a firefighter, I need a knight."

"Have you ever considered being a knight?"

Skye glared daggers at her. "What? Of course not. And I'm not actually waiting for a stupid knight either!"

"Really? As a knight, everyone admires you and thinks you're daring, you get to go on adventures… In ancient Japan we had something similar, well, kind of. It depends on who you ask. Anyway, we call them samurai."

Skye flicked her tail once more and then it turned into two pale legs. She squealed and shuffled in the sand, trying to cover her bare bum. "Don't look!"

Cutting off her laughter, Mayu turned away and stared at the affluent, cobbled town a little way beyond the beach. Red, sloping rooftops and buildings decorated with frescos and carved timber frames could be seen between the trees. It looked so attractive and safe. The real world was so different now. Fires had swept across large parts of Asia and Oceania, floods had covered half of Europe and droughts continued to parch Africa. Ecosystems had been damaged, and an unstable global climate threatened worse to come. Mayu had to stop her thoughts spiralling; thinking about the thousands who had either starved due to the lack of sustainable food or died as victims of the increasingly hostile environment.

The world is changing, she thought. *It can't be too late, please, it can't be too late.*

"Alright, you can look now."

Turning, Mayu saw no one there. "Skye?" She saw the small paw prints in the sand and looked down to see a tubby ginger cat sat by her feet, staring at her.

"What?" Skye mewed. "Okay, fine. I couldn't make any clothes appear."

"Your concentration slipping?"

Kitty-Skye yawned, curling her pink tongue.

"That's a good sign," said Mayu. "Wearing you out is part of the plan. You need to sleep. Want me to create an outfit for you?"

Sticking her button-nose high in the air, Skye stalked past. "No. I'm *fine*. And I don't get weary that easy, y'know."

"Whatever you say."

Kitty-Skye trotted ahead, and Mayu put her hands on her hips, watching her go. *Stubborn, proud little pain in the backside!* Just as Mayu made to follow, a sharp stab of discomfort in the back of her skull stopped her.

On the edge of town, dark figures e merged. Th ey stared at Mayu with shapeless faces and glowing white eyes, before slinking off the coastal strip to the edge of the town. The figures paused and turned, hiding in doorways, watching and waiting.

12

"ARE YOU COMING?" Skye turned to face her. "What are we here for?"

Mayu glanced away from the figures and down at Kitty-Skye, who groaned.

"Come *on*. Please?" Her ears pointed forward. "It's getting cold." Behind Skye, the figures—who were really nothing more than the misshapen silhouettes of human beings—slipped further into the town. Some climbed up onto the rooftops and sat there, watching. Whenever the silhouettes moved, a trail of dark matter followed in their wake, quivering, oily globules that hovered in the air and shrank to pinpricks, then vanished.

Mayu felt in control of her senses and intentions, and Skye showed no signs of mental degradation. So, what was spawning the disconcerting silhouettes? Were they part of another nightmare, or simply a malformed population? Probably the latter, she thought. She *had* been interrupted by a little madam insisting they take a miserable detour to school. The silhouettes were likely fine, just half-complete renditions of people.

"That's it!" cried Skye. "I'm leaving you behind." She carried on waddling towards town, oblivious of the silent, lurking creatures. Mayu followed, already thinking of ways to carry Skye off to another location if something went wrong, and if that proved too strenuous, then ways to reshape the landscape. Alerting Skye to the silhouettes' presence might set her on edge and make the situation worse.

"Are you sure you don't want to be a knight?" Mayu asked with weak enthusiasm, her concentration honed on forcing the silhouettes to change, to morph into people with normal eyes and friendly smiles.

A chill crept up her spine as they passed the first silent, staring shadows. Their glowing white eyes did not blink, nor did their gaze shift from her face. Damn, what did it mean? What was her subconscious trying to communicate with this unblinking attention? She felt she had to be the cause of their presence—they had re-entered her mind space now.

"Why are you obsessed with knights? You be one if you like them so much." Skye peeked back at her, tucking her tail low. "I think you should do it, actually."

"Be a knight?"

"Yeah, I like knights, I just don't want to be one."

Wind rattled through the village in swells, rising and falling to whispers, echoing through the houses and declaring the spaces hollow. Door screens rattled as they passed, and blank faces peered down over the edges of the rooftops, as shapeless and dark as the void. Even the setting sun as it washed the sky in hues of orange and pink could not brighten or cast contours on their bodies. Mayu's concentration faltered; fuzziness tingled inside her head. The pastel twilight colours faded like dialling down the saturation filter.

"Mayu, it's really quiet."

Willing her appearance to change, *ō-yoroi* armour

wrapped around Mayu's body. It took the style of the Kamakura period, her head encased in a helmet with two golden horns, but the crest on her torso was…the Halcyon logo, a bird soaring free from the back of someone's head. She wore no mask over her face, and the typically heavy iron plates of the armour weighed almost nothing.

"That's not a knight," said Skye.

"Not an *English* knight, no."

A hiss echoed ahead and the sunlight turned bleach-grey. It felt like the first world, where Mayu had found Skye, except this was her dream. Her world. Had Mayu slipped into a deeper sleep without realising? Lost a degree of control?

"What was that?" whispered Skye, darting behind Mayu's legs.

"I don't know."

"This place is creepy."

Mayu nodded, feeling confused and anxious enough to believe the armour was constricting tighter around her chest, inch by inch. The town was supposed to echo with children running home to change into summer *yukata*. The air was meant to smell of deep-fried marinated vegetables and glaze-grilled *unagi*. People from another era were meant to smile and wave. Mayu wanted to buy salt-boiled *edamame* pods to share with Skye and to show her how to squeeze out the beans.

Another hiss sounded behind them.

"Look, I'm not being funny," said Skye, "but can we leave?"

"I'll fix it," said Mayu.

As she spoke, the eerie strokes of a *biwa* sounded and set Mayu's teeth on edge. The strings twanged methodically, slowly, its distinctive melody coming from every direction.

"Is that a guitar?" asked Skye. "It sounds broken."

An undulating, female voice burst into song, sad and low. A sinister thrum filled her lyrics. Whimpering, Skye darted back and forth, breathing hard.

"Oh my God. No, no. I'm leaving."

She turned tail, making towards the sea.

"I don't know where…this isn't my memory," said Mayu.

Skye let out a yowl, and spinning around, Mayu saw dozens of the silhouettes in the street, dragging their feet towards them. A hundred whispering words rattled against the paper screens, none of them distinguishable.

Why is this so difficult? Mayu thought. In her worst dream workshops with Tomoya, when one of them could not maintain enough clarity to shape the Parallel landscape, it was often caused by personal stress. Tomoya, for instance, had a habit of taking on too much without complaint, to the point of being sleep-deprived and anxious. Once Mayu had learnt to recognise the signs, she could intercede without hurting his pride but, in the early days of working together, it had created friction between their Parallel Energies. His stress and fear of being a failure had swallowed so much of his waking consciousness that it was too powerful to control in his sleep.

"What are they?" cried Skye, backing into Mayu's shin, tail vertical and spikey.

"I don't know, but they can't hurt us." *They might scare us into a fit, however.* Nightmares consumed the mind and touched corners of the body that human hands could reach. Their imprint sank into bones and muscles, swallowing the dreamer in inescapable fear, until the dreamer woke up…

provided they could sense the difference between the real world and the dream. Was Mayu causing this? Could she not manage her grief even here? Or was Skye hiding something…?

The pitch dark, twitching silhouettes did not look like a dream.

"Let's just back up," said Mayu, "and find a different street."

"C-can't we fly away?"

"I'm tired myself, just give me a minute to build up the energy." Truth be told, apprehension weighed her down more than fatigue. The wailing melody pressed on Mayu's shoulders and she forgot why she'd even brought Skye here.

The *biwa* and songstress fell silent. Only the indistinct whispers trickled through the air. Except, wait—Mayu tilted her head like she might hear better that way.

Skye squeezed between Mayu's shins, puffing little breaths.

"*Where is it?*" the whispers asked.

"Where's what?" Every muscle stretched tighter in Mayu's body.

The shadows stopped their slow procession, heads twitching, the dark matter that had trailed in their wake gathered and sank into the silhouettes' limbs and sharped their humanoid outline.

"You see," whispered Mayu, "nothing to worry about. They're just curious."

"What do we do now?" Skye whispered back.

A single note twanged from the mysterious *biwa* and the shadows burst into action, sprinting up the street, mouths open, revealing gnashing, human teeth, "WHERE IS IT?"

Skye stiffened like a perfect taxidermy. Mayu shrieked and scooped Skye into her arms. Dressed as a samurai or not, she couldn't fight. She had no sword. She had no strength. There were too many of them. Mayu couldn't safely stand her ground, but she could run.

The winding streets flashed by as Mayu ran like the wind, but not fast enough. Her feet felt sticky and her pace slowed. Skye bounced under her arm.

"This hurts!" Skye yelled.

Mayu flung the girl's front paws over her left shoulder and carried Skye like a baby.

"They're gaining!" Skye shrieked, looking back over Mayu's shoulder. "Faster! Faster!" The girl's commands petered off into a groan. "I can't feel my legs."

They heard the songstress start to sing again. In every window they sensed movement, saw white eyes following them. Mayu's armour grew heavier.

"You're a knight!" said Skye. "Can't you…can't you…"

"Just close your eyes, don't think about it. Any minute now we'll fly."

But Mayu couldn't catch hold of the winds; gravity sucked her feet to the floor. What if the figures caught up and sank into the hidden corners of her mind? Were they from the school? Was this the darkness she craved when she took her cocktail of pain relief during the day? Or was it her guilt chasing her—the tidal wave of death she'd seen claim Yūta given legs and now coming for her? *Where is it… Where is the way out?*

Skye's body went limp.

Up ahead, Mayu could see something moving, a glimpse of another human, running towards the next bend.

Someone broad, powerful, and tall. Someone to follow, someone fleeing to a safer place. The man paused on the corner, turned, and beckoned for Mayu to follow, he was there to help them.

"Yes!" she gasped.

"What?" Skye's claws dug into her braided armour again.

"Just hold on."

Pushing forward, Mayu chased after the apparition, one she had been longing to see for months. Fever and relief gripped her, mixing as well as oil and water but pulling her onwards with renewed energy. Her *husband* was guiding them up to a temple at the brow of a hill, the grey gardens surrounding it were a maze of paths and steps. Despite Mayu's determination, staggering over shrubbery and leaping to cut corners, the figures were still gaining on her. They glided up the steps, splashed through ponds, tumbled over hedgerows.

As the invisible songstress wailed louder, Mayu made out a name in her song: 'Yoichi'; a famous samurai from the Genpai War. He rode on horseback into the sea and shot down the enemy's symbol of protection with one arrow. But, in her terror, Mayu heard nothing of the Samurai's feats:

Arrows cut through the air and struck Yoichi into the sea

Betrayal ate him like the depression consuming the Heike

The *biwa's* tune thrashed with violent notes, the melody shuddering into Mayu's teeth. She caught another glimpse of Yūta up ahead. He had reached the temple doors. Turning, he held out his hand to her.

"Come on!" he cried.

Oh heavens, his voice! It electrified her.

But a hissing, gnashing noise at her back was drowning it out. Mayu needed a sword. Anything.

She tripped up another flight of steps, Kitty-Skye tumbled out of her arms and thudded across the stones, rolling to a stop. She twitched, then lay lifeless.

A hand slid up Mayu's back plate, sucking the warmth out of her. Yelling, Mayu reached to her hip and felt a *katana* materialise. Grasping it she tugged it free, swung it in a desperate arc and the curved blade sliced through two figures behind her, their mouths gaping as they vanished in plumes of smoke.

Dozens more ran up the path.

"Mayu, concentrate!" encouraged Yūta.

She stumbled up the steps as a tar-black wave rose over the horizon. Solid and overwhelming, it blocked out the pale sky and loomed over the town. Her head lolled back as terminal sleep pulled at every fibre of her being. It was… soothing.

"Run, Mayu!" cried Skye. A ginger cat scrabbled back onto her shoulder. "Run!"

"*What happened?*" asked one of the whispers. It sounded like Richard's voice.

"*I don't know.*" Fukushima. "*She broke through layer three on the chart readings, but then Skye's brainwaves got stronger. It snapped something in Mayu. She's not responding to stimuli again."*

If Mayu gave in, would she fall into the darkness, with Yūta?

Yūta…

The hoard screamed, the songstress wailed and Mayu ran. She dropped the *katana* and bolted towards the temple doors, both arms hugging Skye tight to her chest. Yūta was holding the doors open, but she almost froze in shock, it was her face staring from his helmet.

"Wait!" she cried, as the face morphed back into Yūta's. He charged past her, down the steps, swept up her sword and charged into the flailing hoard. Skye twisted to watch as they surged over Yūta's body and he disappeared into the gnashing blackness. A white light exploded from within the writhing shadows. It poured over the gardens, reviving the plants with colour and lit up the sky. The town glowed and, as the light ebbed away, sunlight dusted the sky with the last rays of a sunset.

A warm breeze swept over the temple, carrying with it the bustling sounds of human life from the town below. A deer-scare tipped and knocked against stone as the bamboo tube filled and emptied with water. The calmness of it all felt surreal but she closed her eyes and inhaled deeply, smiling.

"Now that," said Skye, "was a knight."

13

"WHAT THE BLOODY hell happened?" asked Skye, who was no longer a cat, of course, as she helped Mayu push their raft away from the water bank. "I didn't make those shadows, so don't you dare blame me!"

Once certain that all the shilouettes were gone and Yūta wasn't coming back, Mayu had taken Skye into town and bought a packet of salt-boiled *edamame* pods. Night had descended in the blink of an eye.

After Skye had gone on and on, exclaiming how pretty the town girls looked in summer *yukata*, Mayu had conjured one for her. It was white as snow with rolling waves embroidered on its sleeves. Multicoloured fish leapt along the hemline and, with a little extra tweak, they actually swam and splashed across the lower half of Skye's dress.

Mayu's was a favourite from her childhood; she had treasured a luscious, peach *yukata* decorated with large plum blossoms. She had long since out-grown it and given it to Fukushima's niece, but tonight it fitted her perfectly, the crimson *obi* comfortable around her waist.

Now, from the other side of town, Mayu and Skye pushed out onto the local lake. It lay at the bottom of the hill, below the temple. The temple windows glowed from within and paper lanterns lifted into the sky. On the water bank, the townsfolk sent lanterns floating across the water's surface, a few shaped like flowers.

The raft drifted out amidst the starry lights and Mayu settled into a comfortable position. She gazed at Skye and sighed.

"Come on, I've waited long enough—more than is polite," said Skye. "What happened today? I thought we had control of this place." Her eyes narrowed. "This *is* a fake world, right? It…it doesn't feel fake."

"I'm sorry," Mayu began. "Today was my fault. We share a neural connection, but you are ultimately inside my head. Everything you see, I have created. Some of it I build from my memories, like parts of this town come from my grandmother's village, but most of it I create anew—I'm often inspired by books, movies, and pictures. Your memories, however, are being held at bay."

"Why? That's not fair."

"Memories stupefy the mind. Yours are kept hidden in case anything lures you from my hold. I've not been at my best lately. *My* memories are warping things."

Skye laughed, clutching her stomach. "Where do you come from to have memories like that?"

"The key word is 'warp,'" Mayu chuckled. "I'm trying hard not to let my feelings interfere with our world, but suppressing the mind can cause negative retaliations. Dreaming is a cathartic process, it allows us to simulate desires, fears, anxiety, secrets, and everything else.

"I'm skilled at what I do, but even *my* subconscious will attempt to manifest what I'm trying to hide. I have things I wish to forget, and some things I'm afraid I'll lose. If I give into my memories, I might sink into a real coma and our connection would break. My dreams are never so perfect, so vivid and so lifelike as when I'm sharing them with someone else. Do you understand? What I want, I can only have in this world."

Skye's shrewd eyes softened and she visibly swallowed. "What is it you want?"

Telling a child her burdens felt self-indulgent. Skye didn't need to know anything else. Mayu's duty was to make her happy, not gain her sympathy.

"Mayu?" Skye leant forward, dipping her head to try to catch Mayu's eye. "Are you lonely?"

Mayu's chest constricted and her throat tightened. Lonely? She hadn't considered herself to be alone, not really. Mayu reached up to clasp Yūta's dog tags, but her fingers curled around thin air. She looked at her palm, as if expecting the tags to appear in her hand.

Huffing, Skye sat straight again and folded her arms. She looked out over the lake and said, "You can tell me things. I'm not a child."

Mayu smiled, unwilling to talk in case the truth spilled out.

"I feel alone sometimes," said Skye gently. She touched one of the flower lanterns as it floated past, her eyes vacant. "Did my parents really send you?"

"Of course."

Skye glanced at her, assessed her, as if searching for a lie.

"They don't talk to me, you know. Not very much. They don't visit me, either. They never take me on holiday.

They go away at Christmas and leave me with my friend. I can go home for New Year." A numb look fell across Skye's face and she cut herself off, gaze fixed on the shore. "I go to boarding school."

"I know." But that explained Skye's original appearance. Her school was the centre of her life. "I'm very sorry," said Mayu. "I'm sure they have their reasons."

"They just can't be bothered," Skye muttered. "One year, I took a train, a bus *and* a taxi to my Aunt's house." Her lower lip trembled. "It was snowing, Christmastime—a year when my parents decided not to go on holiday. I think I was eight. I'd lied to the teachers, forged my parent's signatures, and convinced them I was travelling with a guardian. I just found a woman who looked nice."

A tear grazed Skye's cheek and she swiped it dry with an aggressive flick of her wrist.

"When I got there and walked up the drive, I looked through the window. My cousins were there, I'd forgotten that they get to go home for Christmas. At first I was sad—'cause their parents actually *want* them, but then I realised I'd have more friends to hang out with.

"When Dad opened the front door…" Skye hid her face in her sleeve. "He was so angry. He shouted, and I don't even know what he said. They don't care, Mayu."

Chewing hard on her bottom lip, Mayu shuffled across the raft and firmly squeezed Skye's hand. "They love you. They love you so much," she said. "You should have seen your mother crying over you, Skye. She's worried about you."

"Probably about how much I'm costing them," Skye spat.

Mayu shook her head.

"I know one thing," Skye said, tugging her hand free and folding her arms. "The real world's going to be a right bore after this."

At that moment, a bang echoed across the landscape and a glittering firework filled the night sky. Dozens more followed, raining pearls of light. Looking at it all—the lanterns, the fireworks, the glowing paper dragons bobbing across the lake's surface—Skye's smile completely vanished and she burst into tears.

Mayu put her arm around Skye's shoulders and took a deep breath. "His name was Yūta."

"Who?" croaked Skye, her tone reproachful, as if Mayu had just compared her feelings to that of a snail's.

"My husband. The one you called a knight."

Gulping down her tears, Skye stared at her, stunned. Reaching out, Mayu curled her fingers into a fist, taking an imaginary hold of some of the firework sparks. They whizzed towards the raft, and with a few waves of her hand, the stolen sparks assembled into an image of Yūta. He smiled at them, hovering over the water.

"He was a firefighter," said Mayu. "That's how we met. He came from my grandmother's village. I was visiting her just before a terrible forest fire started. It spread rapidly, consuming most of the village. We were asleep at the time.

"A firefighting team was deployed to evacuate as many people as possible." Mayu caught hold of more sparks, and they rushed down to the water's surface to form images of Mayu and her grandmother, enacting Mayu's story.

"Yūta ran into our house," Mayu said. "It was already filling with smoke. But he charged in, up the stairs, into

Grandma's room. He got her out first. But by the time she told him I was still inside, sleeping, the wind had spread the fire to the rooftop.

"Yūta went back in. He couldn't fully rouse me…I have broken memories of being carried through heat and smoke. There was no one else to help once Yūta got outside. Grandma couldn't carry me, and the village was collapsing fast. He made a hard choice that day, to leave his team, so that he could take me to the lake. When he tried to return to the village, the fire was too fierce. He couldn't get through.

"Later, when I'd been treated, he came to check on me. I think he didn't know what else to do. For hours, those of us who'd made it to the lake could hear people screaming from the village. Air support didn't arrive until three hours after the fires had taken hold."

Mayu shook her head. "I don't know how Yūta and I become so close. I spent the night comforting him, thanking him, apologising. He was a stern looking man and at first his silence scared me but, when he did speak, his words were always thoughtful. We just seemed to fall into each other's hearts."

Mayu smiled at the shimmering picture of Yūta. "Grandma called him the Mighty Manatee. Never used his real name, silly old woman," she said fondly.

"What's a manatee?"

A slow smile spread across Mayu's face. "They're like a friendly sea cow."

Drums began to play along the water's edge, a lively tune involving *shamisens*. It clashed with the grief deep in her chest. "A fire took him in the end. He carried on his work in the city, but one day he sustained serious injuries. He died three months ago."

"That's awful," whispered Skye. "I'm so sorry."

Mayu swallowed hard and watched the fireworks illuminating the temple rooftops. "Me too."

They sat in silence for a while, admiring the view, and soon the boat began to rock as Skye swayed to the music.

"You like dancing, don't you? Ballet?" asked Mayu.

"Absolutely! One day, I'm going to join the Royal Ballet."

"Do you think you can dance in a yukata?"

Skye pulled at the material around her legs. "I don't know. It's a bit tight."

Nodding at the dress, Mayu made the fabric voluminous enough to do the splits in if she wanted. "How about now?"

"Definitely," Skye laughed.

"Try walking onto the water."

Skye's eyes filled with wonder and she sucked in an excited gasp. Without doubting Mayu, the girl carefully got to her feet and stretched one foot out as far as she dared. She placed it on the water, applying more pressure bit by bit. When it didn't sink, Skye suppressed a squeal and hopped off the boat.

She stumbled forward, circling her arms to keep from falling over, then froze a short distance away from the boat. When Skye found her centre of balance, she looked round at Mayu.

"Amazing!" Skye yelled. "This is real magic."

Grinning, Mayu bowed her head. "Thank you. I know this music isn't traditionally ballet, but—"

"That doesn't matter," said Skye. "Those drums are thudding right into my chest. But before I try anything…" With a mischievous smirk, Skye lifted up the hem of her *yukata* and ran across the surface of the lake. She let out a long cheer, almost running a complete circuit around the lake, purple-tinted water splashing around her ankles. When she lapped back towards Mayu, she leapt into the air, arms stretched overhead, the *yukata* swirling and her legs in a perfect position. Mayu's mouth fell open as she actually did the splits in mid-air, then pranced onward with a range of spiralling jumps and steps at tremendous speed. Skye's face was focused, lost in the rhythm. Some of her moves didn't look like ballet to Mayu, the girl's shapes and flicks too loose to be traditional, but whatever she was doing captivated Mayu's full attention. The white *yukata* flowed around her, fireworks continued to thunder across the lake, and the spirit-like paper dragons bobbed over to see what she was doing. They swooped around her, and Skye stared at them as she danced, losing some of her shapely technique.

Warmth melted into Mayu as she watched. Beside her, the sparks she'd captured reformed into Yūta's image. He knelt beside her on the raft, and Mayu struggled not to pay attention to him. Would he distract her from the job at hand, or could it work? Could she be with him one last time?

"You'd make a good mother," said Yūta.
"You always say that. I think today proves I'm not responsible enough."
Yūta leant over and blew hair out of her face, dusting her nose with glowing powder. "Today just needed a little

teamwork. It's not like you'd have to do it without me," he chuckled.

Mayu's eyes blurred, and she waved her hand through his glittering body, dispersing it. "You're not real," she whispered. "I'm not ready for you." She shuddered, taking a deep breath and wiped her eyes.

Paper lanterns began to descend onto the water, and the fireworks exploded in a final crescendo. Mayu forced a sincere smile, watching Skye stare up at the lights. When she turned, making to walk back to the raft, she faltered as a lantern landed at her feet. She flapped, flailed, and finally fell—disappearing beneath the water.

Giddiness hit Mayu like a blow, for a second she almost believed she could spend the rest of her life laughing, smiling, making magic for a girl who loved it, and things would be just fine. The real world never had to touch her again.

Getting to her feet, she walked out to Skye who resurfaced like a coughing and gasping wildebeest, hair plastered over her eyes. Mayu stopped beside her and held out a hand. With ease she pulled her out of the water and onto her feet.

"Well, this is just great," said Skye, flapping her soggy sleeves.

Mayu started laughing again.

"It's not *that* funny."

"You didn't see your face."

Skye skewed her mouth, utterly unimpressed.

14

AFTER DRYING SKYE off, Mayu rearranged the scenery around them. The hills swept past, the lake and village fell behind, and they reached a solitary country house. Moonlight bathed it in silver light and crickets sang in the grass.

"I didn't want to sleep in the village," Mayu explained. "I hope you understand."

"After what we saw today, I'm okay with that."

Leaving Skye to explore the garden, Mayu stepped onto the veranda, slid open the latticed paper door to reveal a cosy *washitsu* room—plain, neat and simple— lined with synthetic *tatami* mats. She hadn't seen a room like this in too long, not since the countryside retreat she'd taken with Yūta four years ago. He had gushed over the alcove, elevated four inches off the floor and displaying a replica sword, saying he couldn't wait to move out of the city with her so they could have a proper *washitsu* too. Mayu slipped off her shoes and stepped inside, wriggling her sock-covered toes against the floor. She took a long, deep breath and closed her eyes, recalling Yūta's warmth as they spent long hours reading by the open sliding doors, content to share each other's company and bask in their lack of obligations.

She could smell incense. Her eyelashes fluttered open, and she turned to the alcove in her shared dream with Skye… There was no sword in it, but a potted bouquet of white chrysanthemums. Smoke curled from the petals, pale and pretty, and scented the air with sandalwood. Her heart began beating hard at the memory of Yūta's funeral, the endless hours of waiting for it to be over as everyone offered their respects, incense burnt deep within her nose. Mayu saw large chopsticks beside the flowerpot and felt sick, punched with the sharp grief she'd felt when picking his bones out of the crematorium ashes with his parents and placing them one by one into the burial urn.

The grief blazed into rage and Mayu stormed to the chrysanthemums, hefted the pot against one shoulder, and launched it into the garden. Pottery smashed across the grass, Skye screamed, but Mayu turned back and grabbed the chopsticks, flinging them into the bushes with a wild shout.

Breathing hard, she met Skye's wide-eyed gaze.

"Do you have a problem with flowers?" Skye asked. "Or did they start growing fangs?"

Mayu looked at the limp, scattered flowers and the shards of pottery, feeling like something in her had cracked too. She laughed. Couldn't stop laughing. Tears rolled down her cheeks, but her smile was wide and open, sucking in great gulps of air to keep up with the laughter. *I want to smash everything*, she thought, *let's just smash everything, because nothing matters. Not me. Not you. Nothing.*

"Oh, my god…" Skye muttered, but she was smiling, if distinctly ignoring her now.

Fighting for calm, Mayu went to the cupboards and dug out two futons, sensing she was one blink away from relinquishing control of herself and inviting in the unbridled mess of normal dreaming. She rolled them out across the floor and patted them smooth. As she finished her work, Skye climbed onto the veranda.

"Those are beds?" she asked.

"Yes, they're very cosy."

With a gleeful expression, Skye tugged back the blanket of the futon closest to the veranda and settled herself on the mattress. She stroked her feet over the fresh sheets. "This is fun," she said. "Can I sleep on this one?"

Mayu nodded.

"How do I get out of this dress?"

Shuffling across the floor, Mayu instructed Skye to turn around and helped her strip down. Once in nothing but her cotton *juban*, Skye flopped onto the thin mattress and wriggled under the blanket. She grinned up at Mayu before turning to stare out at the garden.

"Don't you want proper pyjamas?" Mayu asked.

"This is fine."

"If you say so." Disrobing as well, Mayu settled into her own futon and propped her head up with one arm. She watched the fireflies blinking in the grass and rubbed discreetly at the dried tear tracts down her cheeks. "How are you feeling, Skye?"

"Tired."

"Good kind of tired?"

"Yeah."

"Then—"

"*Where is it?*" The question hissed through the grass, slid onto the veranda, and shook the room.

Skye's eyes opened wide, her body suddenly stiff with alarm. She looked like she could shatter at the slightest touch. Each shallow breath made her body shudder. Outside, the fireflies winked out and the world went still. Only the wind spoke, always the wind, except it came in gusts, like heavy, steady breathing. Deep, and whistling faintly through the trees. Mayu regretted throwing the flowerpot, the superstitions of her childhood declared that she had brought the wrath of evil spirits, she needed salt— they needed to purify. She needed to accept that Yūta's family would not let her have any piece of him for her own shrine.

Instead, shutting her eyes tight, Mayu willed it away. She fought to push back the anger trembling around the house. She wanted a world that would comfort her, a place where she could hide. Mayu brought back the fireflies, silenced the breathing wind, and added a windchime on the veranda. It jingled and plinked, soothing the tremors of fear away.

"Don't be frightened," whispered Mayu, squeezing the girl's clenched hand. Skye forced her gaze around to meet Mayu's eyes. "Nothing can get in, I promise." The girl's tension loosened a little, her lips parting with a controlled breath.

"What is it?"

Mayu shrugged. "I don't know, but it's not real."

"Well it feels it," she snapped.

"Try to sleep." Mayu brushed her hair.

"I can't!" Skye knocked her hand away.

"You can."

"Don't tell me what I can do." A rawness made her voice shrill, and she turned back to the garden, searching the darkness.

"I've an idea," Mayu leant closer to the girl's ear, "how about someone to stand guard?" Not expecting a response, she sought deep within for feelings of safety and protection. A warm breeze blew onto the veranda this time, forming a man's figure. Excitement fluttered in Mayu's chest, focusing on the pleated navy-blue *hakama* trousers that materialised first. His back appeared next, filling out a dark top. Bracers wrapped around his wrists and a black breastplate appeared on his front. Mayu realised that Yūta was dressed for a *kendo* match and a bamboo sword appeared in his hand.

"Who's that?" muttered Skye.

"Don't you recognise me?" Yūta flashed a wink at her. "Don't worry, nothing's gonna get past me."

"*Hmph.*" Despite the noise of contempt, Skye let her eyelids close.

With a chuckle, Yūta did a few squats and kicked his legs experimentally. "I should wear these more often! You could host a party in these hakama. What'll I wear next? Ice skates?" He looked at Mayu, full of vigour and colour, until his face flickered and disappeared. *Her* face grinned at them now but a man's voice left those lips. "I could stay here forever." Her skin prickled as the face transformed again, Yūta turning to watch the garden.

Mayu listened to the windchime until Skye gave in to the sleep tugging at all corners of their shared mind, her breathing soft. Sinking into her own pillow, Mayu closed her eyes. The lull of crickets and the swish of the grass tempted her to let go—to give in to the peace, to let it take control; to let their minds disconnect into separate dreams so that she could go and sit by Yūta on the veranda.

But sighing, Mayu sought out the electric snaps and stings of Skye's mind. She gathered them into herself so that her own brainwaves would amplify Skye's. Throughout the night, Mayu half-rested, cocooning the girl with feelings of reassurance and wellness.

When dawn peeked over the hillside, Mayu opened her eyes to clear blue skies. The *washitsu* was gone, along with Yūta, and their futons lay at the top of a magnificent valley. Below, sunlight gleamed off fields of rice paddies and cranes stretched their legs between the rice stalks.

Nothing had gone wrong. If Mayu's high energy levels were any indication, she had guided Skye closer to consciousness—through one world and into the next.

"*If Matokai dies, I'm leaving.*"

Mayu's good mood shattered like ice on a lake's surface, plunging into the chill of Momo's words as they rang clear across the valley.

"*I should have done something,*" Momo went on. "*If Matokai dies—*"

Fukushima talked over her. "*Nobody forced him to do it.*"

Richard laughed without mirth.

Thunder rumbled in the sky and it started to rain, despite the brilliant sunlight. It splattered across Skye's face and she slowly blinked awake.

"The house broke," she groaned. Yawning, Skye pulled the blanket over her head. Then she threw it off and sat bolt upright. "Where are we?"

"Somewhere," said Mayu.

"Amazing. You're *so* helpful." Skye wrapped her arms around her head. "The lady who can walk on water can't keep a house up."

"I'll take away your futon in a minute." With another sigh, Mayu gazed across the valley, watching the rain. The rice paddies turned murky in the upheaval, and streaks of rainbow patterned the sky. "I know a man who made me think of rain on a sunny day as ambrosia."

"What's ambrosia?"

"It is the sustenance of the Greek gods, a divine drink that makes you immortal. It tastes like honey and flower nectar."

Skye pulled her blanket over her head. "I don't want that in my hair," she said. Puffing out her cheeks, wrapped in white cotton, she looked like a coconut dumpling. Mayu smiled, but Tomoya's name popped into her head like a deer jumping in front of a car.

The valley vanished.

They stood in a familiar office space, next to the window desk Mayu occupied at work. Skye still gripped the blanket over her head. She pulled it off, dazed by the new location. Everything was in its place; the brimming invoice trays, multicoloured binders, the whiteboard by the door, the navy partitions between the desks—memos, charts and schedules pinned to each one like chaotic leaf piles.

Momo sat at her desk, a few metres in front of Mayu. She was scribbling away on a digital sketchpad. Each stroke materialised on her monitor, as she glanced constantly at her notes, like they might vanish between blinks. Rain pattered on the window beside her, casting calm over the office and muting the already drab colour scheme.

Skye ignored everything and went straight to the six-foot bamboo feature in the middle of the room. "Is this real?" She brushed her fingers over the waxy green shoots. "Mayu, is this…" Looking back at Mayu, she frowned. "Why are you wearing that?"

Mayu plucked at her smart black jacket, sinking deeper into an old memory. She stared back at Skye, trying to figure out how this girl knew her name. "Are you new around here?" Mayu asked.

"Huh? Is this a game?"

"I don't think so."

The door pushed open and Tomoya came in with a tray of coffees. "Alright, I think I've cracked it!" As he kicked the door shut, Momo set down her stylus.

Forgetting the pale girl beside her, Mayu sat at her desk, smirking.

"You've got to give it up," Momo called to him, catching Mayu's eye. "I've been trying to get Mayu to like coffee for years. She's a lost cause."

Unfazed, Tomoya set the tray down on his desk.

Momo smiled, "Come on, you've tried everything. I've tried everything. I've even tried tricking her into drinking it, but she'll suss you out."

"My palate is refined," Mayu chuckled, fishing a letter from her invoice tray and pretending to inspect it. She tilted it towards the window beside her, trying to illuminate it better.

"Here." With a soft plink, Tomoya placed a mug on her desk. "Try this."

Lowering the letter, Mayu gave him a sceptical look, but picked it up all the same.

"Seven hundred yen says she doesn't like it," Momo teased.

"How about three hundred?" Tomoya gave an over-exaggerated grimaced, as if conceding that Momo had a safe bet.

"If nothing else," said Mayu, bringing the mug to her nose and inhaling, "it'll be nice to have something warm to hold." She looked out the window at the rain, now streaming in curtains down the glass.

"It is a bit cold," Tomoya conceded.

"It's miserable."

"Not at all." Mayu looked back at him, at his unfaltering cheer and the hopeful gleam in his eye. "It's liquid sunshine. You've got to see things for what they really are." He smiled at Momo too, who shook her head, but there was something like fondness in her frown. "Rain is liquid sunshine," he said to her. "Remember that and you won't ever have a bad day."

In Mayu's ever active imagination, the rain outside turned glittering gold. She sipped the coffee and licked her lips. It was sweet, but not the sugary sweetness that usually made her cringe. Subtle and floral…

"I added a little vanilla," Tomoya explained.

A slow smile pulled at her lips. "I'm sorry, Momo. I like it!"

"Mayu!" cried Momo, in the voice of an eleven-year-old. The office vanished.

Blinking, Mayu no longer stared at Tomoya and Momo, but at Skye Mansfield. The girl had a blanket wrapped round her head again and was shivering. Green mountainsides sloped behind her, down into a valley; the same valley they'd awoken to that morning.

Mayu leapt upright. "I'm so sorry."

"No, it's fine, but I just…started to feel myself fading away and you stopped responding to me. I started hearing things, horrible things…"

Mistakes like this couldn't keep happening. Skye needed strong, vigilant guidance. With two clashing Parallel Energies, like theirs, lapses into memory could mean catastrophe. Skye was fragile, and Mayu was…well, a mess.

She placed her hands on Skye's shoulders. "If I ever seem to have forgotten who you are," she said, "you *must* call me back right away. This is serious. Don't let me forget who you are, even for one moment. And don't go off without me."

"Alright, okay, let go! You already said that." Skye jerked out of Mayu's grip, dropping the blanket.

A beam of white light shot between them. Skye screamed, her feet got tangled in the blanket and she fell with a graceful twirl. She lifted her head to watch as the ball of light shot away over the valley and into the clouds.

"What the hell was that?" she cried.

A harsh gust of wind hit Mayu's back, rippling her clothing. "I'm not sure…"

"What? Do you know anything?" Skye shrieked over the growing wind. "You're useless!"

A dozen more spheres of light shot past, with a gust that flung Mayu's hair forward. Each one made a mewing sound, creating a chorus of noise. "Cats?" she said with surprise.

One of the light balls skidded to a stop, then floated past Mayu's face. It spun in the air, regarding her with deep, sentient blue eyes; a touch of curiosity reflected in their depths. Mayu saw it was a pearly white cat, it flicked its soft tail over her nose, like a feather duster.

Purring, the cat turned and shot away after the others.

"How beautiful," gasped Skye, on her feet again and running after it for a moment. A straggler let out a mournful yowling behind them and Skye held out her arms in greeting. "Aw, did they leave you behind, Kitty?" It yowled again, bobbing around Skye's head. "Why do they glow?"

Balking at admitting ignorance again, Mayu grasped the first answer that came to mind, "They're stars," she said. "Shooting stars."

"Shooting cat stars?" For a young girl, Skye had mastered cynicism.

"Yes."

"Really?" Skye scrunched her nose.

Mayu folded her arms and lifted her chin. "Why ask if you're not going to believe me? They're cats made from starlight." The cat flicked its tail in front of Skye's face, and she absently reached up to run her hand down its length, still glaring at Mayu, unconvinced. The second her hand closed around its tail, the cat bolted through the air, yanking Skye off the ground and dragging her high into the air.

Mayu watched, stunned, as the tiny girl sailed away, her silhouette rapidly shrinking across the distance until, presumably, her muscles went limp from the shock and she let go of the cat's tail. She fell, tumbling head over heels through the clouds.

"I'm gonna die! I'm gonna die!" Skye wailed, her voice distant.

Shaking herself and closing her gaping mouth, Mayu gathered her energy and charged down the steep hillside—gaining wicked speed. Her sprinting turned into colossal bounds, and with a huge leap, Mayu sprang into the air. She swooped down into the valley and then arched upwards. Skye managed to make herself stop spinning uncontrollably and turned to face the ground, spotted Mayu soaring towards her, tried desperately to paddle backwards.

"No, no, no, no, no!" she cried.

They connected, Mayu's arm thudding around Skye's stomach and the girl deflated with a grunt, groaning at the impact. Mayu felt a *little* guilty for being so rough, but taking Skye by the hand, Mayu dragged her higher into the clouds.

"Thanks a lot!" Skye snapped, clutching her tummy with her free hand.

"You're welcome. Want to do it again?"

"Don't you dare!"

"Oops…"

Skye screamed as Mayu released her hold and she slipped down to Mayu's conveniently outstretched leg.

"Don't do that!" Skye dug her nails into Mayu's skin. "Take me down. I'll slip." The girl started to hyperventilate, and with a sigh Mayu stopped their ascent.

They hung amidst the clouds that, as all dream clouds should be, were soft and fluffy. Sunlight warmed Mayu's back. Hooking her arms behind her, she peered down at Skye.

"I thought you wanted to fly," she said.

"Not like this." She sounded vicious. "Take me down, or I'll bite you."

"That's no way to ask."

"Now. Do it *now*! Take me—"

Mayu reached down, pinched the back of Skye's neck, turned her into a tubby ginger cat and held her out at arm's length. Skye blinked at her, frozen stiff, her tail bristling in agitation.

"Now you listen here," Mayu said. "Your attitude stinks. You're bossy, rude, and disrespectful. I don't have to be here. I'm *trying* to help you, mind your manners. Is this how you speak to your teachers?"

"Get lost!"

Mayu gave her a shake, and Skye whimpered.

"That's no way to speak to me."

"Let me down!" she screamed.

"Shall I drop you then?"

Skye responded with a ragged, howling cry. Tears filled her eyes and she revealed her claws, swinging her stubby arms at Mayu's wrist. Maybe this wasn't the best way to lecture her. Years away from home had given her an education but had obviously done nothing for her social skills. The absence of anyone close in her personal life had turned her into a lonely, self-sufficient smart-arse. Mayu wasn't her mother, and she imagined that Skye was too used to shouting at and ignoring her parents.

The clouds turned to powdered charcoal and closed around them. A crackle sparked inside Mayu's bones and, *oh no*…greyscale.

Images moved past in a blur as Skye's mind invaded hers. Her peripheral vision quivered and glowed as Mayu was sucked in towards a bitter memory. Ancient school hallways swirled past, girls in uniforms, teachers leaving offices. They cleared to reveal a sulking image of Skye, her chin tipped down.

"It doesn't matter what she did! You do not *hit* other students," barked the teacher, looming over her.

"She slapped me!"

"I don't care. You could have seriously injured her! Detention for the next month and cleaning duty at five a.m."

"What!"

The images swept forwards and Mayu was in a common room. Skye sat, with four other girls at a low table, doing her homework. She chewed her cheeks and rolled her pencil between her fingers in concentration.

"You're such an unrefined cow," hissed one girl, tucking ringlets behind her ear. The others sniggered.

"And you're a two-faced bitch," Skye replied.

The girls pretended to be offended.

"At least I'm not a *lazy* bitch. I think you're just brain dead and that's why you fall asleep all the time."

"I can't help it," Skye growled, shaking with rage.

"Of course you can't," said one of the others, her voice shrill. "You're so stupid your eyes don't know how to stay open. You can't even take a dump without someone making sure you don't fall down the toilet." Her giggling turned to a shriek as Skye lunged forward and grabbed a fistful of her hair.

"I'll shave your head!"

The girl with ringlets dived at Skye, slapping her face hard, knocking her sideways. "What's *wrong* with you, you stupid cow?" But Miss Ringlet's bravado failed as Skye sat up and locked her in a stare.

Cold, boiling eyes; Skye's jaw clenched.

Skye swept up her ruler in a flash and thwacked the girl across the face. A crack like a whip silenced everyone in the room, and Miss Ringlet let out a banshee's howl. The screams and insults moulded around Mayu and cleared to reveal another scene.

Snow covered the ground, the day was crisp and clear, and on a bench beneath a naked tree sat Skye. Beside her was a young girl with black, braided hair and dark skin— the same girl that had lured Skye away in the school on the seabed. They wore winter robes and thick scarves and mittens; each was reading a book, like two girls plucked straight off a pretty Christmas card.

"What does 'aroo-bes-kweh' mean?" asked the braided girl in an Edinburgh accent.

Skye rolled her eyes. "Honestly, don't you know anything? It's '*arabesque*'."

Mayu felt herself starting to fade. "Skye!" At this rate, they'd lose all the progress they'd made the night before. "*Skye*!" She ran over and shook Skye's shoulder, calling once more.

Gasping, Skye looked up from her book. The scene whipped away, and Kitty-Skye was in Mayu's hand again, both of them falling down to the valley.

Tears filled Skye's eyes that fell away in the wind and Mayu brought her close to her chest. She allowed them to plummet headfirst, blurring out the sadness she'd witnessed with the wind in her ears and the dropping sensation in her stomach. She stroked Skye's fluffy head.

"Stop us falliiiing," Skye wailed, ending with miserable sobs.

Unable to resist a smile, Mayu slowed their descent and curled upright, cradling Skye in her arms. "I'm sorry," she whispered.

Skye huddled against her breast, hiding her face with both paws. "I don't want to wake up," Skye blubbered. "Why can't I stay here?"

"Staying in one place means things will never change."

"Exactly, I don't want this to change."

Mayu stroked the fluff around Skye's ears with the back of her finger, sinking slowly towards the rice paddies like a feather. "It's impossible to stay here," soothed Mayu, "you wouldn't be able to sustain a Parallel world forever and your parents are waiting for you."

Skye bristled and a lance of agony struck the back of Mayu's head. It sliced through her mind, blinding her, and she almost dropped Skye.

"Don't fight me, Skye." She clutched the girl tighter. "It will only hurt us both."

"I think you should get out of my head."

"I'm not in your head. You're in *mine*. I'm healing—"

Skye kicked her with her back leg, scratching her, and another jolt shot right through to Mayu's forehead. Her focus shaken, they fell like a rock into one of the paddies. Muddy water gushed up Mayu's nose and she tasted silt on her tongue. She coughed and spluttered as she surfaced, spotting a bedraggled Skye paddling towards one of the dirt tracks.

"Skye," she called, "the jolt of misinterpreting temporal space—the overload of electrical stimuli to one part of the brain—it could kill us without going through the logical processes. Parallel worlds are imaginary, but real enough that—"

Skye hauled her feline body onto the path, then turned back to yell, "I don't know what you're bloody talking about!"

A hurricane of rice stalks, mud, and floodwater rose up behind Skye. It arched over her head, five liquid fingers sprouting from the crest of the wave as it aimed for Mayu. Throwing out one arm, the assault never made contact; it domed around Mayu with a roar and a crash.

The next revolt took her by surprise.

Mud wrapped around her feet and sucked her into the earth by a few inches. It oozed up her ankles and up her calves. Horror latched onto her, unable to break free.

"Skye, don't!"

But Skye transformed back to her normal body, wearing her school uniform, and did nothing but watch… glaring through red-rimmed, angry eyes.

"Maybe we should die," Skye snarled.

15

I F SKYE'S MIND was like a spider web of cells, Mayu felt threads snapping and disconnecting. She closed her eyes, visualising the flow of electrical pulses, and fought to keep their minds entwined. A warped cry shook Skye's body, and Mayu felt an echo of it in her own nerves. It was working.

Opening her eyes, Mayu saw Skye kneeling in the dirt, gripping her head.

"You don't mean that. Don't do this!" begged Mayu, mud gobbling up to her hips now. "You might end up trapped in a nightmare, or you might render yourself brain dead."

"You're not listening," Skye sobbed. "I don't care."

Mayu took a sharp breath, trying not to freak out about the water soaking her chest now and the mud creeping over her stomach. "What?"

"I have to stay here."

Taking charge of their surroundings, Mayu urged the sun to warm them, sculpting a gentle breeze to carry scents of earthy cultivation.

"I understand how you feel," Mayu said. "Staying here can seem appealing, but we cannot control our dreams forever." Paddy water sploshed against Mayu's chin, and the mud squelched beneath her breasts.

Suffocating beneath the pressure around her chest, she let out a ragged shout and tried to break free, tried to dry the paddy fields, crack the mud, split the earth—*anything*. Nothing changed.

"Skye—" Her mouth filled with water, and she gagged, tilting her head back to keep her nose above the surface.

Mayu struggled harder to rein in Skye's energy levels. Her vision went blotchy red...or was that the clouds? A thousand angry barbs of foreign brain activity fought against hers, like it was trying to explode outward.

Her nose went under. When Mayu tried to breathe, a wave of liquid invaded her lungs and she convulsed, splashing her arms, aching for a mouthful of air. She could breathe if she let go of Skye, everything inside was panic and tension—her reptilian brain roared for her to save herself. But if she let go, both of them might disappear into separate comas. Skye's spirit seemed almost out of reach, Mayu clung on by sheer desperation.

Grasping for anything, Mayu clenched her hands in the air above her sinking head, feeling a sting in her fingers. The only way to free herself was to fuse Skye's spatial-temporal awareness with hers; to use Skye's own energy against her. It crackled everywhere and Mayu embraced it as her own, tried with all her might to believe *this is the best thing for me*, to welcome in the threatening, angry essence of Skye Mansfield.

Willing the merge to happen, Mayu felt an instant energy shift as they re-established a connection, gripped each other tightly with metaphorical hands. Without thinking, she gathered a powerful force beneath her, pushed upwards, and shot out of the mud. Her arms flailed as she soared towards the path. Shielding her nose, Mayu braced for impact. She slumped with relief when it never came. She hovered over the ground and dropped the last inch onto her front.

Mayu massaged her pulsing head.

Looking up, she saw Skye standing nearby, staring at her. The girl's knees trembled and her fists were clenched. Mayu sighed and hung her head, not sure what to say. She wanted to say everything that had been promised to her the past few months, *it will get better, you'll be okay, lean on your friends*. But how could she promise those things when she didn't believe in them? Getting up, Mayu took one step forward and Skye took one step away.

"You've been through a lot," Mayu said, "and I know why you don't want to wake up. I'm not angry with you."

"How could you know?" Skye croaked.

"I've read about you, I know what happened to your friend." Mayu folded her arms, unsure about bringing this up, but ready to try anything. Forcing herself to be open, she held out her hands. "The one you used to stay with at Christmas?"

Skye's whole body shook.

"What was her name?"

"Henri."

The image of Skye with the girl on a snowy bench returned to Mayu's mind. The girl who had pushed through the faceless students to play tag in the underwater school. She recalled reading that, two weeks before Skye fell into the coma, her friend Henrietta had died in a car crash.

Upon impact, her mother's car had spun, skidding off the road, and ended up on its side—Henri's side. The mother was knocked out instantly and Henrietta died in minutes, half the car door wedged into her side.

"She was the best thing in the world." Skye's expression of anger crumpled.

Nodding, Mayu approached her again and drew Skye into a hug.

Taking a deep breath, Skye let out a wail of grief and Mayu froze, trying to remain composed. She knew that wail. It resonated with her own desperation and hopelessness; with the longing she'd screamed into Yūta's cold pillow each morning.

"It's odd to think that any of us could die tomorrow, isn't it?" whispered Mayu. "All we have are minutes, and whispers, and memories. Life is one constant memory as we pass into the next minute, and for you *and* me…that leaves a hole when we lose the person we want to share those moments with. I know it does."

Skye clawed her hands into Mayu's shirt, trembling like a sheet.

"I want to see Yūta, just to see him sleeping on the couch or making himself breakfast. And I could have that if I stayed here, but not for long, in the end it would kill me. It would be the same for you, Skye."

"We're all going to die anyway," the girl sobbed. "In ten years, maybe less, we've destroyed the world, so what's the point? What's the point in school? In friends? In anything?"

Decimated rice stalks quivered in the breeze and Mayu shuddered, closing her eyes.

"A friend told me that we are like leaves and that we

have to make a choice. We either choose to carry on wherever the wind takes us, or we sink to the ground and rot. We must choose, even if it doesn't fix things the way we want. And you know…"

Mayu paused, her stomach twisting with doubt. One should never make a promise to a patient, but what if that was what Skye needed?

"When you wake up, you'll still have me," Mayu said. "I know I'm not your best friend, but I'll be there. I'll be there for as long as you need me."

Skye's arms tightened around her. "Can I live with you?"

A little laugh escaped Mayu, her eyes watering. Blinking tears clear, she pulled away and looked down at Skye. "I don't know about that. I live a long way away from you, and your parents would be hurt. But I'll be with you when you wake up, and I'll be with you while you recover."

"I'm not sick."

"I didn't say you were, but you will be physically weak for a while. Your muscles will need retraining." And she might not remember any of this, or even moments of her life before falling down the stairs.

They fell silent and Skye watched the horizon. She took a deep breath, held it, swallowed hard, and then let it out slowly. Her face struggled to hold a smile and Mayu gripped her shoulders.

"I can hear the whales." Mayu touched her ear for emphasis.

"What?"

"Listen." She pointed to the mountain peaks and, squinting, she could see dark shapes floating through the mist. The whales. Their mighty tails made slow, steady strokes, shifting the clouds like sea foam. Their dull song danced faintly across the distance.

Willing the miles to move around them, Skye and Mayu found themselves at the top of the highest peak above the valley. The rice paddies shone like tiny mirrors below. Skye and Mayu shivered, breath visible in front of their faces, but Skye didn't complain. She hugged herself, watching the whales above her head.

Reaching up, Mayu grasped her hand in thin air a few times, really having to focus on her intention, until her hand finally closed around a length of rope.

"Here." She passed it to Skye.

The girl hesitated before taking it, she looked up to see what it was attached to. She didn't even seem surprised.

"Don't let go this time," said Mayu.

Grasping the rope with two hands, Skye stared at her like a stunned rabbit.

The rope went taut as the whale it was attached to swam further ahead and Skye almost smiled as her school shoes dragged across the ground and rose into the air. To Mayu's pleasure, Skye laughed.

Running after her, Mayu bounded into the air and flew alongside her. Skye grinned into the wind, admiring the view.

With a long cry, the whales climbed higher. The scenery grew flatter and the sky darkened.

"Wait, wait," cried Skye, "we can't breathe in space!"

Mayu laughed. "Do you think whales can really fly?"

Peering up at the mammal carrying her, Skye said, "Fair point."

The Earth stretched for miles below them, the earth's magnetic fields pulsing around the globe visible to the naked eye.

"Hold on tight," Mayu said, "and don't be scared."

"What? Why?"

Mayu floated over to her and took hold of the rope as well. She smiled at Skye's serious expression and started counting.

"One…two…"

Before Mayu even reached "three," the whales leapt forward with lightspeed, and the universe sped past in streaks of dust and light. Stars passed in a blur, planets circled beneath their feet, and nebulas engulfed them in clouds of colour.

Skye let out a shriek that turned into an elated whoop. They cheered and took in the scenery with wonder, unable to absorb the scope of the universe no matter how wide they stretched their eyes.

"I'm going to be an astronaut," said Skye, then she tipped her head back and laughed as if this was the best joke in the world.

The whales halted their journey when they reached a glimmering, swirling nebula glowing yellow, green, blue and pink, and speckled with black stars.

Their rope swung forward with the whale's momentum, swinging them up, and up, and up—until they bounced softly into the whale's underbelly, giggling. They swooped back down, like a pendulum, towards the whale's tail and Mayu let go. Her stomach lurched at the pure elation of hovering without effort. Anti-gravity. Skye stared at her as she swung away.

"You'll be fine," said Mayu. "Everything floats in space."

"That's assuming things aren't just falling very, very slowly," she said, her voice growing faint.

Willing herself forward, Mayu moved at a sluggish pace and held her breath as Skye let go of the rope. The girl hovered, drifting sideways like a starfish in deep water.

"See! I told you," cried Mayu.

Time slipped by unnoticed as they floated and tumbled through the void, racing each other as if paddling in a shallow swimming pool. They climbed over the backs of the inattentive whales, studying their rugged skin. Eventually, tired out, they drifted side by side, staring out into the darkness.

"We're so small," said Skye.

"Maybe *you* are."

She chortled. "I wish I could really see the universe like this."

"Being an astronaut isn't such a crazy idea," Mayu said.

"No way. Too scary. And I'd have to be good at science."

Mayu chuckled and rolled, admiring every possible direction.

"You know, this is the longest I've gone without… falling asleep randomly," Skye said, staring at a distant nebula like it had all the answers she needed. "But my cataplexy still happens."

"That's probably because you're already asleep," said Mayu, "so you're not tired in the same way as when you're awake in the real world. The chemicals that trigger your narcolepsy, or the lack of brain chemicals, I should say, don't really matter if you're already asleep. Your cataplexy, however, is trigged by emotion, which you're still capable of experiencing in dreams."

With a resigned sigh, Skye's gaze regained some focus. "I wish I didn't have any of it. My dad still thinks that half of it is because I'm lazy. I'm not."

Ugh, ambitious parents. "You're not lazy. You have a condition and there are doctors who can help to make the symptoms easier to live with."

"We tried doctors."

"Well," Mayu did her best to sound lofty, "we'll try some more. Why haven't you been given medication?"

"It's too expensive. I've got something for the narco-lepsy, it's okay, but nothing to stop me collapsing when my feelings are intense. It's so embarrassing. You saw me… hit that girl with a ruler, didn't you? I collapsed straight afterwards—I was so angry and afraid they'd hit me back. Sometimes I collapse when I laugh, not often though, thank God. That's even worse."

It wasn't Mayu's field of expertise, but she was all too aware of the expenses involved with brain related illnesses. Narcolepsy and cataplexy were low in priority, even on Mayu's radar. She couldn't pretend to be surprised that remedying Skye's condition wasn't given much funding.

"Ugh." Skye waved her hands, exasperated. "My headteacher tried hippy *mindfulness* sessions on me. Full of 'self-control' guff and 'connecting with my body'. She thinks she's a guru or something. I mean, I like her, she's okay, but she takes the 'close your eyes and breathe deeply' rubbish way too seriously."

It sounded like the headteacher had made an effort to help, even if the complexities were beyond her understanding. Taking time out from running a boarding school to tutor someone in mindfulness seemed generous.

"It really can reduce stress…" Mayu hedged.

"Don't *you* start." Shaking her head, Skye's body language closed off.

To fill the silence, Mayu started humming the first song that came to mind. Giggling, Skye's attention refocused on the scenery. "I wish stars really were glowing crystals."

"Me too. But maybe we'd only try harder to mine them."

"Yeah, my mum and dad would."

The starlight pulsed. The brightness ebbing and dimming.

"My parents tried hypnotherapy once." Skye sounded vacant. "It just put me to sleep."

A reply was on the tip of Mayu's tongue, but nothing came out. Her stomach crawled with something, a nausea she couldn't place. The stars seemed dizzying now. Spinning and pulsing, all gathering together they colluded into one point, and Mayu felt heavier.

"Skye…" But it sounded more like a gasp as she fell, or as Skye rose higher. "Skye!"

Mayu wrenched herself free of the fatigue clutching her limbs, and she finally stopped falling. She hit the bottom of a well, the walls so dark she feared straying left or right. She only knew there was a plinth of rock in the middle of the well because Skye stood on top of it, miles above Mayu's head, illuminated by a violet galaxy.

Drowsiness hit her again. Mayu staggered, unable to shake it from the back of her head, like a virus attacking her ability to see. *Think…balance.* She just had to return to Skye. Get back to her before things got out of hand again.

Studying Skye as she ambled toward the plinth, she saw the girl staring at a single star. It hovered above Skye's head, out of reach, and she stood beneath it, still as stone.

"Where is it?"

That voice. It was down in the well with Mayu. There, a flashlight. Searching for her—for something. The beam of light swung back and forth, coming around the plinth, and the man growled again, "*Where is it?*"

16

MAYU TIPTOED ACROSS the crumbling, rocky well—around the plinth and away from the searching beam of light. She staggered, swallowing bile, and blinked hard to regain some kind of bearing.

Figuring her best bet was to sneak up on her hunter, Mayu hurried after him, hoping it would keep her out of the beam of light. The rough base of the plinth grew a little more distinct in the glow of his flashlight, revealing jagged edges and handholds. She'd get a little closer to the man before trying to climb it to give herself a better head start before he looped around.

Mayu got near enough to see the creases ironed into his white shirt and his perfect, starched collar. His questioning bounced off the stone and whispered between the shadows, over and over, rising and sinking in volume like the tide.

Breathing through her mouth, Mayu focused on Skye. She lowered into a deep crouch and then jumped with all her might. The heavy, sickening fatigue dragged her down, and Mayu only made it up a few feet. She landed on the sides of the plinth, her feet scrabbling against the rock, kicking loose a river of stones. They clattered into the well.

"Where?" the man hissed. The beam of light whipped toward the sound.

Trembling, Mayu jumped again. The rock cut into her hands when she landed this time and she gasped. The noise echoed around and around, her one breath filling the black well like a siren. She pressed close to the rock and shut her eyes, as if he'd never see her if she couldn't see him.

The man shuffled closer, each footstep deliberate and unhurried. "You will tell me the truth," he rasped.

Each breath was harder to inhale, the very air pressing down on Mayu's head. Digging her nails into handholds, she looked up at Skye again—so far away. But she'd moved. Skye's hand was stretched upwards, reaching for the solitary star above her head.

Mayu's hands lit up, bathed in artificial light, the rock around her illuminated in the hunter's flashlight. Her heart thundered, turned into a slamming drum.

"Where is it?" he cried right below her. At her.

Not glancing down, Mayu lurched upward, jumping in short, scrabbling bursts. Panting followed after her, angry and laboured.

"Where is it?"

Where was what?

So close to Skye, all she had to do was make everything vanish and calm down. But the man, he sounded ravenous, seemed so real. Get away first. Think later. Focus on Skye's hair fluttering in a wind not possible in outer-space.

With one last jump, Mayu touched the top of the plinth.

The man's hand closed around her ankle. "Where is it?"

he snarled, and yanked her off the rock. His hand was ice on her skin, manacled to her as they fell.

They hit the bottom and Mayu kicked to get free, twisting and flailing on her back. He grabbed her other ankle and Mayu screamed.

"Let her go!" yelled Skye. The girl peered down into the well, glowing white from head to foot, like she'd eaten the star above her head and turned into one herself.

The man crawled up Mayu's legs, his fingers digging through her jeans. She saw his face at last and almost recognised it through the mania transfiguring his expression. His eyes were wide and mad, blue as summer sky, and his nose strikingly aquiline. His cheeks were sallow and hair greying above the ears. He wanted violence. He wanted answers she didn't have.

Desperate for anything, she lurched at him and clawed slashes into his cheek—bright red streams of blood. He let go with a howl. Flipping onto her front, she tried to fly, but only rose a few inches before the man caught her ankle again, his fingers cutting her jeans to ribbons.

"Let go!" Skye sounded near.

His hands seized the back of Mayu's neck.

"Where is it?"

What? What had Mayu taken, or lost? Was this really about Yūta's ashes?

As he wrenched her onto her back, she gasped, her gaze filled with someone else behind him. Skye: plummeting to the ground, ablaze with light, her hands outstretched for Mayu as the man's hands wrapped around her throat.

Just make it end, Mayu thought, *kill me*. But that was no way to leave Skye.

Dredging the last of her energy, Mayu kicked and scratched until she heard the man howl once more. He sat up, cradling his face, and Skye plunged into Mayu's chest.

The girl wrapped her arms tight around Mayu as the floor stretched beneath them like a trampoline, stretching taut until it snapped. At once, the fog in Mayu's head cleared. They fell, silent, eyes shut and hiding in each other's firm grip. Until second by second, the wind stopped roaring in Mayu's ear and she realised Skye had gone limp. Her grip on the girl tightened as if pinning a precious rag doll to her chest.

She opened her eyes to a beautiful view of the galaxy.

"Thank you," she said into Skye's hair.

"I can't feel my legs," she replied, shaking. "Who was that?"

"I don't know. What does he want?"

For a moment, she only heard Skye breathing into her shoulder. "I don't know. I really don't. I wanna go back to Earth."

Mayu brushed her own long hair out of her face, letting the tension inside unravel with slow, steady breaths. "Great timing, I've just seen our transport on its way."

"Where?" Skye let go and tipped backwards, stretching into all kinds of lazy shapes trying to spot it.

With a long '*meow!*' a glowing white cat zipped between them. It sent Mayu and Skye drifting apart.

"Are you kidding?" Skye yelled.

"And you doubted me!"

A shower of cats blazed past them like shooting stars, and she heard Skye groan.

"Come on, you know what to expect this time."

One of the cats circled around Skye and stopped in

front of her face. It wiggled its tail in offering. Grimacing as if she'd rather have after school detention, Skye reluctantly took hold of it.

The cat shot off, Skye screaming, leaving a trail of stardust.

Snorting, Mayu found her own cat and cried out as it streaked forward. She had to admit, these cats were damn fast.

She hurtled towards the panoramic Earth, trailing in Skye's wake. They burst through the ozone layer and Mayu let go of the cat's tail. She carried on firing towards the planet and willed herself to gain speed with Skye. When they were level with each other, Mayu saw the terror in Skye's eyes.

"Just let go," Mayu shouted.

"Then what?" Skye snapped.

"Fly! We can do it this time."

"Into the bloody ground?"

"Don't worry, I've got you."

Shaking her head, Skye let go of the cat and Mayu dropped back to take hold of the girl's ankle. Their rapid descent began to ease, but not fast enough. The ground came closer and closer…

"Mayu…" Skye's hair billowed around her head, but not enough to mask the train tracks that the pair of them were diving towards. "*MAYU!*"

"You're fine," she shouted back, tugging as hard as possible.

"THIS ISN'T FUNNY."

Unable to stop herself, Mayu laughed, and she halted their fall a good five metres off the ground.

"You see," Mayu panted, "I told you."

Skye sagged, arms dangling towards the ground, and she groaned. "You're bloody mental."

17

MAYU SET SKYE down on the station platform and landed next to her, staring out at the suburban landscape. Many of the houses were single story buildings with amateur mosaics drawn in chalk on their walls. The vivid, cheerful view soothed away the horror of that man in the well until only the rush of falling back to Earth mattered.

"It's good to get the heart racing!" said Mayu, scraping her hair into a bun.

"Yeah, I think it's only healthy when you're exercising, not panicking for your actual life." Skye crawled over to the waiting bench and slumped into a seat. She started giggling. "That was crazy. Wow."

"I knew you'd warm to the thrill of possible catastrophe," Mayu teased.

"No, you're still on your own with that one."

Skye dropped her head back and stared up at the clouds, and Mayu took the opportunity to turn away and cringe. She massaged her forehead, feeling a feverish headache. They were hiding too much from each other and triggering deep-seated fear, both terrified of either accepting something or confessing a painful truth, of being seen for who they really were and what they'd done—something needed to give.

What did her subconscious want? What was it looking for? What was the significance of the one recurring question? Part of it had to originate from Skye's subconscious but searching for answers could be dangerous.

Putting her smile back on, Mayu looked up and down the train tracks, admiring the countryside and squat houses nearby. She could smell home cooking, laundry, and gardening, and—

Mayu did a double take.

Standing on the tracks heading out to the wide world was Yūta with his hands in his pockets. He pulled one hand free to wave at her, smiling. He gazed at her fondly and slipped his hand back into his pocket.

Her field of vision narrowed onto him, filled with warmth and longing.

A scraping, clanking hiss rattled the tracks as a train approached from some distant city, but Mayu didn't turn to look. They'd travelled to this train stop so many times to visit her family—she wanted that time back, needed to feel his hand in hers as the train dropped them off and left in a gust of wind.

Mayu started walking.

"Don't follow him!" Someone grabbed her hand and yanked. "Stop. I'm fading!"

Refocusing on her surroundings, Mayu looked down at Skye and saw the girl's arms had gone a little translucent.

"Sorry. I'm back." Mayu swallowed, pushing the warmth further away. Skye's arms solidified again.

"You should stay away from him," Skye whispered.

Even so, Mayu watched Yūta walk away and vanish. Tomoya's last words to her had been that she could look after Skye as a team, with her husband, so long as she didn't use real memories as a base scenario. Once they were away from this town, she'd have to try.

The train screeched into the platform, filling her view, and Skye rushed to the edge. Mayu pulled her back.

"Are we getting on?" asked Skye.

"Do you want to?"

Skye looked at the polished, neomodern train with a hint of adventure in her eyes. "Where does it go?"

"No idea. Shall we find out?"

They climbed aboard the nearest carriage and stared at the passengers inside. A different coloured balloon was tied to the back of every seat, each one bobbing into its neighbour as the train set off again. The carriage itself was spacious, with plenty of leg-room and a wide central aisle.

"All the seats face inwards," said Skye.

"*That's* your observation?" replied Mayu.

"Well, the balloons are nice, but the seats. They're the wrong way round. And the triangles hanging from the ceiling…"

"What are you talking about? Have you never been on a city train before?"

"Of course I… A city train? I…of course. This is just a weird train."

Biting her tongue, Mayu gripped a support beam and watched Skye head for one of the seats. As she made to sit, a yellow balloon sailed down and hit her on the head with a '*boing!*'

"That's my seat," it said.

"What?" Skye jumped upwards, smacking the balloon away.

"Well, I never," it cried. "Such a rude child."

The other balloons muttered in agreement. Skye only acted surprised for a few seconds.

"You're not even sat on the seat," she said, pointing to the vacant chair beneath the yellow balloon.

"Oh! Point out my bodily disabilities even more, why don't you? Can't sit. I'll bet you wouldn't say that if I was lined with aluminium and painted like Mickey Mouse."

Mouth hanging open, Skye looked back at Mayu as if to say, "Is this for real?" Mayu shrugged. She cupped a hand over her mouth and whispered, "Just go with it."

Skye shook her head in disbelief, spreading her arms wide, then slouched and gave the balloon a hard look. "Where *may* I sit?" she asked. "All of you have taken the chairs."

"Have you no respect for your elders?" wailed the yellow balloon.

"I highly doubt—"

Mayu hissed across Skye's retort, and the girl threw her arms up.

"This is stupid. It's just a balloon."

Their floating rubber passengers muttered in horror. Ignoring them, Skye plonked down one seat along from the yellow balloon. They sprang on her. All the nearest balloons whacked and thumped and bashed against any bit of Skye they could reach. Even the balloons situated on the other side of the aisle soared into the fray.

With an angry cry, Skye burst free from the rainbow cyclone, swinging her arms. She batted most of them away until the last of the balloons returned to their chairs. Mayu stifled a laugh; Skye's hair stuck out in a wild, statically charged mess.

Unimpressed with Mayu's reaction, Skye skulked to the other end of the carriage, sank to the floor, and sat with her legs crossed around one of the support poles in the aisle. This girl just couldn't take a hint.

Gauging her balance, Mayu approached a blue balloon on the opposite side of the carriage from the yellow one and bowed deeply to it. "Excuse me," she said. Skye peered over her shoulder, thinking Mayu was addressing her. Her eyes narrowed when she saw Mayu talking to the blue balloon.

"I've travelled a long way today and I'm completely exhausted," Mayu went on. "I'm sorry to ask you, but may I have your seat for five minutes?"

The blue balloon grumbled a little. "Well, I suppose, since you asked so nicely."

Mayu bowed again. "Thank you very much. I'm sorry to cause you trouble."

"No, no," it sighed, untying itself from the back of its seat. "I get off soon anyway." Its string released and the balloon sailed up to the ceiling. Mayu sat down and watched as it shuffled against the racks and support handles, making its way to the carriage door.

Smiling, Mayu looked back at Skye and quirked her eyebrows. Skye turned away, hugging the pole with her face stuck in a sulk.

At the next station, the train pulled into a tiny countryside platform. More balloons occupied the waiting area, their strings tied to various weights to anchor them down.

The doors opened and the blue balloon sailed out, disappearing from view as it floated directly upwards.

Three more balloons detached themselves from seats, making for the exit, and three more tried to board. Skye stumbled to her feet and dived for one of the vacant chairs. Crying out in disgust, all the balloons on board smacked and bashed against her again.

"Come on! They've gone," Skye yelled. "It's mine now!"

One smacked her in the eye and Skye cried out in anguish. Mayu winced. In all the confusion, the train set off again and the new passengers found the empty seats. Skye hunkered down on the floor, arms over her head, until the balloons finally stopped their assault.

Letting out a miserable sigh, the girl crawled back to the support beam and wrapped her limbs around it, hiding her red eye in her sleeve. Mayu shook her head. All Skye had to do was ask nicely, or to apologise.

Mayu closed her eyes. If she pretended to be sleeping, Skye might try to find a seat without offending anyone. Perhaps she felt ashamed, knowing that Mayu was watching. Apologising was hard, she knew that.

Mayu sat there for a while, sunlight flickering over her eyelids in splotches of brilliant yellow, orange, and black. Eventually she heard Skye heave up onto her feet. Patting and strained sighs followed—she was probably stretching and patting the floor-dirt off her backside.

A series of shuffles. Then:

"Excuse me," said Skye, "I've been sat on the floor for a long time. May I have your seat for five minutes?"

Mayu cracked open one eye and glanced to her left. About five chairs down, on Mayu's side of the carriage,

Skye addressed a green balloon. Her arms were folded so tight that anyone would think Skye's ribcage needed holding in place. Skye smiled a sour, forced expression.

Mayu shut her eyes again before Skye noticed her watching.

"Ah, well," said the green balloon, "you're the rude kid from earlier, aren't you?"

"I'm not rude."

Forgetting herself, Mayu's eyes shot open and she stared at Skye, who noticed her sharp movement. Mayu pretended to look surprised and sleepy, then smiled pleasantly as if Skye was behaving like a model student going about her usual business. Subtle encouragement.

It seemed to do the trick. Skye's smile skewed and she focused on the balloon again.

"Young people have no respect," the balloon went on. "It's all *me, me, me.*"

"If that's the case," replied Skye, "then old people have no respect either. You act like your needs are the only ones that matter, and you treat me badly based on no proof. You don't know me."

"Your tone says it all, young madam."

"I am not a madam!" Skye stamped her foot in an aggressive, precise kick.

"Skye," said Mayu, softly. "It's not what you say, it's how you say it."

"What?" Her glare zoomed in on Mayu.

"You can say almost anything in the world, even something that's potentially rude, but only if you phrase and deliver it carefully."

Chewing on her inner cheeks, Skye regarded the green

balloon again over her up-turned nose. "Look," she said, "I didn't mean to make you mad."

Mayu buried her face in her hand.

"Can I please sit down?" Skye asked.

If the word "no" had multiple syllables, the green balloon would have enunciated every single one. Skye growled in frustration. Spinning on her heel, she stormed to the other end of the carriage scanning the ground, the seats, the racks—she even opened the toilet door and peered in there.

"What are you looking for?" asked Mayu.

"I'm going to find a pin," yelled Skye, "and I'll pop every bloody one of them."

"How daaaare you!" shrieked a red balloon.

Mayu gripped the edge of her seat and leant forward. "Just say sorry, Skye. Don't hurt them."

Planting her feet wide apart, her arms pinned to her sides, Skye skewered Mayu with a fiery glare. "Are you doing this? Do you think this is funny? You're making this world, you fix it."

"It's not really something that requires a drastic solution, is it?" Mayu slumped back into her seat, folded her arms, and shut her eyes again. "I'm not causing it," she added, half-lying. "It must be you."

Mayu didn't control the balloons' actions or their words, but they were a part of her subconscious. Regardless, Mayu didn't see the harm in letting Skye put up with them for a little while longer.

"*Mayu…*" Again, that demanding, vicious tone.

Mayu didn't open her eyes; she just raised her eyebrows and crossed one leg over the other. "What?"

"I know you're doing this. Make the balloons go away." Then, as an afterthought, "Please."

Mayu sniffed and shook her head. "Shan't."

"Stop being a tosspot!"

"A what?" Glancing at Skye, Mayu decided she didn't want to know. "For goodness sake, they're not causing any problems. One balloon gave up its seat for me, didn't it? Are you saying you're not capable of asking for one too? Do you have to *bully* them into giving up their place?"

That struck a nerve. Skye's jaw tightened, her eyes shone, and her face paled. She stared at Mayu as if she'd like nothing more than to slap her with everything she had. But there was something else, something deeper in those round, quivering eyes: a nakedness. A betrayal. Mayu steeled herself. She knew that Skye didn't want to hear a connection between herself and the word "bully," but Skye's silence meant the word rang true.

"I'm not trying to punish you," said Mayu. "These balloons aren't here on purpose, but I don't see why I should vanish them away, either. You're a good person. You're better than this."

Closing her eyes again, Mayu let out a weary sigh and sank into her seat, trying to get comfy. How far did this train travel? And where was it taking them? She yawned, the pull of deep, unconscious sleep whispering in her ear. It promised relaxation, warmth, large hands trailing up her arms…

The orange light flashing over her eyelids grew hotter, painting her inner-eye with the colours of a sun dipping below the horizon. Heavier and heavier… Sinking into the train's rocking rhythm…

"Pardon me."

Skye's voice roused Mayu from the precipice of sweet dreams. Forcing her eyes open, she saw Skye addressing the green balloon.

"Not you again," it said.

Skye clenched her teeth, tightening her lips into a thin line. She took a deep breath. "I'm sorry for being rude to you earlier."

"Just him?" cried the yellow balloon across from Mayu.

Turning slowly, her smile rigid and a little possessed, Skye replied, "No, I am sorry to you as well. And I'm sorry for threatening to find a pin."

"I oughta think so," cried the red balloon. "Disgusting."

"Please forgive me."

The red balloon peered over at the yellow balloon, and they cackled without mirth.

"Forgive an urchin like you just so you can feel better about yourself? That won't do anything," snapped the red balloon. "I've seen it before. You'll get what you want and then carry on being a spiteful little—"

Skye's lip wobbled and her eyes grew wet. Mayu leant forward, looking at the red balloon.

"Come on now," Mayu said, "Skye apologised. There's no need to treat her like this."

"No need!" shrieked the red balloon. "No *need*! She threatened to kill us, and you think a rude, contemptuous little brat can make up for that by—"

Mayu waved her hand and the balloon burst with a loud *bang*. Skye jumped, her mouth springing open, and the other balloons jerked against their strings.

"Oh my God!" screamed the yellow balloon. "Murder! Murder! Get her!"

The balloons near Mayu swooped down and whacked and bashed her body. For inflated rubber, they packed quite a wallop. With an irritated groan, Mayu waved her hand again and a succession of loud bangs and pops filled the carriage. The last one wailed before it splattering against the floor in shreds of yellow.

Looking over at Skye, Mayu said, "Don't take after me. Obviously you shouldn't hurt real people who are…" She almost said "assholes," then couldn't think of an appropriate substitute, so shrugged her shoulders.

"I could have told you that," sniffed Skye. She gruffly wiped her eyes. "Well, looks like I'm spoilt for choice now."

Smiling and feeling a fond tug in her chest, Mayu patted the seat beside her. Skye padded over as the scenery changed from countryside to city buildings. They both jumped, watching cars shoot past, shopping fronts, traffic lights, pedestrians, newsstands, and late evening city activity. Skye's bum barely touched the seat before the train stopped in the middle of a busy street.

They saw an ice rink outside the window, surrounded by leafless trees and decorated with blue and white lights.

"Whoa," whispered Skye. "Where are we?"

"Rockefeller Centre, I think," said Mayu, "New York. I've only been here once in winter time."

"Aren't those lights a waste of energy?"

Mayu shrugged. "They have the resources and money to produce it."

"Huh, that doesn't seem fair. We don't have any

Christmas lights in my town. In Balloch, anyway. Not that it's much of a town…"

"Have you been ice skating before?"

Skye's eyes lit up. "No. Can we?"

"Let's go."

18

THEY HURRIED OFF the train and across the street, although Mayu noticed the train didn't pull away. As for the ice rink, it was empty and no one manned the ticket booth. The ice sparkled in the low evening sun and gleamed off the golden statue of Prometheus looming beside the rink.

"Look, look," said Skye, running down the steps, "I'll produce my own skates."

She ran at the ice and Mayu lurched after her. "Don't run; you'll hurt yourself!"

But it was too late. Skye leapt over the barrier with fantastic grace. Mayu held her breath as two white boots appeared on Skye's feet and the blades on the bottom hit the ice with a sharp clack. Skye wobbled, her blades slipping back and forth, before she lost her balance and toppled over backwards.

Mayu caught up and peered over the barrier. "You alright?"

Skye winced. "Hurt less than expected."

"I told you."

She watched Skye scrabble around as the girl wiped her hands on her socks.

"Um, I need help."

Rolling her eyes, Mayu floated into the air and over the barrier. By the time she landed, she was wearing ice skates as well. She gripped Skye's hand and planted her feet wide apart.

She heaved Skye up with all her might, wobbling back and forth like a clown on stilts. They laughed and squealed, clutching each other's arms. When Mayu finally found her balance again, with Skye hanging onto her forearms, she noticed that Skye's uniform had changed.

The girl blushed, unsure of herself as Mayu took in the glittering gymnastic dress. "It's more suitable, right?" she said.

To be honest, she looked adorable. "It's lovely!" Mayu chirped. Skye clung on tighter. "You know, if you stop focusing so hard on what you think you can see, you'll find it a lot easier to do what you want."

"What does that mean?"

"It means you're dreaming, and you're an Olympic ice dancer now."

Skye blushed a deeper red and pushed away from Mayu inch by inch. She scudded further out across the ice with heavy footfalls, leaning over like a hunched monkey. Mayu stifled a snicker.

Looking up at the surrounding buildings, Mayu noticed the waning sunlight. Not wanting to skate in the dark, she concentrated on keeping the sun from sinking any lower. They'd have the Christmas lights, certainly, and the city itself to light the rink, but like all things, this was based on a memory. A night memory. It was best not to tempt things.

Shaking her body, a thick black coat wrapped around Mayu and black stockings melted up to her thighs. She patted her skirt. Some bits of a memory couldn't be altered, it seemed. Mayu chuckled to herself.

With a clap of her hands, cheerful, bouncing music blared from the ice rink's speakers and, kicking off, Mayu glided past Skye, who was turning in a slow circle. Her limbs were locked stiff, gauging the weight and pressure needed to alter her course.

"Stop thinking so hard," Mayu cried. "You're a ghost across water. A nightingale in the breeze. A ballerina on ice."

"You make it sound so easy. I can't stop seeing what I'm seeing!" Skye tried to push off with the same momentum as Mayu, but she wobbled and shot forward into the nearest barrier. She flailed her arms in an attempt to stay upright. When she hit the side, she groaned and kicked the barrier.

"You do better," Skye cried.

Oh, no, no, no. Mayu wasn't any better either, but she couldn't admit that now. Mayu forced a smile that made her skin feel like stretched rubber. "I don't—"

"Come on. I want to see a pirouette, a jump, and a perfect landing." Wicked, teasing child. Her grin showed just how much she doubted Mayu had it in her.

"Alright, kid, you're on."

Light as a feather, skilled as an athlete. Slicing her blades against the ice, Mayu set off around the rink. She gained speed quickly and her feet overlapped with precise fluidity. Finding her centre of balance, Mayu pirouetted just as she passed Skye, her body bending and controlled just as it needed to be. She heard Skye gasp.

Slicing forward again, Mayu prepared to jump and, holding her breath, she leapt into the air to do a three-point turn. She made it around twice before crashing back down.

She let out a short scream as her feet buckled. No way out of this one, the only place she was spinning was onto her face. But she stopped mid-fall. Mayu felt two arms hook underneath hers.

Peering up, she looked into Yūta's confused face.

"Beautiful," he said, "except for that last bit."

Her frown transformed into a grin.

"Mayu! Get rid of him! It's me—it's Skye!"

Shifting onto her own two feet, Mayu waved her hands in placation as Skye slammed her blades against the ice. The girl approached at a snail's pace.

"Whoa, whoa. It's alright. This isn't a memory. I've never been ice skating with Yūta, and I've never been to New York with him. He's totally unconnected to this place, aren't you?"

"New York?" he repeated. "That's where we are?" Yūta tipped his head back to admire the buildings. "Aren't all those decorative lights a waste of energy?"

Skye glided to a stop. "That's what I said."

He regarded Skye in his familiar, penetrating manner; his golden-brown eyes twinkling and alert.

"What did one air purification ship say to the other?" he asked Skye.

Mayu groaned but couldn't hide her smirk.

"I don't know?" Skye replied.

"If you're not part of the problem, you're part of the precipitate."

Mayu watched a range of emotions pass over Skye's face, ranging from confusion to looking at Yūta as if he had a few screws loose. A short laugh came out at last.

"Is that meant to be a joke?" she asked.

Yūta jerked his chin and put his hands on his hips. "Well, not if you have to ask."

Laughing properly this time, Skye made to skate off in style, gliding on one foot. She lost her balance at once; setting her other foot down only made things worse. Yūta lunged forward and caught her in one arm.

"Honestly," he said, "you're both as bad as each other."

The look on Skye's face was priceless. Mayu covered her mouth to hide her smile and turned away. Yes, Mayu never got tired of Yūta holding her, either. The lovestruck look in Skye's eyes was understandable.

Yūta straightened Skye up with the same ease as placing a doll back onto her feet. Towering over her, Yūta held out both of his hands. "If you're going to skate, why don't you let me teach you?"

Skye nodded, but then glanced at Mayu. "Is that okay?"

"Of course."

Skating in a weaving path around the sidelines, Mayu watched with flushed cheeks as Yūta guided, pushed, and pulled Skye around the rink. She didn't know if he'd really be any good at ice skating, but it amused her to see.

In no time at all, Skye didn't need his help anymore. She blitzed around the rink like a swan in flight and her natural flexibility rendered some stunning movements.

"How is it?" she cried, looping around Yūta.

"You'll have to slow down, I can't tell."

Cackling, she leapt into the air, sunlight shimmering

off her dress. Skye twirled and landed without incident, and both Yūta and Mayu applauded. Stronger and faster, Skye dominated the space around them, and Mayu felt a warning sting in the back of her head.

"Do you have children, Mayu?" Skye asked, skating backwards in a figure of eight.

A stab of grief almost knocked Mayu over. Yūta replied first.

"Not yet we don't. But we're thinking about it."

Too late now.

Yūta intercepted Mayu and wrapped her up in his arms. She smelt the spice of his aftershave and remembered the prickle of his woollen coat. Swooping her around, he led Mayu in a clumsy waltz.

He tossed his floppy hair and waved one hand in exasperation. "Really, you're clumsier than I am!"

"No, I'm not!"

He grabbed Mayu around the waist and hoisted her off her feet, spinning her about in a careless circle. She shrieked with laughter and clung to his shoulders.

"Put me down. We'll fall!"

Tripping on his own boots, Yūta dropped Mayu onto her feet and, still laughing, they clung to each other's hands as they slipped and kicked all over the place. They broke apart and Mayu flailed on the spot. When she looked up again, it wasn't Yūta skidding towards her, but Tomoya Matokai.

He laughed so hard that he wheezed as Mayu caught him in her arms.

"Matokai!"

"You're really good at this," he babbled.

He was so close that she noticed the sweet smell of spirits on his breath and the intensity of his grip. A heated wooziness came over her too.

"Are you sure you're not cold?" she asked. His business suit felt thin beneath her touch.

"Of course. You keep my coat." Tomoya patted the black padding on Mayu's arm. "You suits you very well." He giggled. "*It* suits you."

"Thank you," she gushed, her legs beginning to slide away from her. "Matokai, I don't think…"

"You should call me *Tomoya*," he said, patting her shoulder.

Embarrassed, Mayu looked away.

"I've known you *so* long now. I insist."

"Tomoya, I don't think I'm sober enough to—"

At that moment, Momo crashed into them, and Mayu's legs finally buckled. They landed in a heap, with Mayu at the bottom. Keiji Obinata and Fukushima cheered from the sidelines, clapping hard at their spectacular fall.

Lying on her back on the soggy ice—pinned beneath Tomoya and then Momo—Mayu exploded into a fit of giggles. She laughed so hard she couldn't breathe. She laughed at the stars far above her head. And she laughed at Momo's ridiculous face as she too wailed with inane, wheezing, giggles.

"We're never gonna find our way back to the hotel," Mayu cackled.

"Airport," laughed Tomoya. "*Airport*."

"Jesus Christ," said Richard, skating over, "what is this cluster-fart?"

Something slapped Mayu's face and her laughter

drained away. Her chest felt lighter without Tomoya and Momo on top of her. She stared up at Skye, the stars dim behind the city's glare.

"My name is Skye Mansfield," she said.

"Skye…"

"I'd say, 'I come in peace,' but I just slapped you, so maybe not."

Still tingling with drunken laughter, Mayu reached up and pulled Skye into a hug. The girl cried out in surprise and toppled into Mayu's arms.

"Get off. It's wet."

Letting go, Mayu sat up. "I'm sorry. I should have got rid of Yūta sooner. I thought it would be alright, mixing him with a memory he didn't belong to. I'm clearly just… At the end of the day, seeing him is just another part of myself. I can't handle it." Maybe she'd give it one more chance. "You brought me back pretty quick, though."

Skye grinned and raised her chin. "I didn't fade so much this time. Last time I felt a really sinister *pushing*, you know? It felt like it was trying to erase me. This time it felt different. Easier." Her mouth compressed into a serious line. "Are you sure it's okay to keep Yūta around? I like him, but he drags you away a lot."

Mayu nodded. "You're right. I thought this time would be different. You're smart, Skye."

Her cute smile returned before stretching into a yawn.

"Shall we get back on the train?" Mayu asked.

"Just a second." It took a lot of wobbling, but Skye got back onto her feet and then just stood there and admired the Christmas lights. "So many…" she whispered. She stared at them until the sun returned to its original, late afternoon position.

They climbed the stairs out of the rink and Mayu glanced back at the top to appreciate the ice and sunlight one last time.

Her smile faded. A stack of three lockers stood in the middle of the ice rink; isolated, out of place, like a lone figure emitting a shadow that blanketed the area around it. Keeping a firm hand on Skye's shoulder, she pushed them onward and turned her back on it.

As soon as they boarded the train, it set off without delay. Mayu returned to her original seat and Skye transformed into a cat as she sat down next to her. She curled up on the cushion like a croissant. It looked much comfier.

Concentrating, Mayu willed herself to change as well. Her limbs shrank and the carriage grew larger, until she sat awkwardly with an ebony tail between her legs. Mayu shifted and curled up beside Skye. She poked the girl's fluffy head with her paws.

Skye looked up with a feline grin.

"It looks like this will be a long train ride," said Mayu, "and I don't fit very comfortably on the seats as a full-grown woman."

Humming in agreement, Skye closed her eyes and settled her chin on her fluffy arms. The girl fell asleep just as the sun disappeared and the light outside grew smoky.

Mayu half-slept. Lights flashed in her dreams like a network of veins. With Skye's sleep pattern completely under Mayu's control again, she manipulated the outputs and signals to convey healing and safety. If a coma was a reaction to danger, bringing Skye out of it meant giving her assurance that danger had passed.

There was very little resistance. In fact, Skye's mind seemed lethargic and malleable. The day's activities had really worn her out.

After a while, the electrical impulses changed into new shapes. The strands bent into a snowy park path lined with trees—their leafless branches decorated with Christmas lights. City skyscrapers loomed on the other side of the park and a water fountain shone at the end of the path. Blue lights glowed in the fountain's jumping water, the liquid calculated to eject in patterns, creating the illusion of fish or a sentient water dance.

"This is…" Mayu whispered.

"Osaka, Namba Parks."

Like he'd been in front of her all along, Fukushima buried his hands in his pockets, pushing his lab coat behind him. His serious mouth seemed incapable of kindness. The tree lights reflected off his glasses and hid his eyes behind the glare.

Mayu shuddered and turned her back on him, startled to find him stood right in front of her. Maybe it was the cold sheen of his glasses or the feel of snowflakes on her hands, but Mayu bit her tongue and remained totally composed, sensing it would be far worse if she revealed any hint of fear.

"What's wrong?" she asked.

"Are you serious?" His hands shot out of his pockets, reaching for her, and Mayu darted backward. "When you wake up, are you going to deal with anything properly? Do you expect the rest of us to trail after you, picking up your snotty tissues? When are you going to start feeling okay?"

"Never."

"You hypocrite." Fukushima undid his tie and pushed past her, returning to the fountain. Sitting on the basin's edge was Yūta. She felt a rush of joy that twisted into horror when she noticed his hands tied behind his back.

With a flick of his wrist, Fukushima whipped his tie across Yūta's face. It cracked like leather against stone.

"What are you doing?" Mayu shrieked, her voice giving out mid-sentence.

"You'll tell Skye to wake up," spat Fukushima, dropping the tie and punching Yūta's other cheek. "But you're not telling yourself the same, are you?" He drove his knuckles into Yūta's stomach, and Mayu forgot how to breathe, felt the blow as if he'd hit her instead. Her vision blurred, wanting to run over and restrain Fukushima with teeth, nail and foot, but she couldn't. Her body felt stretchy, unwilling to bend at her command, stretched taught with guilt and denial.

The path narrowed, the tree lights vanished. Only the fountain's blue spotlights illuminated Yūta from behind.

"Where is it?" Fukushima demanded, like he was asking Yūta.

"What? What do you want?" Mayu cried.

Her colleague turned on her like he was seeing her for the first time. The lenses of his glasses shone white hot, the rest of his body black as shadow. "Where is it?" he bellowed, teeth flashing, storming at her. It was not Fukushima's voice anymore. Language barriers were wonderfully muddled in shared dreams, there was never normally a distinction in the words used, only innate understanding. But Mayu heard it now—a well-spoken, male British accent.

Her legs didn't work, everything was numb. Mayu stumbled away and fell down a flight of stairs. She tumbled head over heel, unable to tense for the inevitable crash at the bottom.

Mayu jolted out of it and forced her eyes open. No longer falling. Her body still felt unresponsive—pinned down.

Moonlight spilled into the train carriage and a steady *cha-cha-cha-cha-cha* rumbled inside the seat cushion. The thing pinning her down tightened around Mayu's chest, forcing her feline arms to straighten out. She twisted her head back and saw Skye's human face. She lay across three seats, snoozing softly, with one arm wrapped around Mayu like a cuddly toy.

Relief flooded Mayu as she relaxed into the warm embrace. She watched the stars outside the window, comforted by Skye's firm grip, safe from their nightmares for a while. Mayu hadn't fallen asleep in someone's embrace in so long, she had forgotten how blissful it felt to know that someone was with her. Someone needed her.

Skye pressed her cheek against the top of Mayu's head, and Mayu curled around the girl's arm.

19

THE STILLNESS WOKE her. Pale light soaked the sky and a cool breeze blew in from the now glassless windows. Wriggling out of Skye's grip, Mayu pushed onto her front paws to better assess their altered surroundings.

Moss and rot decorated the train carriage walls. Mud trailed over the aisle floor, and most of the seat cushions looked as if they had been chewed by mice. A bird squawked outside but all Mayu could see from the windows opposite them was open sky. Through those behind them was a building with ornate stone arches.

She jumped down to the floor and, as she leapt onto the seats opposite them, Mayu transformed back to her own body and knelt on the shabby cushions. She peered out the window and her heart soared; a field of yellow tulips stretched for miles. She was tempted to climb out of the window to run through the swaying flowers right then and there. But she clenched the window ledge, resisting.

"*I never want to go through that again.*" Momo's voice. It seemed to come from the sky. "*She's merged with Skye way too closely.*"

"*Yes, but what else could she do?*" Fukushima. "*Those*

energy spikes a few days ago were violent—Skye would have rendered her vegetative."

A dull whimper. *"It looks as if she still might. I can't go through last night again. We almost lost Mayu. We're not prepared for this. Skye's PDE is so strong, Mayu is going deeper just to keep the girl afloat."*

"We made it, didn't we? You did good last night, everyone did."

"It's been six days! We've barely gotten any sleep. This is dangerous, even for Mayu. No wonder Matokai struggled. None of us predicted this. Look what it's doing to her."

A sigh. *"We can't know for sure."* A pause. *"How is Matokai?"*

A long pause. *"He still hasn't woken up. No change in his vitals though."*

A loud yawn from Skye brought Mayu back to the moment and she got to her feet, ready to say good morning.

"What's all the noise?" asked Skye.

"Noise?" said Mayu. "Do you mean the birds? Good to see you waking up. Did you sleep okay?"

Skye pushed into a sitting position and beamed. "Great. I…feel great! Where are we? Wait…wait, let me guess; you don't know?"

Cheeky little thing. "No, I don't. Want to find out?" She pointed over Skye's head to the building outside. It was an effort not to acknowledge the field of tulips.

Skye got to her feet and straightened her pleated skirt, taking in the mouldy carriage. "You're not very good at holding everything together, are you?"

Mayu folded her arms, detecting the child's teasing

tone, and chose not to bite. Smirking, Skye skipped to the open carriage doors, swinging to a stop in the doorframe.

"Let's go then!" she cried and jumped onto the abandoned platform.

The sun rose behind the building, throwing the platform into shadow. They stared up at the black, lifeless windows, the cracked brickwork, the aged stone decorations and then at each other.

"After you," Skye muttered.

Despite the building's ominous appearance, Mayu did not feel trepidation. She didn't recognise the building either, so her memories shouldn't affect their exploration.

Walking up to the large oak doors, Mayu peered back at Skye before heaving them open to a long creaking sound. Beyond lay a rotunda hall with a split marble staircase. White sunlight shone through the glass ceiling and illuminated the space. The following silence was layered with ageless secrets.

"Skye, look at this," she said, crossing the threshold.

Marble pillars stood around the perimeter of the hall and multiple corridors stretched away into the building around them. The wooden panelled walls must have gleamed with polish in times gone by but looked dry and neglected.

"Echo! Echo!" Skye shouted, making Mayu jump.

Skye smiled as her cry rebounded off the marble floor. She kicked her feet through the dust, then smiled, as if she'd thought of a new game, she began dragging one foot through the dirt, creating grey trails.

Leaving her to it, Mayu peered down one of the corridors.

She saw tapestries, Roman suits of armour, crinkled books in glass cabinets and a half-clad statue of a woman.

"Look, Mayu."

Turning back to Skye, who stood admiring her handiwork on the floor, she returned to see that Skye had marked out a girl's face.

"Very nice. Who's that supposed to be?"

Skye shrugged. "No one." Her smile slowly faded as she stared at the floor. Beneath the pale light, Skye had the posture of a wilted daisy, like a crow had swooped down and plucked her out at the roots.

"What's wrong?" Mayu asked, tilting her head.

Skye shrugged her shoulders, suddenly dejected. "You say I've been sleeping for almost a year?"

"Yes."

"So I've missed my twelfth birthday?"

"True, but next year you can make up for it: two parties!"

A little smile returned to Skye's lips. Mayu hunched forward, her black hair slipping over one shoulder, and she tried to summon up as much reassurance as she could.

"You can always begin again," she said. "When you wake up in the real world, you can wake up to a new life. Think of it as a chance to change what you didn't like before."

"There's only one thing I'd really change."

A susurrating wind blew into the hall, disturbing the edges of Skye's drawing. The braid twisting around the dust-girl's neck swayed across the floor and Mayu saw it was meant to be Henri.

"We can't have them back, but aren't we so lucky?"

"What?" Skye stared at her with hard, inquisitive eyes.

"We spent time with great people. Doesn't she still make you smile, if you search deep down? Important people are like bamboo. Once they set roots in our life, they are there for good. Their effect on us continues to grow, to strengthen our personality, even when we can no longer see them."

Skye smiled, not completely replacing the sadness in her eyes. "You're full of weird stuff, aren't you?" she said.

Mayu laughed. "There you go. Life lesson, kid. People are like bamboo."

"Whatever you say."

They wandered down the corridor with the Roman armour and Skye announced that this was clearly a Greek museum. The half-naked statue was (apparently) Aphrodite. Skye's theory fell down around her ears, however, as they entered a new wing; covered in paintings from the Western Renaissance.

"Look how realistic they are," said Skye. "I wish I could paint like this. Can you paint, Mayu?"

"Not even slightly," she replied. "But I can create parallel universes, if that counts for anything."

"Show off," Skye clucked, heading into the next gallery, which was much darker than the others. She disappeared into the shadowy room, humming a tune Mayu didn't recognise.

Mayu ambled behind her, hands clasped behind her back. As she entered, her eyes narrowed. Skye wasn't there but her humming was still audible. Speeding up, Mayu peered into the next room, still no sign of her.

"Skye," she called in a sing-song voice. "Where are—" She cut herself off, remembering the school at the bottom of the ocean. Clearing her throat, she tried again, steady and flat, "Where are you?"

"I'm through here."

Her voice came from a narrow corridor ahead. Fiery orange sunlight illuminated the doorway from within—a welcoming sight; being alone in the galleries made Mayu uneasy. She sped up to find her companion, when movement in one of the paintings caught her eye. Mayu paused, turning to look. It was a dark painting, all blacks, greys and dark emeralds with a splash of cream. Creeping closer, her lips parted in surprise, recognising a younger Skye in her school uniform. Squinting and leaning so close that her nose almost touched the surface, she watched as the miniature, painted Skye twisted around to look at something behind her. A sparkling pink badge with the number seven on it gleamed on her chest, and an aggressively fluorescent birthday card was in one hand. In the painting, Skye turned back to a telephone pad on the wall to finish tapping in a number.

Mayu traced her finger down the curve of Skye's acrylic spine and gasped as she heard a dial tone, electronic pips and then a ringtone. Mayu kept her finger on the canvas, listening as the ringing continued, before the screen lit up to show a woman's face.

"Mum!" cheered Skye.

Mrs. Mansfield checked her watch, bobbing in and out of the screen as she prepared to go out somewhere. "What are you doing calling at this time of day?" she asked. "Shouldn't you be in lessons?"

"They said I could call you, because I know you're going—"

"Rupert, your daughter wants to talk to you!"

A voice off screen yelled back, "Unless you want me to drop this…"

Mrs. Mansfield sighed. "Is there something you wanted, sweetie? We're busy right now."

Skye clamped her lips together and clutched her birthday card so tight between her hands that it crackled and bent. She shook her head, her eyes dewy. "No, sorry."

"For goodness sake," Mrs. Mansfield sighed softly. "Don't skip lessons like this. We'll see you at Easter. Don't call unless it's important."

"Yes, Mum."

Skye hit the "end call" button, and a series of pops chirped from the dial pad. The girl sniffed and stared down at her card. She bent it to and fro until she had crumpled it. With a tearful gasp, she seemed to realise what she'd done and tried to flatten it out again. She opened it and kissed the name at the bottom of the card.

Love from, Henri.

"Mayu? Are you coming?" called Skye from the distance.

"Sorry–" Mayu gave the painting a final brush with her fingers. "I'm on my way."

She turned to face three statues that hadn't been there a moment before. The hairs on her arms prickled, but the light from the next corridor drew her on and seemed a reason not to panic. She was in a museum, there would be statues. Backing away, the light caught their faces, their eyes set with amber stones. Three faces, two of which she recognised: Mr. and Mrs. Mansfield. The third seemed to grow less distinct as she withdrew. Mayu worried at her lip, trying not to read into the symbolism of the gemstones eyes. Wasn't it said that amber represented disdain?

Backing into the lit corridor she finally looked to see where she was going. The floor was paved with paintings, they stretched along the hallway to form a continuous image of a staircase, each step carpeted in crimson and roughly painted in broad strokes. Uncertain, she stepped cautiously along the first few canvases, waiting for some kind of admonition; it felt so wrong to walk on them. As she tiptoed warily along, it felt like she was walking down a gradient. At the far end, a tapestry hung across her path, fluttering slightly, the only indication it hid a passageway and not a wall.

Just as she reached to push it aside, there was a thud behind her.

Mayu snapped around. A new painting covered the entrance she'd passed through moments earlier, and in it she saw the statue of Mr. Mansfield. The statue she hadn't recognised sat in a chair behind him, features masked by shadows. They were in an attic-like room, with a sloped ceiling. Mr. Mansfield punched the man in the chair, his movements sharp stop-motion. The next second, he stood facing the hallway stairs again, staring at Mayu through those expensive gemstone eyes.

But then, down the stairs, a two-dimensional lump was rolling and bumping towards her. It whimpered and grunted, tumbling closer and closer. She jumped back against the wall as it rolled past. When it hit the last canvas, a three-dimensional lump rolled under the tapestry. Clenching her jaw, Mayu pulled the cloth aside to find Skye. But her body was made of fabric, she lay in a tangled heap; a rag doll.

Mayu crouched and brushed thick strands of woollen hair from Skye's face. The girl blinked, her eyes two huge white patches of thread.

"I can't feel anything," she whispered. "We've gotta go. Quick! Help me!"

Pushing the tapestry aside to reach the painted staircase again, Mayu tensed at the sight of Mr. Mansfield inching from frame to frame. She was in two minds about which way to turn, but the image of Fukushima and Yūta in Namba Parks came back to her…the beating, falling down the attic stairs; Skye's coma.

"You fell down the stairs," Mayu mumbled.

"Yes, idiot, and it hurt!" Little silver drops formed in the corners of her eyes. "Please. Please run!" The silver flakes fluttered to the floor.

Mayu dropped the tapestry, scooped the girl into her arms, light as cotton stuffing. She jogged to the door at the end of the hall, a horrible thought gripping her. Skye was hiding something, a secret that made the girl feel so awful it kept pushing through Mayu's defences. She could crush it now, she could get them away, through the next door, shutting Mr. Mansfield and the rest of them in the museum, then step into the field full of tulips and pretend it was all just a nightmare.

She squeezed the doorknob.

But Mayu had to know.

As she opened the door, she let it act as a transition between Skye and Mayu's dominance. It was like stepping aside in the ethereal space between their minds. She let Skye fill the gap Mayu had occupied, the girl's energy levels simmering at the newfound freedom, eager to create what she wanted. It fought for more space by crushing a corner of Mayu's mind—*make way for me!* it cheered. She groaned, resisting, the air fizzing with static.

"What's wrong?" asked the ragdoll in Mayu's arms.

"Nothing bad. I'll fix it."

When the struggling settled into a fresh equilibrium, Mayu's cheeks felt numb, like she wasn't quite there anymore.

They'd entered a square room with a dais against each wall. On each dais were mannequins depicting still-life scenes. Silence reined.

"You can put me down," said Skye.

Mayu set her soft, rounded feet onto the polished floor and then took the girl's plush shoulders in each hand. "Skye," she looked into those round, white eyes, "you're in a coma because you fell down the stairs. Do you remember?"

"Kind of."

"Did your father push you?"

Somehow, her eyes went rounder. "No," she whispered.

"You can tell me, he won't know."

Skye wrenched free of Mayu's grip. "He didn't push me!" Her voice echoed off the glossy floor, shrill like the stab of warning in the back of Mayu's head.

"Okay, okay. I believe you." She glanced at the mannequins in case they depicted an answer. "What did happen?"

"I fell."

"Yes, I know. How did you fall?"

Skye backed away a step. "I—my legs, they went numb."

"Why did they go numb? Did something scare you?"

They both jumped as movement on every dais cut off

her questions. Each scene had changed in a blink. Skye crept to Mayu's side again and took her hand. She squeezed the girl's padded palm, an unspoken promise: *I won't leave you.*

"These are memories," the girl murmured, "my memories. We should go. Right?"

To their left, the dais held mannequins of Skye and her mother shouting at each other—Mr. Mansfield frozen mid-stride near them.

The scene in front of Mayu was more complex. In the forefront was a desk with Mr. and Mrs. Mansfield studying inside the desk drawer. The statue she hadn't recognised stood beside them, its face bruised and lip split. Behind the three of them, more mannequins were posed mid-revelry—expensive dresses, tailored suits, glittering glasses of wine in their hands.

The dais on the right held only a stack of three lockers. There had been a mannequin, Mayu was sure of it. She scanned the room, but there was nowhere to hide. Maybe it had run to the party on the other dais.

Skye pulled on Mayu's hand. "I hate this. Make it stop. Let's go back to the sea."

As Skye tugged her across the room to a door near the party dais, Mayu heard a whisper, "Where is it?"

She looked at the mannequins. All of them were staring, following their movement. One stood in the middle of the room where they'd been moments before.

Mayu pushed Skye through the door and banged it shut behind them. They held their breath, glancing around the balcony they found themselves on; it had a view of the entrance foyer. After three heartbeats, a knock rapped at the door.

"Skye," someone said from the other side, "where is it?"

Mayu clutched the girl's hand tighter. Neither could move, both holding their breath. Something slammed into the door from the other side and, by the *thunk* it made, it had to be one of the mannequins. Skye collapsed, now solid as iron, dragging down on Mayu's arm.

"No! Come on." The words came out raw and shrill. "Wake up!"

The pounding on the door became a thunderous rhythm; something was determined to get through. Skye moaned, her fabric eyelids fluttered, she was no longer dead weight.

"Yes, come on, up, up!" Mayu hooked her arms under Skye and propelled her off the ground. The girl staggered, her fabric limbs stiff, and she seemed short of breath, but the slamming against the door roused some urgency in her.

They ran to the other end of the balcony, into a winding corridor lined with display cabinets. Tiaras, necklaces, earrings and broaches twinkled behind the glass—each item made of pasta and glitter.

The pressure in Mayu's head increased, compressing her thoughts into a flat, confused line. No one had been asking *her* for some lost object—she'd just been standing in the way of a nightmare, unable to manifest its true intent.

Skye had something her parents wanted.

Wood splintered as the mannequins rammed the door blocking them off, it wouldn't hold for long. Mayu needed to sever this dream now, regain the control she'd leased Skye, but Skye grabbed her hand and ran.

"Wait…" No other words came to mind.

Why had she given Skye control? What did she need to know? Was there something else she was missing?

The door gave way behind them. Skye skidded to a stop on her woollen feet and picked up a stool beside one of the cabinets. Mayu watched the mannequins approach, their steps jerky but quick.

With a shout, Skye hurled the stool above her head and smashed it into the nearest cabinet. She reached through splintered glass and seized a pasta necklace, then dragged Mayu down the hall again.

With each step Skye transformed back into a real girl; and with each step the fabric crawled up Mayu's arm. By the time they reached the foyer, her whole body had become soft and the sound of pursuit had faded.

"We did it," panted Skye, her face fell when she looked at Mayu. "Are you alright?"

Every tilt of Mayu's head, every twist of her joints felt fluid. She felt wonderful, soft, light but hazy. "Where next?" she asked Skye. Sunlight in one of the corridors caught her eye and Mayu beamed. "This way."

"No, I want to leave!" Skye said.

Such a silly girl.

Reaching the corridor, Mayu saw that most of the ceiling was missing. Grape vines twisted around bare metal beams, and a fruity scent accented the air with sweetness. She looked at Skye, beckoning her with a thin, stuffed rag-doll arm and turned to carry on. She took three steps before noticing the photos on the wall and stopped dead.

Yūta stared back at her from an oval frame. His eyes were heavy and miserable, staring at her. It twisted Mayu's stomach into knots. His eyes consumed her and held her captive. Drawn towards him, like the tide to the moon, Mayu raised one shaking hand and touched the photo. It rippled beneath her slubbed cotton hand. Inside the white-washed wall where the photograph hung, Yūta appeared at full height, no longer bound by the frame. Mayu realised it wasn't a wall at all, but an endless void. The photograph became part of Yūta's creamy sweater and his head bent forward, over the frame. He reached out with ghostly arms and Mayu felt them tingle around her back. The smile lines around his eyes were clearer than ever and his gruff-cut jaw clenched.

"I'm fading," he whispered. "If you keep ignoring my signs…"

"What signs?"

"Don't you like tulips anymore?"

The field outside the museum.

"Mayu," said Skye, "you seriously—Mayu!"

The shrill cry made Mayu jump and her hand fell from the photograph. Yūta's eyes filled with panic and he vanished.

Skye ran over and gripped Mayu's hand, but something felt wrong—empty.

"Remember," said Skye, "you can't get lost, or…or… you know, lost in memories."

No, no, this was important. How dare this girl chase him off? The fear in Yūta's eyes—Mayu couldn't help him. She pulled her hand free.

"What have you done?"

The girl went pale. "I didn't…"

Mayu's emptiness expanded into a hollow pit and she clutched her stomach. *I'm dreaming.* But what if she wasn't? *No, stay with the girl.* Yūta only lived in this world. *What is the child's name? WHAT IS HER NAME?* But Yūta needed Mayu to find him, delaying like this only made it worse.

"What's happening to you?" the girl asked, voice trembling. She pulled her hands into her sweater sleeves.

"The tulips."

"What?"

Of course! He'd been calling for her all this time. Whipping around, Mayu sprinted into the main marble hall. She heard the girl running after her, telling her to stop, telling Mayu she was wrong.

A sharp pain hit the back of Mayu's head and her eyesight blurred. Skye Mansfield. That was her name. Oh gods, what was she doing? What *was* the real world? Mayu tried to pinch herself with her nails, but she had none.

Skye's footsteps sounded closer.

The sound became meaningless when Mayu saw a flickering image of Yūta through the main doors.

She ran to him, but he vanished, and Mayu stumbled onto the platform outside. Tulips spread for miles on the other side of the derelict train carriage, and in the distance, she spotted Yūta racing towards her.

Fear gripped her as she recognised, behind him, the shadow people, their white eyes glowing. They were chasing him—as they had chased them on their first day together. Their writhing numbers doubled with every stride Yūta took.

Mayu leapt off the platform, shedding her rag-doll looks for her own skin.

20

A S SHE SPRINTED through the tulips, scattering petals and covering her pants in pollen, Mayu felt the distance tearing her from Skye. Maybe someone else could finish the job; someone else could take Mayu's place. Even though she saw death in the shadow peoples' eyes and felt the struggle in her mind, Mayu refused to go back.

"My name is Skye Mansfield and you promised you would stay with me!"

Mayu faltered.

"Get back here right now! What the bloody hell are you doing?"

Skye had family, she had her whole life ahead of her. Mayu wanted to die every night she curled up in an empty double bed. Her husband had died once because of her mistakes, she couldn't let it happen again. She had to… remember that this wasn't real.

Mayu squinted as the colour of the sky, the tulips, the shadows and Yūta glowed with such vibrancy that her eyes watered.

"Don't leave me, Mayu." Skye's plea cracked in her throat. "It's me. It's Skye!"

Mayu slowed.

"I'm sorry. I'm sorry. Whatever I've done, I didn't mean it."

Yūta cried out as one of the shadow figures launched onto his back and bit into his shoulder. Mayu stopped running altogether.

She felt so very sluggish, like Skye's mind was pressing down on every fibre of her being. She looked down at her hands, they glistened grey and transparent: faded. With no will or direction left to latch onto under Skye's intensity, Mayu's mind was compressing and Skye was eclipsing her. Yūta called out her name as another dark figure clamped onto his arm.

"Your memories are dying," he cried. "Focus. Where did I propose? Where?"

Her eyes darted from shadow to shadow; her mouth moved with unknown words. Mayu smelt salt water but couldn't think why. Had she ever met Yūta before? Had they ever coexisted in real time?

A small body crashed into Mayu's back and she staggered forward.

"Later, remember him later!" Skye said, gasping and wheezing. "We have to go!"

Staring at Yūta, as he fell to the ground beneath the writhing creatures, Mayu raised her arms in a trance. Yes, she was right, they had to go. Why should she care about some man she barely recognised? Did she recognise him?

Time to go home.

Skye squealed as the ground shook beneath their feet. A column of rock broke upwards and carried them up to the sky, the force of their ascent buckled them onto their knees, but Mayu paid no attention. Bricks and sheets of glass flew in, like a constructive tornado, up and up, until the swirling cyclone settled and Mayu felt carpet beneath her fingers.

A clock ticked nearby and she smelt jasmine fabric softener. She regarded her apartment as if observing a blank wall. Nothing registered quite as it should and, although Mayu studied every piece of furniture, the tulips by the window, the view of Tokyo beyond the window, the shrine in the corner, she felt no attachment to any of it. If this place belonged to her, it held no value anymore.

Skye sprawled on the carpet by the coffee table, watching her, as if waiting for Mayu's anger.

"Are you alright?" Mayu asked pleasantly.

Mistrust coloured Skye's expression. "I suppose. Are *you* okay?"

A wild event had just occurred—they'd been running from something dangerous, but Mayu couldn't grasp what had happened. "Of course," she said, getting to her feet. What did people do to reassure others? A smile. How did one smile?

Tightening the corners of her mouth so it stretched into a thin curving line, she said, "Would you like tea?"

Skye hugged herself, her lips parted but no reply came and she stared at Mayu as if waiting for something else.

"Do you not like tea?"

"I love tea," Skye mumbled. "Yeah, okay. Tea."

Stretching her mouth in that curved line again, Mayu wandered into the kitchenette and pulled out a traditional tea set. The glossy black pot, decorated with red and white calligraphy, piqued Skye's interest. Shuffling onto her feet, the girl crept closer and stared across the counter.

"What does it say?" she asked.

Mayu picked up a cup and twisted it between her fingers. "The cups have different stanzas from a famous poem written by Princess Shikishi on them. She was a high-priestess of the…" She paused, searching for the name of the shrine, without luck. "Of a shrine in Kyoto. *This* cup has the last two stanzas."

Mayu raised it and read, "Who grows up living here? A hut; with a brushwood fence; buried; in the falling snow." She twisted the cup in her fingers to read the other side. "The kind of place; where the way a traveller's tracks; disappear in the snow; is something you get used to…; such a place is this world of ours."

Skye scrunched her nose. "Huh. Odd poem."

"Do you think so?" Mayu filled a kettle and set it to heat on the sideboard. "I've never been much of a poet myself. My grandmother gave this set to me and Yūta as a wedding…" Her words trailed off and a spark of a memory burnt through her foggy mind. She put the cup down, staring at Skye, who took a wary step back.

"Skye…" A part of Mayu struggled to resurface to full awareness, but the apartment finally had meaning—a private world of memories. "I'm so sorry for almost leaving you."

Skye chewed her bottom lip and shrugged.

"You were right, I should be moving on," Mayu said. "I don't know why I keep losing control, I'm not usually this distracted."

No response. Skye peered at her from under her lashes.

"You did the right thing," Mayu continued. "Thank you for calling me back. You did exactly as I asked."

Skye pulled her hands into her sleeves and played with the elastic hems. "I think you're hiding something from me," she said. Outside the large window opposite, snow floated past. Fluffy, thick and luminous. "Today felt different—I mean really different. My head is buzzing, and that museum we visited? I went there on a school trip a few years ago. I don't remember much about it, but I'm pretty sure *I* built the world today.

"Before you ran off into the flowers, I heard you whispering inside my head. I feel like I've swallowed a planet load of…" Skye sighed. "I feel too small for whatever's happening to me. I know things about you…your life."

Mayu clenched her hands to check she could still feel them. She couldn't tell Skye that she had almost died. The results of the merging process lay on Mayu's shoulders alone, she had gone too deep, lashed their minds together too tight, and then let the reins slip. Her arrogance caused this, *or my nosiness*. Whatever her reasons, Mayu should've known better. Skye's PDE was stronger than hers, and if she hadn't pushed Skye's memories and feelings to the point of revolt, they might not be in this mess. *Maybe I want to be in this mess.* Mayu took a deep breath, shoved the thought away.

When Mayu didn't reply, Skye went on, "He proposed to you on a pier."

A flash of sunset, the sea, Yūta cheering and sweeping Mayu into his arms.

"Skye, I don't think it's a good idea to remind me. I mean, thank you, I don't want to lose that one, but it's safer if I let them go."

"But aren't you disappearing?"

The kettle beeped and Mayu smiled, shaking her head. "No, don't worry." It was better to lie. As she poured hot water into the teapot and filled the extra thermal jug, a flake of snow fell onto the back of her hand. She peered up.

"The ceiling's gone," said Skye, unsurprised.

"Uh-oh. Come here." Mayu pulled a crimson table-cloth out from a cupboard under the counter and flicked it at Skye. The girl flinched, and then giggled as the cloth transformed into a cosy knitted scarf. It wrapped around Skye's neck and half of her face.

"Can I help with anything?" she asked.

"No, no. Go sit."

Mayu carried over a tray of sencha and knelt at the coffee table. She smiled to herself when Skye shuffled off the couch to join her on the floor. A dusting of snow already covered most of the surfaces.

"What's your favourite animal?" Skye asked, watching Mayu dribble tea into a cup and across half of the table. It sizzled and steamed on the wet surface.

"I'm not sure. I love jellyfish."

"*Jellyfish?*" Skye sounded horrified. "But they sting you and they're so ugly."

"They're not ugly at all," Mayu replied, passing over the handleless cup. Skye gripped it with the tips of her fingers, trying not to burn herself. "They're graceful and soothing to watch. Some of them even glow different colours."

"No, they don't."

"Yes, they do. Look." Mayu waved her hand and three jellyfishes popped into the air with a little squelch. They bobbed up and down around the room, their mushroom bodies rippling with white lights. "Well," said Mayu, "they don't produce their own light. They disperse it."

"Whatever that means. You could make anything you want glow. Even me!"

"If you like," Mayu teased, and with a wave of her hand beads of light shimmered beneath Skye's skin. Skye stared at her hands in amazement, sploshing hot tea into her lap.

Crying out, she slammed the cup down onto the table. Mayu fetched a damp cloth. "Good thing I don't have school in the morning," Skye said, scrubbing her stained skirt.

"Why are you still wearing that?"

Skye paused and studied the snowflakes on the table. "I don't know. I guess I didn't notice. It feels like my skin."

"I see. You do live at school, so that makes sense."

Skye picked up her cup again and blew on the green tea before taking a sip. She coughed and cringed and held the cup as far away from her as possible. "Yuck! What is this? This isn't tea."

"It's *my* tea," Mayu laughed.

"Maybe it will taste better with milk."

"I seriously doubt that."

Holding the cup in two hands, Skye closed her eyes and wrinkled her brow in concentration. A few flakes of snow landed in her tea, before the liquid changed to a caramel brown colour. Skye opened one eye and smiled at the sight. She took another sip.

"Oh, much better," Skye sighed.

"English tea?"

"Of course."

Shivering as a jellyfish tentacle brushed over her hair, Mayu patted her stomach and a white cardigan enveloped her. Giving her hair a quick shake back and forth, a snug yellow scarf appeared around her neck.

"You look pretty," said Skye. The unexpected compliment sweetened Mayu's mood, she felt bubbles of light blossom across her cheeks and pop into the air around her. Skye focused on drinking her tea.

"Is this where you normally live?"

Mayu nodded. "Yes, usually with a roof."

"Obviously."

Mayu drank the salty-grassy tea, by now accustomed to Skye's tone. She no longer focused on the note of derision, but on the irony. From Skye's perfected expression—boasting of self-assurance and wisdom—Mayu understood that she spoke like this to both undermine her own value and to turn the joke's focus onto someone, or some*thing* else.

A snowflake fluttered past Mayu's nose and landed in her cup. No, not a snowflake. A cherry blossom petal. She looked up and saw more pink petals spiralling down with the snow. Flakes stuck to her lashes and the petals decorated her hair.

She looked over at Skye. The girl stared up at the white abyss, set down her cup, and held out her hands to catch the falling seasons.

"Is this usual for your country?" she asked.

"Oh yes. All the time."

Skye gave her a cheeky smile, not missing the way Mayu mimicked her derisive tone.

A shrill ringtone broke their peace. Vibrations tickled

through Mayu's cardigan, and with fumbling hands, she pulled a flip-phone from her pocket. She sighed at the name shining on the preview screen and answered, "Hello Mother."

"I hear you went back to work. You're no good to them anymore."

"I'm fine, how're you?"

Skye raised her eyebrows, like she'd heard what Mayu's mother had really said.

"Don't change the subject. You're not fit for work anymore. You should have left years ago, when you still had everything." A lump formed in Mayu's throat and her gaze diverted from Skye to the beautiful tea set. "Just sell the Parallel Dream Project—you'll make enough money to pay for me, your father and yourself until the sun explodes. Stop trying to control everything and *let go*."

"I'd like to let go, but—"

"But you've just got to make sure everything goes your way."

"No, I don't."

"Now, don't get on your high-horse—"

"Fine, I'll quit and leave everyone alone." Mayu hung up and tossed her phone across the room. It sailed through the sliding bathroom door. They heard a splash and plunk as it dropped into the toilet.

Skye folded her arms. "Very mature."

"Let's talk about school."

"No."

"Dance?"

"Fine."

"Oh, are you going to dance?" said someone new.

Skye and Mayu both sloshed tea over their fingers at Tomoya's appearance. He knelt at the end of the coffee table like the happiest man alive, bouncing to a tune only he could hear. A dusting of snow had settled on his suit.

"I'm too hungry to dance!" cried Momo, sitting at the opposite end of the table.

Keiji appeared on Mayu's left. "You're always hungry," he said.

"Who are these people?" Skye looked affronted at the intrusion on their privacy, eyeballing Keiji in particular, perhaps due to his platinum hair and stern countenance.

"Nice to meet you too," he said, staring right back. The girl blushed and fixed her eyes on the teapot.

Mayu introduced her colleagues, and in a matter of seconds, her living room was abloom with friendship. She felt their support in her bones, something she was aware of when awake, but that seemed all the more tangible here.

"You still owe me *champon*," said Momo, pointing across at Tomoya.

"What, you want me to cook it right now?" he replied.

"Yes! Tell him, Skye." The young woman reached over and poked Skye's arm. "Tell him to make me *champon*."

"Uh, make her *champon*?"

Tomoya threw his arms up. "But I don't know how to cook that!"

With a belligerent moan, Keiji got to his feet. "*I'll* make some."

"Hooray!" cheered Momo, like she was watching a sports match, and Skye started laughing. She reached across to shake Momo's hand, a business woman in the making, used to copying her parents.

"Nice to meet you."

Momo looked at the hand and then tapped her own against it, like a joint effort at clapping. Chuckling at some private joke, Momo then shook the offered hand. "It's great to meet you too. Wait, no one's offered me tea! Never mind, I'll do it myself." Without pausing for breath, Momo poured three new cups without spilling a drop.

They all sat together eating steaming *champon*, the broth salty and flavoursome, the noodles tender, topped with fried pork and vegetables. Mayu wondered if Keiji was a great cook in real life.

"I can't forget one of our first dreams together," Tomoya was saying. "You turned us into goldfish. Do you remember, Mayu?"

She remembered that Yūta had goldfish when they'd first moved in together. *Serene*, he'd said, two beautiful creatures blissfully ignorant beyond the bowl. He'd watch them as he made tea, or after a grim day at work, or late at night just before bed; admiring water patterns and the flick of their tails.

An earthquake shook the bowl off the kitchen counter one morning—they heard the smash from the bedroom. Even over the rumbling, Mayu had heard his sharp in-take of breath and noticed his arms go taught. He crouched over the broken glass afterwards, water soaking his slippers and stared at the lifeless fish for what seemed an age. Mayu remembered hugging him from behind, kissing the soft skin behind his ear, as Yūta lifted their slippery bodies into the palm of his rough hand. Tiny, ill-fated things, glittering under the ceiling light.

Mayu took a deep breath, focusing on Tomoya. Everyone, even Skye, had gone rigid mid-motion.

"I remember."

The tableaux unfroze and everyone resumed eating as if they hadn't noticed a pause.

"We swam around the office," said Tomoya, "looking for pencils…Why pencils?"

"I don't know," answered Mayu, "but I lost control and whenever someone in the office took a deep breath, we got sucked up their nose!"

"Oh, yes. That wasn't so fun."

"Eww!" Skye laughed, wiping broth off her chin with the back of her hand. She smiled at Keiji, "This is delicious," devouring hers faster than everyone.

Keiji bowed his head. "Cooking is an art."

"You're saying you're an artist?" Momo teased, sharing a look with Tomoya.

"Modest," Tomoya added.

"Smart too." Keiji's mouth twitched with a smirk as the others' pretended to be flabbergasted by his boasting.

As Skye reached out to touch Momo's hair, complimenting her on the pink tones, Mayu noticed Tomoya disappear. He quietly faded away, taking his near-empty *champon* bowl with him. Keiji went next, his bear-paw of a hand on Mayu's shoulder as if to leave a trace of reassurance.

"Didn't someone mention dancing earlier?" asked Momo. "You've not seen anything until you've seen Mayu dance. If you can get her on the floor, that is! Absolutely hilarious." She nudged Skye with her shoulder and promptly vanished.

Skye blinked, taking in the quiet room without much surprise or disappointment. "They were lovely," she said.

Rising to her bare feet, Mayu pushed the couch on her side of the coffee table to the other side of the room. She gave her arms a vigorous shake and the sleeves of her cardigan lengthened. The material hung down to her knees, as if the cardigan was part of a formal robe. She tied back some of her hair.

"What are you doing?" the girl asked.

The jellyfish still floating around the room started to loop and swirl through the snow petals.

"You play an instrument, don't you?" Mayu replied.

"Not very well."

"What is it?"

"A cello but, when I play, it sounds like a stork having its legs ripped off. That's what Mum said."

Tutting, Mayu reached inside one of her big sleeves and pulled out a cello. Its polished body gleamed in the snowy light as she set it down in front of Skye. The girl's eyes shone and she jumped up, stroking her hands over its curving belly.

"Wow…I can't believe you had this hidden."

Mayu giggled. "Don't listen to your mother. Have you ever had dreams about playing the cello?"

Skye nodded, a wistful smile coming over her.

"And did you play beautifully?"

Another nod.

Mayu put an encouraging hand on Skye's back and the girl wrapped her hands around the fingerboard. Reaching into her other sleeve, Mayu produced a bow.

"When I was little," she said, handing it over, "my

culture club teacher told us to make a dance that told a story. I was never talented at dancing, I had to focus constantly and to memorise precise techniques. Even still, I was not a natural. But I remember that challenge, to perform a story, because I never quit practicing."

Mayu backed into the open living space, and giving the hem of her cardigan a few tugs, it elongated and fanned down to her feet. Now wearing a white dress, Mayu pointed one foot and turned in a slow circle, drawing a line in the snow with her toes.

"What kind of story?" asked Skye. She brushed her bow across the cello's strings, producing a steady, low note.

"A sad one," Mayu replied, "about Yuki-Onna. She's a snow spirit." Twisting her wrists together, Mayu felt the childhood dance waiting to flow through her limbs. "Two woodcutters lost on the mountain tried to take shelter from a snowstorm: Minokichi and his elderly father Mosaku. They lit a fire and decided to wait out the cold. But in the night, Yuki-Onna paid a visit."

Skye brushed out a few quiet notes experimentally. They quivered and trembled with the beginnings of a tune and ribbons of light curled around Skye's fingers. She gasped in admiration, sweeping the bow more confidently just to watch the light show.

It heartened Mayu to watch. "The spirit flew into the hut where the woodcutters took shelter, blowing open the door and putting out the fire. Only Minokichi woke up. He stared at Yuki-Onna and thought she was a woman from the heavens. Hypnotised by her beauty, he did nothing as Yuki-Onna covered his father with her body and blew out a deep breath."

Leaning into the cello, Skye nodded at her words and began a tune that pierced Mayu to the core. Low, stretching notes dipped into sounds of hope—high and quivering, tender and meaningful.

The music moved Mayu and her dress swooped as she enacted old patterns, spraying snow outwards. "As Yuki-Onna breathed onto Mosaku, it covered the old man's body in ice, and he died without a sound. Weeping only a few tears, Yuki-Onna rose up again.

"No human could withstand her kiss and she was doomed to live unloved forever. She had become accustomed to killing those who wandered in the snowstorms. The Moon spoke to her—told her to kill again and again. It told her she had no other fate."

A warning, desperate edge entered Skye's melody and Mayu could picture Yuki-Onna running through a thousand snowstorms, desperate to find someone who could withstand her touch.

"Turning to Minokichi, the spirit forgot her sadness and she stopped. He was so handsome and his eyes so youthful that Yuki-Onna did not even want to try to embrace him. Minokichi backed away. 'Please, spare me,' he said. She felt torn between longing and obedience.

"Leaning over Minokichi, she said, 'I'll try.' As gently as she could, Yuki-Onna kissed Minokichi's forehead. The young man's lips turned blue and his body shook, but he did not die.

"The Moon spoke to Yuki-Onna: 'If he survives one more kiss, I will give you a human body,' it said. 'If the boy lives, he must promise never to speak of you again. But if he tells anyone about this night, you must kill him, and if you do not, you will die in his stead.'

"Minokichi survived one more kiss and swore to Yuki-Onna that he would never tell anyone what had happened. A year later he met a woman called Oyuki who lay sick and dying in the summer heat, and being kind, he took her inside and nursed her to health. In time, they fell in love. They married and lived many happy years together, producing three children.

"One winter night, as Minokichi watched his wife sewing, he said, 'Oyuki, whenever I see you next to the snow, I am reminded of the mysterious night that took my father's life. When I was young, I met a woman with your beauty. Sometimes I wonder if it was a dream or whether she was Yuki-Onna.'"

The snow petals in Mayu's living room came up to her ankles now. When she leapt into the air, the resulting spray arched high over her head.

"Oyuki jumped up. 'You promised never to talk about that!' she cried. 'I warned you I would kill you if you told anyone.' Her heart broke as her pale skin grew even paler, until she looked like the translucent spirit from all those years ago. Minokichi gasped, recognising her true form.

"But how could she kill the only soul to ever love her? Now that she was no longer human, who would take care of their children if he died? Holding in her tears, she said, 'I wanted to live happily with you forever. Why did you tell? Take care of the children.'

"Yuki-Onna left the house and entered the snowstorm outside. She looked up at the Moon. It bathed her in silver light, and just as Minokichi ran into the garden to save his beloved wife, she melted into the blizzard, leaving behind a single tear. Her voice still echoes in snowy mountain winds."

Mayu dropped to her knees and stretched backward, baring her throat to the white abyss above. She watched the tendrils of light from Skye's cello illuminate the snowfall. Mayu had been such a morbid child, and to think that this story of Yuki-Onna was one of the happier ones she had heard. But it had suited her, it still did.

The musical lights from Skye's cello grew brighter, flickering in time with the melody. Mayu fell back in surprise as Skye's face appeared above her. The girl's auburn hair tickled Mayu's cheeks, a necklace made of pasta swinging around Skye's throat.

Looking at the cello, Mayu saw the bow gliding back and forth on the strings by itself.

"It got carried away," said Skye. "I couldn't keep up."

With a giggle, Skye jumped into the air and threw her arms and legs out. She landed in the snow petals on her back sending up a wave of white and pink flakes. The snow was so deep that she almost disappeared.

"Hello!" cried Mayu. "I seem to have lost a little girl. She looks a bit like a cat…"

21

THEY TOSSED SNOW around the room, the jellyfish continued to bob above them like nightlights and the cello went through a range of emotions. Eventually, the snow was so deep that the cello hopped onto the kitchen counter to keep playing, while Mayu and Skye pretended to swim in a cottony soft sea.

The white abyss above faded to indigo and stars sprinkled the night sky. A rainbow of music lit up the heavens like the Northern Lights. Sheltered, and yet exposed to the heavenly wonders, Mayu's living room was the best world she'd ever created. Skye taught her how to do a basic barn waltz and they spent a while spinning around to the music. When they eventually lost their footing, Mayu picked Skye up with both arms and continued to twirl through the snow, singing a discordant version of the cello's tune.

As the snow piled up to Mayu's waist, however, it started to feel oppressive rather than fun. Concentrating, she willed all the snow and blossoms to vanish, leaving her living room spotless—if still without a ceiling. She pretended not to notice the smell of aftershave coming from the open bedroom door. Mayu turned to the cello and shushed it. "Something soothing, please." It screeched on its current note, as if affronted, and the bow flicked through the air to punctuate its rage. Rolling her eyes, Mayu turned to Skye. "How do you feel?"

Skye yawned. "Tired."

Plonking a hand on top of Skye's head, Mayu turned her around and guided her over to the couch. "Better settle down and catch some of your own dreams, then." Skye flopped down onto the cushions. She smiled as warmly as summer sunshine, before breaking into another yawn. Like a well-fed cat, Skye slouched forward and observed the room with half-lidded eyes, obviously content. In the corner, the cello stopped having a tantrum and began playing a tender lullaby, one she had heard on the radio earlier that year and never forgotten. The sweet melody melted the silence, and Skye lay across the couch as Mayu fetched a blanket from the closet. She threw the silky material over the young girl and tucked her in, kneeling beside the couch.

The pasta necklace bunched around Skye's neck. Mayu gestured to it. "Why did you stop for that?" Skye twisted the dried shells between her fingers, struggling to hold Mayu's gaze. She shrugged.

"It must be important—to stop and grab it in the museum. Is that what everyone has been asking us for?" Skye rolled and nestled deeper into her pillow, not looking at Mayu. "Did you lose something that doesn't belong to you?"

Skye shook her head.

"Did you steal something?"

A glassy sheen filled her eyes. She glanced at Mayu,

a picture of misery, her lips pressed tight together as if it would stop the tears from spilling over. Mayu sighed.

"You stole a necklace, I take it?"

Skye shrugged.

"Why?"

The answer exploded out of Skye in a gust of anger. "Mum said she hated me." Every line in her body was tense, her breathing harsh as she fought to hold onto the mirage of composure. Words pushed past her teeth. "She said I was selfish and did nothing but take, take, take. So I took some stupid necklace they'd been waiting for. They were too busy with their party to see me."

"What do you mean?"

Skye took a long-suffering breath and curled into a ball. "They were having a party to talk about their jewellery and to show off in front of business people. The necklace arrived during the party—but they didn't show it to anyone. They locked it in Dad's office drawer and I know where he hides the spare key." Her anger crumpled, giving way to a few breathless sobs and a mouth twisted with fear. "Don't wake me up. *Please*. They just want the necklace, they don't want me. They're so angry."

Mayu brushed the girl's hair, unsure what to say. "They're not—I'm sure they're not angry any more. They just want their daughter back." It must have been the wrong thing to say, because Skye shook her head and turned away. "I'm sure you're imagining things are worse than they are."

No response, only stifled wheezing.

Mayu slumped against the couch. As she stared at the back cushions, tulips sprouted between the fibres on the couch. Shoots wriggled through the top of the cushions, petals springing open in the moonlight.

Skye rustled under her blanket. "What is it with you and tulips?"

"Yūta used to buy them," Mayu whispered. "He said yellow suited me, cheery flowers for a cheery woman. And tulips for perfect love."

They said nothing else for a long time but, when Mayu was about to get up, Skye spoke. "Dad was beating someone in the attic," she murmured. Mayu stiffened. "He thought he'd stolen the necklace or that he knew who had. The party made Dad suspect everyone. I was gonna put it back, but…he was scary. I didn't mean for someone to get hurt. I didn't want him to hurt me."

It took a lot of effort to stay serene but Mayu placed a soothing hand on the girl's arm. "Skye, how did you fall down the stairs?"

She took a few shaky gulps. "I—I just kind of shouted, 'I took it.' Dad stopped beating the other guy. I was so scared, I couldn't—my legs were numb. Dad ran at me, and I fell. I stepped back and went out the door. I couldn't stop myself."

Mayu gripped her arm tighter. "You'll be okay. No one can hurt you when you wake up. I promise it'll all be okay. I'll be there." She'd finally said the right thing. The tension uncoiled from Skye's limbs and her eyelids fluttered with weariness but, before she sank into sleep, she touched Mayu's hand and gave a little squeeze.

"Goodnight, Mayu."

"See you when the sun rises."

She stroked Skye's forehead for a while, admiring

the freckles peppering her nose. As her face relaxed, Skye looked so angelic that Mayu caught herself longing for Yūta—for her own children. She peered over her shoulder and looked at the cello.

"Don't stop playing tonight," she told it. "I want to hear every lullaby under the sun, you got it?"

The bow played two staccato, harmonised notes; Mayu took that as a 'yes'. If music filled her ears, instead of the memories whispering in her apartment walls, tomorrow morning might rise without further danger.

She crept into her bedroom, resolutely ignoring that Yūta's aftershave smelt even stronger there, and took a futon from the cupboard. Back in the living room, she rolled it out on the floor, close to Skye, and settled down for another night of brain mapping. But just for a while, Mayu gazed at the stars, the musical lights, the inky shades of night…

As she fought to keep her eyes open, the stars rearranged themselves into a man, a woman, and a smaller version of Skye.

"Surprise! I'm home," cheered Star-Skye, throwing her arms wide. "Merry Christmas!"

The man and woman, her parents, reeled in shock.

"What the hell are you doing here?" shrieked the mother.

Star-Skye's arms fell. Her father lunged forward and yanked his little girl into an invisible house. "Who brought you here?" he demanded.

"N-no one."

"Did you steal money to ride the train?" asked the mother.

"No!"

"Did you take the train?" asked the father.

Star-Skye started crying. Her father slapped her hard on the back.

"I asked you a question."

Nodding, hunching smaller as if to protect herself, Star-Skye burst into full-blown wailing.

"Get her upstairs," said the mother, "otherwise everyone will hear."

"Go on, you heard your mother," said the father, pushing Star-Skye onto an invisible staircase. "Go back to the others," he told his wife, "I'll get to the bottom of this."

Crying, and leaving her luggage outside, Star-Skye crawled up the stairs like she'd rather lie down and never get up again. Then she screamed, "I never loved you anyway!" and raced up the stairs before her father could slap her again.

Mayu sat up and reached over to the real girl sleeping beside her. "Hey now," she whispered, stroking Skye's hair. She noticed dream tears flowing over Skye's freckled nose. "Don't think about that. Don't think about them. Dream of tigers and giant fish. Be a mermaid, paint the sky like Picasso, turn into a nightingale and sing for an emperor…"

Mayu peered up at the stars and felt relieved to see the pictures change into a tubby cat wearing a giant hat, captaining a ship with massive sails.

"Or be a cat," she chuckled. "Of course."

The glittery pasta around Skye's throat sparkled with dazzling light for a moment, blurring its outline. When the glow faded, a fantastic necklace sat against her skin. Shaped like a vine of ivy, the main chain was made of eighteen rose gold sprigs, sprouting at least eighty white diamonds decorating the tiny leaves. Hanging from the apex was the largest yellow diamond Mayu had ever seen—flawless. She stared at it, mesmerised.

Before she felt tempted to touch it, Mayu lay down once more, sighed, and finally surrendered to sleep. The sluggishness from earlier still weighed her down, and only as she explored Skye's sensory network, did Mayu find the cause. While Skye's mind gradually restored itself, closer and closer to true consciousness, Mayu's mind sank into the depths of her medically induced coma.

She tried to make herself care. She pictured Momo flirting with Richard. She sought to recall feeling elated at winning recognition for her work. She smiled, thinking of long walks with Keiji when the lab got too stressful. But these things existed without Mayu, she didn't need them anymore. She didn't care to see them again. Mayu deduced that one more day with Skye would be enough to wake her up, but she also suspected that this final transition might push her to the depths of no return.

Yūta's voice reached her ear as if riding the cello's lullaby. "If that happens, I'll find you. I should have tried harder, I'm sorry. I'm so sorry I left you."

"It's not your fault," Mayu whispered back, wet droplets falling across her cheekbones and into the shell of her ears. "I know you didn't intentionally die, you sweet fool." Feeling pathetic, she clenched her hand, imagining Yūta's calloused hand in hers.

"Do you want to hear a joke?" he asked.

Mayu laughed already. "I swear, if it's one of your puns…"

"I wouldn't *dajare*!"

Mayu groaned, spilling over with genuine laughter and tears.

As the hysteria faded, Momo's faraway voice reached through the night and cried through Mayu's unconscious mind: "*Listen everyone. Matokai's awake! He's okay. He'll be okay.*"

Thank goodness.

Richard: "*Really? Can we visit him?*"

A door closed and things went quiet. Mayu forced her tired mind to realign Skye's brain. The task seemed to take forever. She'd forgotten all about her team by the time the door opened and closed again.

Richard: "*It's happening. The top floors have been evacuated.*"

Momo: "*Who else is left up here?*"

Richard: "*Just one other patient. The window shutters will come down in a minute.*"

Momo: "*Oh hell… What strength is the hurricane predicted to be?*"

Richard: "*Category three. It could go up to four.*"

Fukushima: "*Boot up the second generator. Make both of them our primary power sources, we can't miss anything.*"

A clattering of metal and a dull whine cut him off.

In an effort to blot them out, Mayu sank deeper into the recesses of her mind until everything was silent.

The night passed without further drama. She focused on pooling Skye's Parallel Energy into one small section of her brain, compressing it into a tight ball. To wake up successfully in the real world, without being dragged down by Mayu's fading mind, Skye needed to spring away with little to no effort. Their merge needed to end in one quick, clean action.

Just before dawn, Tomoya's voice whispered around the room. "*We should have put this off for another month,*" he said. "*Look at you… Please look after yourself, Shirakawa.*" Mayu felt a gentle squeeze on her hand. "*Don't give up now.*"

"It's time you called me Mayu," she tried to say, but only a puff of air passed her lips.

A blistering sun rose that morning, beaming into the living room. The cello had stopped playing an hour ago and Mayu could hear it snoring on the counter in the kitchenette. Mayu attempted to roll into a sitting position, but her limbs dragged as if steel rods had replaced her bones. She panted with the effort just to roll onto her front.

Slumped in her new position, Mayu studied the carpet's plush fibres.

"*Mochi, please, I was trying to help.*" Richard's voice.

"*Don't call me Mochi,*" Momo snapped. "*Don't even speak to me.*"

"*Mo—Kuramochi, you deserve better. You're only making things worse for yourself.*"

"*It's late. I'll take my break now.*"

"*Mochi…*"

"*Let go of me.*"

"*Why are you angry with me? You wrote the thing!*"

A door slammed.

"*Argh!*" A pause. A sigh. "*Don't leave us, Shirakawa. We're in deep shit.*"

Mayu cringed as he addressed her unconscious body, her real body, lying in a hospital bed a thousand miles from home. Even if she could reply, Mayu didn't think she would. Not this time. It sounded like Momo needed a friend to run after *her* for a change. If only she could just…how had her mother put it? Let go. Slip away from everything that hurt and from everything that demanded her energy.

"*Do you hear me, Shirakawa?*" His voice sounded louder, like he was speaking into her ear. "*Come back to us.*"

Skye jerked awake and stared in confusion at the living room. "What?" she murmured. Sunlight hit the necklace, throwing dazzling multicoloured rays around the room.

Mayu tried to respond, but her lips only opened a crack and another puff of air came out instead of words. Her heavy breathing caught Skye's attention and she heard her laugh.

"Are you comfortable like that?" she asked. "What are you doing?" Her cheer died when Mayu didn't reply. "Mayu? Mayu, wake up!"

Still unable to respond…only a few strangled puffs of air.

Skye slid off the couch and onto her knees. She shook Mayu's shoulders and tried to roll her over. The shaking roused a sliver of life in Mayu's heavy body.

"Help me sit," she said.

"What's wrong?"

I'm dying. I'm ready to go. Gripping the edge of the coffee table, Mayu put all her effort into standing up. The sun's heat made things doubly difficult and sweat broke out on her face. Skye tugged on her other arm, doing her best to help.

Finally on her feet, Mayu lost her balance and staggered

forward. She hit the ceiling-to-floor window and pressed against it for leverage. Breath fogged the glass. Sweaty handprints. Turning to face Skye, she straightened.

"If you say you're fine," warned Skye, "I swear…"

Mayu smiled. "I'm very tired. You have abnormally strong Parallel Energy—I mean, a strong brain. You could grow up to do my job one day, if you wanted. You have great potential. It's gets harder for me to wake up the closer I guide you towards the real world."

The girl's eyes narrowed. "What do you mean?"

Taking a deep breath and letting it out with a huff, Mayu avoided her gaze. She studied her apartment as if seeing it for the first time. Flutters of movement caught the corner of her eye. Looking up, it surprised her to see falling snow and pink cherry blossoms.

"This again?" she said.

Skye stalked closer. "What do you *mean*, Mayu?"

"I made you a promise," she said, "to be around for as long as you need me. That…may only be for as long as you're in the dream world."

Skye paled. Hands clenched. Shoulders stiffened.

"You won't be alone, and your parents—"

"If you say they don't mean to be tosspots, I'll hit you." Her lip quivered. "What are you talking about? Where are you going?"

"I'm not going anywhere."

"Then…you're staying here? In the dream?" Skye's eyes widened and rage transformed her face. "HOW IS THAT FAIR?"

Mayu jumped and her knees trembled. She looked away. "I'm not sure it is but I… I can't do this anymore.

You've got your whole life still, no commitments yet, and I… Everything's disappearing, everything I love is broken or gone. I'm a weight holding everyone back. But for you—"

"That's stupid!"

Skye shoved her in the chest and Mayu gasped. She caught a glimpse of Skye's furious expression, her watery eyes, before flying backwards. The window smashed against Mayu's back and her stomach lurched as fresh air billowed through her dress. She caught one more glimpse of Skye— no longer raging but paralysed with shock—and then the building filled her field of vision. Sunlight glared off the glassy apartment complex and the world turned upside down, a blazing white sky, air purification ships and sky- scraper rooftops. Mayu fell headfirst in a shower of glass, snow and blossoms.

So far to fall…

Wind tossed her hair as she stared at the ground coming ever closer.

So heavy…

Your face is going to smash into the floor and turn inside out, Mayu thought. *Your neck will snap, your skull will pierce your eyes, your spine will crumple. This is it.*

She heard Skye scream her name and peered up, unable to spot where she might be calling from. Turning back to face the ground, a person hovered in the path of her fall. Mayu jolted—tried to pull back. Yūta held his arms open, as if to catch her. She only saw him for a second before she fell right through him and he vanished like smoke. No… how could she stop this? *Mayu, you're so selfish.*

A dark wave washed into the street below, absorbing

everything it touched. Mayu wouldn't hit the ground and crumple after all. She was falling towards fatal sleep. Closing her eyes, she focused on saving Skye. Every ounce of energy she had left, Mayu poured into their mental connection.

Wake up, Skye. You're ready.

The girl's mind roared to life.

22

S KYE COULDN'T STOP her breath from heaving. *What have I done?* she thought. *Fly! Fly!*

How could Mayu desert her? Did everyone have to be so bloody incompetent? Skye hovered at the edge of the broken window ledge, trying not to choke at the overwhelming drop. The wind tugged at her as if trying to pull her off, and she growled, sick to death of things not behaving as they should.

A sharp stabbing pierced Skye's head and she doubled over. She felt icy cold and panted at the terrifying sensation—as if little bits of her mind were being plucked out and crushed.

That's when she noticed the sticky black gloop oozing around her shoes. She cried out, watching as it flowed out of the broken window and, creeping back to peek over the ledge, she saw Mayu's dress flapping far below. The yawning abyss waiting to swallow Mayu sucked Skye's breath away.

"Why don't you fly?" she screamed.

Gaping black abysses never meant anything good.

The ground softened, absorbing Skye's feet, and the whole building toppled forward. Her terrified cry strangled

itself, arms flailing, and plummeted after Mayu. "Help—
I'm gonna die!"

Do it like before, Skye prayed, *fly into me, sling your arm
around my tummy—anything!*

Beams of light warped the void and churned it into a
black and white vortex. How did Mayu fall so gracefully?
The swirling made Skye's already aching brain dizzy as she
tumbled head over heels. A thumping headache assaulted
her, and she longed for numbness, or for things to make
some sense.

No sooner did she wish it than the swirling abyss
turned green and blue, it twisted into rolling hills on a
clear sunny day. Skye landed in the grass heavily, sending a
bolt of shock up her legs. She fell onto her knees, panting
with relief, and pressed her hands onto the earth.

Where the bloody hell was Mayu now? Staggering
upright, Skye saw Mayu still falling headfirst towards the
ground. "Bugger!" Skye took a few steps and started to run
towards her. Mayu disappeared over the brow of the hill,
and a fraction of a second later, the ground shook as if with
cannon fire.

An eruption of mud and grass blasted into the sky from
where Mayu had fallen and Skye stumbled to a standstill.
Horror gripped her as the shockwaves vibrated underfoot.
Repeated waves of soil and rock thundered out of the hillside, travelling closer and closer to Skye. A cry built up in
her throat, she turned, she ran and unconsciously a yell
burst out: "Oh my god, oh my god, oh my god, *oh my god,
oh my god*, OH MY GOD!"

Streaks of white light blasted through the dirt tsunami
threatening to bury Skye alive. Squeaky mews caught her

ear and her hand lurched out to catch a passing star-cat. Choking now, suffocating, she was falling beneath a mountain of mud. Skye caught the star-cat's tail and it almost wrenched her arm off as it shot them back towards the crash site. She shut her eyes and tried to shelter her face beneath her arm, pressing her mouth closed against the dirt, she could not surrender to the dizziness, her cataplexy was setting in strong.

Too much panic. So much panic. Breathe. Breathe. *Don't die.*

It took all her strength to tighten her fingers around the cat's tail. Her arms were going numb, but she just needed her legs to run to Mayu and kick her sorry arse into next Sunday.

Just a bit longer.

They burst out of the earthy tsunami and Skye sucked in a deep, clean breath. Trembling with effort, her grip finally went slack. She soared to the ground in a dusty arc and braced for impact. Her back hit the ground with a wicked crack and her chin rebounded off her chest. She bounced and hit the ground several times before rolling to a stop. Everything hurt. *How am I not dead?* Rubbing her throat, Skye peered up, expecting to see endless grassy hills.

Instead, a lake spread before her, rippling with moonlight. A red bridge lined with paper lanterns stretched across it. On Skye's side, the bridge led to a magnificent Japanese temple. It had curving rooftops, balconies overlooking the landscape and thick timbre pillars. But her attention was drawn to the mass of people crossing the bridge. They rioted in the confined space, pushing and shoving and clamouring to get into the building. "In an orderly fashion!" shouted an attendant, flapping his arms in desperation. "We all have to cross the bridge one day, there's no getting around it!"

She was deaf to the noise. An icy chill swept down her back and her vision blurred as, for a few seconds, *she* became *Mayu*. She had a woman's body and felt death grip her lungs as she kissed a man in the rain, standing on a flight of steps to reach him.

She shook her head and returned to herself, lying by a lake in the middle of nowhere. Trembling and wincing, she managed to sit up.

Mayu.

Skye spotted her on the far end of the bridge, walking away from the mass of people who were trying to get into the temple. Where the heck was she going? Groaning, Skye heaved herself to her feet, not trusting her arms to take her weight.

What possessed Mayu to keep leaving her like this? An ache crept into Skye's chest as she thought of the harsh words, rudeness and bad behaviour Mayu had taken from her. Had she pushed Mayu too far? Stupid, stupid, why had she done it? Her parents were right, she pushed everyone away, she didn't deserve friends or praise, and she definitely didn't deserve Mayu.

Her mouth twisted into a heartbroken frown. She thought of dancing in Mayu's snowy living room, of being picked up around the waist…how warm and safe she had felt, how wonderful it had been to have someone gentle and kind twirl her around the room.

Skye clenched her hands. "MAYU!"

Don't die. Don't leave me.

Skye looked at the heaving bridge—there was no way through *that* mayhem. Steeling herself, she splashed into the inky shallows of the lake, water soaking her shoes and socks. But the lake started to bubble. It boiled and frothed, and Skye gasped as a colossal tentacle erupted out of the depths. Four more rubbery arms burst out of the water, each as big as a whale. Skye screamed and ran back to the shore.

Shivering, she watched as the blinking stars were gradually extinguished by a wave of deeper blackness that absorbed the night and washed over the moon. Skye looked back across the lake and spotted Mayu wandering off into a twinkling town on the other side.

As the giant octopus thrashed at the surface, the commotion on the bridge grew wilder. The crowd crushed together, desperate to escape before it destroyed the bridge with its swinging tentacles. Skye's legs threatened to buckle, her arms were limp, and as her heart hammered against her ribs. With one large gulp of air, she let her eyes glaze over and focused her mind on finding Mayu.

The bridge was her only option. Letting out the deep breath, Skye launched into a sprint and charged at the crowd. She barrelled her shoulders into peoples' chests and lunged against anyone in her way. Her trembling grew stronger—if only she had use of her arms! But her cataplexy wasn't easing off.

The octopus threw up a wall of water as it slammed into the middle of the bridge. Skye skidded to a stop and watched as dozens of people were swept away, flailing and screaming—the water gushed up Skye's legs. She clenched her teeth, mentally pushing back at the mist that fogged her vision. She rushed into the stragglers at the rear of the bridge, her arms flopping from side to side. "Mayu, please. Don't leave me here!" Skye couldn't even see her anymore.

A curtain of lake water fell, drenching her and she skidded on the slippery wooden surface. She heard more screams and an almighty wooden crash as she was sent flying into the air. Her useless arms flapped around her, and with a groan, she hit dry land. Relieved but now caked in a thick layer of dirt and dust she rolled to a stop in someone's muddy garden and whimpered, smelling sweat and earth.

She peered over her shoulder to see the giant octopus breaking the bridge in half, flinging people into the night sky. As it started to drag its wooden prize into the depths, the ominous black veil spread over the temple, smothering all its lights.

Skye scrabbled to her feet and sprinted onwards, already out of breath. She charged down the steep path and into the small town. When she reached the outskirts, Skye bent over to catch her breath and let out a few desperate sobs.

"Where are you?" she cried, voice hoarse.

A roar from behind her was the only answered. No longer in its watery lair, the giant octopus scrabbled over the top of the hill leading into town. Limbs lashing, eyes burning, it crashed down the narrow path and straight for Skye.

Her legs finally gave out, sheer terror would have disabled her anyway. As her muscles spasmed and she fell to her knees, she stared at the malevolent octopus. The cataplexy spread to her jaw and her face went slack. She'd never suffered with it for so long—surely her arms should have recovered by now. *Move, just move.* Shudders enveloped her whole body like a seizure as the octopus thudded into one of the outlying houses. It ripped up brickwork with a sweep of its tentacles, she felt the vibrations from her knees and to her teeth.

Barrelling onwards, the octopus drew near. It destroyed buildings in its path, toppled lamps, which fell in plumes of white sparks, and pulled up to Skye with a deafening growl. She stared up at the tentacle rearing above her head, its suckers covered in dust. Just as the colossal arm came slamming down, a searing pain assaulted her forehead—bursting from the inside out. Use of her arms returned and Skye gripped her head and screamed in agony. She braced for the blow of the octopus's tentacle. It never came.

"*Fukushima, that was way too much!*" A man's voice.

People! Where?

Skye looked up and saw a blur of moving images, like she'd landed in a film on fast-forward. The giant octopus was gone.

"*It was that or lose her.*" Another man, his voice richer. "*We…we have to choose. Kuramochi, get those readings cleared up.*" Skye scrutinised the people rushing past but couldn't distinguish who was speaking. The man's words echoed in a language she didn't speak. Her brain seemed to be piecing it all together into something she could understand. "*We have to choose between Shirakawa and Skye, their Energies are diverging, we can't maintain the connection. Skye's Energy is more sustainable. Focus on—Matokai! What are you doing here?*"

Skye lost focus on their words as, through the blur of

movement, she saw her father stride forwards. Her body still not responding, she tripped and fell, tried to scrabble backwards. Her father's lean figure, hollow cheeks and razor-sharp cheekbones loomed closer, ghostly grey.

"Get inside," he said through his teeth.

"No." The retort escaped Skye's lips before she could stop herself.

"You will get inside right now—before I smack you."

"I want to play. It's not fair."

"Get inside! You bit his arm, that's disgraceful!"

"He dared me to. He kept hitting me and said I wouldn't dare. So, I did!"

Her father's cheeks quivered with frustration, "Probably because you pissed him off, you wretched child. I won't say it again. Get inside."

"No. I *hate* you!"

His eyes narrowed and he lunged forward. He caught Skye's arm in a crushing grip. She thrashed and twisted and dragged her weight, but he was stronger. As he tried to pull her through the front door of their house, Skye let her legs sag in an attempt to thwart him.

With an angry bellow, he kicked the back of her shins. She choked in shock, throbbing with pain.

"I hate you. I hate you!" she wailed.

"And *I* wish you'd never been born."

His words cut her. *How can he tell me that?* This couldn't be happening again. She had Mayu on her side now.

Her father's grip vanished. The house disappeared, and she stood in a washed-out shopping district. A semicircle of women stood around her, with her mother at the head of the group, they were talking about Skye, as if she was deaf.

"I just don't know what to do anymore," said her mother. "I can't wait for the summer holidays to be over. If she's not causing trouble with the neighbour's kids, she's screeching on that cello. If she's not murdering my few hours of peace and quiet, she's trying to start an argument."

"No, I'm not," snapped Skye.

"Do you see what I mean?"

Skye hung her head, aching with shame. Mrs. Mansfield's friends consoled her and shook their heads at Skye, unable to offer any sound advice.

"I put my children on the naughty step."

"I take away my son's night light."

"My husband only has to give ours a *look* now."

And so they went on, until Mrs. Mansfield sighed and said, "Maybe when she goes back to school I'll tell them to teach her proper manners. Honestly, you spend good money…"

Behind Mrs. Mansfield—outside of the group—she recognised an indistinct figure. Skye's mouth fell open, forgetting the ache in her chest.

Don't forget Mayu. I must stay with Mayu.

The white fabric of Mayu's dress fanned behind her as she walked away from the group, her kind eyes staring dead ahead, as if possessed. Skye shook life into her limbs, and as she batted her mother aside, the image of her shattered apart.

"Why won't you listen?" Skye yelled after Mayu. "Come back!"

Her eyes fixed on Mayu's back, sprinting in an effort to catch up. The people in the shopping district scrolled past even faster, zooming around Mayu and Skye like the two of them were in a slow-motion tunnel. Skye pushed her legs harder, arms pumping. Her breath became so ragged it ripped inside her throat until she tasted blood.

Not much further now, if Skye could just stretch far enough she would touch Mayu's billowing dress… Fingers splayed, arm locked, a brush of cotton against Skye's fingertips…

Swish.

Everything vanished. Without even a blink—Mayu, the shoppers, the district—it all ceased to exist. Infinite blackness. Not an echo or a whisper. Skye froze and crossed her hands over her chest, stiff as a brick.

"Hello?" she said.

Hundreds of hissing voices mimicked her, and Skye twisted and spun about, desperate to see *anything*. The voices hissed like beasts from nightmares.

"*No! You haven't recovered. Get back to bed.*"

"*But I can save her.*"

"*Give Skye three shots of—Matokai, do not disobey me.*"

"*I can save them both, Fukushima. I can. I can do it!*"

"*Richard, take him back to his room.*"

"*Understood.*"

"Why do I have such an ungrateful daughter?"

"*Shirakawa's PDE is 50 percent less than it should be. You've seen my papers. Obinata has done* some *testing. Create a third link that synchronises me with both of them and I can—*"

"*Matokai, we are not in a position to use your theory. Kuramochi, get Skye responding again.*"

"*Yes, sir.*"

"Go to your room and rot for all I care. I'm sick of your attitude. I'm sick of you."

"*You don't have to put me under! Just—just—just use the helmet. It's only electrodes, I'll be fi…get* off *me, Richard!*"

"*I won't let you do this, either.*"

"*Just listen to me! Kuramochi, look at the circuit in Skye's lateral amygdala. Information is firing along pathways to her prelimbic cortex. Without Shirakawa, your stimuli are just turning into nightmares. By my calculations—*"

"For God's sake, just smack her."

Twisting and turning in the blind void, Skye yelled, "GO AWAY."

Her outburst died on her lips as she came face to face with someone. Her chest heaved with one long in-take of breath.

Henrietta, full of colour and life, stared back at Skye. Her best friend had come to save her. Henri was here. Not a bloodstain on her. Her forehead creased and her earthy eyes shone with an untold burden. Henri had always been good at empathy, her gentle manner won people over as soon as they gave her a chance, but somehow Henri looked older, like she'd seen a lifetime of wrongdoings.

"Skye, hurry," she said.

Henri grabbed Skye's hand and she held on tight, cherishing the touch of their skin and the strength of Henri's fingers. Her long black hair bounced as they ran, brushing Skye's arm. She couldn't take her eyes off Henri's face.

Until a dim light emerged in her peripheral vision.

Looking ahead, Skye saw a splash of grey light in the distance, flecks of white drifting in the air like fireflies. Two shimmering figures stood in the hollow spotlight: Mayu and a man. The man stood with his back to Skye but she guessed it could only be Yūta.

A raging wind hit Skye in the face.

"Keep going," cried Henri, before the gale wiped her away and Skye clutched nothing but thin air.

Demonic creatures emerged from the darkness and slid towards her, leering and groaning. On one side, a ten-foot-tall headless knight stamped towards her, swinging his enormous broadsword. "You will tell me where it is!" rumbled her father's voice.

Skye's arms went slack again. Her uselessness burned a hole in her chest. "Mayu!" Gasping and blinking back the haze in her eyes, Skye forced her legs to keep going.

"Give me your hand!"

She stumbled and turned to see one of Mayu's colleagues bursting towards her on a motorbike. It was the serious one who cooked them food. He leant out, reaching for her, and Skye clasped his hand as he passed. Keiji effortlessly swung her onto the backseat and they weaved between oversized monsters who grasped at them. The headless knight charged in pursuit, still swinging his hefty sword.

"The generators can't cope—the hurricane—"

A howling, whistling wind blew the demonic creatures to dust, funnelling her and Keiji into a wind-tunnel.

"Don't stop!" he cried, before disappearing as well, taking the bike with him.

Skye dropped onto all fours and tried refocusing on Mayu up ahead.

"You promised me!" she cried. "You can't be a bamboo or whatever. You have to wake up!"

The wind pummelled Skye's face, stealing her words. Screaming didn't sound any louder. She tried again and, on the final note, the wind dropped. Panting on her hands and knees, startled by her own scream, Skye gaped at the colour surrounding her, as if blinded. She felt smooth wood panels beneath her hands, heard bird song and rustling trees, and in front of her stood a man she was starting to recognise.

"I've always wanted to revisit this temple," Tomoya said.

23

"ARE YOU TOMOYA?" Skye asked.

They were on a magnificent balcony, close to a sloping red rooftop, offering a view of a city beyond the gardens. The building looked...spiritual, unlike Tomoya, who wore a suit and polished shoes, the wind toying with his short black hair. He bowed to her.

"Yes, that's me," he replied.

"What's happening? Where's Mayu?"

He sighed and glanced over his shoulder. "She's inside the temple. We have to save her together. You're still dreaming, but I've come to help. I'm in a coma as well."

Wobbling onto her feet, Skye gripped the orange painted wood railing for support. "I don't know how," she said.

"I think we need to get through to her emotionally." Tomoya folded one arm and tapped his lips thoughtfully with a finger. "I've got her fairly well stabilised inside the temple, using your energy to keep her alive and mine to shape the world with boundaries. When we go in, things will get...complicated. Mayu's not fully with us at present, all three of us might as well be sharing one body. It's hard to explain. Let's just say, the three of us are one big mind. Have you met her husband?"

Skye nodded. "He didn't help. He made her forget about me."

"Okay…" He paced back and forth for a few seconds and then sprang his hands open as an idea struck. "I've got it!" Tomoya hurried over and placed a hand on Skye's back, guiding her towards the lacquered double doors. "I know who she needs to see." Just before opening them however, he stopped and looked down at Skye.

Sunlight danced in his eyes despite his grave expression. "Mayu's imagination is strong," he said. "I've always struggled to beat her at that. Even if her Energy is diminishing, she might try to turn you and me into what *she* wants to see. What I need you to do is to focus on the room. Look at it and remember the details. If anything starts to fade or change, tell it to stop. You can keep the world from breaking, and I'll try to bring Mayu back."

Skye's heart tried to gallop again, but she took deep breaths. "Okay."

Water splattered against the top of her head. In a few blinks it was full on raining, the balcony glossy in the waning sunlight. "Perfect," Skye groaned. "We just need some lightning and that'll sum up the whole thing."

Tomoya laughed. "You're looking at it wrong. Think of it more like liquid sunshine."

Déjà vu and nostalgia hit her at once, making her long to see Mayu again. "Oh yeah…"

A bird landed on Tomoya's shoulder, brown and speckled yellow. It trilled, a word lost in its song. The bird tried again.

"What's it saying?" asked Skye.

"Uh, 'kelp' maybe?"

She studied its beak, as if she could lip read the message, but Tomoya's face went pale, drawing her attention. He stared at something over Skye's head.

"Help!" said the bird. "Help me!"

Skye whipped round to see a wall of black in the garden, stretching from the earth to the heavens, absorbing everything with silent intent, gaining distance on them with alarming speed.

"Quick!" Tomoya gripped Skye's shoulder, threw open the temple doors and pushed her inside, slamming the doors shut behind them. A moment later, the building rattled and groaned, darkness blotting out light from the windows.

"Look at that," said Tomoya, his grin not good enough to fool Skye. "Everything's fine. Now, uh…"

She followed his gaze to the middle of the room where Mayu stood, the centre of the floor sunken and paved with oak panels, the circumference raised and lined with mats. The woman had become a ghost. Her body shifting and translucent, no warmth in her once beautiful smile, and fatigue marking dark circles beneath her eyes and making her long dark hair dull and lifeless.

"Study the room," Tomoya said, stepping onto the wood. "I'll do the rest."

There wasn't much in the room but Skye had never seen anything like it before. The walls were made of sliding doors and panels, each one painted in gold and depicting the story of their dreams, the first showing Skye chasing Mayu downhill to a fishing bridge.

"I've missed you, when did you last visit?" asked a cheery, crackling voice.

Skye looked over at Tomoya, who now had the form of a tiny old woman.

"Grandma?" murmured Mayu. Colour returned to her cheeks.

"That's right. Do you know how much I've missed you?" The old woman tried to grip Mayu's hands, but they passed through her skin. "I'm getting lonely in my old age. Will you come and see me?"

Shaking her head, Skye carried on studying the paintings. In every scene, each blending into the next, she spotted Yūta in one form or another. His shadow lurked around the edges, both dark and light, a memory that hurt Mayu no matter how he appeared.

"You don't need me, Grandma," said Mayu, interrupting. "You're dead."

Looking back at the first painting, Skye sucked in a hard breath. Mayu's face had melted, the sockets of her eyes turning black. "Stop it," Skye tried. But the painting of Yūta's face dribbled and blackened as well. All along the wall, figures in the paintings turned to corpses, apart from the ones of Skye, in which she started to look terrified; running to hiding spots within the scenery.

"Stop it!" Skye's voice wobbled.

"Well, I can't bear it if *you* die too." A new voice, another woman.

Skye recognised the new apparition in front of Mayu as another of her colleagues. The lady with pink hair and earnest eyes. "You must try," she said. "It's me, Momo. Please come back us. We need you. We care about you."

"*Stop*," Skye told the room, but the paint turned a disgusting grey-brown, bubbling in places, like the room was deteriorating at the bottom of a lake. Water dripped from the ceiling. "Enough! Go back to normal!" Staring at the painting of them ice-skating, she felt relieved to see a hint of gold reappear. It blossomed across the walls in patches, recolouring the hideous pictures of Mayu and Yūta.

In the middle of the room Momo flickered and changed into Tomoya, who looked as if he was fighting an internal wound, before quickly morphing back into Momo, arms folded tight to keep standing upright. "Look at me; I'm your best friend. You can't—I'd be distraught if you—"

Mayu stirred at the mention of best friend.

Tomoya's image flickered over the woman but the figure settled at last as Momo and a bit more gold blossomed across the paintings. Looking relieved, Momo said, "I'm here for you." Her face fell. It was a man's voice that left Momo's mouth. She cleared her throat. "Mayu, it's me." Again, it wasn't her voice.

"Yūta," said Mayu, her pale lips smiling.

"No!" cried the shape shifting figure.

The paintings of Yūta reached out for Mayu, crawling off the soggy panelling. Whimpering, Skye stumbled off the mats and down onto the wooden centre piece. "Stop!" she shouted. "No, *no*!" Yūta's jaw had gone slack, his skin, spotted with mould, flaked off to reveal dried flesh beneath.

She turned to see Tomoya looking like himself.

"Remember me, don't do this, Mayu." Tomoya gripped the woman's shoulders, but a second later his hands fell through her ghostly body. "You're leaving everyone behind! And you're—you're hurting me. Hurting Skye!"

The air smelt of vomit and Skye gagged. Retching, she clenched her fists, ready to beat the hell out of any of the images of Yūta slithering further out of the walls and onto the floor.

"Stop!" Skye yelled. The walls rattled as the wind picked up again. One of the panels ripped out of place, revealing the darkness outside, and the panel tumbled away into the space.

Skye closed her eyes, focused on what the room should look like, aware of the hideous Yūta figures only a few paces away.

"We love you, I know it's not the same as him, but we do!" yelled Tomoya. "You have family, you have friends, there is so much more for you."

Skye opened her eyes and saw one Yūta swiping for her face. Fighting with everything she had against the wind, Skye drew her arm back. "Leave her alone!" Her fist hit a fragile, but solid, figure. Yūta cried out in agony before shattering into a hundred pieces that fell twinkling to the floor. "*Stop*!" she screamed for as long as her lungs held breath. Until the wind ceased.

Turning in a slow circle, Skye trembled from head to foot and her teeth chattered, she could see nothing around them but impenetrable blackness. Tomoya was gone. It was just her and Mayu, who seemed oblivious to the absence of her husband and that the two of them were alone.

Panting, Skye squashed the hopelessness of everything deep down into the pit of her stomach. What would trigger Mayu? How could she express the conflicting emotions she felt?

"Do you know what I dreamt of last night?" she said, voice dry and rasping. "I dreamt I woke up in your real apartment, I was living with you and I accidentally called you 'Mum', but you didn't mind."

Yes, exactly that. It hurt so much to admit. Was it wrong to feel this way? Did it make her a terrible daughter?

"Don't give me back to my parents. Can't you look after me instead? Why does no one want to stay with me? I'll learn Japanese, I'll behave. You won't even notice I'm there. I'll do anything—anything, *anything!*"

The pressure around them grew stronger and Mayu started turning grey.

"Stop it!" Skye instinctively tried to slap her but her hand passed straight through Mayu's cheek and down her long, elegant neck. Despite passing right through her body, Skye's swing left a blue, smudged handprint streaking down Mayu's skin.

"If you don't snap out of it, I'll follow you and stay here. I'll die, but at least I'll be with Henri."

Mayu's dead eyes slowly lowered and focused on Skye. Her cold gaze only strengthened the hopelessness Skye felt.

"You know who I am. Make an effort. Why won't you try? You're a stupid idiot! Stupid, stupid, just stupid. I'm not sorry if—no, I am sorry, don't listen to that. Don't…"

Exhausted, Skye hung her head back, closed her eyes, and let every feeling of betrayal pour down her cheeks.

"*No…Matokai.*"

"*Get him out of here. Kuramochi, get it together.*"

The voices echoed louder than before and Skye sensed

the next world. She was waking up. Her parents were going to stand there and offer pleasantries, but she'd see the tension in their eyes and feel the absence of their touch.

With one last try, Skye willed for a world where she and Mayu could exist. She looked at the blue handprint on Mayu's neck and, reaching up, hovered her hand gently on top of the mark. "Please don't leave me. I'm sorry."

Skye focused hard, searching for that warmth of mind and soul, for the unseen hands that had cradled her up until now. They'd been like unborn twins, wrapped together in mind and body, sharing dreams in a way the real world denied. Now that Mayu's…well, she didn't know what to call it, her spirit? Now that whatever it was about Mayu had vanished, she already struggled to remember what it felt like, but she needed it. Skye held her breath. She needed it more than air.

The silence continued and Skye dropped her hand, sobbing. "I'm sorry."

Soft arms wrapped around her body, pulled her close and held her tight. Her tears dried up at once, choked into nothing as she looked up from the folds of white cloth.

Mayu stared back at her with glistening eyes, her mouth twisted in a grimace and a smile. Skye saw kindness, gratitude, sorrow, regret, and love in that one mixed expression and her legs collapsed under the weight of it all. She wanted to explode from the unbearable complexity of having to exist.

Mayu caught her and dropped to her knees. Skye managed to fall into her lap. She clung on tight to Mayu as she sensed that she was about to pass out.

"Let's wake up," Mayu whispered against her hair.

Skye shivered, feeling lighter, as if something had been removed from her head. A quietness more absolute than before shrouded her mind, as Skye no longer hugged anyone but herself. Mayu was totally gone.

24

HER FOREHEAD BURNED. Her body felt like cold concrete. Breathing hurt. Water leaked from her heavy eyes. Her face was stuffy. A steady beeping pierced the air.

Mayu cracked open her eyes and a shaft of artificial light blazed into them. She winced, blinded. Where was she? Was this real? What happened to Skye? She turned her head on her pillow towards the ragged breathing she could hear close by.

Squinting against the unbearable light, Mayu saw Skye lying in the bed beside hers. Joy ballooned to bursting point at the sight of her round, freckled face—Skye's outline growing too blurry to see through her wet gaze.

She heard Skye groan behind her breathing mask and Mayu forgot her body could no longer fly. She reached out one leaden arm, dangling it off the bed, searching for Skye's hand. Blinking her eyes clear, her pillow damp with sweat, Mayu saw Skye cringing against the light.

A shadow fell over Mayu as a frantic Fukushima blocked her view. His shining glasses hid his eyes and the light from above cast his features into darkness. She shuddered, remembering the shadow people from her shared dreams with Skye.

"Mayu, stay calm. Don't move." His hand cupped the

side of her face. "I'm going to remove the probes." As reality far outweighed her hazy nightmares of shadow people, she sighed happily.

Swallowing against her sandy throat, Mayu shut her eyes. Fukushima accidentally knocked the breathing mask over her nose, and the stuffy, claustrophobic feeling in her face made sense.

"You're alright now," soothed Fukushima. She heard Richard saying the same thing to Skye. Other voices she didn't recognise fluttered around them like a squall of sparrows—nurses come to assist with the after-treatment.

A feeling of relief and sorrow overcame Mayu. She was alive. The light hurt. She felt disgusting—limp and drugged. *Why cry over any of that, Mayu?* she asked herself. *I'm alive and all I can do is cry about it.*

She smiled despite the lump in her throat as Fukushima stroked a cooling agent onto her de-probed forehead. Oh, how she loved his seriousness and dependability; his round glasses and compassion.

Someone squeezed her other hand. She looked up at Momo's red-rimmed eyes. Her friend caressed her hand, trying to look cheerful, but Mayu saw the dark circles beneath her beautiful, fluttering eyelashes. Momo couldn't have slept much these past few days…or weeks. None of them had, in fact.

A loud bang shot through the room. Momo's grip tightened on Mayu's hand. She thought she saw sparks in the corner of the room and heard the plinking of glass. "It's just the wind," she told Mayu, forcing a smile. She patted Mayu's leg.

"What's going on?" Mayu tried to ask. It came out as a strangled moan.

"Just take it easy," Fukushima told her. "Everything's fine now. You saved the girl." He twisted around as if to double check, then stepped aside so she could see Richard reassuring Skye. He checked her vitals and answered questions from the nurses about what the girl needed next.

Mayu looked back at Momo, but the woman only had eyes for Richard. Moaning, howling sounds caught Mayu's attention, as if the room had quietened and she hovered in time, listening to the wind outside. The spell broke and everything resumed moving in a blur.

"We'll get you set up in your own room," said Fukushima. "I'm sure—"

"No."

"Pardon?"

Mayu sucked her tongue in an attempt to make it less wooden. "Keep me with Skye."

He nodded. "Okay."

Momo continued stroking her arm, staring at Richard, until the nurses descended. Momo gave Mayu's arm an extra squeeze before following Fukushima out of the room. Richard came over and removed the breathing mask from her face.

"Hey, Sleeping Beauty," he said. "How ya doing?"

Mayu smiled at him, adjusting to the fresh, chill air.

"You gave us a real scare, you know. Glad to see those pretty eyes again."

His flattery lessened the tension coiling inside her gut.

"What happened?" she whispered. "Everyone…" She conveyed the rest of her question with one look.

Richard's smile tightened, and for a moment he didn't reply as he stretched Mayu's eyes wide with his thumb and forefinger. Once satisfied, he placed a hand on her mattress and hung his head, sighing.

He took a deep breath, about to speak, but changed his mind.

"What is it?" she pressed.

"It's nothing," he replied. "We just...There was a difference of opinion. It's nothing."

"All of you?"

Richard nodded. He checked her drip, then put on a smile and straightened his shoulders.

"What about?"

He glanced over at the nurses, the machinery, searching for an answer. "Just...procedure. We had to make a hard call. Nobody liked it, but it worked out in the end, right?" Richard cleared his throat. "Everyone's just...sim-mering down, and the storm has everyone on edge. Anyway, I'm sorry, Mayu. I'm very tired. Would you mind if I left you in the capable hands of these nurses?"

"Okay."

"Thanks. I'll check on you later." Richard bowed his head and left.

Wind whistled round the corners of the room. Looking round, Mayu noticed that the exterior metal window shuttering had a hole in it; jagged edges punching inwards through the glass, nothing but darkness outside.

It was only as the nurses left, one of them promising to return with water, that Mayu realised she hadn't seen Tomoya. When the nurse returned, Mayu asked after him, but the nurse was vague and said she had to plug the window against the cold. Mayu felt too weary to argue.

25

"LOOK AT ME, darling, come on. Look at me."

"Stop, she doesn't understand."

"She does, or someone's going to pay."

"Rupert…"

The man sighed, and Mayu took a deep breath, registering the room as she looked around in slow blinks. A blank wall, a metal door, a generator. Everything went silent. Recognising the blurred shapes in front of her, Mayu stopped trying to make sense of the voices on the other side of the bed and let her eyelids droop heavily again.

"Is she awake?" the woman whispered, quieter than before.

A chair squeaked, clothes shuffling. They meant Mayu. A puzzle piece clicked into place and her foggy stupor lifted just enough to tell her: the voices belonged to Skye's parents. She did her best to look peaceful as she felt their gaze studying her.

"No," said Mr. Mansfield. "She's not."

Sighs passed between them like Morse Code, a series of statements Mayu could only guess at. She fought to pay attention, to push away the sleepy haze still blanketing her.

"Skye's just…staring at nothing." Mr. Mansfield's voice

was gruff. "How long did they say we have to wait until she improves?"

"They don't know."

"For God's sake. I thought this was supposed to be better than normal therapy."

"What if she's never going to come back?" croaked Mrs. Mansfield. "What will we do with her?"

Mayu clenched her teeth.

"If she doesn't come back, I can't… I want her back." Skye's mother sounded like a foot-pump that was upset about being trodden on—huffing, like she wanted to cry but didn't know how. "Oh! Oh, she looked at me! For a second, her eyes… Did you see? Yes, darling, look at Mummy. I'm here for you."

"Or you can look at me," said Mr. Mansfield. "I'm here for you too."

A song cut the air, the James Bond "Diamonds are Forever" chorus. It died a few seconds in, followed by Mr. Mansfield saying "hello?" and Mayu realised that it was his ringtone. In the peaceful room, the voice on the other end of the phone was just about loud enough for Mayu to distinguish; deep and gravelly, the voice of a middle-aged man, who measured the clout of every word.

"Ah, hello, Fabio. How are you?"

Fabio said something Mayu couldn't make out, before he mentioned Skye's name.

"She's…" Mr. Mansfield shuffled in his chair. "They said she's awake."

An awkward pause stifled the room.

"Tell me what's wrong," Mayu heard Fabio say.

"Her eyes are open, but she's not…responding or

moving. The dream therapy was supposed to reduce recovery time—to restore her to how she was. I'll get more answers. But, so far, no one's said anything conclusive." Panic edged Mr. Mansfield's voice with every sentence. Despite his impatience and demand for an instant cure, Mayu couldn't begrudge him that.

"That is worrying," Fabio concurred. "Has she said anything?"

"Nothing. It's like…she's not here."

But Mayu knew otherwise. Skye was there. Listening. Recovery started with consciousness and comprehension. Even if it seemed like her body was empty, Skye was probably aware—begging her lips to let her reply.

"Keep me updated. Maybe she'll improve in a few days."

"What if it takes longer? What if…" Mr. Mansfield couldn't finish.

"We'll cross that bridge when we come to it. Hang in there."

They said their goodbyes, and Mrs. Mansfield whispered, "Let's go. I can't take it."

Mayu knew she should pretend to wake up, intercept them and convince them to stay by Skye's bedside and talk to her. Coming out of a coma and being immobile was frustrating, terrifying. Maybe Skye wouldn't remember this stage as she regained full consciousness and independence, but company would speed recovery. And yet, Mayu stayed quiet. After what she'd seen of them in dreams, she wasn't motivated to ease their worries.

They stood and headed to the door in broken, back-and-forth steps.

Shame grew heavier in Mayu's chest with every second she stayed still.

"Get off," Mrs. Mansfield hissed at her husband, a small rebuff.

"We'll figure this out," he replied.

The woman finally charged at the door, her heels clopping, her husband close behind.

"Wait," Mayu said, just as they shut the door behind them.

A flutter of fabric made her look over at Skye. The girl had turned her head, staring at the door. Her gaze slid to Mayu.

"Don't worry," Mayu said, "you'll be doing cartwheels soon." But her smile weakened.

Skye looked miserable, she couldn't help but look that way with minimal muscle control but it tugged at Mayu all the same. So she told her a story about a girl who defeated a dragon god at the bottom of the ocean, and then another, as many folk tales as she could remember, until her voice rasped on every word and Mayu fell asleep mid-sentence.

∽

After propping Mayu into a sitting position, Richard told her the news late that evening while Skye slept. He removed his tie and held it in both hands, as if seeking a distraction or a piece of normality.

"They declared him comatose five minutes after you woke up," he said.

Mayu went rigid as the words settled in.

"Whatever he did, he managed to stabilise the

connection between you and Skye, right before having a seizure. It weakened him too much."

"Tomoya…" Mayu bit down on her finger, hand clenched against her mouth.

"I've never seen anyone work so fast," Richard whispered. "He drew out the calculations for a third PDE connection in minutes. I mean, he said he'd been sitting on the work for ages now. Maybe if he'd had time to refine it…"

"You shouldn't have let him."

"And then we would have lost you when we had a potential solution." His grey eyes shone. "'She'll die,' he said, 'and we'll always wonder if my theory might have worked.' We couldn't live with ourselves, *he* couldn't live with himself, if we didn't at least try."

Mayu drooped forward and cupped her face in her hands.

"It's not your fault," said Richard. "You should have seen Skye's PDE readings, I'm amazed you managed to save her at all—she practically drowned you. Your mind kept trying to protect itself by shutting down any unnecessary processes. We had a hard time keeping the electro-magnetic pulses at the right frequency, you both required constant vigilance. That girl could be a potential recruit when she's older."

"Don't talk to me about work," she snapped.

"I know, I'm sorry, I just meant…"

A fuzzy ringing filled her head, her skin tingling with pins and needles and her eyes glazed over as if she and the hospital existed in two different time paradoxes. Indeed, Richard could have been talking from behind a pane of glass.

"We're worried that he's…vegetative."

Mayu coughed to clear the tightness in her throat. "He seems as good as dead?"

"He might not be gone."

"Then hook him up to Morpheus immediately and find out!" she snapped.

Richard shook his head, looking pained. "Do you remember a loud bang as you woke up? The motherboard fried—it got so hot that wires were melting. With the storm going on, the lights were flickering, the walls were groaning and the generators only just held out. You woke up just after the lights came back on, thank God, because a minute later the voltage surged and the generators overloaded."

A familiar emptiness drained her of energy. Richard sat down next to her and looped an arm around her shoulders. Taking deep breaths to calm herself, Mayu looked across at Skye, her thoughts churning into meaningless noise. The floor between their beds looked as if it was moving, she squinted at it but it only made the floor look more liquid, the tiles sliding together like the surface of the sea. Mayu stared at the water, focused on its soothing slosh and spray melody. She swayed with the waves, vaguely aware it was Richard jostling her shoulders. As she tried to pull her mind away from the haze blanketing everything, tiny, multicoloured handprints seemed to float on the surface of the waves, surfacing and submerging, like leaves falling into a river.

"I need to talk to you about Skye's parents," she said.

He gave her an odd, inquisitive look, searching her eyes and perhaps making a private assessment. The question probably seemed out of context, but she needed something to latch onto.

"What about? I don't think they'll press charges, the treatment worked, and they can damn well wait a week or two for Skye to get better."

"No." Mayu pushed his arm away. She sounded weak and tired already as she denied any feelings of grief about Tomoya. The internal strain made her throat tight and her voice tremulous. "Something else."

"There's something else I need to tell you first." Richard looked sombre. It shot nerves through Mayu's stomach, squeezing tighter when he placed a reassuring hand on her arm. "Our labs are gone."

Mayu stared at him. Not daring to question it, waiting for further explanation.

"A magnitude 9 earthquake hit Tokyo, half the Bay area has been washed away."

Ice trickled down her arms. It couldn't be true. Equipment they had taken years to design would be gone if it was. They didn't have the money to rebuild. They didn't have anything. Did they even have homes anymore?

"Are you serious?"

Richard's frown deepened. He nodded.

People suffered every day. She'd already lost Yūta and the fact that any one of them could die at any instant, from almost any cause, left her breathless. But without their equipment they couldn't do anything to help Tomoya. If only she had been the Dream Guide from the start, maybe Tomoya wouldn't have been injured, he may have been able to save Mayu and Skye and still been able to live to tell the tale.

To think, he'd followed her throughout her life, and now he was gone. No longer there to cheer for everyone, to bring them coffee during the late shifts, to leave passive-aggressive sticky-notes when someone ate his rice balls, to chew on pencils he didn't own and to make a mess of the filing cabinet, or to share parallel dreams with Mayu…

"What about Keiji?" she managed, staring at the floor again as the waves thrashed harder against her bedposts. Maybe she hadn't woken up at all, maybe this was her new reality—*she* was the one in a coma and these hallucinations were all part of a bigger dream. "The others? Are they safe?"

"I don't know."

Dread scooped out every other feeling as the terrible news mounted. Her breath grew heavier as the world grew wider in her imagination; no home, no job, no person to hold the walls in place. There would be tsunamis along the coast, severe flooding, and fires. How many were dead already?

The door handle to the room clicked open.

Richard glanced over his shoulder, got to his feet, and folded his arms, trying to avoid eye-contact with someone.

Glancing over, Mayu saw Momo slip inside. By the ugly twist of Momo's mouth, her gaze fixed on Richard, a gut reaction told her there was something else she hadn't been told. Her friend looked petite and smart in a snug, grey vest-jacket, and as sharp as the creases ironed into the front of her trousers. Neither of them acknowledged each other properly, just a mumbled hello. Mayu clenched a fistful of sheets in each hand as Momo strode to her bedside as if the water reaching up to her knees wasn't really there, her voice airy as she made formal inquiries after her health.

Richard pushed his shirt sleeves further up his elbows. "I'll give you two some space."

As he left, a flicker of feeling revealed Momo wasn't just upset. Her lashes framed betrayal in her eyes. No matter how sharply dressed she was, how flicky her pink-tipped hair, or how pretty her eyes—none of it hid Momo's exhaustion in that one look.

"Do you want to talk about what just happened?" Mayu asked.

Momo covered her eyes with one hand, the other clutching Mayu's shoulder. "It's not important."

"Liar."

She smiled. "You remember Halcyon offered me a full time job? I told Richard. He said I should have taken it. Except he started talking to their lab scientist—you know Klaus, right? Started setting things up for me as if I was going to accept. He even told Fukushima—who's hacked off with you as well, by the way, for not telling him I might be leaving and that he might need to find a new bio engineer."

After Richard's devastating news about Tomoya and their labs, Mayu struggled to feel the indignation her friend needed to hear. "He shouldn't have done that." It sounded as lame as she felt. "But maybe it's for the best. We've lost everything."

Perhaps her apartment was still standing. Maybe she had a home, at least. Her heart clenched to think of the black tea set from her grandmother, given as a wedding present, shattered and lost within a city-wide river of devastation.

"What are we going to do?" Momo whispered.

Feeling heavy, Mayu sank into the pillows, staring at the wall without seeing it. "I don't know." They wouldn't be able to monitor Skye for more than a week, by which time Mayu should have regained stable autonomy.

The prospect of half her life's work being lost sent a sick jolt from Mayu's head to her feet. A dull throbbing hit her temple. She draped her arm off the bed and trailed her fingers back and forth through the water, surprised at how warm it felt.

"What are you doing?" asked Momo.

"The floor is covered in water…" To confirm it, Mayu held her hand against the waves, watching water pool over her fingers, but frowned when she didn't actually feel any resistance.

With a firm push, Momo rolled her back onto the pillow and gripped the hand Mayu had dipped into the sea. Her friend stroked her forehead, feeling for a temperature, and then gently pulled Mayu's lower eyelid down. "You're hallucinating," she said, her tone as soft as her touch. "You know you're not dreaming anymore, right?"

"Right… Momo, I really need to talk to someone about Skye's parents."

Momo replaced Mayu's arm on the bed and pressed her hand into the mattress, as if to state what was real. "Those idiots? What about?"

Glancing at Skye, to be sure she was still sleeping, Mayu whispered, "I've been trying to remember details from my dreams but, you know, parts are unclear. Something I saw… I don't think they're good parents."

Momo looked over at the girl, as if trying to see parental issues written across her forehead. "You know, I'm trying to be surprised, but I'm not. Mr. and Mrs. Mansfield are cold. They live in another world of 'my life is so difficult.' Richard had to spend two hours with Mrs. Mansfield because she had a breakdown about how stressful it is being a mother and that she can't cope."

"Stressful?" scoffed Mayu. "Skye only goes home two months of the year."

"That's what I said, sort of." Momo's shoes tapped against the linoleum as she went to Skye's bedside and carefully took hold of the girl's fingers. Her gaze wandered to the readings on the monitors. "She has such a beautiful neural network," Momo whispered. "You'll love the charts." Then she sighed and returned to Mayu. "Anyway, there's not much we can do about her parents. Some parents are just shit."

Despite shaking her head and the unsettled feeling deep in her gut, Mayu had nothing substantial to go on. "I guess you're right."

26

SOME PARTS OF their parallel dreams were so vivid; it was hard for Mayu to accept they weren't true memories. Whenever she wasn't retraining her leg muscles or trying to shake off the effects of the drug that had induced her coma, she lay in bed near Skye, recalling their dreams.

"And you were skating round the ice rink like a professional, do you remember?"

Skye smiled, lop-sided.

"You got to see thousands of lights at nighttime. And your dress was blue and glittery. Oh, and you turned into a tiger!"

A gurgling sort of laugh escaped the girl. She tried to form words. "Weh—weh…" It ended in a low, lulling sound. It took a few more attempts before Mayu guessed it.

"Whales? Yes, the flying whales. And we rode them into space."

Sometimes, when Mayu thought she was speaking, she'd stare right at Momo or Fukushima or even Skye, the walls alive with lichen behind them and the ceiling rippling with music—aquatic life swimming against the surface—only to find that no one understood her. Fukushima told her she wasn't recovering as well as her previous coma excursions, which he deduced from her preoccupation with the giant koi carp above his head.

Glorious images of nebulas sometimes filled Mayu's imagination. If she concentrated, she could see one painted on the ceiling in shimmering purples, blues and yellows. But then the imagery snapped to a dark black well, a man clambering up to crush her face and squeeze her neck. She pushed past it, to Skye diving into her arms and holding her tight like a living star.

For this reason, as the hallucinations grew less frequent, Mayu wondered about discussing what had happened in the dream-museum. She couldn't remember all of it—only Skye as a rag doll and the mannequin room. For a few days, she held off bringing it up, questions squirming inside, afraid it was better forgotten. Mayu feared it would upset Skye but, more than that, she also feared it might make Skye withdraw from her. She didn't want to risk that.

Bad news greeted her every morning. Keiji still hadn't contacted them and the earthquake in Tokyo had triggered tsunamis along the south-east coast of Japan as she had feared. As the death toll kept rising, so did the nausea in Mayu's stomach. The loss of their labs seemed meaning-less with the possibility that their families and friends were amongst the dead.

On the fourth day of their recovery, as the two of them rested in the afternoon, Skye spoke her first clear word.

"Mayu."

It rang in Mayu's ears and made her jump. She stared, dumbfounded, the nausea shoved aside by a blazing beam of joy. "Yes?"

"Ma… Ma… Mayu."

For the rest of the afternoon, Mayu focused on recalling the part of their dream at the museum. Paintings had paved the floor, she'd walked on them and found Skye behind a tapestry at the end. But what was in the paintings? All Mayu could grasp were shadows and shades of red and brown that filled the hospital room and left her cowering into her pillow.

During the early evening, Mr. and Mrs. Mansfield stopped by. Perhaps Mayu should have feigned sleep, considering the way they now grumbled at her about Skye's recovery during every visitation.

"She understands you, but she might not remember these visits when she's fully conscious," she explained.

"*Fully* conscious? I don't understand, I thought she was conscious." Mrs. Mansfield looked Mayu over like she wore trash bags for pyjamas.

"No. When patients emerge from a coma, they can appear conscious but mental capacities take time to return. Our project means patients sometimes recover faster, usually with memory and knowledge almost intact. I'm doing better because I wasn't comatose due to the result of an injury."

Their questions only grew more indignant, their disappointment that the dream therapy hadn't been a miracle cure made plain.

"We told you—" Mayu sighed, thankfully interrupted by Momo sweeping into the room and then by Mr. Mansfield's phone ringing. He dragged a hand down his face before answering with strained politeness. "Fabio, hi. No, she isn't talking yet but it's early days. You can say hello if you want, apparently she understands what we're saying." He offered Skye a smile to show he hadn't forgotten she was in the same room.

With firm hands, Momo helped Mayu off the bed and onto her feet, saying, "Come on, let's get you some exercise. We'll try the stairs today."

"Only if you're carrying me on your back."

Momo chuckled. "You'll be lucky."

Neither of the Mansfields said anything as they left, Mr. Mansfield busy with his phone call, and Mrs. Mansfield holding onto Skye's hand, patting it as if that might spark a reaction in her daughter.

"My mother called this morning," said Momo. She held Mayu's arm tight, shuffling one step at a time along the corridor and out onto the balcony that looked down on the lobby. "She says she's okay, but my brother is still missing."

"Oh Momo... We should go back to help however we can."

They reached the staircase and Mayu wobbled as she went down the first step, but her balance got stronger with each one. Her nervous system and motor-skills were still sluggish.

"Yeah, once you're better. Perhaps it's just as well we don't have any work right now." It rang hollow. Mayu wondered what state the earthquake had actually left their labs in. Were they reduced to rubble? Were they superficially damaged or structurally weakened?

"But what about Halcyon?" asked Mayu, hiding the sharp, knotted anxiety in her stomach at the thought of finally losing her friend as a colleague. "You'd be great in their PTSD program."

"I can't leave you guys now!"

"But I thought, what with Richard getting involved—"

"Don't talk to me about Richard." Momo huffed and paused their descent, partly to give Mayu a breather. "It feels like he's trying to get rid of me."

"I'm sure that's not true."

Tugging on her arm, Momo continued to lead her downstairs. "Whatever. I don't want to make things difficult. I just want to do my best for the project we've built together."

As pleased as she was to hear it, Mayu stopped at the bottom of the stairs, gripped both her elbows, looked her dead in the eye. "Thank you so much. But we all need a job, and you've had a fantastic offer. Halcyon bought half their tech from us, so you'd be very valuable to them. You might even learn more about interpreting dreams with them. Just know, you would always be welcome to return, well, if there's anything to return to."

Gratitude shone in Momo's eyes as she swept Mayu into a hug. "Halcyon can wait a little—"

A jaunty ringtone cut her off. Momo dug her phone out of her pocket. The second she read the caller ID, she gasped and answered, "Obinata!"

Mayu leant in close, trembling to her bones. On the tiny screen glowed a video feed of Keiji, the usual news banner scrolling at the bottom.

"Thank goodness," said Momo, "we've been so worried. Are you alright? Where are you?"

His white-blond hair looked dull and unwashed, his angular face haggard from lack of sleep. Bleached sunlight glowed around him, washing out the blurred buildings in the background. His leather jacket suggested he was probably parked on his motorbike.

"One: I feel like a corpse, but hey, I'm still breathing," Keiji shrugged and took a deep breath. "Two: I'm in Kiyose."

Momo and Mayu glanced at each other. Kiyose was on the outskirts of Tokyo, a solid hour's drive inland from their labs in Akasaka.

"The quake hit while I was on my way back from lunch," Keiji explained. "It didn't hit hard to start with, so I carried on, made my way back to the labs. Then the first real slam came. I've never felt anything like it. First chance I got, I ran inside and hit the evac alarm. The place was already shook up bad. The lobby ceiling had come down.

"I'm pretty sure everyone got out. I checked all the rooms but then the next quake hit and, damn, I… I just had to get out. I was almost buried under rubble." Keiji shook his head, mouth pressed in a grim line. "It felt like forever. A giant crack ripped across the front of the building. I could barely crawl across the street to get away. I thought it was gonna collapse on top of me."

Mayu bit her tongue, desperate to reach through the screen and comfort him.

"When it stopped, we ran to the cafe on the corner. Some people were stuck in there. We dug for hours—the whole day but then the sirens started. The police came through telling everyone…evacuate immediately; Tokyo Bay has flooded, it's collapsing…"

He paused and closed his eyes. Mayu had never seen him in pain, never seen him upset or even angry. It was like seeing a bird with a broken wing, seeing him so helpless was distressing.

"I saw the water coming. I got on my motorbike and dragged Shiori, the new intern, onto the back. I keep telling myself I grabbed her because she was the person closest to me—I didn't have a choice, I couldn't have chosen anyone…that's all I could do, right? I just…rode away and didn't stop. I never thought I'd regret having a bike instead of a car."

Tears welled in Momo's eyes, but she held it together. "You did what you could. I'm so glad you and Shiori are alive. Perhaps the others got out earlier, perhaps some were too tired or injured to help dig. Don't be so hard on yourself."

Mayu could picture the scene, it made her feel weak. She knew that by the time a tsunami reached the labs it would have been a fast wave of debris—a wall of water full of wood, metal, even cars and boats. She was unaware of her surroundings or Keiji on the phone, visualising the horror so clearly that she had to clench the banister to remain in the present. The moving lights of the news banner on the small screen caught her eye: *Smash-and-Grab Jewel Heist* it still proclaimed, flicking to show a gorgeous necklace…a *diamond* necklace, one that looked all too familiar now.

She grabbed Momo's arm, stiff with shock.

"Sorry, Obinata, Mayu's still recovering." Momo straightened her shoulders. "I should take her back to bed, but I'll call you soon."

"Yes, of course." He seemed to focus for the first time. "I'm glad you got through it, Shirakawa. I told you so, didn't I?"

Either he didn't know about Tomoya yet, or he was deliberately not mentioning him to make her feel better. Mayu nodded, her skin shivering with cold flushes.

As the call finished, she jerked Momo's arm to stop her from closing the chat app.

"Hey, careful! What's wrong?"

"That necklace." Mayu didn't feel steady enough to point to or touch the screen, so she gestured to the phone with her head, just as it flicked to an advert for business hotels. "I saw it in our Parallel dreams. Skye had it. It belongs to her parents."

"Slow down, what are you talking about?"

They waited for the necklace report to reappear.

"Skye told me that she hid that necklace from her parents. It's so unique, it has to be the same one."

"If it's the same necklace," said Momo, "then why does this news item say that it was stolen?"

"I don't know."

The confusion on Momo's face made Mayu wonder if she was deluded.

"I recognise it, Momo, I swear. Can we look it up online?"

"Ah!" A man's voice.

The two women startled and peered up the stairs to see Mr. and Mrs. Mansfield.

Mayu was deaf to whatever the two said next. All she could see, as Mr. Mansfield led the way down, was an attic at the top of the stairs and a man beaten bloody behind him, painted in shades of red and brown.

27

"MAYU, THIS CAN'T be the same necklace."
Momo leant back in the padded chair between
Mayu's bed and Skye's, reading her phone.
Skye was excluded from their conversation as they spoke
in Japanese but she looked relaxed now that her parents
had left the room.

"It belongs to some woman in Singapore. It's called the
L'Incomparable, its unique *and* famous. Not only that! It is
one of the most valuable necklaces in *the world*. The whole
world, Mayu."

"Let me see."

With a theatrical sigh, Momo put her phone in Mayu's
outstretched hand. Leaving the news page, Mayu began
searching images, but she already felt positive this was the
right necklace. She tapped on an image that linked to the
website for the 'Mouawad' company—luxury jewellers and
the creators of the stolen diamond necklace. There it shone,
the *L'Incomparable*. Ninety-one white diamonds adorned
the rose gold branches of the design and, suspended at the
apex, the world's largest, *flawless*, 407 carat yellow diamond.
The complete necklace was worth over fifty million dollars.

"Come on," scoffed Momo, "if this belonged to the

Mansfields and Skye hid it, like you said, why would the news say 'smash-and-grab'? How would Skye have had the chance to take it? You think it would be lying on her mother's dresser and not locked in a bullet-proof safe?"

"It was a nightmare, alright?" Mayu snapped. "I'm trying to figure it out. A little support here." She glanced at Skye, who was watching them without confusion or curiosity. Inhaling softly, Mayu made herself murmur, "Her father said she was a good liar."

"There you are. Maybe Skye saw the necklace somewhere and—"

"I meant, maybe she didn't want to show me the whole truth!"

The nightmares had sprung from a real sense of suppressed terror. Mayu ordered her body to get out of bed.

"Come on, stop. Mayu!" Jumping up, Momo didn't stop her but helped Mayu up, so that she didn't get tangled in the sheets and fall.

Clutching Momo's phone tight, Mayu shuffled over to Skye and leant on her mattress. The girl followed her with her eyes, unintelligible sounds passing her lips. Mayu held up the phone so that she could see the picture of the necklace.

"I saw this necklace in our dream, didn't I?"

Skye went quiet, eyelids lowering evasively.

"I will protect you, Skye, but you must tell me the truth, otherwise I can't help you. Is this the necklace you hid from your parents? Just nod for 'yes' or shake your head for 'no'."

They stared at each other. Skye look scared, her mouth

twitched. How could Mayu show the girl that she cared by expression alone?

Momo placed a comforting hand on Mayu's shoulder. "Maybe she hid her mom's favourite necklace and in your dreams—"

Skye nodded.

Mayu smiled and pushed the hair back from Skye's forehead gently. "Yes? You're telling the truth? This is the necklace you hid?"

She nodded again.

Mayu looked back at Momo, who bit her bottom lip, still unsure.

"Thank you," Mayu said to Skye. "You are very brave." As she started shuffling back to her own bed, Skye threw her arm out. It dangled off the bed, reaching for her. Mayu turned back in surprise. "You moved! Look at that! I'm not leaving you, don't worry, and we won't tell your parents."

The glimmer of emotion in Skye's eyes could have been gratitude or some kind of plea. Mayu gave a reassuring smile.

"We've asked the hospital for eye-tracking communi-cation equipment," Mayu said, as Momo tucked her into bed. "You'll be able to talk to us then, Skye. You're on course for a quick recovery."

The girl made a toneless sound, perhaps a cheer, but she turned her head away and stared at the wall. Mayu frowned. Returning to her first language, she said to Momo, "If the necklace that Skye hid is the same one that's been stolen, what's going on?"

Momo shrugged and looked about the room, as if for

the answer. "I don't know. This seems…impossible. Dreams are full of symbolism. What could a diamond stand for?"

"I'm not sure," Mayu murmured. Her friend's shoulders stiffened and, clearly holding her tongue, Momo held out her hand for the phone. Mayu held it close. "Let's look-up her parents? Maybe we'll find something."

Momo sighed and massaged her forehead. "Fine."

All they found was that the Mansfields' business had a charity offshoot called *Clear Skies* in Mrs. Mansfield's name. The environmental damage caused by diamond mining had made it an increasingly expensive business, so the Mansfields had installed twenty-three-foot-tall towers around London that sucked in smog and compressed it into glass gems. The pieces of smog glass were turned into jewellery and trinkets and the profits were being donated to environmental protection projects. Mrs. Mansfield was quoted as saying, "We cannot just take from the Earth without giving something back, which is why we've set up *Clear Skies*. We believe diamonds are wonderful but that they should be mined responsibly and not excessively."

Before Mayu had a chance to search further, Momo demanded her phone back. "I said I'd call Obinata back, he's probably waiting for my call. Come on. There's nothing to find."

A chill traced its fingers over Mayu's skin, unsettling her further. How could she be wrong when all her instincts suggested that she was right?

"I know you don't like her parents," Momo held her hand out, "but maybe there is nothing bad to find. Just because they're not good parents doesn't mean they're bad people."

As Mayu slapped the phone against Momo's palm a flicker of pink caught her attention. A blossom petal fluttered through the air and settled on her sheets. She brushed it to the floor, only to see another petal land on her leg. The ceiling hadn't gone anywhere but she squinted at it, searching for holes. When she looked at her blanket again, blossoms covered her legs and she gasped, brushing her fingers through the soft petals.

"Mayu, I think you need to get some rest."

The frown on Momo's face made her feel crazy. Doing her best to ignore the petals, Mayu clutched at the sheet, unable to totally push past the haze swimming round her head.

"We need to get answers," Mayu shot back. "We need to look into this."

"No. No we don't. You're not well."

"I need you to help me."

"I am helping you!" Momo glanced at Skye and lowered her voice. "You know who else needs help? Obinata. Our families. That's real, Mayu. We're not detectives, we're scientists. You're sick and hallucinating. I'm sorry. I really am but just…get some sleep."

"I've slept enough." Mayu thumped back into her pillow and rolled away from Momo, covering herself as much as possible, her eyes peeking out and focused on Skye. The girl looked as if she wasn't in a bed but in a rock pool; her hair tangled with seaweed, her body laid uncomfortably over the stones, water lapping against her face. The sound of waves hissed inside Mayu's ears and she shut her eyes against the unsettling image.

"You know this happens sometimes," said Momo,

"patients find it hard to distinguish dreams from reality. We didn't think it would happen to you, but it will pass."

Maybe she had not woken up at all. Maybe Mayu had died and the afterlife was just one unending dream, a tumble of regrets and unfinished business.

"I'll find an answer with or without you." Mayu failed to hear Momo's reply as a Shinto prayer chant arose from the sound of the waves and quickly washed away again.

She heard a door click and turned over, Momo was gone.

Alone with Skye again, Mayu studied her as she faded back and forth between lying on a bed and lying in shallow water. What did she need?

Skye stared at her without embarrassment. "Ma…yu," she said.

"Why did your father beat someone up when he suspected they'd stolen the necklace, rather than report them to the police?"

With visible effort, Skye shook her head from side to side, before slumping and staring once more.

"You don't know?"

Skye nodded.

Mayu sighed. The Mansfields sourced diamonds and sold luxury designs. Their daughter said she'd hidden a valuable necklace from them. Mr. Mansfield hadn't gone to the police…

All at once, the answer came to her and Mayu gasped. Skye burbled a few almost-words, asking for her to spill the secret. The girl went silent at Mayu's expression. They were no longer in a hospital but on an isolated beach, Skye sinking in a rock pool and Mayu stranded on the wet sand nearby.

Maybe Mayu's eyes were deceiving her, maybe she was still dreaming, but it didn't matter. She had the first answer: the Mansfields weren't victims of theft, they had to be thieves.

Keeping her voice as steady as possible, she said, "Skye, do not tell your parents where you hid the necklace. *Promise* me you won't tell."

Like the air was being sucked out of the room, Skye's chest rose and fell faster, and she nodded again.

28

NEUROLOGISTS CAME TO set up the eye-tracking device the next morning. Having barely slept the night before, it had seemed to take forever, especially with the staff spending a lot of time chatting to Mayu about the Parallel Dream Project. She felt a pang in her chest at the mention of her lost project and agitated by the delay in setting up the communication device. She would normally have gushed about the Morpheus machine, how it worked and how they had developed the therapy. Being with others who were equally excited about the science involved was usually exciting. But today she couldn't engage, her thoughts were focused on the problem of the stolen necklace.

They propped Skye into a partial sitting position and placed a monitor and keyboard on a hinged stand over her bed. Once they found the correct position and calibrated it to Skye's eyes, it was ready to be tested. They waited and watched Skye's gaze tracing across the digital keyboard and, one by one, letters appeared on the screen forming words, until finally the 'enter' key lit up.

"Am I really awake?" asked a computerised female voice. "O m g," Skye said through the device. "It works!"

Mayu laughed, unsure why she felt overwhelmed at hearing her communicate.

"Wonderful!" All heads turned as Fukushima arrived with a briefcase under his arm and Richard hot on his heels. They introduced themselves to Skye, explaining that they had come to evaluate the way her brain reacted to certain requests and to test her short-term memory.

After fifteen minutes, Richard drifted away to check on Mayu. "How're you feeling?"

"I don't know. Are you and Momo still not speaking?"

"Ah…" He rubbed the back of his neck. "I just… wanted her to do something for herself. Especially now we've got nothing to go back to. I wasn't trying to sign the contract for her, I only… She drafted the acceptance email herself, you know. We wrote it out together, just to consider it, but she wouldn't hit send. So I…" Groaning, he tried to move on. "Can I help you sit?"

Mayu let him. As he started pinching her fingertips and tapping her inner elbow, she said, "She thinks you want to get rid of her."

"What?" Richard looked mortified. "I don't want that!"

She made a show of rolling her eyes. "I don't know why I keep the two of you around. Just apologise and tell her that."

He shovelled his hands through his hair. "Perhaps I should get her a gift? What do you think?"

Mayu sighed. "If you figure it out, let me know. She's not happy with me either."

"Uh oh. What happened?" Looking relieved not to be the only one in Momo's bad books, he folded his arms.

Glancing at the staff nearby, especially Fukushima,

she gestured for Richard to come closer. He leant forward, eyebrows rising.

"It's complicated, but I'm pretty sure Miss Mansfield's parents are diamond thieves."

"Whaaat?" He elongated the word like she'd announced something both incredible and ridiculous. "That's… absurd!"

"I need to question her in a minute—but Momo doesn't believe me. She thinks it's just dreams."

Richard nodded, pulling at one of his earlobes. "She did mention to us that you were acting…strange." Mayu glared at him and he raised a hand in self-defence. "Look, we all agreed that dreams are unreliable and don't necessarily reflect reality. Even Halcyon have to be careful when assessing their value and don't use dreams to diagnose people."

"Please!" Mayu almost gripped his hand. "I'm not stupid. I've done this enough times to know I'm awake and hallucinating." At least, she hoped she was. "But what I saw in my dreams literally connects with real world events. Can you…can you talk to Momo for me? Try to convince her to listen to me?"

"You'll have to tell me how I can get her to talk to me first."

Digging through her memory-bank of 'Things Momo Kuramochi Loves', the only thing that didn't seem too much like a tacky bribe was food. "You know Momo loves a broth. Why don't you buy her chicken *gyoza tanmen*. There's a real Japanese restaurant nearby. Buy her a big cup of that and tell her you're really sorry for going behind her back."

He cringed.

"Do not use the word 'but', either," she added, levelling him a serious stare.

Grimacing, Richard dropped the subject as Fukushima came over. With a swift goodbye and mentioning something about lunch, Richard hurried from the room. Her Co-Director studied the monitor at Mayu's bedside and made notes.

"I'll be leaving you with Richard and Kuramochi soon," he mumbled.

"How soon?"

"We need to get Matokai back home. His parents say Matsumoto hasn't been badly affected. Their health insurance together with his is enough to get him back and set-up."

Set-up for what, though? she thought, as she slumped against the pillows, watching Fukushima's stylus glide across his tablet. How long would it be before they knew whether keeping Tomoya on life-support was actually keeping him alive or just hanging onto an empty shell? She wanted to see him, to study his brainwaves for herself.

"When do you go?" Mayu repeated.

"Tomorrow afternoon." He slid the stylus into his tablet and placed a comforting hand on her shoulder. "There's not much point staying here to monitor Miss Mansfield right now. We've got nothing left. We can't analyse her results properly and I can't afford the hotel for much longer. Also…I haven't heard from my sister or my niece since the earthquake. Please, forgive me."

"It's okay." She smiled at him while her insides twisted and ached. "I understand."

Not long after everyone left, Mayu mentioned the museum to Skye, hoping that confronting this problem would lessen the ache of everything else beyond her control. The only thing she had left was this girl and finding out the truth before Momo and Richard decided they'd be better off going home too.

"After I carried you into the mannequin room, the dream gets fuzzy for me. What were the mannequin's doing? There were three groups of mannequins, right?"

"Yes," intoned Skye's device. "In the first group, I argued with my parents. It made me angry. The second group was the party. A man I've seen at the house before came and my parents took him to the study. He showed them the necklace. When they went back to the party, I sneaked in and took the necklace from the false drawer."

"What about the third set of mannequins?"

After a pause, "I don't remember—I don't think there were mannequins on the third stage."

But there had been something…

"I don't remember where I hid it. I know it's somewhere I didn't mean to put it, I can almost see where. I think I panicked. Stuffed it somewhere safe. I thought they'd find it, I remember, but they never asked. After school sent me home, I found Dad blaming that man." Skye sighed, but Mayu reassured her that not knowing was best for now.

"Keep thinking all the same."

They lapsed into silence for a moment and then Skye said, "Dad thought the guy who'd brought them the necklace was the one who took it."

Mayu watched as Skye wrote out the next bit on her

monitor, feeling frustrated that Momo hadn't arrived yet to discuss this further.

"He's the one Dad punched in the attic. I'm sorry."

"Hey, don't be sorry for what your father's done." Unable to swing out of bed without a bit of help, Mayu rolled onto her side instead, clutching her pillow close as if it could replace hugging Skye. The girl stared back at her, miserable as ever. "Your father made his own choices. You aren't to blame, no matter what."

The girl looked up at the monitor, selected letters with her eyes. "I wish you were my mum."

A breathless knot grew in Mayu's chest. It felt so wrong to love hearing her say it. It filled her head with all kinds of stupid ideas and dreams and hopes. She held it together though.

"Wait, I put the necklace in a bag," said Skye.

Just outside the door, they heard a ringtone playing "Diamonds are Forever". They both jumped.

"Don't say anything," hissed Mayu.

She heard Mr. Mansfield's voice behind the door and Mayu rolled to face it, pretending to be asleep.

"Yes, you can ask her," said Mr. Mansfield, "but I don't know if it'll do any good. Hang on."

Mayu heard the door click open. Holding a deep breath, she focused on looking serene despite her heart thumping in her chest. She heard shoes scuffle inside, one set of heels.

"Oh, darling, look at you," said Mrs. Mansfield. "You look frightened. It's only us. You see? Is that your new talking device? How are you? Tell Mummy you love her, please?"

"I love you," intoned the machine.

Mrs. Mansfield fluttered around her daughter and started to drag a couple of chairs closer to the girl's bed, the noise half-drowned her husband's phone conversation. Straining to block out her own heartbeat as well, Mayu heard the father say, "She can talk. If you want to ask—yes, yes, I understand. Alright, just let me check her roommate is asleep."

Mayu suppressed a shiver as he walked to *her* bed. His breathing grew louder as he stood by her feet and watched her sleeping. She felt a gentle bump as Mr. Mansfield tapped her leg to get a reaction. When he deemed her to be sleeping, Mayu considered she deserved an Oscar for not freaking out.

"Why is that woman still in here, anyway?" asked Mrs. Mansfield. "It's becoming inappropriate."

"I want her here," said the computerised child's voice.

"Skye," said Mr. Mansfield, "Fabio would like to speak to you." A second later, a soft, tinny crackling came from their side of the room. "You're on speaker, Fabio."

That deep, gravelly voice Mayu had overheard a few days before echoed into the room. A hurried clicking noise followed. Mr. Mansfield lowering the volume.

"Hello, Skye, I'm glad to hear you're on the mend. I know we haven't met, but I'm afraid you've taken something very valuable from me."

Since her back was facing the group, Mayu dared to open her eyes, every line of her body strung tight.

"It's a beautiful necklace, do you remember?"

"Yes," said Skye.

Don't tell them, don't tell them, begged Mayu, squeezing her eyes shut again.

"Where did you hide it? I'll forgive you right away if you tell me. If you don't… Well, Skye, I'm afraid people might get hurt. You don't want that, do you?"

"Good evening, ladies—oh." Momo froze in the doorway, one foot across the threshold like someone frozen in time. She composed her smile and bowed, then looked self-conscious for it.

"Uh, Mayu, good," she said in English.

"Hang on, Fabio," said Mr. Mansfield.

Way to have her cover blown! As hot and cold swept through Mayu's body in waves, she put on a show of being disturbed from sleep. "Oh, Momo, what time is it?" She could feel Mr. and Mrs. Mansfield's eyes burning holes in the back of her head. All the nerves going taught inside her body collected and bunched into a ball in her stomach.

Not daring to look at Skye's parents, she accepted Momo's hand and got out of bed. "Careful, I'm still woozy," she said, determined to convince them that she'd only just woken up.

"Really?"

"Just go with it," Mayu mumbled in Japanese. "Get me out of here."

They hurried to one of the quieter balconies, words pouring out of Mayu's mouth before they even reachcd a table. "The Mansfields stole the diamond necklace. That's the only answer." Neither of them sat, Mayu could barely stand in one spot.

"How the hell could those two steal, I repeat, one of the world's most valuable—"

"They didn't do the actual stealing, they had someone else for that." Mayu described the night of the party when Skye had seen someone deliver the necklace, the beating she'd witnessed in the attic, and how that had triggered her cataplexy resulting in her falling down the stairs.

"This isn't my dreams talking—Skye just told me all this herself. And remember, Skye's parents didn't pay for this treatment—their friend 'Fabio' did." Adrenaline was well and truly firing through Mayu now. "I just heard Fabio ask Skye where she hid the necklace because it belongs to him."

Momo stared with her, mouth hanging open, wearing a mixed expression of confusion and horror. "But the news said it belongs to a woman in Singapore."

"Didn't you just hear me? Skye's being threatened right now! This Fabio guy didn't pay for Skye's treatment because he cares, he wants to find the necklace and keep it, or sell it, or because he stole it. Maybe he's the one who organised the whole theft. Maybe the Mansfields have a crooked business."

Faced with such a bewildering choice of bizarre possibilities, Momo's face warped with disbelief. She gripped Mayu's biceps. "We don't have any *evidence*, you saw it all in a dream!"

"I know, you've got to help me. We've got to see if it's true. He's *threatening* her. If they get to the necklace before us, then yeah, we've got no proof. I need you, Momo, please!"

"Alright, calm down." Like a panicked bird, Momo pushed Mayu into a chair and gave her a brisk shake. "Think. There must have been some clue in the dreams.

Where did Skye hide it? Close your eyes." Mayu obeyed. "Sometimes we channel our fears or secrets into recurring symbolism. Sometimes it's literal, or sometimes we hear repeated phrases."

"I don't know, you're not helping."

"I am trying to. *Think*. Think of all the different worlds you created. Remember them like a story, in chronological order if you can."

Mayu placed a hand on top of Momo's.

"Skye's a child," Momo continued. "They hide things in places that make total sense to them, sometimes in the most obvious place, but the least obvious to their parents. My brother's kids hid the TV remote under the piano lid."

As best she could, Mayu recalled each major event, the school at the bottom of the ocean, her grandmother's village, screaming at each other in the rice paddies, riding whales in space, ice skating, the museum, the snowy apartment, and dying.

"Where did Skye go before her coma? Do you remember? What did she tell you about the time between taking the necklace and her falling down the stairs?"

There was one thing that had followed her. The harder she focused, the clearer Skye's hiding place became, seeing it in her memory like a glowing shape amidst a crowd of people.

Mayu opened her eyes with a gasp. "Her school locker."

29

EELING STRONGER THAN she had in days, Mayu limped back to their hospital room with Momo. She held her breath upon re-entering their room and felt her heart drop at the sight of Mrs. Mansfield still sitting there, without her husband.

"I hope we didn't wake you," the woman said, smiling like a shark.

"No, my friend woke me, don't worry." It almost felt as if Mayu wasn't allowed to approach her bed. She glanced at Momo out the corner of her eye. "I hope I didn't scare your husband away. My morning face is awful."

Momo faked a chuckle, an infectious one. They stood there giggling like two idiots on helium until Mrs. Mansfield cut them off with a sharp inhale.

"No, he had business to attend to at home."

"Home?" Mayu pinned her smile in place. "In Scotland?"

"Yes. He's only just managed to book a flight, an important business deal hangs in the balance. The diamond industry can be fickle."

She couldn't help it, Mayu glanced at Skye and saw

the first real emotion on her face since she'd regained consciousness; fear.

"Oh, well…" Momo said, seeing as a stone had blocked Mayu's throat. "Good luck!"

"Thank you."

Clearly the woman planned on staying a while longer. It would seem rude to leave again, so Momo helped Mayu into bed, although she needed less help than before. Either adrenaline was still shooting through her system, or she was doing better than she'd believed.

"I've asked that you be moved to another room," Mrs. Mansfield said, that crinkled smile unflinching. "I've already got permission. I hope you don't mind."

A chill swept over Mayu's body, and she wondered if her recovery might back-track at this rate. "Of course not," Mayu responded but, then to Momo in Japanese, keeping her tone as neutral as possible so as not to alert Mrs. Mansfield, she said, "Get Richard. We need to talk to the police, even if we fly to Scotland ourselves. He'll explain it better than we can. Get Fukushima here too. Tell him everything and make sure he believes us. And get me released from hospital!"

To her surprise, Momo didn't fight her on that last part. She pulled out her phone and left the room. Mrs. Mansfield excused herself a moment later to go to the bathroom.

Mayu counted to five.

"You told them where it is, didn't you?" Mayu whispered.

Skye nodded, tried to speak with her own voice, "Ssss… Ma…yu—"

"It's okay, I'm not angry. Just tell me, is the necklace in your school locker?"

A nod.

"Is your father going to get it right now?"

Another nod.

"What's the name of your school?"

The girl's eyes shone as she looked at the eye-tracker. "Faragreen Boarding Academy. I'm sorry. Fabio said he'd hurt people," the machine intoned.

"Don't worry. Everything is okay and I'll make sure you're okay."

Mrs. Mansfield returned. Her bum must have barely kissed the toilet seat to be back so quickly. Summoning a calm and cheerful voice, Mayu refocused on Skye. "Do you remember dancing across the lake with all the fireworks going off?"

For a moment, Skye only stared at her, then at her mother, who sat and watched them.

"There were candles on the water, and people playing drums on the shore," Mayu added. "What about the balloons on the train? Do you remember what I did to them when they were mean to you?"

At last, Skye played along.

It felt like an hour had passed by the time Momo returned with a bag over her shoulder. Mrs. Mansfield had probably underestimated Momo, assuming she was a frivolous young woman of little consequence, but Momo played it cool, she was not one to let her emotions get the better of her. She dropped the bag at the foot of Mayu's bed casually.

"Alright, let's, uh, move you to that other room."

"Already?" cried Skye, as Mayu dangled her legs over the bed and Momo started pulling trousers up over her ankles.

"I'll be close by, don't worry. I'm Senior Director of the Parallel Dream Project, I'm not going anywhere until you start walking again."

Momo met her eye as she wriggled the trousers over Mayu's hips. Her friend did such a good job of keeping her face neutral that her true feelings were unreadable. Mayu stared back and Momo lifted off her nightgown.

Once dressed in her black suit and white shirt, Mayu almost believed she was fit enough to leave the hospital. Skye ogled at her smart appearance.

"I thought you were just moving rooms," said Mrs. Mansfield. "What's with the suit?"

Mayu swayed, her skin feverish, not sure what lie to spin. "I am, but I feel okay. I…want to sit in the canteen and…catch up with my colleagues."

"A bit pre-emptive, aren't you?" Mrs. Mansfield pursed her lips. "You seem to be rushing your recovery; I do hope you're not overdoing it. I'll have to put you to bed myself at this rate." Despite her words, concern didn't show in the woman's face, her lips still puckered as if chewing a sour candy. "I'll come visit you later."

The hair on the back of Mayu's neck tingled uncomfortably. "There's no need. Thank you." She itched to go over and squeeze Skye's hand.

"I insist. I have more questions, anyway."

Mayu's mouth went dry but she tried to nod confidently and to look reassuring as she spoke to Skye, "I'll see you soon."

She turned to leave and Skye flung h er a rm o ut, moaning.

Mrs. Mansfield sat on the bedside and took her hand. "I'm here, darling, don't worry. I'll never leave you." Without another glance at Mayu, Mrs. Mansfield patted her daughter's hand as they left.

It was hard for Mayu to tear herself away, every step felt like it created a chasm between her and Skye, one she'd have to leap over if she ever wanted to go back.

Richard met them by the elevator and took Mayu's other arm. The ride was made in silence, Mayu stuck between her awkward chaperons. She bit her tongue to resist commenting on it and, since neither of them spoke to each other, she tried to remember any relevant details from the dreams with Skye, unwilling to play third-wheel.

They led her to one of the cafes where Fukushima sat waiting at a table. Momo had briefed them as best she could, so Mayu only had to fill in the gaps. Richard was already looking for plane tickets to Scotland.

"So, Fukushima, I need you to stay here and keep an eye on Skye. Make sure her mother doesn't do anything stupid to protect their secret."

"I'll do my best." Like a military general, he gave a firm nod. "But are you sure you should travel anywhere? This is only your fifth day of recovery. Are you still hallucinating?"

"I'm fine." But he was right, Mayu shouldn't be travelling. Her earlier energy had already seeped away with the adrenaline. "I don't feel great, I admit, but as a witness, it's important that I'm available for questioning. We need to act fast."

That only increased the concern on Fukushima's face.

"I've got tickets," said Richard, "but we have to leave right now."

Fukushima grumbled under his breath and got up to personally help Mayu out of her chair. "Don't overdo it. We almost lost you once." Despite working together for years, it was always a surprise to remember that he was older than herself, because they treated each other as equals. But she saw the twenty years that separated them now. Specifically, she saw the fatherly concern behind his glasses and Mayu swallowed the sudden lump in her throat.

"Try not to worry," she replied, "it really makes you age faster."

A smile twitched at his mouth.

Half an hour later, they were racing through the airport. Momo carefully mopped Mayu's sweating brow with tissues, Richard held her tight as if guiding a tired partner, concerned that she shouldn't look unsafe to travel. The flight itself was cramped but short and Mayu slept on Momo's shoulder.

On arrival, she felt light-headed and weak, as if all her limbs had turned to rubber, and her vision swirled. Richard shielded her from view and waited until most people had disembarked. With some effort, and Momo's help, Mayu was up and edged into the aisle. "You've got to hang in there a bit longer or customs will pull us aside, alright? Fight through it. We're almost there now." Richard placed a comforting hand on her back. "You can do this, just think about Skye."

Mayu nodded.

"Is everything alright?" asked a flight attendant.

"Yes, thank you." Richard flashed his best smile. "She

just has a massive phobia of flying. How're you feeling, honey?" He looked back at Mayu. "Let's get some fresh air."

Mayu nodded again and smiled at the attendant, mumbling an apology.

At Customs, the official glared at Mayu for an agonising minute, as if her photo had been taped under the desk with the word 'wanted' in bold font. She'd gone pasty and was struggling to control frequent shivers. She managed to answer his questions and he let her through.

Fifteen minutes later she was slumped on the backseat of a hire car. Richard drove while Momo discussed the plan and what they should say. "We might still get there before Skye's father," she said. "Her locker will require a key, right? Let's hope he took a detour home to find it."

Mayu loosened her seatbelt and lay across the seats, too tired to contribute to the plan. She'd wing it when they arrived. As soon as she shut her eyes, she saw Skye reaching for her, asking her to stay. But she couldn't think about Skye, she needed to rest. Instead, Mayu imagined herself curled up on her grandmother's couch with Yūta squeezed in behind her, holding her close, their gentle breathing almost in rhythm. She was barely aware of Richard and Momo's voices, the tone changing from conversational to heated discussion.

"Maybe I'm afraid of moving somewhere totally new," Momo hissed. "Maybe I'm terrified of being alone in Germany, where I don't speak the language. Just maybe, Richard, I'm comfortable where I am."

"And now that we've got nothing left?"

Mayu drifted again in the silence that followed.

"If you cared about me you wouldn't make that choice for me."

"I'm sorry." Richard sounded miserable. "I'm so sorry." After another tense pause, he spoke first. "I like you, Momo. Thinking of you leaving…it honestly…I hate it. I thought I was doing that in your best interest, because really, that's all I want for you; the best. I just…can I ever make it up to you?"

Another long silence passed, and Mayu slept. The stillness woke her.

Bleary eyed and exhausted, Mayu heard both the front doors open and close. A moment later, the back doors opened and Richard pushed her into a sitting position, while Momo pulled from the other side.

"I'm heading into the police station," Richard explained. "I'll do my best to tell them what's going on but the rest is up to you two. The school is about twenty minutes away. If Mr. Mansfield has already arrived, delay him however you can." He tapped Mayu's cheek as if to rouse her a little. "Don't do anything stupid, you got it? Mochi, keep her in line." They straightened her seatbelt and left her in the backseat. Before Momo got behind the wheel, Richard pulled her into a hug. She even held him back.

Only once the ignition was running and Momo was pulling out of the parking lot did Mayu think to say, "Do you know the way to the school, *Mochi*?" Despite the weary shadows under Momo's eyes, her spark had reappeared. "Yes, *honey*, don't worry." Mayu relaxed and watched out the window. Further out of town, the buildings vanished between forested hillsides and valleys of grass.

They turned onto a long, smooth driveway. As the grounds expanded on either side of them, Momo cast her a look in the rear-view mirror. Mayu blinked hard and opened her eyes wide, fighting to shake off an exhausted trance. Lush green fields stretched towards the most isolated and imposing building she'd seen in a long while. It was built from grey stone, the roof sloped and pointed at intervals, shingled in black and green tiles. One side looked like the square end of a castle with turrets crowning each corner. In the centre were a set of solid oak entrance doors.

Kids in uniform crossed the courtyard and there was a game of rugby going on in the playing field. Checking the dashboard clock, it said four o'clock. She didn't know how the days were structured in a boarding school, but she prayed they could quickly locate staff to help them.

Momo parked and helped her out of the car. She'd followed Skye into a pseudo version of this place once before, so headed straight for the oak doors.

Inside, the receptionist straightened at her desk, her big brown eyes assessing them with both alarm and curiosity. "Can I help you?" Compared to the historic appearance of the building's exterior, the furnishings inside were sleek. The desk countertop was made of frosted glass and curved around the receptionist in a horseshoe shape. A digital tablet faced visitors, displaying the options 'sign in' for visitors or the staff. Photos of students hung on the walls, printed onto large canvases, making the space feel almost like an exhibition.

Mayu shook Momo off her arm and pulled her wallet from her pocket. "We need to speak with the head teacher urgently." Hoping to look professional, Mayu held up her

ID card from work. "It's relates to the safety of one of your students."

"I see. Then…I'll pass it onto the headteacher. What is the name of the student?"

"Skye Mansfield. Can we see the headteacher ourselves, please?"

"She's busy with someone at the moment. Can I take your contact details?"

A sickening tension started tripping Mayu's heart.

"No, we have to see her now."

The receptionist tapped at her computer. She frowned. "Miss Mansfield hasn't been at school since—"

"The police are on their way," Mayu snapped. "Please tell the headteacher this can't wait."

The woman behind the desk folded her arms. "Why don't we wait for the police to arrive, then, and you can all go in together."

Shaking, no matter how hard she tried not to, Mayu pressed her hands flat onto the desk. She didn't feel good about forcing the issue but what if Mr Mansfield was the person already with the headteacher? "We have reason to believe that someone who poses a danger to you and your students is on their way here right now. If you don't take me to the headteacher immediately, you will have to answer for whatever happens."

As if to emphasise the threat, Momo folded her own arms, braced tall, chin raised and expression severe, despite her pretty features and pink dye.

Scowling, her body language signalling her annoyance with every movement, the receptionist flicked a setting on her headset and spoke to the headteacher. She briefly relayed the situation to her boss.

"Follow me," she said, dropping her hand from her ear and standing from the desk.

They were taken down stone corridors Mayu half recognised. Their guide knocked on a door a short distance down the hallway and a woman inside called, "Come in."

The door opened, and Mayu felt needles erupt under her skin as Mr. Mansfield turned to look at her.

30

THE RECEPTIONIST LEFT but didn't close the door, leaving Mayu's back feeling exposed, especially under Mr. Mansfield's harsh gaze. He stood from the armchair he'd occupied opposite the headteacher. Mayu fought not to ask if she could sit there instead.

Momo stood close, placing a discreet hand on her lower back as a gesture of support.

"What are *you* doing here?" sniped Mr. Mansfield. "Shouldn't you be in hospital?"

The headteacher stood as well. She had a long, brown plait coiling over her shoulder, and a fringe that had started growing into her eyes. Dressed in a cream shirt and grey trousers, she fit perfectly with the school's colour theme. Karate trophy shields hung on the wall behind her along with framed newspaper clippings about the school and its martial arts competition winners, with photos of the girls in their white karate suits, the headteacher standing proudly beside them in a white uniform of her own.

"My receptionist tells me these women have relevant safety information regarding your daughter," the woman said. "Do you know each other?"

"Yes." Mr. Mansfield dug his fingers into the back of

his armchair. "They recently brought my daughter out of her coma. Except *she* should be recovering alongside her. What delusions do you have regarding Skye's safety to bring you all this way? *She* is safely in hospital."

Mayu read the nameplate on the headteacher's desk and took a deep breath. "Headteacher Douglass, I'm sorry to burst in like this. Please forgive us but I believe Mr. Mansfield and his wife have involved their daughter in a serious crime. The evidence is hidden—"

"How dare you!" interrupted Mr. Mansfield.

The shakes hit Mayu in the legs. She'd already done too much today. The room had a watery haze at the edges and a shadow in the corner had a grinning face that she couldn't blink away.

"Are you here to accuse me of being a threat to my daughter? You have no right to—"

"Mr. Mansfield!" The headteacher's voice cracked like a whip. "Let her finish."

"No! I will not stand here and listen to some woman accuse me of anything because she saw it in a dream!"

"What are you talking about?" Douglass came round to the front of her desk and folded her arms. She had sharp eyes, the kind that analysed every hair on a student's head and plucked the truth right out from the roots.

A wicked breathlessness hit Mayu then. She gasped and placed a hand over her chest, feeling the irregular rhythm try to correct itself. Douglass unfolded her arms.

"Are you alright?" She dragged the armchair away from Mr. Mansfield and across the small office. "Sit down."

The prickling heat under Mayu's skin only intensified

as she sat. Momo crouched beside the chair to check her pulse and temperature.

"This woman is a doctor," said Mr. Mansfield. "She created a dream world that somehow woke Skye from her coma. The two of them have been recovering. You shouldn't be out of bed, Ms Shirakawa. It's clearly doing you no good. Now," he squared his shoulders before the headteacher, "I'm going to collect Skye's phone from her locker. Thank you."

"No!" cried Mayu.

Momo jumped up in her place and snatched his arm.

"Get off me." He jerked his arm free. Momo stood in front of the door to block it off.

"Wait there, Mr. Mansfield," said Douglass. "Skye's phone can wait a few more minutes. The locker is hers until she graduates from Faragreen, it's not *going* anywhere."

"Well, I can't wait. These two may no longer have a business to return to but some of us don't have that luxury."

Until that moment, Mayu hadn't actually hated him. She'd almost empathised that his 'friend', Fabio, had put him in a horrible position. But to refer to the disaster, still haunting Tokyo and half of Japan, as if they were somehow fortunate; she loathed every speck of him. Darkness crept in from the corners of the room, the leering shadow stretching tall over Mr. Mansfield's head. Its grin split wider, revealing sharp canines.

"How dare you," growled Momo. She looked at the headteacher. "He's a diamond thief. One of the world's most valuable necklaces is hidden in Skye's locker. Our colleague is with the police now. Call them and convince them to get over here and—"

Mr. Mansfield pushed Momo aside and ran out of the office.

"Mr. Mansfield!" bellowed Douglass. She seized the phone on her desk and rang for the police.

Momo recovered and sprinted after him.

Still fighting to control the stutter in her chest, Mayu heaved herself onto her feet.

"No," said Douglass, stopping mid-sentence in making her emergency request, "you stay here."

"Just get the police," Mayu wheezed.

She stumbled into the corridor, willing herself to fly down the hallway like in a dream. To the left, she caught sight of Momo's legs disappearing around the corner in pursuit. What if Mr. Mansfield hurt her? One hand on the wall, Mayu jogged like a drunkard after them. Sweat beaded thick on her forehead, and in a blink, the corridors vanished. Never ending blackness stretched as far as she could see and water splashed under her feet. Was she drowning? Always water, like her lungs were filled with it.

"We need you, Mayu." The last of her breath skittered away at the sight of Tomoya. He held his arms open, and she shuffled towards him. She'd barely taken a few steps when he exploded into a thousand fragments and Skye came charging towards her, blue light pinging to life like fireflies beneath the girl's footfalls.

She flung her arms around Mayu's waist. "Leave her alone!"

Light dappled around her, and in another blink, Mayu stood at the end of the school corridor. Tomoya and Skye gone. The solid feeling of stonework under her fingers. She heard shouting nearby. Taking an angry breath, Mayu thought about Skye, focused on that feeling of holding onto her, of making this right, like she'd promised. Letting go of the wall, she ran towards the shouting, pushing past the sensation that everything was swaying. Students backed out of her path, while others flocked towards the commotion.

"Move aside!" Mayu shouted. "I said move!" The kids nearest obeyed without question.

To her credit, despite their weight difference, Momo was putting up a good effort to drag Mr. Mansfield away from Skye's locker, but his elbow connected with her mouth and sent her reeling. He paused, realising what he'd done and aware of the people gathering to watch.

He spotted Mayu and paused to straighten his jacket and tie, then dived back to the locker, jamming the key into the lock. Mayu charged at him, instantly deflected by a solid shove. She hit the floor and felt it spinning out of control beneath her. But Momo was there, caressing her face, shocked to see blood on her friend's teeth.

"Stop him!" Mayu breathed.

"Everyone, out of the way!" Headteacher Douglass parted the audience like she could command mountains to move. In a few strides, she came upon Mr. Mansfield, hooked his arm behind his back and had him face down on the floor. "Mr. Callaghan, get everyone to their classrooms."

Another teacher's voice rang out, following her orders without hesitation.

Mayu saw the headteacher touch her ear. "Gilly, I need a first aider at B Classroom."

As she spoke, another teacher rushed forward to help

Douglass pin Skye's father to the floor. He writhed beneath them, shouting protests and threats about his lawyer.

Minutes passed in a haze as someone came to help Momo sit Mayu against the wall. Only when Richard appeared, bringing with him a wave of people in navy uniform, did she rouse. Officers arrested Mr. Mansfield, another two came to check on Mayu and Momo, while the remaining officer looked inside Skye's locker. He pulled out a P.E. bag from the depths. As he opened it, a rainbow of light reflected out and illuminated his face.

31

"DO YOU DENY allegations of child neglect and emotional trauma?" asked the Prosecutor, Miss Capello, from her bench. She had a loud, emphatic way of speaking. Whenever she turned her head to look at the jury, Mayu could see blonde cropped hair beneath the woman's white wig. "Do you deny ever being violent towards her? Do you, Mr. Mansfield, deny ignoring your daughter's medical conditions for years by moving her to Faragreen Boarding Academy, where you didn't have to deal with them?"

"I resent such questions! I would never hurt her," snapped Mr. Mansfield, his eyes bulging and blinking fast from stress and sleep deprivation. "Have you done any research? Do you know how much it costs to send her to that school? Have you ever had to live with someone who's got cataplexy and narcolepsy? It involves a constant and excessive need for attention. We couldn't manage our business with Skye at home, so we sent her to a prestigious school where someone could monitor her full time. We work hard to send her to that school—somewhere that *can* help her; they give great support. We wanted her to have a normal life and to learn to cope in the real world."

"So you sent her to an isolated community where all her peers know that Skye has to use the bathroom with an adult standing in the open doorway?"

Mayu got chills of satisfaction from the Prosecutor's condescending tone.

"You sound like you hold a personal grudge against boarding schools," sneered Mr. Mansfield. He smoothed his palm against his head, flattening an imaginary tuft of hair. "What are you implying? That Skye gets teased? We all get teased. Skye is treated with dignity, and if nothing else, you've highlighted how much attention she does need. Yes, despite her age, she does still need to be monitored twenty-four seven! She needs help and we have provided the best for her. Twist it however you want, Miss Capello, but the truth is we love our daughter and we've tried to give her the best."

"I see." Miss Capello paused to flick through her folder of paperwork, white wig bobbing as she scanned to-and-fro.

Mr. Mansfield's Defence, a man called Mr. Young, half rose from his chair and piped up, "Your Honour, I don't see what this has to do with an investigation into alleged robbery. I'd like to call someone else forward."

"Its relevance," replied Miss Capello, "is that Mr. Mansfield is an aggressive and calculating individual, even when it comes to his own child. Although our main witness saw events occurring in a dream, this is backed by the evidence of blood in the Mansfields' attic that doesn't belong to any household occupant." Slapping one hand on her folder, Miss Capello returned her searing attention to Mr. Mansfield. "You and your wife worked together to steal the world's most valuable diamond. You didn't provide dream therapy to wake your daughter from her coma out of love, you wanted to be able to ask Skye where she'd hidden the necklace from you, isn't that so?"

A grimace bent Mr. Mansfield's mouth into an ugly shape, as if wounded at the suggestion. "We wanted our daughter back, nothing else. We've got no reason to steal anything. We've been framed—down to the last drop of blood!"

"Except you struggled *very* hard to stop Doctor Shirakawa from getting to Skye's locker, where the necklace was found. You even injured Doctor Kuramochi in the struggle as she, quote, 'tried to stop you from taking the evidence.'" Miss Capello raised her brows at the jury, as if standing on a theatrical stage and not before the Crown Court.

"That was an accident." Mr. Mansfield's hand fumbled for something to cling to, but the witness stand had low walls and offered no support. "She was attacking *me*. It disturbed me that they were trying to break into my girl's locker—they were like women possessed. It was self-defence! My daughter asked for her diary and I was assured that Skye's belongings were still in her locker. We wanted things to be left the same until she had recovered, so the headteacher agreed to leave her locker and wardrobe assigned to her until after her expected graduation date. That's why I was there."

Licking her lips, Miss Capello did not look convinced. "You went to get Skye's diary?"

"Yes."

"Not her phone?"

"I—her phone, too."

"I see." Miss Capello pursed her lips for a moment. "Who do you think put the diamond necklace in her locker then, Mr. Mansfield?"

His Adam's apple bobbed, his face the perfect picture of stony indifference. "I don't know. But I'd guess Ms Shirakawa is in on it."

Miss Capello coolly conceded she was done questioning Mr. Mansfield, *for now*, and settled down onto the hard wooden bench. Mayu's palms sweated as her eyes met Mr. Mansfield's, the faintest smirk touching his lips. Straightening his shoulders, he left the stand with all the outward confidence a winner should possess. Court officials escorted him back to the defendants' box at the back of the room, where he joined his wife behind a wall of clear plastic.

On the front bench, the Defence got to his feet. "I'd like to call forward Doctor Mayu Shirakawa." Her mouth went dry, her stomach leapt, and the thumping of her heart made it hard to concentrate. She barely recognised Momo's voice beside her as she offered a murmur of encouragement. Wobbling to her feet, Mayu made it to the witness stand without tripping and met the Defence Barrister's hard gaze.

"So," he said, "in your statement, you say that Skye revealed to you that the necklace was in her school locker. But that's not the whole truth, is it?"

Mayu clenched her hands, hoping it would hide her shaking.

"Did you deduce the whole thing from a dream?"

"Although I had suspicions after a dream, Skye confirmed them once we were both conscious."

The Defence pointed to a line of text in his folder and read out, "'As a Dream Guide, it's your responsibility to control the world around you and your patient; to manipulate the patient's brainwaves into seeing your dream creations.' Is that true?"

"Yes." Mayu was glad she had a microphone; she couldn't speak above a whisper. "When connected to the Morpheus machine and the patient, you share your dreams with them, it's like entering another world." Taking a deep breath, she fought to strengthen her voice. "I could ask you, 'How do you know you are awake now?' If your worst nightmares appeared here, in this room, you would have to admit they were real. The dreams we share seem real, as if you are awake. Nightmares have to be controlled or they would be so frightening the fear might cause the patient a seizure, or a heart attack. I had to keep Skye's fears from surfacing."

"And what does Skye fear?"

Mayu raised her chin, daring to meet Mr. and Mrs. Mansfield's cold stares. "Her father. He was constantly a figure of terror in the dream world we shared. Hunting us." He had the audacity to look surprised. Mrs. Mansfield shook her head, savaging her bottom lip as if to contain her outrage.

"Do you deny having met with the Mansfields' previous business partner, Fabio Socratous, before Skye's surgery?"

It wasn't the question she'd been expecting. Blinking, Mayu fought to translate the words and rearrange them. "I never met him."

Pointing with his pen, the Defence said, "Did you not fabricate the whole ordeal to create a witness out of

Skye, so that Mr. Socratous could plant the necklace and destroy the Mansfields' business? They refused to help him sell counterfeit diamonds, they threatened to expose him, but now he's vanished into thin air and suddenly the Mansfields are accused of theft. You saw their alleged crime all in a dream, isn't that convenient? The only other witness is one you've had mind-control over for two weeks."

"N-no!" How could anyone believe that? But when he said it with such conviction, it sounded like a possibility even to her ears. "I don't know who Fabio is. I've only heard him talking on the phone to Mr. Mansfield—on speaker. Fabio spoke to Skye and said, 'You've taken something valuable from me—a beautiful necklace. If you tell me where it is I'll forgive you, if you don't, someone will get hurt.' He threatened Skye into telling her parents where she hid the necklace."

"But Mr. Socratous paid for Skye's treatment." The Defence shrugged and shook his head. "How could you not know him before coming to the UK? Was he paying you to frame Mr. Mansfield for theft?"

A shake entered Mayu's voice, the thudding of her heart interrupting every other bodily function. "I didn't know he was paying for the treatment, not until I met the Mansfields. Their name is on all the bills."

If lions could speak, perhaps they would sound like the Defence Barrister, as if, with his fierce smile and cold tone, he was sure he would have Mayu for dinner. Maybe she'd dream about it later that night.

"So how, from a dream," he pressed, "did you accurately deduce a crime, down to the very last detail? What reason could Mr. and Mrs. Mansfield have for stealing when they have a well-established business and international recognition?"

"I don't know their motive," whispered Mayu, starting to hope she'd throw-up just for an excuse to stop the questioning. "I don't know why they'd do it. But what I saw was real. Maybe using 'dream' is the wrong word." She glanced at Momo, seeking courage from her. Her friend managed a smile. "You say 'dream' and to you it means 'fake', or 'illusion'. But dreams don't fall out of the clouds; they come from our minds. And, like I said, Parallel Dreams are so real you wouldn't know the difference if you were in one right now. We make dreams from our experiences. Skye showed me hers."

The Defence sighed, as if tired of her dodging some obvious answer. He pointed at his notes again. "Aren't your experiences also a cause for concern?" When he didn't elaborate, Mayu had to suck her tongue to loosen it.

"I don't understand."

"Well, according to your records and your colleagues, you are also susceptible to nightmares and to being influenced by your experiences. By combining your dreams with Skye's, did you fabricated the whole thing and create a story that even you believed? That way, you absolved yourself from being involved with Mr. Socratous by no longer remembering it. Could you not distort the truth and change what you believe?"

Mayu glanced at the Prosecutor. She'd spent long hours with Miss Capello talking about what she might be asked and what she should reply. But the woman's lips only thinned, she couldn't do anything for Mayu right now.

"No, that's not possible," Mayu replied. "We've got no reason to think it."

"Except," said the Defence, making Mayu's heart sink, "your colleague helps a company called Halcyon, who work on PTSD patients to convince them that their fears can no longer control them. Is that not the same principle? Altering their reality to make them see and feel differently, to disconnect from the events that really happened to them?"

"No. Not at all! It's therapy, not day-to-day mind-control. When you're not dreaming anymore, the world is…" She paused. Hallucinations could be considered dangerous and manipulative—making someone unreliable. Mayu wiped the sweat off her palms onto her trousers. "The world is too real to ignore. Being awake does feel different from dreaming, but you only notice that when you're awake. We can't control people. We can only influence…" Dammit, this was a disaster. "We can influence what they believe, sure, but we can't make the patient accept it right away, that takes more time."

The Defence raised his eyebrows, a picture of innocence. "Two weeks, perhaps?"

Mayu gritted her teeth. "No. It takes months."

"As does preparing to be someone's Dream Guide, does it not?"

Pressure built up behind Mayu's eyes. She dared a glance at Mr. Mansfield in his plastic booth. His smug face churned her insides to paste.

"It does," Mayu conceded.

32

MISS CAPELLO TUGGED off her wig and wrung it in her hands. "Why didn't you tell me that Parallel Dreams can ultimately change the way you think and feel?"

Alone with the Prosecutor in her interview room, Mayu finally felt able to breathe. She went straight for the couch beneath the misted windows and collapsed. "Because we don't do that!" Not really, not Mayu's team. She dug her fingers into the creased cushion beneath her, bouncing her heels against the worn grey carpet. "Maybe Halcyon do something like it, but we don't. That's not how our project works."

"But is it possible?" The question loomed as tall as Miss Capello, who stood motionless, expression grim. "Could you brainwash yourself?"

Mayu shook her head. That was delusional. And yet, why couldn't she remember even a few events from her life before accepting Skye's case? What had she worked on? Who had she spoken to? Tingles crawled down her arms as the simplicity of it all trickled back to her in glimpses of early morning light and mouldy teapots. "I…spent a whole month doing nothing. Before Skye's case, I mean."

"What do you mean?"

"I barely spoke to anyone." Mayu played with her wedding ring, watched the light bounce across the tiny diamonds. "You can check my emails, my phone—I only spoke to colleagues and friends, but barely. I…I don't think I left my apartment."

They were quiet a moment, listening to the ping and clink from the nearby radiator. It made the room smell of warm dust. Mayu kept her eyes averted, aware of Miss Capello studying her; trying to read her story from the cut of her fringe to the ring on her finger.

"How long ago did he die?"

"Almost four months ago now." It already felt like a year, time having blurred and stretched over the past three weeks between dreaming and recovery. If only her grief had dulled too.

"I'm sorry." Miss Capello slumped into a chair at the table and drummed her pen against her notes. Her voice no less kind, she said, "We need another angle. If you'll let me, I'll use the fact that you were too grief-stricken to be plotting fraud."

Mayu nodded consent, before remembering it had to be given verbally. "Okay."

Miss Capello stared at the wall as if it had answers, her eyes darting across the scuff-marks and chipped cream paint, before asking, "Are you sure you don't remember any names? From the dreams?"

"None, I'm sorry." The dreams were hazier day by day. Mayu would never admit it out loud, but she only remem-bered half her story because she'd repeated it so often.

Seeing the images was harder than ever, the details had gone. *Had* she invented the whole thing?

Being banned from seeing or speaking to Skye made it harder. If she could just get Skye to say she wasn't crazy…

"Look, I want to help you." Miss Capello leaned across her notes, not making her any closer to Mayu, but somehow it made the space between them feel smaller. "Unless Skye is deemed fit to appear in the witness stand, we've got no one else to testify. We should have an ID on the blood found in their attic later today, but we still have to locate the guy."

"Can't you see if they've sold stolen diamonds before?"

"We need something easier than that." Sighing, Miss Capello massaged her forehead, stretching the lines around her eyes. "Money usually talks." She scribbled a few words into her folder. "I'm waiting to see what their bank accounts tell us. Maybe that'll clear some of the smog."

The word sank deep in connection with the Mansfields. Mayu frowned.

"What is it?"

"Will you be checking their charity business too?"

Miss Capello tilted her head. "Why?"

"They make smog-glass by compressing carbon from the atmosphere. They use it in jewellery or giftware. They say all profits go toward environmental causes."

"Do they now?" Miss Capello chewed her pen, eyes sparking. "I'll double-check."

❧

She met Momo at a coffee shop in Southwark, a few minutes from the court. It had got colder in the few weeks since their arrival in the UK, with less crisp sunlight and more rain. Everything was washed in it. She tugged her woolly cap tighter over her ears, already shivering, and refused to sit at the table with her friend.

"Do we have to sit outside?" she grumbled, accepting the paper cup from Momo.

"I thought it was nicer out here that's all…" Momo peered up at the arched roof that protected the shopping avenue from rain, but not from the wind blowing in off the Thames nearby.

Sparing one longing look for the warm yellow lights inside the café, Mayu dragged out a chair and sat, too tired to protest. Besides, Momo must have hit 'call' as soon as Mayu approached, because her phone chirped with a dialling tone. Just as Mayu settled into her seat, Richard's face appeared on vid-call, and they greeted him in unison, Momo waving.

"How was your flight? Did everything go okay?" asked Momo.

"All good. No complications." Richard pushed a hand into his hair and yawned. His image froze and unfroze, bouncing with the rhythm of his footfalls. Streetlamps passed above his head, making shadows flicker across his features. "Staff met us at Matsumoto airport and took us straight to the hospital. Matokai is safe and sound, his condition didn't fluctuate much."

"Thank goodness." Mayu's entire body sagged with relief, as if Richard had cut a piece of string that had been holding her taught all day. But the feeling sputtered out just as quickly. She clenched the paper coffee cup in her hands, noting the subtle smell of vanilla. How many years of Matokai's life would disappear before they could help him?

"Where are you now?" Momo fidgeted with her black scarf, bits of pink hair poking out the bottom of her cap. "It's midnight there, isn't it?"

"Yeah. I'm still in Matsumoto. I found a cheap room for a couple of days, just until I can check the state of my home, but when Obinata gets here I can stay with him. Apparently, his family have a summer home somewhere close by." He sniffed and tugged up the collar of his coat. "It's icy for September. What about you, how's the trial?"

The only response Mayu could muster was a hefty sigh. Momo watched, waiting for her to speak, until the silence stretched into awkward.

"They're spinning an angle that Mayu hypnotised herself during the dream to forget that she helped Fabio frame the Mansfield's."

Richard stopped walking. "What? That's crazy!"
"We shouldn't talk about it," Mayu grumbled. Closing her eyes, she finally took a long draught of her flavoured coffee. The sweetness flowed across her tongue and warmed her face; soothing. Forcing a smile, she looked into the camera. "They've got no evidence. It'll be fine."

Momo cupped her face in her hands, downcast. "But neither have we."

❧

The next day, the barristers briefly questioned one of the guests who had attended the Mansfield's infamous party, used as a smokescreen to conceal the presence of the diamond courier at their house. But this potential witness insisted that he hadn't noticed anyone or anything suspicious.

The court then called on Mrs. Mansfield to give evidence. She had taken care to apply her make-up and wore a homely faded purple sweater, the stitching loose with age. Mayu noticed that, unlike on previous occasions, she wasn't wearing much jewellery, just a faint glint of silver in her ears. It gave the overall appearance of someone cosy and well-kept, and Mayu couldn't stop herself from thinking it was a strategic outfit.

"You have a charity called Clear Skies," said Miss Capello, hands on her hips. "Do all the profits earned go to environmental protection agencies?"

"Yes, they do. It's our desire to balance out the damage caused to the world by diamond mining. It's like the Yin to our Yang." Mrs. Mansfield beamed at her joke, but Miss Capello did not look warmed by it.

"So, you take none of the money? It goes directly to fifteen different agencies?"

"Most of it, yes. We keep one percent to cover the running costs of Clear Skies." Mrs. Mansfield shrugged like that was obvious. "The condenser towers need specialised maintenance, amongst other costs."

Miss Capello's sour smile turned predatory. "When this case first opened, I asked for copies of your bank statements," said Miss Capello. "Did you also bring copies with you, as requested?"

If Mayu hadn't been watching so intently she might have missed the twitch in Mrs. Mansfield's jaw. An usher approached the witness stand and took the bank statements from her. No one spoke as Miss Capello compared the copies side by side.

"This year, two lump sums of ten thousand pounds appeared in your business account. One in February and one in May; a total of twenty-thousand pounds. You'll find it in your handouts," Miss Capello added to the jury, who began flipping through booklets of paper. "The identity of the sender, however, is given only as an eight-digit number. Who sent you such a generous sum?"

The muscles in Mrs. Mansfield's neck flickered as she swallowed. "It was Fabio. He wanted to invest with us in Sierra Leone, production at a mine there has been very successful."

"Wait, so the money was to be invested on his behalf?"

"Correct. He didn't like to get his hands dirty."

Mayu rolled her eyes and Momo nudged her arm.

"That's odd, because I've looked at the Clear Skies transaction reports. On the version you have just given me, it puts the total sum of money in the charity's account during January at forty-five-thousand pounds. However, on the copy sent to me by your bank, the total is sixty-five thousand: a difference of twenty-thousand. I'll ask you again. Where did the twenty-thousand pounds in your business account come from?"

No more smiles. Mrs. Mansfield looked pale. "It was from Fabio. He's hard to trace, as you've probably noticed."

"Why is twenty-thousand missing from the charity's report that you've just provided?"

Chest rising and falling, Mrs. Mansfield looked flustered. She said nothing.

"Have you just lied to me?" Miss Capello gripped her

lectern and leant forward. "Did you alter the charity's records to make it look like it had taken less than it really had?" She held up one of the papers the usher had handed over. "This isn't a print off directly from the bank. This is from a register in one of your gift shops, which are easily altered."

"There must be a mistake." Mrs. Mansfield shook her head. "Our manager may have put in the wrong number, or altered it. We're being framed."

"Well, someone's lying!" Miss Capello threw the statements onto her bench. "How can twenty-thousand be reported as going into the charity account, by the bank themselves, and then twenty-thousand go missing—the same figure as ends up in your own profits? Why take money and lie about it?"

"We didn't!"

Laughing, Miss Capello raised her hands, in a gesture of incredulity. "These documents show that the charity paid out twenty-thousand pounds to a mysterious account. Just like the mysterious transaction paid into your profits. Is it an offshore bank account? Are you struggling to pay back loans, your taxes, or to keep your business going? Is that why you colluded to steal the world's most valuable diamond?"

"That diamond was planted! We did nothing—"

"You took twenty-thousand pounds out of your charity fund, set up to support environmental agencies—you took it as tax-free profit and spent it on diamond mining in Sierra Leone." Miss Capello paused to savour the silence in the room. The Defence, Mr. Young, looked mortified. "You looked at the devastation caused to the world and it wasn't the chance to make amends that you sought—to 'provide the Yin to your Yang'—but the chance to make money off the world's suffering. You then took that money, money spent by people to *help* the environment, and you and your husband threw it down a mine." Running her tongue over her teeth, hands on her hips again, Miss Capello shook her head like she couldn't bear to look at Mrs. Mansfield for a moment longer. "If we care for our world so little, maybe we deserve it to turn against us."

As she resumed her seat on the bench, Momo grabbed Mayu's hand and shook it. They smiled at each other.

With some apparent effort, Mr. Young got to his feet. "It seems we might have to open another case under new circumstances. However." He shot a glance at Miss Capello. "Laundering tax-free money from Clear Skies does not prove whether or not my clients are guilty of stealing the *L'Incomparable*. It was stolen by armed robbers in Madrid where the necklace was on show. We still don't know how or why it ended up in their daughter's locker. Our only lead was provided by Dr. Shirakawa based on scenes she saw in a dream, this does not amount to evidence. It is still possible that Dr. Shirakawa worked with Fabio Socratous to invent the whole story. She's desperate for sponsors to keep her business running, is she not?"

Miss Capello stood up like she'd been dragged there, exasperated. "Misleading, my Lord. There are no monetary links between Dr. Shirakawa and Fabio Socratous. The Mansfields have been shown to have falsified their accounts. What else are they lying about?"

With that, she thumped back down and folded her arms.

"Indeed," said the judge. "Court is adjourned for an hour."

33

WHEN COURT RESUMED, Momo was called to the stand. Dressed in one of her suits, the collar and pockets of her jacket trimmed in azure blue, she looked both striking and professional. Shoulders back and pinching her fingertips, Momo stood ready for the barristers' cross-examination.

The Mansfield's' Defence readied his questions first. "In recent years, you have been at the forefront of developing technology that can affect the brain as it sleeps. Can you explain that a little more for us?"

Momo raised her chin. "Yes. I have worked on the detection of nightmares or stress in coma patients. These patients' brains don't fire signals like regular people, so we can't know how they're feeling. But our Morpheus machine acts as a gateway between the patient and the Guide, it connects them. The Guide then acts as a mirror of the patient. The fusion of their bioelectric signals and chemistry can be read. The patient's brain patterns can be assessed by those of the Guide, so we can now detect when the patient is scared or stressed. It's like turning two people into one mind.

"When we detect signs of fear or stress, the dose of

certain drugs that we developed can be increased to coun-
teract the chemicals firing in the brain, or we can stimulate
certain areas of the brain with electro-therapy."

Mr. Young lifted a piece of paper from his notes.
"You've been working with Halcyon. They buy these drugs
and you provide training on how to use them."

"Yes."

"For the past two and a half months, you've also been
acting as their consultant on the manipulation of a patient's
thoughts and feelings, isn't that so?"

"We work with people on their projects, Halcyon
patients are—"

He cut her off by slapping the paper onto his open
folder. "You're also working on the manipulation of dreams
and whether it's possible to translate them into images so
that the brain could become some kind of TV soap on a
screen."

"That is being researched, yes, but it's not currently
possible." Momo tugged at the bottom of her jacket and
held it taught. Mayu wanted to leap over the gallery bench
and shout 'enough'. This was an irrelevant line of questioning, but she feared where it was headed.

"But you are involved in viewing and controlling a
patient's dreams?"

"No, that's not possible!" Momo's voice went up an
octave.

Mayu's heart fluttered when Miss Capello jerked to her
feet. "Why are we interrogating the witness on technologi-
cal speculation?" she asked the judge. "There is no current
ability to see what anyone dreams and no way to control
what a patient dreams. Not unless you're hooked up to the

Morpheus. Mr. Young is suggesting the impossible: that an observer can control thoughts."

The judge nodded his head in agreement and Miss Capello sat down again.

Mr. Young cleared his throat. "You have said that you can affect the patient's brain though. So answer me, Momo, for clarity: can you manipulate a patient's feelings and beliefs, or not? Isn't that what they're trying to do at Halcyon?"

"No." It looked as if Momo was trying not to grit her teeth. "I can stop the brain from entering shock, flight or fight. I can ease it into a feeling of calm. But I cannot tell it to love, to lie, or to feel happy. At Halcyon, the patients have suffered a different kind of metal trauma. Halcyon don't put people in comas, they create dreams that help patients with cathartic scenarios or just to help them sleep without pain. Their patients sign documents agreeing to their therapy and the results they want, which is normally to get back to their daily lives. They want to cope with invasive thoughts and feelings. No one is being mind-controlled. We can't do it with Parallel Dreams and we can't do it in PTSD therapy."

Mr. Young's cocky demeanour withered. Head bowed, he took his folder off the lectern and took his seat. Mayu let out a breath she didn't know she'd been holding.

Lips pressed tight, Miss Capello took over the questioning.

"Halcyon offered you a job recently. Why didn't you take it?"

Momo's gaze turned to the gallery and found Mayu, who felt just as interested in her answer. "I couldn't. I couldn't leave Mayu."

"Why?" The atmosphere in the court changed at the softness of Miss Capello's voice, like snow muffled everything after a bout of raging wind. Everyone waited as Momo chewed on her lips, her cheeks flushing pink as she struggled to control her emotions.

"She is not only my colleague, she is my best friend. She had recently lost her husband. I thought…I worried… about what she might do if I left…"

Everything started to spin. Mayu pressed a hand to her mouth, ashamed and yet deeply touched. All those times Momo had tried to hug her; when she had stood up for her even though she obviously wasn't pulling her weight at work; she had even tried to follow her into the bathroom when she could—she'd been worried. Mayu hadn't hidden it from her, like she'd wanted.

"What made you think that?"

Momo's brows furrowed as if she were pained, eyes on her fingertips. "I found a lot of painkillers in her apartment. Empty packets, like maybe she had taken too many. I realised I had to be wrong because she never went to hospital and she was still alive." Momo paused to suck in a deep breath. "But our colleague…he told me to keep an eye on her, that she'd said things to him that had made him concerned."

Mayu shut her eyes—she didn't want to see her best friend looking pained to admit these things. It had clearly hurt Momo that, despite their friendship, Mayu hadn't turned to her for help.

"What kind of things?" asked Miss Capello.

"I'm not sure what was said, he didn't want to betray her trust, but he said…he was afraid she felt suicidal."

Wanting to vanish and never reappear, Mayu's hand slid from her mouth to her eyes. She wanted to run away but didn't dare draw too much attention. The air felt thick but, having had plenty of practice over the last few months, Mayu let her mind cloud over. She let the room spiral into another world of reality, one that felt separate from the guilt and misery eating her alive, a world that didn't matter and couldn't touch her and that left her sitting like an empty shell.

"You've been friends with Mayu for a long time, haven't you?" said Miss Capello. Mayu opened her eyes, upset that she hadn't quite succeeded in cutting herself off from all that she felt. "You've been working with her for almost seven years?"

"Yes."

"You're someone who knows her best then. In your opinion, would you say that Mayu was too grief-stricken to be making elaborate plans to sabotage someone's diamond business?"

Momo looked back at Miss Capello, the emotions on her face regaining composure. "Absolutely. None of us even knew of the Mansfields until they requested our services. Even then, Mayu didn't want to work on the case. She had lost her husband in Parallel Dreams. She was terrified of doing it again."

Miss Capello smiled, both reassuring and victorious. "Thank you."

34

TWO THINGS HAPPENED within a matter of days to tip everything against the Mansfield's claim of being framed. First, the court cleared Mayu of any involvement in the theft of the *L'Incomparable* on account of poor mental health prior to Skye's treatment and afterwards. This meant that some part of her story had to be acknowledged as true, since she had no other way of knowing where the necklace had been hidden. Secondly, forensic results on the blood in the attic identified the victim, who confessed to being part of a network involved in smuggling the *L'Incomparable* from Madrid, and ultimately to the Mansfield's house on the night of the party.

With the evidence stacking up against the Mansfields, incriminating them in GBH, criminal conspiracy and handling stolen goods, evading tax, and breaking environmental laws, Mayu was told she could go home, and the jury found the Mansfields guilty. When the depth of the Mansfields' involvement was revealed, they were found to have stolen money from their charity to cover business losses. They had previously been handling stolen diamonds on a smaller scale with the intention, they claimed, to return this money but had only dug themselves into a deeper hole.

Their involvement with 'Fabio' and the *L'Incomparable* was 'meant to be their last false deal'.

Meanwhile, the case caused a media storm. Mayu's unusual involvement didn't go unnoticed; *Diamond Heist Solved in a Dream!* Despite the sensationalised headlines, they did attract some beneficial interest. The Parallel Dream Project received large donations for the reconstruction of their labs, while their local government created a charity to provide funds for their research.

It all happened so fast that, somehow, it seemed like months had passed since Mayu awoke from the precipice of fatal sleep. Checking her digital flight ticket one last time, she tucked her phone away and took the elevator to the children's ward. Shortly after Skye's parents were arrested, she'd been moved from her private room. Staff promised Mayu that she seemed much happier for the company of other children.

Trees and star-filled skies painted the walls. Storybook characters decorated the play area, where a few children were working at the activity table. Skye sat slumped in bed, watching the TV screen above them. Mayu crept into the girl's peripheral vision, afraid to find out if their friendship still held any glue. She shouldn't have worried. Like sunlight rising over the hill, Skye's eyes lit up at the sight of her.

"Mayu!" She reached for her, leaning forward to offer a hug. "How are you?"

"How am I?" What a question. Sitting on the bed, she kept a respectful distance and shook one of Skye's outstretched hands instead of accepting the hug. "I'm good. But you look better. You've recovered well."

Skye slumped again, shrugging. "Kind of. I get tired so easy and walking is still hard." Her words were a bit slurred too, but she had regained some weight and her hair had a healthy shine.

"You'll get there." Mayu knotted her fingers together in her lap, watched the way her own skin creased when she pulled at it. "I'm sorry I wasn't around to help."

"That's okay. It wasn't your fault."

Well, it kind of was, since Mayu had instigated the whole investigation. "You're not angry with me? I've basically sent your parents to jail."

Skye took a big breath and looked down at her own hands. "I'm not angry. You did the right thing. And I told you, they don't love me anyway."

"No, I think they do, they just don't know how to show you."

Another shrug. "Can I live with you now?"

"I'm afraid not." Although Mayu had considered asking to be her legal guardian. She'd told Momo, broken down in her friend's arms at the joy Skye had given her. But Momo had made her see reason. Not only did Mayu lack a stable income at present, her home was potentially uninhabitable, she lived on the other side of the world and, also, she wasn't in the right head space to be taking on a child. No one would consider her before Skye's blood relatives.

It hurt to say goodbye. She'd worked so hard for a life with Yūta and lost it. Now, she had to let go of that glimpse of another life with Skye.

"I think you'll be going to live with your mother's sister and her family."

"They're okay, I suppose." But Skye looked far from happy. "Why can't I live with you?"

'I want you to' was on the tip of Mayu's tongue, but she bit it back. What she wanted didn't matter, she'd only be making the moment harder for Skye. "The law says you have to go to your aunt."

One of the kids at the activity table shrieked with laughter, making them both cringe. Skye took a deep, juddering breath and took Mayu's hand.

"I'm sorry I upset you in the dreams," Skye said.

"I'm sorry I upset you too."

They smiled at each other.

"Skye, I have to go back to Japan today."

The smile vanished. Skye fought into a sitting position. "No, you can't go yet. You promised you'd stay until I got better. You can't go. Please."

"I know, I'm sorry."

Skye's eyes glistened as she scrabbled to get a hold of both of Mayu's arms, as if she could physically restrain her from leaving. "Please!"

"I will visit you. Here, keep this card, it has my number and email on it."

The girl took the business card with both hands like she'd been given a piece of treasure. She chewed on her lips, distraught, but swallowed hard to hold it all inside. If only Mayu could take her home, give her the love she needed.

"Goodbye for now." Mayu went to stroke Skye's hair, but the girl let out an almost inaudible cry and fell apart. She cried, it rushed up on her so hard she could hardly breathe and her distressed sobbing sounded like a tired, bleating animal. Before the girl could see the regret in Mayu's eyes, she broke the barrier between them and hugged Skye tight.

❧

A different kind of family greeted Mayu and Momo at Matsumoto airport. Not their parents, although Momo's only lived an hour away, but a few people who, in some ways, knew them better than family. The colleagues who had stayed up late with them at the office, when street lights had gone out and dinner had been an instant packet of ramen. Three friends who had devoted too many hours to work instead of being at home, forging something else, equally as precious.

Without saying hello, Momo rushed to Richard and wrapped him in her arms. He pulled her close, one hand stroking the back of her head as she buried into him. His laugh lines had deepened over the past few weeks, his youthful face looked haggard.

Averting her gaze, Mayu greeted Fukushima instead, overwhelmed with gratitude to see him there. It *felt* like coming home to a parent. Keiji hovered by his shoulder, a pillar of stone apart from the blithe tilt to his lips.

"Welcome home," Keiji said.

Mayu inclined her head, turning to Fukushima again. "It's good to be—"

Her Co-Director reached for her, arms outstretched, cutting her off with a gasp. Mayu couldn't remember whether she had ever hugged Fukushima before, but certainly never like this. He locked her in his arms, his breathing harsh in her ear.

"What's wrong?" Mayu peered at Keiji, hoping he'd give her a clue.

"I'm just glad you're okay." Fukushima sounded strained.

"Well, of course… It was only a trial. They couldn't put me in prison."

"I know."

Keiji didn't mouth anything, but his frown showed empathy, his usually stoic features soft and vulnerable. It squeezed Mayu's insides. Pushing Fukushima to arm's length, she peered into his eyes, noting the dark circles beneath.

"What is it?"

Staring at her seemed to make it worse and Fukushima fractured. His whole face crumpled with the effort to control himself. "My sister, my niece…" Watching him choke and struggle was like a physical blow. What else had the world taken from them? He covered his mouth with a hand. He didn't need to say it out loud. Mayu pulled him back into her arms and held on with all her strength. "I'm just so glad you're okay," he repeated. "You're like family to me. I hope you know that."

They hired a car and Keiji drove them twenty-five minutes north to a small village nestled among dozens of rice fields. His hands gripped the steering wheel so hard his knuckles were white, his shoulders hunched stiffly the entire ride. Despite Richard and Momo's attempts to start a conversation, Keiji didn't say a word. Mayu watched him, worried that he was remembering the day of the tsunami, recalling him saying that he had wished he'd had a car.

When Keiji pulled up at his parent's' summer house, even Fukushima strained against his seatbelt to get an eyeful of the place. The house had a beautiful view of the rice paddies, colours dancing in the water as it mirrored a gorgeous sunset—purple, blue, yellow, and pink—darker clouds sitting on the western horizon.

The house had three small, sloping, black tiled roof-tops, the eaves flicking upwards like the point of Arabian slippers. Its white walls had grown discoloured, but nothing could hide its charm. A maple bonsai stood watch by the front door, waving five-pointed red leaves at them.

"It's nothing special really," said Keiji, sliding open the front door, "but you're welcome to stay here as long as you need." They lined their shoes up in the foyer and tiptoed across the polished wooden floors in their socks.

"Have a look around." Keiji shrugged at the sliding doors that led deeper into the house. "You can decide for yourself where you want to sleep, the bathroom is down that way." And with that, he headed to the kitchen with four canvas bags of supplies.

"I'll sleep wherever," Fukushima murmured. Pushing his glasses up his nose, he headed for the dining area and settled in a chair on the floor. The low table had eight beautiful, legless chairs around it, pine backs and cushioned seats. As if already feeling at home, Fukushima pulled out his phone and Mayu saw him open a news feed.

"*Wooow*," Momo whispered, "it's so big. Where shall we sleep, Mayu?"

"Huh, you're sharing with me?"

Richard pretended not to hear and crept off to the bathroom. Not missing a beat, Momo shoved Mayu's arm.

"Of course I am. I mean, you give much better cuddles." Tittering at her own joke, she gripped Mayu's arms and turned her to face the hallway leading to the stairs. "You pick a futon for us. I'll help Keiji make dinner."

The house let in plenty of natural light, some of its windows almost ceiling to floor. The frosted, sliding glass doors, framed in black wood, moved to reshape rooms. She found Richard upstairs pulling open one of the bedroom walls to reveal another sitting area looking out across the paddies.

"I haven't been in a house like this in, well, years. not since I came as a tourist," he said.

Mayu joined him at the windows, soaking in the serene view. "How is your place, by the way? Did you find out?"

"Yeah. It's gone."

She hugged herself against the chill still lingering in the walls, wondering how the rice managed to carry on growing. "It doesn't seem real, does it? That the world can be so beautiful and so deadly at the same time. I wonder if we can save what's left of the planet." The colourful sky faded in the encroaching night and a few residential lights popped on across the fields. "Why did it have to end up like this?"

Richard huffed. "It's probably down to money."

Money made her think of work, made her think of being jobless, and lead to Tomoya, who she couldn't save without that job. "This place makes me think of home. Tomoya and I lived in Fukuoka Prefecture, way down south. Our village grows rice." Her mind's eye filled with luscious green fields, so neatly kept that they formed patterns over the hills. "I'm glad my parents are safe."

"We'll help Matokai, too." Richard squeezed her shoulder. "I promise."

They negotiated who got what bedroom and joined

Fukushima at the table. Dinner was served up in one bowl each: noodles in *miso* soup, topped with a poached egg, *pak choi* and spring onions; simple, salty and delicious. Each mouthful lightened the mood around the table.

"I'm sorry it's not much," said Keiji.

"I put my heart and soul into this," interrupted Momo, "don't you dare apologise for it!"

Mayu chortled, dropping a load of noodles and splashing herself with soup. "Oh, come on. I saw you use miso paste from a jar, Momo. You're ridiculous."

"It's the thought that counts."

Speaking for the first time since dinner was served, Fukushima raised his sake cup. "I'm happy to be here with all of you." Everyone lowered their chopsticks, almost hesitant. "It will take time, but if we work together, we'll rebuild what we lost. We've got support again, and so long as there are people who need us, it's our responsibility to help them. I'm proud of you." But his gaze fell on Mayu. "I'm especially proud of you, Mayu. Without you, Skye Mansfield would be suffering in more ways than one. We know it's been hard for you. Thank you."

Tears stood out in his eyes for a second before he blinked them away. He now understood her grief better than anyone at the table.

"Besides," he said, raising his cup higher, "if nothing else, Kuramochi has enough energy for all of us." With that, he grinned and downed his drink to cheers of agreement.

Mayu looked around the table, her joy turning sour as she took in the three empty chairs. Reality flickered and the empty seats filled with Tomoya, Yūta, and Skye. Snow fell into her soup and a jellyfish tentacle brushed her shoulder.

"*I'm too hungry to dance,*" she heard Momo say.

"*You're always hungry,*" replied Keiji.

"Are you alright?"

Mayu jumped, focused on Momo beside her. Her friend looked as if she half-expected Mayu to start sobbing. The snow kept falling but the chairs were empty once more.

"I'm fine. I tuned out for a moment. Sorry."

If she hadn't been so self-pitying, embracing fatal sleep, Tomoya never would have tried his three-way dream connection; he'd still be here. But Momo had pointed out how deep Mayu had gone in distorting her own grasp on reality, just to keep Skye on track. Still, her lapse in judgement had been disastrous, she eyed the chair where a young man should be sitting and mulled over *his* lost dreams. She closed her eyes and thought of Skye—of the mixed dread and joy she represented. The fake snow soothed Mayu's hot face and she opened her eyes again. A new clarity settled in her chest as she studied each of her colleagues.

Keiji was still very quiet, but Mayu sensed that seeing his friends around the dinner table satisfied him. Of all of them, Keiji probably needed a break the most. The earthquake's destruction hadn't wreaked havoc here, unlike many other places, and the look in his eyes spoke endless gratitude for that. His cheeks had flushed pink, perhaps from the sake or the warmth of the room, but he seemed proud to be able to provide them with shelter.

Momo had plenty to be optimistic about, Mayu was comforted by that. She could still decide to work for Halcyon if she chose and Mayu noticed how her fingers often brushed Richard's hand or leg. From the buoyancy in her voice and the carefree way she talked with her hands, she felt Momo wanted to pass that optimism on to the rest of them. Despite catastrophe and heartbreak, Momo still saw goals worth working toward.

Richard had mellowed somewhat. He hadn't thrown his head back in laughter all evening, his blond hair had not been gelled into place and he hadn't sought attention. Usually, he was first to break any pause in conversation, but tonight Richard let the silences hang, his face pensive.

Finally, Mayu looked at Fukushima. Whenever the conversation turned to the future, Fukushima stared into his noodles looking lost. Mayu saw herself in the lonely twist of Fukushima's shoulders, the sombre curve of his lips. If she carried on burying herself in work or ignoring her feel-ings, she'd be left with nothing in her life.

She needed to embrace a new future, even if it wasn't the one she had planned. A new space had to open up and Yūta had to move aside a little to make room. She had to let him go and accept that, in some way, he'd still be there.

It was okay to stop blaming herself.

35

Three months later

KEIJI SLAPPED A letter on Mayu's desk, pulling her attention away from her monitor. Their new logo, a cherry tree growing from a boulder, stood out at the top of the page. "I hope you wanted one hundred million yen, because we sure have it."

"What?" She picked up the letter, scanned it, and half-screamed, half-whooped for joy. Without pausing, she leapt out of her chair and hugged him.

"I don't like you *that* much," he muttered.

Mayu laughed and shouted the news to Shiori across the room.

"Awesome!" the woman cried, clapping her hands above her head, her long black hair swinging. No longer an intern, Shiori was Tomoya's partial replacement, but seeing her fresh face still hadn't become easy. Personal feelings aside, Mayu liked her work ethic and energy.

"What's going on?" asked a voice from Mayu's computer.

Rain hit the window beside her desk, the light casting odd reflections over Skye Mansfield's face. When Mayu explained that they now had enough money to rebuild almost all of their lost equipment, Skye cheered too.

Their new offices were, in some ways, much nicer. They'd added more plants, the desks were curvy and spacious and the testing lab was a beauty. In the lobby was a memorial to the three colleagues who had lost their lives in the tsunami, a simple but glossy golden plaque.

"Oh, Auntie Vera says it's dinner time." Skye rolled her eyes and pretended to puke.

"Alright kid, I'll talk to you again soon."

"If the casserole doesn't kill me."

Even Keiji laughed.

As Skye ended the call, her face was replaced with the image of a fluffy, white kitten, its dew-drop blue eyes fixated on a bubble. Skye had insisted that Mayu chose a profile picture too, because she 'couldn't stand to look at a hideous grey silhouette any longer.' To deliberately nettle her, Mayu had chosen a close-up photo of a pug with fries poking out of its mouth.

A line of text from Skye appeared in their private chatroom. *That dog is still ugly.*

Mayu's fingers flew across the keyboard. *He's modern art. Go and eat your dinner.*

Patting Shiori's shoulder as she left the office for the labs, Mayu heard someone jog to catch up with her. She turned and beamed at Fukushima. His hair looked greyer around the edges these days.

"Going to check, in light of the good news?"

"You got the message quick," she teased.

With a chuckle, he gestured for Mayu to go first. She entered the lab down the hallway, a sterile place but not a cold one. Shiny metal tables lined the walls. Above were glass-fronted cabinets filled with drugs, solutions, vials, empty beakers—some cupboards completely empty. But her eye was always drawn to the great glass screen dividing the room, partitioning off an occupied bed.

A holographic monitor by Tomoya's bed displayed his heart rate and electrochemical impulses at six cycles a second. Tomoya, that bright spark, was still awake in there. Mayu approached his bedside, studying the breathing mask on his face and his hollow cheeks. She felt comforted by the sound of the rain against the window and of the machinery surrounding them.

"I've just heard—I'm so excited!"

They turned to see Momo rush into the lab, her white coat fanning around her. The pink in her hair had faded to blonde over the past few months and grown closer to her collarbones. Refusing Halcyon's salary to stay with the Parallel Dream Project meant everyone's budgets were tight, hair salons were a luxury she said could live without for now. Plus, Mayu was sure that Richard had *somehow* helped make the choice to stay a little sweeter.

"We'll be upgrading our lab to a penthouse within the year," Momo laughed, clutching onto Mayu's arm. Not even a dream could be this good. Mayu leant into her best friend's touch, glad their levity brought out a youthful grin on Fukushima's face.

"Matokai will be awake in no time," he said. As he pushed his glasses up his nose, the rain caught his attention. "At least we've got something to be happy about on such a miserable day."

"It's not miserable." Mayu's whole body felt like it could

fly, head already tumbling with Parallel Dream ideas. As a ray of light pierced the clouds, illuminating the rain and warming her cheek, Mayu took a deep, refreshing breath, "It's liquid sunshine."

AUTHOR NOTE

I wrote the first draft of this novel in 2013 in a span of thirty days for National Novel Writing Month (NaNoWriMo). I had not long graduated from university and I felt utterly lost, all I knew was that I had to write this book while I still had plenty of free time, and no novel since has poured from me quite like this one did.

I've always felt it's important to put aside a completed draft and forget about it for a while, so that you can return to it with fresh eyes and energy. So, after I wrote this book, I worked on another with my cousin, *Bloodshot Buck*, which was published as a serial until 2016. Throughout, I flitted back to this one, paying for it to be edited, seeking help in making it better.

While I struggled to find agents, I began another novel in 2017 called *Witching Knight*, and briefly found excellent support from an agent until he just…ghosted me. Throughout this briefly described timeline, something awful was happening to me inside. With each rejection (and there were many), confidence in my writing died, until I couldn't face looking at any of my work.

Only in 2020, when I couldn't take solace in meeting friends face-to-face to play Dungeons and Dragons—being the Game Master has the similar buzz of writing a novel—I realised one day in a sudden rush, as I sobbed my eyes out behind the sofa, aware that I was overreacting to a minor argument: *I am depressed.* And my next thought was about Mayu Shirakawa, abandoned and depressed on my hard-drive. My self-esteem had fallen so low that I hated myself for failing to achieve the one thing I had only ever wanted with a burning passion: write novels and publish them. It wasn't all that dragged me down, of course; work, money, housing, isolation... But in many ways, I am grateful that lockdown forced me to confront and acknowledge what I love in life, what I need, and that I had to seek help.

The past two years have been a long inner battle to rebuild my confidence, but support from colleagues, family and friends have made it possible that *A Headful of Skye* is finally in your hands, and it has been hard to let go. I hope, as you read it, there were moments that made you smile, that made you feel warm, that moved you, and most of all, I hope you enjoyed the time spent reading.

ACKNOWLEDGEMENTS

Thank you to Mikey Wyatt and Mitch K. Allen for always reading my early drafts and for being kind, loving friends. Thank you to Suresh Ariaratnam for your time. The plot would never have improved without your probing questions into plot-holes and motives. Thank you to Amanda Meuwissen for proof-reading the whole thing and knowing exactly what was missing, including a better title!

Thank you, Mum, for being my stalwart champion, cheering me on with the genuine vigour of a battle cry, even though I don't write anything that's your cup of tea! Thank you, Dad, for reading the early draft and telling me, honestly, that you didn't like it and couldn't finish it, but then still reading a heavily edited version years later. Your emotional reaction after you read the final page is like a beacon I cling to, thank you for that hug.

Thank you to Rachael Dewhurst and Laura Hollick for *asking* to read this story after I finally admitted 'I write books,' and for such enthusiastic reviews. Thank you to my partner, Aaron Gaffney, for holding me as I sobbed into his lap when I believed, 'I cannot write,' and for gently propping me back up.

Finally, thank you so much to my aunt, Jane Porter, who gave *A Headful of Skye* the most intense line-edit it has ever received—any remaining mistakes are my own. I am grateful for the hours you spent helping me refine every single word. I am so lucky to have you.

Printed in Great Britain
by Amazon

25947901R00209